QUEEN OF
IRON YEARS

QUEEN OF IRON YEARS

LYN McCONCHIE
and SHARMAN HORWOOD

WILDSIDE PRESS

Published by Wildside Press LLC.
www.wildsidepress.com

DEDICATION

To Georgina Beyer, whose assistance when she was an MP hasn't been forgotten, and to Cheryl Johnson, a friend who helped when it was needed and is appreciated more than she might realize.

ACKNOWLEDGEMENTS

First and foremost we would like to thank our editor Carla Coupe. She helped us both in developing the shape of this story for its new edition.

We would also like to thank the people who got us the reference books when they were needed: Phil Robbie of Griffin's Books in Victoria, B.C., in particular, and to the people online, especially at About.com, who were willing to find answers for some rather odd questions about Boadicea's time (believe it or not, the Iceni and other English tribes did not raise chickens). And to Andre Norton for providing books that described the social side of that history.

Further, we would also like to thank the person who, back in 1995, butted into a discussion Lyn was having (on the Spartans of Thermopolae and Alexander of Macedon), to inform everyone that no gay man or woman had ever really changed history. That person inspired the idea central to this book.

1

Despite the controversy surrounding her life, there is no evidence that Boadicea regretted her position as queen of the Iceni. However, as daughter of the former king, wife to the current king, and priestess to her people, the irony of her position could not have escaped her: her blood and spirit embodied power that she could not in herself wield. Power was the purview of the ruling male, even though the line of descent was carried by a woman. Personally, despite scribe Anla's claims of their happy marriage, I doubt Boadicea had a normal relationship with her husband. She bore him two daughters yet I am sure it was a marriage more of state than love.

Given her position, she had to have experienced a great degree of frustration comparable to that of any modern woman facing a glass ceiling. This has often proven to be as impenetrable as steel, or as in Boadicea's case, iron. Her frustration may even have been the source of that strength. But, as in the ancient Trinovantes' saying, a strong woman has been cursed; the gods made her so only to endure a hard life. Boadicea had an incredibly harsh life when she overturned the world as queen of the Iceni.

—from *The Warrior Queen*,
by Leceister Murrane

Who would fault Boadicea for inciting rebellion? She had very good reason to do so. Her husband dead, her daughters raped, her nobles goaded by the Roman soldiers stealing from them: what ruler could stand back and accept that treatment for either herself or her people?

Several of the other tribes had done so, however. They'd signed treaties with Rome and accepted the unfair treatment of a conquered people. Since they hadn't been accorded the status of client kingdoms as the Iceni had, they'd been viewed by the Romans as good for nothing more than slavery and extortion.

With that example before her, Boadicea had ample cause to doubt the future well being of her people. In England, trusting the Roman governor had never been a wise choice.

—from *Queen of the Tribes*,
by Leceister Murrane

The Romans called her Boudicca, but we never named her so. That was their crude attempt to render her name into their tongue. While their soldiers and their swords strutted across our land, we could not openly say they were wrong. But alone, away from the Roman procurator and his men, we called her by her real name: Boadicea, Queen of the Iceni.

—from *The Journal of Ancha*, 2nd Edition,
translated by Ericia Thromheart

Spring, Calan Mai, 61 C.E.

Within a shallow cave beside a grove of trees, a strong slender figure bowed before an altar.

"Brighid, Goddess of women, give me strength to endure, and power to alter this life. Make of me a sword to guard those I love. Let me walk in your great path, the way of hearth and home. The Druid priests claim you are one of many gods. But to me you are the highest, the most powerful. From you the blood of life flows and thus you are all. I pray to you where I bow to no other. Hear my plea; give me the strength to protect my people, my children. Send me a sign, a path to lead me to my desire ..."

She turned to leave, her long red hair flaming in the shaft of sunlight reaching inside the cave. Behind her the blood splashed across the altar flared, too, in the light. It seeped down between the gray stones, no less vibrant, no less red than the woman's hair. Fire, light and blood.

Los Angeles: November 2, 2048 C.E.

Night blazes. They rose from the blank areas, the dark areas of what once had been urban sprawl. Where power failed, fire surged to light the night between old, abandoned houses now to burn with the fire of gang anger, gang violence, and the primitive emotions that flared with hatred of everything that was *other*. Each night the fires spread, here one night, and there another, gutting what many had once called home.

Cean (pronounced, unlike the original Irish version of that name, as 'See ahn') stared out of his apartment window. He was high enough, far enough away, but the high-rises where people lived now in safety were hostage to the street violence that burned below. The flames flowed, following the paths of the pavement. And in the dark streets, the security of what was left was eroded. The apartment enclaves like his were the safest places to live. That illusion was fast disappearing. Instead they'd been taken hostage to the street violence that burned below, wiping out what had been—so briefly—middle class America.

Cean was thankful he'd moved out of the urban neighborhood he'd known all his life, but he feared the fires reached out for him even here, and lapped now at the doors of the building in which he stood. What had once been safe was not so any longer. He wouldn't miss it at all.

Had anyone been with him they would have observed a slender wiry figure, a little over five and a half feet in height, with pale skin, eyes of a clear blue, and a benign appearance. He looked like the sort of person who was nice to cats, kids, and old ladies. What he appeared to be however, was not entirely who he was. Cean had secrets, and now in the year of 2048, he was in danger of being having those exposed—and secrets of the kind he had could be lethally dangerous in that year and in that place.

* * * *

A year and a half later, Cean's first sight of England was disappointing. He'd expected ivy creeping up gentle walls, quaint streets and even the thatched roofs of the past, but of course that just wasn't the case. The weather in England at this time of year was pleasant, a fall filled with exotic colors on unfamiliar bushes, trees, and wandering ivy.

As the plane landed at Gatwick, Cean thought they were descending into sunlit clouds, and that London was socked in with more of its frequent rain. Victorian fogs, he hoped. Once on the ground, though, he realized the clouds were a mixture of more pollution. The thick layer filtered the sunlight, creating a false, early sunset to mask the looming threat of the dark sky.

The buildings were as etched with acrid air as they were in Los Angeles, and in the downtown core of London, the tall structures hung over the narrow, shadowed streets. Just as they did back in California. London had become one more city overgrown with high rises, choked with a large population. It shook him. England in his mind had been that pleasant land of old stories, of Dickens' Christmases, Jane Austen's gentle, elegant dinners and balls, a promise of the type of home he'd never felt he had in North America.

Instead, the bad air, the bad water, and the closeness of the buildings tightened his chest. This wasn't her world. Indeed, it wasn't even his. Not what he wanted it to be. No more than Los Angeles was to him.

But when Cean left London and arrived in Norwich, he felt easier. He'd halted for a brief lunch, and soon closed in on North Walsted. The car swung to the right, plunged downhill between tall hedges, and ahead Cean saw the small shopping area that comprised the town's high street.

It was a pleasant place. Shops, cottages, all the conveniences of a reasonably-sized country community. The hotel clerk quickly gave him directions to the site where the remains of an Iceni dun still rucked up the ground in a circle, undeterred by the two thousand years of farming since it had fallen.

Cean stepped from the car onto the grassy shoulder of the road and quickly caught himself on the door as a flaring shock ran up through his body. In that moment it was as if Boadicea herself had spoken in his ear. Had the feeling been in words, it would have said:

"Welcome, kinsman. It is good that the blood returns."

For a moment Cean swayed, one hand holding himself upright. He looked around, but no one was there to notice his sudden tremor. The feeling went as quickly as it had come and Cean straightened up. Had it been his imagination? Jet lag? He didn't believe it. No, that had been real. A sensation as if he was rushed along by a moving walkway, faster and faster. Ahead he could see his goal, and his increasing speed seemed suddenly natural, like the flight of an arrow.

He took the time jumper from the trunk of the car, along with his pack. Fort had stayed in Los Angeles, keeping the second jumper with him.

"I'll get Mel out of here, once she's mobile again," he'd told Cean, patting him tentatively on the shoulder, then flinging his arms around his friend. "And the others, too. Can't leave the Coalition behind, can I?"

Not when everyone profiled with Tensen's was being herded into camps, the police forces very unclear on how and when they would be released, he thought.

Cean quickly unpacked, pulling out a large, roughly sewn bag. This carried all of the goods he'd prepared to take back in time with him: the copies of Roman coins, the medicines safely packed in small twists of cotton or fleece, even a metal box, figured on the outside with Celtic designs. This held a small solar-powered computer, on it the information that would help his survival in some very rough times.

And the Iceni's as well, Cean added to himself. He wasn't going for himself; he was going for them. For her.

He tucked the car keys into the glove compartment. This was farming country, someone would come along and return the car to the rental company. Slinging the pack over his shoulder, he carried the time jumper towards a small grove of trees. Dusk was beginning to fall; he had to hurry. In a slight depression beside the young birches, he unfolded the pads and flat keyboard. The jumper's power supply and circuits were small, no more than a shoebox in size, and he pushed it to the side while he readied himself.

Pausing briefly, he set the Celtic box next to the jumper. His old clothes he flung aside, including his briefs. He couldn't take those, not even the belt or sneakers. Then the rough woolen tunic settled over his head and shoulders as if it belonged there, the cloak, too. Picking up the Celtic metal box, he held it to his chest. It looked too new; he'd have to scrape it with a rock and rub dirt into the scratches to make it look older.

It took a moment before he heard the footsteps behind him.

Cean whirled, rising to his feet, the box held to his chest. Behind him several paces downhill stood a man Cean had seen the night before in the pub. Jonathan Smith. A large broad-shouldered man, with muscular arms, and strong hands. A digger, the barman had told Cean. Looking for treasure, he'd added, laughing. "Thinks he's got an educated guess where to find it," he'd snorted, walking away to pull a beer. The barman did not have much sympathy for archaeologists of any kind.

Closer now, the man swayed slightly as he stood before Cean. One hand clutched a shovel, propping himself up with it as much as anything else. Cean gathered himself. The man wanted something and he was drunk. That much was clear from the smell of him.

"You found it," Smith grated out. The wind and the undergrowth had played havoc with his hair, messing up the expensive cut that Cean recognized: neither long nor short, but certainly American, favored by professors and graduate students alike. Like the tweed jacket with elbow patches the man had worn the night before, it was a mark of where he'd got to, where he wanted to be.

"Found it? This?" Confused, Cean held the metal box up. "I'm sorry but you're mistaken. This is mine. I had it made for me. A few months ago before I came over here."

Smith glared at him and Cean realized with a sudden, slow dread, that the man was furious. He must have been drinking for hours. Since dinner at least. Smith snarled, wordless and animal.

"Give it to me!" He lunged towards Cean.

Smith had paid to be here. Years of hard work and education; money and time poring over old books and ancient maps. *He'd earned this!* Now he was paying again to greedy farmers just to let him dig on their land! And this stranger had the arrogance to come wandering out holding the very casket he'd spent the last two years trying to find! Holding it in front of him. Flaunting it. Sneering at him. Like the barman. Like everyone else.

"That's mine! Mine, you thieving bastard!" Thick fingers jabbed, accusing and erratic as he lurched unsteadily on his feet.

Smith advanced, glaring down at the smaller Cean, the casket in hand. The setting sun glittered on the Celtic knots, taunting him. On the ground lay a case, a couple of small lights and a computer motherboard. But none of that mattered. *This bastard had found his casket!*

"Give it to me now!" The outrage in his voice convinced Cean the man hadn't heard a word. He'd been up the entire night before, working on his map of the area, consoling himself with his favorite drink, 40-year old Scotch. He'd worked all day, the Scotch near at hand. He was re-checking the farms he'd marked off after each one was searched. Somewhere he'd find the Iceni queen's casket

He'd read about it, suggested in the Roman records as part of Prasutagus's legendary wealth, discounted by experts as exaggeration and myth. But Smith was sure something like this had existed. *Why else would the Romans have plundered the Iceni duns as they had? And if he could only find the site of Boadicea's royal dun, he was sure he'd find it. He would! The casket existed. He was sure of it.*

But this weakling had found it. A stranger who hadn't worked on this as Smith had. The interloper would claim the discovery and reap the very rich rewards. Smith's rewards. The discovery that should have been his. Mostly drunk and wholly dangerous, he was in no mood to listen. *This weak idiot was not going to reap what he'd worked so hard to find!*

He'd been in dangerous places over the years of what he referred to as "exploration and discovery." Known to others as his unprincipled looting. He'd dealt with dangerous men. He'd learned that violence often *did* solve problems.

He advanced, his body tightening, the blood pumping to his well-exercised muscles in anticipation. This bumbling cur wasn't going to stop him.

"Give me the casket." His voice was a buzz of anger.

"It isn't yours, damn it."

Cean was starting to panic. The man was crazy. If Cean gave him the casket what would happen? He feared he knew. The idiot would force it open somehow, wrecking it, and find the computer inside. Unfortunately, Cean had kept a journal of his attraction to Boadicea and his plans to aid her. All of it on that computer. And there was no time left. He needed to activate the time jumper and be gone before anyone else could turn up to prevent it.

Smith was contemptuous. To him, Cean was a weedy youth bleating about "his" casket. He stepped forward to seize the treasure he'd set his reputation on. Cean still tried to explain.

"You don't understand. I had this made for me."

Smith didn't hear him.

"It belongs to *me*. It isn't *hers*."

Smith half-heard that. "It belongs to whoever holds it," he added, partly to himself.

"But it's *mine*!"

Cean had used the wrong word. Smith heard only the last one as their opposing obsessions clashed on that one point.

"Give it to me!" He pushed Cean contemptuously. "Come on!" He caught at a corner of the casket, wrenching it loose from Cean's hands. Smith stepped back, the casket triumphantly in his hands. "Got it, by God! It's worth more than gold."

And it was. Desperate, Cean swung his fist, flailing at the other man to make him let go but missed. If he didn't go now, he'd have failed! It would all have been for nothing. He'd never have a second chance at it if he was caught. Boadicea and the Iceni would still be slaughtered, and the future would stay unchanged for them. And for those in this time with Tensen's, his friends, like Mel, like Fort, like everyone else in the Coalition, the future would be agonizing.

He closed with the man who would deny him his dream. His hands clamped down, not over the casket but over the arm locked about it. Smith shook him off.

"Fuck off, you idiot! It's mine. Now run away and play with your toys." Smith had no idea why Cean was here.

Cean continued to attack. Smith's grip on the casket loosened. The man struck out before dropping it. The flush of a bruise rose across one of Cean's cheekbones as he staggered back. He grabbed for the casket again and with a growl of anger Smith knocked him to the ground. Smith then kicked savagely as Cean rolled away.

"Stupid fucker! Get out of here before I really hurt you."

"It isn't your casket. I had it made!" Cean made one last attempt to get through to his opponent. "I had it made! Don't you understand? It's not Iceni!"

Jonathan didn't listen. He was prying at the lid, "Damn thing won't open. How the hell …" He was inserting the blade of a knife under the lid as Cean grabbed him. The knife quickly flickered towards Cean's throat.

"You'll damage it. Only my disks are in there." Smith was not listening. He still pried at the lid with his fingers, his knife holding Cean at bay. Cean was frantic. It would be too late! Boadicea would die all over again. This greedy looter would ruin the work of years. Smith was silhouetted in the dying light, struggling with the box. Cean staggered to his feet, charging desperately. He snatched the casket from the rough hands and tossed it to the ground behind him.

"Go away!" he shouted, all thought of danger gone. "I have to go back, I have to save her."

The knife still in his hand, Smith whipped around at him. Alcohol and rage twisted his face into deep, savage lines.

"Give me the casket back, you little bastard, or I'll ..."

He thrust Cean aside, reaching down for the casket at the same time. Cean grabbed his free arm, panic erupting like wildfire in his chest.

"No!"

He grabbed at the hand which held the knife. He wrenched it loose and the blade nicked his palm, drawing blood. That tiny pain was enough. He tore at his opponent and for brief moments they whirled in a mad dance, feet tangling in the long grass, eyes blinded at the swipe of branches. Cean temporarily broke free, but Jonathan Smith advanced, knife at the ready. His eyes wild, he dashed at Cean, tearing his sleeve, and readied himself to stab downwards. *This youth was small fry, ultimately easy to deal with.*

With the sudden certainty brought on by weeks of practice, Cean slid his hand behind his own collar and drew the steel knife he'd strapped beneath his tunic. As Smith struck again and his blade slid through the air, missing the smaller man, Cean stabbed him once in the shoulder, then twice in the chest, not even knowing when the blade bit deep between the man's ribs and into his heart. Cean stabbed again even as the body fell.

Jonathan Smith died in less than a moment while Cean still gaped down at what he'd done. Slowly he straightened. Some part of him had always thought he could return here, back to this time. If things went wrong in the past, if he was badly hurt. Once he'd persuaded Boadicea to listen maybe he could return for the necessary surgery of his final change and then rejoin her.

He could have come back. If he carried the machine with him as he was sent, it would go back in time with him. Then, in an emergency, he could use it to return to his own time again. He'd never spoken of it to Fort, but that had always been an unrealized part of all his plans.

He looked down at the body, nauseated. With Smith dead, there was no chance of returning. Cean had killed a man. Leaving a body behind him here would guarantee he couldn't ever come back. Even if he could hide the violence, the death, he couldn't survive the close scrutiny of a murder investigation. Not after he'd killed the man who'd attacked Mel. Not a second time. The authorities would never believe that was an accident, not if they knew about Smith.

Behind him ... The words formed in Cean's mind as if they came from somewhere else.

"I don't have to leave Smith here. The machine can send him elsewhere."

Somewhere where there was no one to call Cean to account. He'd still never be able to return here but at least he would never be known as a murderer.

Cean hurried to the case, changed one setting, a second. Then he dragged the body over to the open pad. Cean shoved, rolling his victim over onto it. As Cean touched a button, the departure circle opened. There was a flicker like a blinking eye and the body vanished. What had been Smith was gone.

Quickly leaning down to the machine, he altered settings back to their original position. He took up his backpack and paused a moment looking at the machine. Slowly, he wiped his knife blade on his pants, then sheathed it. He stood, the present time distanced by the hovering darkness, the pad open and ready at his feet.

Fort had told him something when they'd parted in Los Angeles. Lost Angeles. That had been Mel's nickname for it: lost people, lost souls, and little future ahead. Fort had grimaced, so much to say with little time and words left in which to say it.

"I can't leave them here," he had said. Not his friends. Cean had shaken his head, not understanding. "I can't go with you," Fort continued. "Who'd look after Mel? Or the others? I have to go and help them. Maybe all of us in the Coalition can help other worlds, the other timelines created by going back to the past. What do you think?" He looked sheepish. "If I send everyone back to different times, each one creating a new world in the process, could we make those worlds different? Better?"

Cean knew. "Of course we can."

Fort had gripped his shoulder. "You're the first, my friend. God speed."

Saying nothing more, Fort had then stepped forward and clasped his friend in long arms. His voice shook, with weariness as well as emotion. This would be a final parting, with no chance of a future reunion. They clung to each other for a moment, then each had stepped back.

Here, amidst the low rolling fields of Norfolk, Cean took one long look out over this land and time that had been his until these last few moments. Then, scooping up Smith's flashlight, he stepped forward, touched the button and paced to where the pad waited. He stepped onto it, his eyes fixed on the ground.

* * * *

Cean reeled as he crossed, the world rushed up in a swoop and then thudded back down again. A dazzle of lights went off in his head. He felt sick, giddy. A sudden sense of swift flight overwhelmed him. Then he was standing firm on the ground again. The lurching earth caught up with him, stopping as suddenly as it had started. The dizziness disappeared.

He glanced hurriedly about him. No one was nearby. But close to him a large area of trees blocked much of the farther landscape from sight. Within their shelter he could plan his next step. And rest. The shock of what he'd just done still surged through him. He walked across, slipped under the shadowy branches and sat on his heels. He listened. Nothing. Darkness weighed heavy in this sky as it had in his own world.

He rose to drift through the trees to the copse's far side.

They blanketed the slope, but beyond and below he could dimly see what had to be the Iceni dun, the wooden stockade and smoke rising from a circular dwelling inside it. Now the time was upon him he hesitated. He felt a disassociation from events. Somewhere two generations ahead of this time he had dumped a dead man. A man he, Cean Rowan, had killed. The sensation of his knife sliding home so easily through living flesh suddenly caught up with him. The astonished look in Smith's eyes.

Cean turned abruptly and vomited into the undergrowth, again and again until he was retching dryly.

Exhaustion swept over him. His chest ached savagely from several of Smith's blows, his slight breasts stinging. He had to rest. He had to adjust to the knowledge of the death he'd caused. He had to acclimatize to this new place in time. He could lie up for the day. Watch how life was lived down there, be sure he'd come through to the right time and place. He had food and a leather flask of water. If he made no sounds, no fire, he should be unobserved.

Finally he was here, all his plans proven true, yet all he felt was exhausted. As his breathing slowed, the ache subsiding, he drank some water, then crawled under a large clump of low-lying brush. He curled beneath it, pulled the lowest branches down around him, and with his backpack as a pillow, fell into a daze which was more a retreat into shock than honest sleep.

* * * *

He woke later that morning. By the look of the light, it was around eight a.m. so he'd slept a good five hours. His body seemed to have accepted the time change while he slept; at least he no longer felt as strange, as if the events of the night before were days in the past. Cean rummaged through his pack to don a tight leather vest which would flatten his chest. Over that he placed a loose wool shirt. He'd prefer they didn't know what he was. It wasn't as if the garment wasn't familiar, in his own city he'd worn it constantly. Now what mattered was what he must do here and now. He'd tried to arrive before Boadicea's husband, the king, died. That way maybe he could convince the man not to risk writing the original will he'd made. To alter it so that Rome had no covenant with the inheritance of his kingdom.

According to Tacitus, Prasutagus and his nobles had amassed considerable wealth. In order to preserve his kingdom from Roman plundering, he left all of his own wealth to his two daughters and the emperor, then Nero, to be shared equally. After all, he only ruled because he'd married the Royal Woman. He thought that writing his will as he had would preserve the peace, save his family and his kingdom, leaving his wife to rule in his place.

But under Roman law, a woman could not rule, nor own property, no matter who—or what—she was. Thus the daughters' inheritance was disallowed, and the Roman procurator had immediately moved to wrest the balance of wealth away from the Queen, and seize her nobles as slaves.

The scent of horses, and of the evening's cooking fires rose from the dun below. Beyond him in the compound the faint sound of wailing drifted over to him on the wind. Cean listened for some time, watching as he could. The machine had been off, possibly by weeks, even perhaps months. It must be 59 A.D. Prasutagus was dead. From what Cean had heard, the wailing mourned the loss of a king. The man had died the night before as Cean had come through.

Damning his luck, he knew there was now no chance to talk to the man. No way to find out what had caused him to write the will as he had.

Cean recalled the results of that stupidity. The governor of Britain and the veterans of his legions had ignored the will's stipulations. They had plundered as they wished, taking from the wealthy Iceni aristocracy whatever they chose.

With truly incredible folly they'd tried to reduce the Iceni to the status of conquered people, seizing many of them as slaves, and taking their property, especially the prized horses of the tribe. Cean snorted quietly. Idiots! Did they really believe the Iceni would willingly suffer such treatment? That Boadicea would shrug and accept her flogging, the rape of her daughters in front of herself and the tribe as merely standard treatment under Roman rule?

He'd arrived too late to change Prasutagus's mind, but perhaps he could still prevent the destruction of Iceni people. Things moved more slowly in this ancient era. It took time for news to spread, for soldiers to march. A year would still pass before the continued Roman brutality provoked Boadicea's rebellion. But by then, Cean should be well-placed in Iceni society. Ready to caution and advise. He had to ingratiate himself quickly, show the Iceni he could be trusted, and believed, before he gave warning. That was his only hope.

Down the slope the Iceni dun sat dark against the land as night settled upon it. He shivered in a mixture of fear and excitement. Let the revolt begin, and this time it would be the Roman side which lost.

He stood slowly, hefting his pack onto his shoulders. The casket was safely stowed in it, the computer inside, along with his disks. He took up a light leafy green branch, held it aloft, and began to walk steadily towards the dun. In his reading the branch was supposed to be a sign he came in peace. He only hoped that the Iceni recognized it.

As he marched forward his gaze was fixed on the gates. Who would see him first? He must convince them of his essential harmlessness, his good will. Cean walked on, beginning to wonder if anyone would notice him before he entered the stronghold.

* * * *

In that he was wrong. He'd been spied the moment he left the shelter of the trees. Even now warriors had him covered with arrow tips. It was Boadicea who had bid them hold bowstrings. The red-haired Queen watched with her archers as Cean walked up to their gate. She had her reasons. She'd dreamed the night Prasutagus had died. And like all good druids, she believed her dreams were gifts from the gods. It could be this stranger was the man of whom she'd dreamt. If so, the stars and the gods had sent him to her. If not, her warriors could always kill him, but for now she wanted to see what this stranger brought to her dun.

* * * *

Cean passed through the gates and halted there to stare about him. Nothing moved. Everyone watched him, arrows and spears pointed his way.

Perhaps it was up to him to announce himself. He raised his voice, speaking slowly and clearly.

"I come in peace to heal. I am Cean, lately of far lands who comes now to the greatest tribe in the land. I can heal sick eyes, aid those whose wounds have gone bad. I come in peace," he repeated, waiting. Hoping with all his might that his accent was intelligible.

It was. Just! In moments, with guards at his side, he was led to the Queen's hearth. Cean barely let the thought surface of what was about to happen: finally! He was to meet her. But the meeting lasted only moments. In the dimness of a hut Boadicea sat, waiting. She'd left her warriors to bring him to her. Cean repeated what he'd said at the gate, still unsure they understood. But she turned to him after he spoke. She nodded.

"He speaks strangely yet he may speak truth. Take him to Dauldi's son. The boy's arm has gone bad where he broke it. See if he can heal that. If he does so, he's not false. Then we shall honor him as our guest."

Two men obeyed her order, one Dauldi himself, the sick child's father. He glanced gratefully at his Queen as he obeyed. She missed little; it was a clever thing she did, to test the stranger's claims. He led Cean out of the hut, explaining quietly.

"I am Dauldi, a man of the Iceni and cousin to our Queen. My son is ill. He broke his arm some days gone, and now the wound is gone bad. All treatments have failed and my son dies. Will you aid him, healer?"

Cean allowed his instincts to guide him. He did not see the weapons, only the anxious eyes of a man who loved his son. He strode along with the man, somehow unafraid now that he was actually doing what he'd trained so long and hard to do.

"Take me to the boy, quickly. All I can do, I shall."

They strode on to his hut, Dauldi leading, Cean at his heels, with a second warrior following close behind them. Cean halted. Inside it would be dark, stuffy, and certainly none too clean. Better to look at the boy's arm outside, where he could see what he was doing, and the tribe could be assured he did the lad no harm.

"Bring your son out to me, Dauldi. Let someone bring a blanket to keep him warm. The sun is leaving us, but good air away from the hearth is a healer also."

He heard indrawn approving breaths at that. Dauldi sprang through the door, thrusting the curtain aside. He returned with a child in his arms. A boy of ten or twelve who tossed and muttered with fever. Dauldi laid his son on the blanket which his wife had brought out with them.

Cean bared the injured arm, cutting through the rough bandaging. He bit back the impulse to vomit here in front of these people. It had been splinted. They had known that much. But what had originally been a compound fracture had become infected where the bone had broken the skin.

The immediate area of the wound was stinking with yellow pus. Red streaks shot up the arm. It looked as if they'd tried various salves, all of which had made things worse, binding the poison within the wound. He could cure the infection, he knew he could and save the boy, but he just wasn't sure if the lad would have a working arm when he was done.

He spoke without turning. "Bring me a cup. Also take water in a pot, boil it so long as you may sing two songs of moderate length. Bring that water to me, then set another pot to do the same."

Dauldi's voice was hushed. "Why for, healer?"

"The water must be boiled." He wasn't certain of the Iceni word. "Heated until it starts to rise into the air because in that way it imitates the sun which is also hot. Do you not often sear wounds with fire to prevent wound sickness?"

"That is true," a woman's voice agreed from the watching crowd. "I will see to the water, Dauldi."

Cean scanned the people, keeping his face impassive. Some amongst the men looked disapproving. As if they felt any aid a stranger could give was unworthy, unwelcome. He'd thought long and hard about that as well as other possible problems. Trust was not easily won, not for a stranger come from the outside, unknown to these people who'd lived all of their lives together. Cean lifted his head to look openly about him.

"Do you have a healer of your own within the tribe?"

Dauldi answered that, a scowl drawing pale brows together. "Aye. Lubran, but he has tried and failed."

Cean glared. "Failed, you say. Not for want of skill or knowledge, I am sure. But how is it if a warrior must fight more men than he can overcome. Is he the less?" There were mutters.

"No," one answered aloud.

"Not so," another added.

"No man can overcome odds too great for him," a third joined the gathering judgement.

"Then if he sees these odds, does he not ask for a friend to stand with him if such a friend can be found?" This time the mutters agreed more quickly. "It is thus I ask. Let your own healer come to ask the Gods for our strength to be combined. Does he not know the gods of the Iceni best? Do they not know him? Let his prayers rise up to be heard while our strengths battle the evil which strikes the child. Surely with two of us we shall prevail in this war of illness."

Already a woman was ushering a man forward, presumably the healer. He was an elderly man, with an alert but steady eye. Intelligent by the look of him and no fool. His gray hair was bound back in a long tail, and he was dressed in a finely woven wool shirt. A cape of thicker, rougher wool was drawn over his shoulders, better than those worn by most about him, and secured too with pins of enameled silver. To Cean's eyes, though, what was striking was that both his person and clothing were clean. Slowly, ceremoniously, Cean bowed his head.

"Lubran, healer and wise man to the people. Have you heard my words?"

"I have heard."

"Will you stand beside me in this fight?" Cean nodded at the putrid swelling on the boy's arm.

There was a long silence. Cean understood, waiting patiently. The old man must decide freely. Yet it would not be easy for him. If he agreed, he was admitting before all of his people that his knowledge and skill were insufficient. Still, with the way Cean had stated his request it would also look bad if the old man rejected the offer and Cean cured the boy without his help. Lubran had to be a shrewd man, living in this time to the age he had. Cean believed he knew which way the healer would choose. To accept would be to share the credit.

At last Lubran lifted his head. "Let us stand together against this enemy," he hesitated then added a final word which brought wide smiles to the faces of all who waited. "Brother."

Two healers to share knowledge, to aid the tribe. Not just one.

Cean bowed his head again. "Lubran the healer is generous twice over to lend his spear-arm to a stranger and to name that stranger brother. Let us be alone now with the child. What healers do is for healers."

The crowd edged away, looking back, until Dauldi's woman shooed them off like scavenging crows. Then she went inside her hut to put on more of the water to heat. Cean looked at his new partner in medicine. He kept his voice low as he spoke to the man. Beneath them the boy looked from one to the other with fever glazed eyes.

"I come from over the seas." He paused, brushing the boy's hair back away from his face. His skin was flushed.

"There is much knowledge in my own lands but too many think there is no skill greater than their own. I know that for folly. Therefore, I wander to learn more from others who are wise, sharing my own knowledge to such as will hear of it. I have no wish to take honor from you. Brother have you named me, Lubran. Brother let me be in truth. Share with me your own cunning and anything I can teach you shall be yours in return."

The old man's eyes lit, but he hesitated. Was this stranger about to trick him? To use Lubran's own knowledge to heal the boy and then claim the victory as his own? The Iceni healer's voice was low and fierce.

"If you heal this lad you will share what you know?"

"On my knife."

Lubran considered his options. If this stranger did in truth have healing knowledge that would save the boy, then at least the boy would be healed to live a good life.

"Then let us to work. The boy fell from his pony a week gone. I did thus …" He detailed his treatments as Cean hid a shudder. "Everything failed as it often does when a wound goes bad and wound fever strikes. What can you tell me?"

"That all around us is life. Some can be seen by the eyes. Other life can be seen only with the mind."

Lubran nodded. "I have dreamed in the night. Surely that is a life known only to the mind?"

Cean thanked the stars that he'd had the luck to find a healer in the Queen's camp who was not threatened by another's skill.

"That is wisdom. Now, my people learned that where the skin breaks life unseen may enter to torment the flesh beneath the skin. There it fights with the life of the one it invades." He grinned. "Do not the tribes and the Romans have similar troubles?"

Lubran smiled grimly. "Even so. Then one must seek to prevent the unseen ill spirit from invading. How may this be done? I know herbs which help if the invasion is small. This one is great, and grows greater with each day, even with each hour."

"It is, but your valiant battles against it have held it back. I have a medicine, only a little that I may not use wastefully. But if you bespeak the Gods of the Iceni, I can give some of the potion to the boy. Beg them to aid, to give him the strength to fight. The Iceni strength lies in their children. The Gods will hear you who are a healer."

The woman had brought them a pot of boiled water, which should have cooled just enough yet still be very hot. He tilted the pot to drip a little over the back of his hand. It was hot but not too much so. Carefully, he poured it over his hands, scrubbing his fingers together under the clean water. What was left he used first to bathe the boy's arm, before holding a hot compress to the site of the infection. When that cooled, he repeated the action with more of the heated water, Lubran copying his actions.

Then, with the small bit that remained, he rinsed out the cup, filling it halfway. Into that he dropped one of his tiny antibiotic tablets. The boy looked to be about ten or twelve. Any child of the tribe must have a good immune system to have survived this long, Cean knew. In this time, the weak were rapidly weeded out, often before three years of their life had passed. One tablet should work miracles but not so swiftly as to look like magic.

Lubran had stepped aside, where he stood praying, looking up to the sky, speaking softly in a quiet sing-song, which broke now and again into a more harsh extemporaneous pleading. His face was earnest, the petition fervent. Cean tilted the cup to the boy's lips, and allowed the water and tablet to slide within his mouth. Lubran ended his prayer and Cean touched his arm.

"Let them bear the lad under cover. He may drink only water which has been boiled beforehand, then cooled. Later he may have broth which has been long-cooked." That should be safe enough.

"When should he begin to heal?"

"In the time from sunset to sunset. He will be improving before darkness falls tomorrow night." He reached out to grasp the man's hand. "I thank you for your aid. Once I heard a saying which seemed good to me: Bare is brotherless back."

Actually he'd read it in a book about the Vikings, he thought, but it was the sort of maxim the Iceni would also appreciate.

Lubran's face lit with approval. "That is well said. Then, brother, let us go to my hut to eat and talk. At tomorrow's dawning we shall see how the boy does."

Cean plucked at the hair of one arm as they walked towards Lubran's own hut. It stung sharply. Yes. He was finally here.

2

The first instance of time travel occurred when Dr. Leogold Fortescue predicted the location of a small wormhole in the future. He was thus able to pinpoint the other end's presence "the wormhole's location in the past" simply by taking a deep breath and stepping through. He emerged at a point in time 6 hours, 12 minutes, in the past.

From this he drew a broad mathematical formula with which he could predict worm hole presence. Other events occurred when a group of young physicists at Darguelle University were able to duplicate Fortescue's experiment by entering the past terminus of a wormhole and exiting its future point, a temporal distance of 1 hour and 5 minutes. By measuring the time accurately, along with the wormhole's dilation, they were as a result able to predict its recurrence, and duplicate the great doctor's results, improving the formula's accuracy.

A wormhole signature is like an echo of itself reverberating very much like the ringing of a bell through air, only in this case through time. In tracking one, they could predict its traces in several temporal zones. It was only a short step from there to discovering a mechanism by which a wormhole's appearance could be induced. Hence, the future as well as the near and distant past both became very accessible.

—*Time's Echoes: Through the Future and Into the Past*,
by Levanna Sudholm

To T. S. Eliot, time was but an instant of spiritual epiphany, a poetic moment singular to each person's life. Hawking measured time from its birth to reveal its dimensions, qualities that are not transparent to the human senses. I, on the other hand, saw time "as humans know it" as a physical measurement that we have imposed on the universe. Actual time, real time, is the universe, and wormholes a part of its atrophy, opening like strands of sticky glue between all the possible realities that are shaped by time's matter.

They were there. I just had to find them.

—*The Time Doctor: How I Discovered the Universe*,
by Leogold Fortescue

It had been a bad dream, all of it. As if Cean's whole life had been wrong from the beginning. From his first breath. It wasn't his fault he was a woman born into a man's body. And the way his co-workers had treated him had been the first episode in a long series of bad experiences. But it had also been the beginning of the end. Or perhaps the start of something else. When he returned to work from his first round of physical treatments, the writing was on the wall.

"Mr. Rowan, I'm glad you're *finally* back."

That wasn't the truth. There was just sufficient sarcasm on the middle word to register, yet not enough for Cean to complain about without appearing silly.

"Glad to be back." His tone was edged with the same rancor.

"Then perhaps you'd like to start clearing up your work file. I think there's enough to keep you occupied until ..." His supervisor allowed the last word to trail off into thin air as she walked away.

Cean walked slowly along the long aisle between desks in CHECK SYSTEMS, INC. He moved in a way which suggested residual discomfort, but with a hesitant gait that promised that, too, would pass, and soon.

Fingers flicking over the keyboard, Cean opened his work file only to glare at the long list of orders scrolling down the screen. Hell! There were enough systems amendments here to keep him busy until the middle of next year, let alone until he needed time off for his next appointment at the clinic. Didn't anyone else do any work around here? Sighing with fruitless rage, he started in.

The day didn't get better. Lunch was miserable. He sat alone, a soggy sandwich leaking raspberry jam onto his fingers. He knew no one would join him. Not these days. Overhearing some of the comments, he couldn't ignore the fact that his supervisor's were the worst. But still not vicious enough for him to report a hostile work environment grievance against them—or her.

"Oh, yes, there was an update on that during the Winslow Murray Hour."

"What did it say?"

"That it really does seem to be a transsexual disease." Someone must have protested. "No, it's okay to tell the truth, they said. Statistically nine out of ten of those who are coming down with it are transsexual. They think it's attacking those who have a greater concentration than the average of either male or female hormones. Something about triggering certain enzyme production that infects others so that either female-to-male or male-to-female hormone profiles are susceptible. Normal hormone balances don't create a good environment for the virus, not like the unbalanced ones do."

"Like …?"

Cean didn't see the gesture, the quick nod in his direction, but he knew it was there. He tried to continue eating as if he hadn't heard it.

"Yes, just like *him*."

That attracted a number of replies below Cean's ability to distinguish actual words but he heard the emotionally charged timbre of their conversation. He couldn't help but flinch from the tones which reached him: the fear, the disgust. The almost gloating sounds from some.

He was a woman born in a man's body. He wasn't gay—someone attracted to other men. But he wasn't a man in more than his outer shape. That it was unfair he'd known all of his life, and endured it. He suppressed a bitter sigh. But he'd realized long before that there wasn't much he could do about other people's narrow opinions. What he could do about himself, however, he was doing. Finally.

For a good portion of his life it hadn't been so bad. When he'd first understood the real problem, any stigma of being transsexual had almost vanished. Hospitals routinely assessed those who wished to change their gender, then performed the necessary procedures first with the required psychological counseling, then with some years of stabilizing hormone treatments—with the amount being gradually increased—and finally the main operation. It was found that this method produced the least physical or mental and emotional disturbance.

But in 2035 Tensen's Virus struck. It attacked both males and females with certain hormonal profiles. Cean had known this for a few years, even though his co-workers were just now hearing it for the first time. In the beginning most researchers thought this occurrence among transsexuals was a coincidence, that the majority of those affected contracted the disease as a result of the depressed immune systems brought on by their difficult lifestyles.

Finally, after almost a decade of inadequate treatment and frustrated research, scientists realized that it was the hormonal abnormalities in themselves which caused transsexuals to be vulnerable to the virus. For that there was no cure so far. Coincidence or not, Tensen's Virus had been more disastrous for the transsexual community than AIDS had been for the gay one, the scourge of earlier years. AIDS had eventually been conquered, and the subsequent generation had been able to accept that it was not a "gay disease." But when Tensen's Virus was found to be linked to transsexuals, people's attitudes changed. Severely.

Cean had just started the hormone treatments that would culminate in his permanent gender change, and since at that time there hadn't been much prejudice about transsexuality, he hadn't kept it a committed secret although he maintained his personal pronoun as "he" since he continued to wear male garb. That was the modern custom—those who were to change didn't use the pronoun of the change until they came out as that gender. When he'd had the operation and was living as a woman, then he would become known as "she" and stay that way.

As it was, none of his colleagues were really his friends, just people he chatted with over lunch or coffee breaks. When they used to sit with him, that is. So he made his first appointments without much concern to keep them private, ignoring the initial rumors about the virus. But, as it turned out, they hadn't been just bloated speculation born out of fear and ignorance. They'd been quite real.

Cean had been placed on the hospital list and accepted that the treatment would take years, beginning with two years of counseling, even before the initial hormone treatments. That time passed, but by the time the initial hormone implant effect escalated into visible changes in his body, the rumors about the virus had become fact, and the background of his social set had changed dramatically.

Thousands around the world had already died because of the virus. Now there was a growing swell of popular opinion that transsexuals had brought this plague down on themselves because of their "sinful" ways, and that they threatened the rest of the world with infection as well. Transsexual bashing surged over night. Within days bars that had catered to drag queens, as well as others with supposed gender dysfunction, had to bar their doors to their usual clients.

And fashions had changed to reflect the prejudice too. More and more males allowed facial hair to grow, beards, moustaches, and long sideburns proliferated, while trousers became tighter to show the leaner outline and genital bulge. Women's necklines dropped to show breasts, dresses drew in at the hips to show a womanly shape. In some of the street gangs the costumes were becoming an exaggeration and cod-pieces were back in favor.

The problem was that the disease didn't affect transsexuals alone. Through coitus—and transsexuals could have sexual intercourse with either gender—the virus was passed on to their partners, causing in them an enzyme reaction similar to an allergy. A lethal allergy. People who had sex with the wrong partner died from something very much like anaphylactic shock, literally a deathly allergy to sex itself. If it had passed in the same fashion as a cold or the measles, people could have forgiven transsexual carriers. But because it was initiated by an act so intimate, it terrified most people.

And even though the public was informed, as with the first hysteria regarding AIDS, no one believed that casual contact couldn't trigger the reaction as well: The touch of a hand, a bit of unguarded breath. Known transsexuals had to change jobs, move to other cities, but many were found beaten or worse, dead, on the streets. Cean had already taken to binding flat his developing breasts so that casual encounters on the street would not turn dangerous. He also remained wearing masculine clothing, as it made him less of a target to strangers. But he'd never considered for a moment stopping the treatments. This was something he had to do. His co-workers at the nearby tables were still talking.

"Well, no one else can pass it on." A sidelong glance to see if he heard.

"I think it's *disgusting*. Expecting us to work ..." The voice dropped so he missed the next part of the protest, but he could guess.

Even after they were told by the World Health Organization that the virus was not transmitted through touch, or the germs of a sneeze, the public still flinched at the thought of contact with a transsexual. Three years ago if he'd heard this sort of comment he could have complained to the Labor Relations Board and been heard. Not now. The Human Rights Laws were more honored on paper than in the workplace when it came to any possibility of Tensen's Virus.

The fact that Tensen's struck slightly more women then men hadn't helped, either. In some countries their own families had killed a number of women if people suspected they might have transsexual leanings. People didn't wait for the certainty of sexual contact: fear of the disease brought out violence and hate before sexual activity was even initiated.

There'd also been a rash of marriages, people eager to show to the rest of the world that their sexuality had not been ambiguous at all. The divorce rate dropped. People were less likely to have casual sex with strangers, or want to be in the position where they would, no matter how bad the marriage was. Thus there were more instances of domestic violence where divorce was no longer an option, and even an increase in homicides to end particularly unfortunate relationships. And many transexuals did as Cean had done: they made it clear in clothing, and by use of the pronouns that fit their outward appearance, that they were "normal".

Police forces in most cities had instituted Marriage Squads, specialists in domestic violence, even though they were rarely called in until after murder had occurred.

Cean hadn't flaunted his changing body at work, but it had been too late to hide the effects of his new hormones at the office. Although still verbal, the attacks by his co-workers had become much more vicious. And open.

"I say we should protest to management."

"They won't listen."

"Not yet they won't, but we can't wait until someone dies. We shouldn't have to face it at work. If that's not a 'hostile work environment,' I don't know what is."

That was his supervisor and her tone was both ominous and satisfied. Cean gritted his teeth at the unconscious irony. She lowered her voice so he missed all but a few phrases:

"… change, the CEO … yes. They aren't relevant now … *our* rights, too."

Cean couldn't sit still any longer. He stood up and quietly left the room, tossing the soggy remains of his sandwich into the trash as his stomach twisted into a knot. It was only a matter of time. What would he do?

Iceni Homeland, Spring, 59 C.E.

Cean remained with Lubran that evening after the old healer had offered guest privilege. The hut was ill lit with lamps, shallow bowls of oil in which wicks floated, two lit braziers adding to the smoky haze. But it was warm, the lamps' soft light glowing upon the wood walls, the smoke filtering away through the thatch above their heads. He shared Lubran's meal as they talked. To his surprise the old man wasn't ignorant of many of the principles of medicine. He knew his herbs, often using honey as an antibiotic, although that was not the name he called it.

"It is difficult to obtain, though. Our bees do not always provide enough, and some years most of the hives die out." His face twisted into worried lines. "I fear for our people now that Prasutagus is dead."

"How so?"

"He was not a wise man," Lubran said shortly. "He believed the Romans, at least until they desired us to go without weapons. Even then he trusted where he should not have and failed to trust where he should."

Knowing the bloodbath that was about to come, Cean agreed, but it was interesting that Lubran should have come to the same conclusion beforehand. His respect for the old man increased.

"He trusted the Romans, I know. Who then did he not trust? His wife?" The words were only half question.

Lubran nodded, "Aye. She is the royal woman. Through her and her daughters descends the blood of the tribe. She was thus chosen to be his wife, that the line will not be lost. And so Prasutagus ruled; now he is dead and it should be for her to order the tribe and her daughter after her."

"You fear the Romans will not agree?" He caught his breath. He could begin now, this night, to warn the Iceni. He went on, planting the right seeds, he hoped. "It is true they believe only a man may rule. I have seen this of them in other places. Women may not even own property in their cities. I've heard, too, that they topple a queen, often in favor of a man of their own, or one who will look to them. They are greedy men, taking much and giving little. They seek any excuse to seize what is not theirs."

He fell silent. That was enough for now. Lubran would think on his words, almost certainly repeating them at some time. People of any age loved rumor and gossip. If the talk was on the ominous side, it would only be passed around the faster. In his own time he'd had too much experience of that himself.

Lubran was already listening, though. "The Romans have said we are a free people." His tone was noncommittal as he passed an oatcake smeared with a paste made of sweet berries.

Cean kept his voice quiet, his sentences short so that his meaning might be plain even through his accent. To their ears at the moment it was thick, almost guttural, but it would improve with practice. He accepted the food as he spoke. They'd had fresh milk to drink and clean water. He'd stayed with the water: he wasn't yet used to mare's milk, nor had he even tasted it back in his own time. The stew had been excellent; the oatcake was dry but the jam was sweet. He chewed his mouthful and swallowed, washing it down with water.

"You were free, your king was a man. Now the royal woman rules. What will they say to that?" He shrugged. "Let us speak of something else. I have no love for the Romans."

They began to speak of medicine again until Cean was shown to a corner where dry bracken was heaped in a long wooden bed-box. Lubran gave him sheepskins and a woven woolen rug. Those below the warrior-aristocracy had only skins as bedding so he knew he was being given the old man's best.

"Sleep well."

"And you. May the night bring you dreams of good council."

Lubran smiled reminiscently in the lamplight as he left. "I have dreamed before. Look also for a true-dreaming, brother. It may be that between us we find truth."

Cean did dream that night. The old familiar dream of swords and blood. Boadicea screaming defiance as she died, her dead heaped on the ground about her. Cean watched in anguish as small children, like the child he'd seen this day, were casually murdered by laughing soldiers, older children chained in long lines to be taken for sale in the slave markets.

He cried out in pain and fury and woke, Lubran bending over him, holding his shoulder. For a moment Cean could place neither the man nor his surroundings. He panted for breath, half sitting up. Lubran released him looking anxious.

"Friend, you dreamed, crying out the Queen's name. What was your dream? It was ill?"

Cean took in a long slow breath, sorting out the language before he could speak. "Ill dreaming, Lubran. Ill dreaming."

"Aye. I feared so. I too dreamed and what was shown to me was death and blood." He sat to rock back and forth, murmuring to himself, "*Ochone, ochone*. I fear for my people. Tell me your dream, then I shall share mine with you."

There was no problem with that, Cean thought. He'd genuinely dreamed and even if that was because he knew what would happen soon, that didn't make the dream any less true.

"I dreamed the Romans approached the Iceni," he said slowly, recalling what he'd read, what he'd dreamed. "They spoke arrogantly, saying that the Queen was only a woman and not a ruler. Proudly, she bespoke them, saying she was the Royal Woman, the life and blood of her people. That her husband had ruled, not in his own right, but through her. My dream broke off then as I fell deeper into sleep. Later I dreamed again, that the Romans returned to take all the Iceni wealth in horses and enslave the people, who were free no more but slaves. The smallest children they murdered, others they chained. The Queen was dead with her daughters and there were no more Iceni."

Lubran sucked in a breath. "The Queen?"

"That was the second dream. I cannot speak more of it, Lubran." He shuddered with genuine dread. What he had dreamed still haunted him. "It was too terrible." The old man took the bait, sitting down beside Cean in the dark hut, alternately coaxing and pleading to hear more. Cean relented.

"If the dreams came to you while you were in my dwelling, I believe I would wish that you tell them to me. The gods are wise, in dreams they share wisdom. I dreamed the Romans came again as I have said. To take the wealth of the tribe, to steal away free people as slaves. Yet that was not the worst for the queen who stood against them." He rocked, hiding his eyes, using the old man's lament as his own.

"*Ochone*, evil befell her and those of her blood. I cannot say it, Lubran. Truly I cannot." Cean covered his eyes with one hand as if he felt great sorrow. If he could not stop it from happening, sorrow would in truth be his.

"Say it, brother! How else shall we be warned."

"They tore her robe, beat her with a whip as though she were a dog. Her daughters," he paused then forced the words out. "The soldiers used them as women before the tribe."

Cean recalled Tacitus's words, to come almost 50 years from this time: "Prasutagus's wife, Boadicea, was disgraced with cruel stripes; her daughters were ravished, and the most illustrious of the Icenians were, by force, deprived of their rightful positions given to them by their ancestors." Simple, polite words for such savage violence.

Cean continued. "They laughed and said no woman should rule within their lands. Let the three learn from Roman teaching and keep silent before men lest their superiors return with a harder lesson to teach them."

He looked up, into eyes which seemed to have taken fire from the single lit lamp. "Forgive me that I speak this, but you demanded truth of me. It was thus I dreamed."

Lubran nodded. Dreams were sacred to the Druids. "I believe it for also I dreamed this. Not so clearly, yet enough to know you speak truth."

Cean blinked. Telepathy? Had Lubran picked up the dream from Cean's mind as it played out? Or was it only emotions that he remembered, and now hearing Cean's words, Lubran had given the emotions shapes and events? It was certain that the old man had dreamed, perhaps not truly remembering the content save that it was something savage towards his people. Or had a portion of what Cean felt in coming here transmitted to the old man, adding to the fears already surfacing due to the uncertainty caused by the king's recent death, the Romans' presence in their land? Cean didn't know what was truth here, although he did know most of the Celtic tribes had lived by omens and portents, seeing dreams as harbingers of the future.

"Should we speak of this to others? I know not the right path here, and I will be guided by your wisdom, Lubran." Cean laid back on the bracken bed, the smell of dust and straw rising as he did so.

"Aye. When dawn comes let us see to Dauldi's lad first. If he improves then I shall go to the Queen to tell her of my own dreaming, then of yours. If she will speak to you of that, I will have someone come to bring you to us."

"That seems wise. Let it be so." He yawned and the healer smiled. "The night is not yet passed. Let us sleep again."

With that he returned to his bed, leaving Cean thankful that he'd slept in his under-clothing. The tight vest that bound his breasts flat was not in view when the old man had come in response to Cean's cry. He had a second within his pack and must be careful to wear one at all times. He relaxed back to fall asleep once more, nested comfortably in the dried plants, the thick blanket over him. Sleep returned quickly, and he dreamed nothing else.

The morning brought good news. Dauldi's boy had slept comfortably. The fever was fading while the wound had already lost some of its angry look as the infection receded. As Lubran went to speak with the Queen, Cean gave the boy a second potion in boiled water. Only a half tablet this time. He would give the other half last thing later that evening.

These tablets were intense and worked quickly, swiftly flooding the system with antibiotics so that the infection had no time to adapt and become immune to them. The boy would probably need no more.

After the next tablet, and more of the hot compresses to draw the poison from the lad's system, Cean thought the boy's own immune system would deal with the problem adequately. It might even be that the boy would keep the use of his arm. That would be good. He would keep his rightful place in the tribe then.

At the same time, Cean made sure to speak admiringly of Lubran, saying that without the healer's prayers and strong aid, the outcome would not have been favorable. The Iceni were fortunate to have such a strong and wise healer. There were approving nods all around at his words. The foreign healer was an honest man, not claiming all the credit for himself. Dauldi's woman left the group briefly to return with two finely cured foal skins.

"Healer, one of our mares bore twins last season, losing both as sometimes happens with twins. These skins I cured with my own hands. Let you now choose one, bearing the other to Lubran. My man and I give thanks for the return of the life of our son."

Cean accepted the skins knowing to refuse would give offense. On the practical side, his knowledge had saved the child and a laborer was worthy of his hire. They would suspect something odd if he refused. They might accept he wandered to trade knowledge and learn in return, but how else was he to live if he accepted no gifts? He inclined his head, a smile breaking through.

"A fine gift from the woman of the house. Lubran too shall be pleased, I think. I thank you in his name."

He took the skins back to Lubran's hut, placing one on each box-bed. The foals had been bright chestnut and the cured skins were the size of sheepskins, incredibly supple and soft. He thought that in this time they were a valuable present; they were certainly beautiful. He stroked one foalskin gently, wondering what Lubran was saying to Boadicea—and, more importantly—what she was saying in return. He didn't have to wait long to hear. Lubran returned within minutes.

"Come. The Queen would hear your dream from your own mouth."

"I'm coming. Look what Dauldi's woman gave to us." Lubran paused to touch a skin.

"Very proper. The lad is her eldest boy; it would have shamed her family to give a gift of less than his worth. But come, follow me. Boadicea asks for you and it would not be well to keep her waiting."

Cean swallowed. Hard. Finally. He was to meet her. Really meet her.

He obeyed, trotting after his companion towards the largest hut within the dun. "Hut" wasn't the right word he thought, if you indicated poverty of size or luxury by that word. Lubran's hut was small, yet it was spacious enough to take in Cean without cramping. It had an almost modern open-plan to it which allowed a considerable amount of space inside. It was simple yet comfortable as well, nor was it as dirty or pest-ridden as he'd feared.

He hurried at Lubran's heels, aware that several people watched them as they walked past two other huts before they came to the Queen's. The adults among them dressed in rough woolen cloaks and the children in belted tunics. The path they walked was moist without being muddy, and Cean's sandals caught in it a little with a soft sucking as he strode along after the healer.

One woman winnowing grain tossed it high on a two-pronged fork made from a tree branch. She watched them out of the corner of her eyes as they went by, the chaff caught by the thin breeze dancing lightly before settling to the dirt at her feet. She tossed another fork-full, smiling. It had been a good harvest.

Cean expected to enter another hut but instead Lubran conducted him around the side of the Queen's house to where a woman sat on a short bench covered in fine skins. Now that he was to see her in daylight, he wondered if she would have anything like the face of the painting he'd had in his own time. He halted, bowed low as he approached, then walked forward again as she turned.

The sunlight glowed on her hair so that for a moment he was deceived into thinking she was beautiful. She wasn't. She was more than fair. She glowed with vitality, with a blazing intelligence and ferocious driving will. Her eyes were an indeterminate shade of either green, or hazel. They'd take color from whatever shade she wore. Just now they had the green hue of the dull mantle about her shoulders. Her face was almost harsh, angular, with fine pale skin, lightly freckled.

Her hair blazed a wonderful shade between red and blond. Titian, a molten cascade of fire as it fell down her back to her waist, the copper fillet which bound it from her face dimmed by the shade of the surrounding hair. It was the hair that deceived one into thinking her beautiful at first. There was too much strength in that face for vapid beauty, Cean felt. Instead it was stunning. But beauty or not, here was a woman who would change his world and hers, for good or evil.

He felt the power touch him. She was a woman men would follow wherever she led, even if it were through the gates of Hell itself. He hid the shiver prickling his spine. If she listened to him that could indeed be what would happen to them all. This was the woman who would now change time for him. He bowed slowly keeping his gaze on her face. Waiting for her to speak.

"Lubran tells me you have dreamed." Cean suppressed surprise. She did get straight to the heart of things. She was not a woman for polite greetings.

"I have. I know not the truth of my dreaming yet Lubran is wise and he also dreamed, saying after he heard me that his dream was similar to mine. So I bade him tell it where he thought best."

Her voice was dry. "Thus he came to his Queen and spoke of both dreams. Now speak of yours to me, leaving nothing out. But stay," she held up a hand as he opened his mouth. "Have you dreamed truly before?"

"How can I say? I am a wandering man. I have dreamed, but rarely do I remain to see if my dreams are truth. Nor have they been of great portent before, being of small things."

She nodded slowly. "This dream was no small thing. Lubran says you called out my name, spoke as if in horror at what you saw." She paused, eyes turning from him to Lubran at his side. "Dreams are from the gods. It may be the great goddess Brighid, or Lugos himself has sent to you these dreams for I, too, dreamed four nights gone and I believe that to have been a true-dreaming as well. Tell me now what your dream was, man from afar." She rested her chin on one hand as she watched him.

Cean looked about him meaningfully. "The dream was long and I was wakened early."

Boadicea waved at one of her women just coming out of the hut. "Bring him a seat and some ale. Immediately."

He sat on the small backless stool hastily provided, accepted the proffered wooden cup, drank a little, determined not to think about what he was doing, and began.

"I dreamed twice. In the first dream a Roman came to the Iceni. A small man who strutted as a cock-bird displays to entice mates to his nest and enemies to battle. The man said now the ruler of the tribe was dead, the people belonged to Rome. To Rome also would go the wealth of the tribe now under Rome's rule. The people's horses, gear, and goods would all go with the slaves whose number came from the people of the tribe."

Boadicea's eyes blazed. "What was said by the people to this?"

"That they were a free people under a queen."

"And the Roman?"

"Said they acknowledged no queens. He said, 'Let women go to their huts and keep their silence. Under Roman rule it is men who speak, women who obey.'" Cean watched her fury gather. "I have seen the Romans in other lands, lady. But this I dreamed—I swear it—and from what I have seen in my wandering, I say also that this is their law."

"You dreamed again you said?" Her words were not gentle. She was angry, but not at him.

He feigned reluctance, dropping his eyes. "I did, my lady. Yet of that second dream I would not speak before others. Lubran must have told you something of it."

She briefly considered. "He did." She turned and spoke quietly to one of her women who left quickly, drawing the watching people with her. Lubran, however, came from the shadows to stand at Boadicea's shoulder.

"None remain now to hear save you and I, and one I trust. Speak plainly, man from afar. Let all be made plain that I may know what I may face."

She believed him!

Cean forced down his elation. She listened, at least. Perhaps she'd believe him entirely and turn aside the doom looming in the future. He kept his voice slow, his words simple. Now was not the time for any misunderstanding.

"The Romans came again. The cock still strutted in their midst. He spoke that your people were no longer free. Without their king, they were Roman slaves. Yet they did not bend to the Romans' demands as expected, this defiance because of your example. The cock crowed his anger. Thus, he said, you should learn the hand of Rome was heavy, and you must bear the lesson he and his would give."

She leaned forward, intent on every word, seeing in her mind the scene he described. Cean faltered.

"Lady, forgive me. I do not wish to tell you more. You will mislike what else I have to say."

"No, go on." She waved her hand at him. "I would hear it. Your dreams could not be worse than my own fears for my people."

Cean continued, quietly. "The soldier seized you, your robe was stripped from your shoulders, and like a mongrel hound underfoot you were beaten before your tribe. Then they seized your daughters." He faltered again, licking his lips. But again her hand gestured impatiently for him to go on. She said nothing. "They were flung down, used by a number of the soldiers before all present. Then were you warned. Learn to bow to Rome as a woman should, else Rome will see to it you have further lessons. You and your daughters both."

"Was that the dream's ending?" Her eyes were gold furies, her voice a rasp.

"In a way, my lady. I saw only one final thing. A great line of horses which were driven by soldiers. With them walked young men and women in the clothing of the Iceni, some only children. They went in chains, guarded by soldiers, and ahead rode the one who had come strutting into the dun. He smirked as he rode as if he counted to himself the wealth he had gained this day. My dream grew dark then, and I cried out in my sleep, '*Ochone, ochone* for the Iceni and for the Royal Women, dishonored by this Roman dog. Surely the gods will not stand idly by and let this be so?'"

Boadicea rose from her seat, stalking rapidly back and forth, in lion-like strides. Cean noticed that by Roman standards their report of her had been right. She must be at least five foot six, and her bones, while not heavy, were strong. Definitely not clumsy, he thought, seeing the pantherish pacing, the graceful powerful movements. She walked like a dancer, or a trained fighter. At length she spoke.

"The dream may be true. I too know the Romans. And unlike my husband I never trusted them. I have seen their gaze when they visited the dun. They have cast greedy eyes on our wealth before. The will Prasutagus made was foolish, tempting trouble for his people. As I told him, though he had no mind to listen to my words. And so I must prepare to defend myself and my people. At the same time I must grieve officially for my husband."

She spoke bitterly, breaking off the last few words as if they burned her tongue. If she had been chosen for him, she could have been unhappy in the marriage. She said then, "And have you advice as well as dreams for me, man from afar?" There was irony in her voice. She was testing him.

Cean calmly met her fiery gaze. "One thing only, lady. What is not known cannot be acted upon. Which buys time."

She smiled grimly. "My husband died three nights gone and none but you have come since that time. None outside the dun know he is no more. If word does not go forth, how long may it be before others find out?"

"Longer if it is given out that he is yet ill in bed." Even though her smile was cold, it warmed him. Now she listened!

"That could well be so, and there is a man of our tribe who has the look of my husband although somewhat older. He was far-kin of Prasutagus's line and drove his chariot. If any come we can show them a man who is ill and speaks wildly with a fever."

Lubran who had been quietly listening, spoke up. "There are ways to make a man appear ill. I can place fever sweat upon his brow, put that in his eyes which will make them seem larger and crazed with the illness that has struck him down. Between us, lady I think none from outside our people shall question this. But will all hold their tongues about this lie?"

"Our people will not speak—not once I have explained to them why this must be." Boadicea's voice was thoughtful. "They will hear my reasons well. I know many already fear Roman greed. Their soldiers trade with us, but always they make certain their laws allow them to cheat us when we may not gain from them in return. Nay, I shall tell the people of the danger in which we stand. I shall send messengers to other tribes who have no love for the Romans either."

She sat again, her eyes fierce as she stared out over her dun. "I am no slave to be whipped. Nor are my daughters fodder for the beds of Roman filth. Before such happens I shall rise and slay them all if necessary." She spoke with the conviction anger brings, and Cean wondered at the years she must have dealt with Romans unwillingly.

"'Bare is brotherless back,'" Lubran quoted to her. "Thus my brother Cean said to me. Best we seek out kin swiftly to stand beside us, my lady. Then when this man struts here in pride we may take him, once we are certain his thought is as my brother has dreamed."

Boadicea eyed him. "That is wisdom. And you?" She turned to look at Cean. "Do you remain with us?"

"How not? This time I have a fancy to see how my dream turns out. I have said to Lubran that we shall learn healing of each other, and besides." He looked carefully into her eyes. "Would you be so joyful to see me depart—now?"

He saw she understood his meaning. He would not have been allowed to leave anyway, not with what he could tell of a man's death before she wished it known. Nor with the knowledge of her intent towards the Romans. And she wanted to be sure his tale of dreams was not a lie.

"I do not wish to leave so that is well," he concluded comfortably.

"A wise man makes the best of things," she agreed, standing again with restless energy. "Your dreams may be of much use to me and your knowledge to the healer. For that Lubran may provide you with a roof, and I shall see that food comes from my table. Dream again if you can, and if you do, be sure I will listen."

She would indeed. Cean looked back at her as he walked away. She had listened because what he'd said of his dream fitted all too well with her own fears. Of course, she wouldn't have necessarily believed all that he'd said, and she would wonder if he was somehow in the pay of the Roman governor.

His own belief in what he said, however, had gone a long way to convincing her. As had Lubran's words and experience of him. And if she was the queen he believed her to be, she would guess that there were other secrets he withheld. Yet he wondered what her people had already endured trying to co-operate with the Romans that she would listen to what he told her so easily. She feared the Romans, and distrusted them. That was enough.

Lubran left him in the hut for the afternoon, certainly to return to the Queen. She would want to be sure that the stranger had not said more to him alone than to her. But Cean was still tired, worn by the entire change in time so he needed to sleep. That evening, when Lubran returned and they ate a meal together, the old healer was somewhat withdrawn, however, and met Cean's eyes little.

Finally Cean spoke, "What bothers my brother?"

"The Queen," Lubran replied. He stuck his knife into the deer meat he was eating. "She saw the tears in your eyes as you spoke of how she was whipped, her daughters ravaged. She was only surprised a stranger should feel for women he did not know. Perhaps you had once had a women of your own house, lost to you by death or some ill-treatment at another's hands? No matter," Lubran quickly continued. "Tell me as you will, or not. In these times, it is not uncommon. But the Queen saw. She thought that might be why you wandered, why you dreamed and why you wept at what you saw."

Lubran had smiled affectionately at her when she asked if he had believed the stranger. He'd known Boadicea since she was a child and she was kin, his mother a cousin to her grandmother.

"I believe he believes," he'd told her. "I think him honest and his heart is kind. He shares what he knows with me and I see his pleasure in doing so. He has wonders."

Lubran did not tell Cean what else they had said although he thought of that now. "Maybe he was sent. I have not questioned him too closely. He does not wish to speak of some things. He bears a bronze casket which is strange, nor have I been able to open it. But I have read the stars and I fear the omens' warning of what is to come. I have seen the portents, but understood only dimly. Perhaps he has come to make clear what I read in the stars."

Boadicea's breath had caught in her throat, and Lubran knew why. Did he mean this stranger was sent by the gods? Someone to advise a daughter of the blood more plainly where the gods spoke usually in riddles? Lubran's thoughts had been the same as hers.

"Treat him with all honor, kinsman, and what of Dauldi's son?"

"He heals, and I say to you, kinswoman, that as I know healing, no man could have saved the boy. This Cean is open-hearted. He gives me a part of the credit before the people when he need not. I know my own skills. Seven years I studied, seven more I trained. I could not have held back death another sunrise. This man defeated death almost as if he knew death could not stand against him.

"I shall treat him with all honor," Lubran had continued thoughtfully. "I can learn much more of my craft from him. But let you be cautious with his words, my lady. Withhold belief until some be proved, but I think the coming days will show that he has been sent to us. If he is proven true, let us listen to what he may then suggest."

The Queen had nodded. "That is good council, old man. First let the boy survive and be whole. Let me make my plans with others. Then we shall wait to see what comes of our king's folly. In that shall be the final proof of what this stranger tells us. If all is as the stranger says, I will hearken to his words. Moreover," her face had lit with rage, her eyes darkened in anger. "No Roman shall whip me before the people. First shall he kiss my spear though he come with a thousand soldiers."

Lubran agreed. But he didn't think trouble would start with such a heavy hand. Even a Roman was not that foolish. "If he come with a thousand it will be a sign. Yet at the start I do not think he will. Did not the stranger dream twice? It is to my mind the Roman will come twice seeking riches. Only when we send him away once is he likely to return in strength to steal what is ours. Talk to our friends in the other tribes. Many of them also chafe under Roman law." Lubran had then sighed softly.

"You fear?"

"For the people I fear. The stars are turning in their paths. There is great change to come upon us, my lady."

"I agree, kinsman. I fear that we may be close to war over this business of my husband's will. It was a foolish thing to do."

Lubran had kept his eyes bent to the ground. It was not for him to admit to the wrongs a king may have done, to criticize a king, even a dead one. He had counseled moderation, though, when he'd spoken to her then. All her life, he had known the wildness in her, the pride. He'd feared what she might do once Prasutagus was gone.

"Be sure I shall consider all things," had been her only reply. Today she told him, "Go now, seek out the stranger, bind him to us with friendship, and learn of him all you may, not the least from whence he comes and his people. You see stars, but I smell secrets. If he is sent to dream for us then when the time comes, we must know it."

Lubran had inclined his head before he left her. "That is the word of the gods. Surely they will show one of us if it be their will."

From Boadicea's side, he had then gone to the trees outside of the dun, looking for what he had kept hidden there over the years. On these he had looked very long and soberly before he replaced them in their hiding place beneath some stones. A healer who was also one trained on the Druid's Isle had responsibilities. Care for the work or not, he must be ready to do as might be required of him.

In his hut, as he finally looked up at Cean's friendly eyes, Lubran wondered how much of that duty he would in fact be called upon to finish.

Los Angeles, Fall, 2048 C.E.

Other people, in another time, had greeted Cean with more trust. When Cean attended a meeting of the Coalition for the Profiled for the first time, a support group for those susceptible to Tensen's, he met Fort and a woman introduced to him as Mel. Cean was immediately taken with her as a person. She was small, had glowing dark hair, and bubbled whenever she spoke.

"Fort's not profiled," she quickly told him. "I am." She grinned. "You'd never know it, would you? I should be big-boned and flat-chested. But I'm not. I simply stay with saying 'she' for myself, it's safer these days. Yet all my life I thought I was a boy my mother dressed in the wrong clothes." She mimicked the sway of a long skirt and laughed. "I was scheduled for hormone treatments to begin next month when they blew up at me at work." The smile faded. "Someone had read my private e-mail, and my colleagues started giving me unpleasant looks. Me, a scandal!" She laughed again at that, her voice a little dry, brittle. "More likely I'd be the boss's pet example, I'm so well-behaved."

"Don't you believe it," Fort put in. "She's the most subversive person I know."

She giggled at him. It turned out Fort and Mel had been close friends since childhood. Fort wasn't transsexual or profiled; he had joined the group out of sympathy for Mel and others who didn't deserve the harassment they were receiving.

"I didn't know what was going on at first," Mel explained. "I just thought they were angry at me for something. I often imitate people, and sometimes it makes them mad."

Someone had handed Cean a cup of coffee, and he drank it. He was a bit shy, and something in his hand made him feel more secure.

"Then they fired me on the spot," Mel continued, a small wince accompanying her words. She had apparently liked her job.

"So now she works with me," Fort put in.

"Where is that?" Cean asked.

He'd become quite curious. Leogold Fortescue—Fort—he'd insisted to Cean, was smart and calm, very unaggressive, an unusual combination for business. Fort hesitated. But Mel nudged him, another grin on her face.

"A think tank," Fort explained. "I do some of their research, even some of my own on the side." He grimaced. "Of course, any patents that come out of those are in the company's name. So far I haven't lost them anything."

"You've actually made them money," Mel quickly said in his defense. "They'll do anything to keep you at this stage."

"Let's hope so. Mel's now my assistant," Fort added for Cean's benefit, then went on: "They let me pursue my research any way I want. As long as I keep them informed of everything I do. Scientists usually work alone in any case, sometimes with an assistant or two, and I don't have graduate students available to me, so whoever I want as a co-worker is fine with them."

Mel broke in quietly. "The prejudice is getting so bad though, that I've stayed undercover. I don't want to cause trouble. Fort does some fascinating experiments anyhow and I'd hate to lose out on watching some of those."

In Fort's personal experiments, he worked on time travel. Cean whooped when Fort first said this.

"Time travel! Science fiction ... er ... crud. You can't believe you can get anywhere with that."

He took a drink of his coffee before he said anything more damning. The first people he'd met in a long time who were willing to be friendly and he'd come that close to insulting them. Not socially skilled, he reminded himself, and took a firmer grip on his tendency to blurt out whatever he was thinking.

"I don't know." His new friend looked thoughtful. "I have a theory about using wormholes." Cean looked blank and was quickly treated to a brief lecture on the theory of wormholes as Einsten-Rosen bridges through space along with their possible connections to time as a quality of space.

Fort smiled at Cean. "Isn't there some time or some place, even some one you wished you could go back to meet? Or even stop them from making an enormous mistake? In theory at least, these bridges would make it possible."

The Boadicea painting flashed across Cean's mind, one that was certainly not like the real woman, but enough to have taken Cean's fancy. He'd carried that picture with him for years. He spoke from his heart.

"God, yes. She needn't have died."

Fort raised his eyebrows. "Well, if I succeed maybe I'll let you go back and warn her." He was joking, of course, and smiled to show it, but Cean wasn't as he answered him.

"I'll remember that. Maybe I'll take you up on it one day."

Mel chuckled. "Maybe we could go back and stop Tensen's from ever happening."

Cean wished. "It would save so much pain and suffering, wouldn't it?"

He almost whispered the next thought aloud. There were rumors surfacing that some countries were forcing their profiled into fenced camps. Just as the Cubans had initially done to their AIDS patients.

"It wouldn't do you any good," Fort was brief, and grim.

"What? Why not?"

"Because if you made a major change you probably wouldn't come back to the same world." He studied their puzzled expressions. "You really don't read science fiction. You probably should." He smiled. "In my opinion, everyone should. Look, the theory used in a lot of stories is simple. If you make a major change the world which eventuates subsequent to that change is no longer the same one it was before you went back in time. That one still exists in its own parallel universe. Many think that what you are actually doing when you alter past events is just create another universe, similar but different in the way you've changed it. In that world, you might return to the same friends but circumstances would be very different."

Fort eyed his own coffee cup then put it down on a nearby table as he held up his hands, as if he was holding a globe between them. "For instance, in the new universe, if you'd stopped the virus early before it affected people, money that was used in doctor's visits, medicine and research, would have gone into other things instead, like space research. We could be substantially further along in that." He lowered one hand, as if he turned the imaginary shape in his hands.

"Or the same money might have funded a major breakthrough which in three years has changed our society in ways you'd never considered. Another possibility," he raised the first hand and lowered the other then, "could be that someone who dies of Tensen's in our world, might have discovered anti-gravity in the other timeline, changing society in ways we cannot even imagine outside of space travel. Drug manufacture, for instance. There are other possibilities, too, major ones. A man could have died here who in a different world would have stopped the never-ending African conflicts, and the entire continent of Africa might now be technologically developed and richer than the United States. It's possible—the natural resources are there."

Cean looked disbelieving. "In only three years?"

"Why not. Thailand recovered from economic collapse in less time than that, with strong leadership, and some draconian laws. They forced their people back into poverty for a short time, but after three years, their economy was improving again."

He coughed briefly before continuing with his original explanation. "Look at retrograde viruses. They made the breakthrough in research only five years ago with that attachment gene. Suppose you went back and killed the person who made the breakthrough, destroying all his notes and files. Then, all the people who'd survived because of his work would be dead. That one breakthrough has saved a lot of people in the past five years, by the way." Cean and Mel nodded. "And what's more, everything they would have contributed throughout their lives would be gone too. Like dominoes: if you change one thing, what follows is changed too, and each change streams out into another universe." Fort was so excited he picked up his cup again, looked at it and set it down once more.

Mel had obviously been thinking about the whole unpredictability of time changes, too. "If you went back further you'd get a progressive effect, like a fan opening out, the further back, the more changes would have been made that would lead to other changes, and so on, spreading out down the years."

"That's right. The further back you go the more likely it is you'd get a major alteration in our civilization today by quite a minor change having happened back there. Someone once said if you stepped on a bug a million years ago, we might now not have a society we'd recognize."

As Cean listened, he went quiet. In his mind a building burned, a woman and two children were savaged. He saw the flaming hair, the eyes that seemed to search his face for answers, and he had none. Injustice triumphed and there was no one to stop it. But if there was any possibility in Fort's work there was also the chance …

"Cean? Cean? Where've you gone?"

"Sorry … just thinking. I wonder what sort of a world you'd get if you went back and shot Ghengis Khan?"

"Or got rid of Hitler before he ever gained power," Mel added. One of her great-grandmothers had died in Auschwitz.

Fort grinned. "That one's been done. An interesting book too. And someone wrote a brilliant short story about Napoleon dying young and obscure. No, take any crucial point in history and change it and you would end up with a completely different world here and now. The other world would carry on its own universe, but this one would be changed irrevocably. But," he went on, lifting his cup to acknowledge a woman passing them, "however you look at it, time travel won't save this world so they'll just have to find a cure for the virus soon, and then we can return to life as it should be, all things being equal. Everything will sort itself out in the long run. Hopefully."

But the grimness in his eyes belied the cheerful tone, and his friends took the cue to change the subject. Mel had lost her smile, and Cean was certain her life had not been as easy as she made it seem. Hard as it had been for him, he thought that a woman who wished to be male might face still more levels of prejudice.

But when Cean left the meeting, he knew what he was going to do. He would go back to Boadicea's world. He'd create a different universe, a kinder one that healed instead of punished, one without Tensen's, a world in which Mel, himself, and others like them would not suffer.

In this world he had never found love, and now that Tensen's was so feared, he was afraid to look; if he revealed himself and was rejected it could mean a beating—or much worse. And in truth, while he had felt desire for an occasional attractive woman now and then, love eluded him, all but his fascination with Boadicea, and his yearning to see her and her people, to give them the chance at life they had lost to the Romans. He saw again in his minds eye the face of his picture, the wind-tossed hair, and the proud harsh-planed features. Would she really be so or was that an idealization? He didn't know, but his mind was made up, and he would find out.

3

Before the Romans arrived in Britain, the Iceni were a simple, passionate people. They measured their wealth in horses and cattle as well as coins, and they believed in their land as a spiritual force in their lives. In Druidic belief, this is not so unusual. But the Iceni had a quality that made them greater than the other tribes: a belief in themselves as a people, enhanced through their family relationships.

This gave them a certain pride as a distinct tribe of the region, and while neither of these aspects reflects economic principles, in the Queen's hands it did. As they united their belief system with their attitudes about their families and land wealth, they initiated a method of tribe management that was peculiarly their own. Consequently, as I plan to show in the course of this chapter, because of these two factors they developed a leadership system and economic structure unique to their tribe. It opposed outside rule, and encouraged female sovereignty in business relationships with outside communities, a system that I call sovereign economics.

—from "The Life and Rule of the Queen,"
Leceister Murrane, in *The Making of
the Tribes: Iron Age Economic Management*

Iceni culture emphasized the land. That was their wealth, that and the horses they loved so well as living expressions of the world. Anla states that "Boadicea paced the land each morning, greeting the sun's rise as it floated above the eastern hills at dawn."

Other sources say that the Queen also lit a lamp every night of her life to represent the light of the sun while it was gone. The exact reason for her doing so is lost, although many state it was a part of her personal worship of the Goddess Brighid, but it also suggests that in her life she maintained a continuous link, a thread tying all life, day to night.

In these stories about her, there is certainly a reflection of the spiritual connection with the land that modern life repudiates with every step of its technological development. Buildings crush the ground, the land that has given us life. Vehicles like cars, trucks, or trains separate us from this spiritual essence and so we are cut off from that vital spark of the world with all that we do. This is the curse of modernization, a curse that will eventually destroy us, from the spirit out.

—from *Spiritual Definition and Loss by Her Holiness*, by Priestess Lianad Riarven

Iceni Homeland, 59 C.E.

If proof was what they sought through Dauldi's son, Verli, then they had it swiftly. The following night the boy was sitting up drinking broth. His arm, studied carefully by both Lubran and Cean, was showing no heat and the red streaks had drawn back so that the angry hue of infection infested only the wound itself, its edges beginning to pale.

"Waste no more of your potion if it be so rare." Lubran urged. "The lad heals now."

"Aye, but the unseen enemy is cunning. Like the Romans, if battle ceases too early it may rally and return."

Lubran understood that. He helped Cean lift the boy to a half-sitting posture as Cean handed him the cup, the boiled water and the other half a tablet that would ensure there was no backward step in Verli's improvement.

As the boy drank obediently Cean looked him over. A slight, lithe child, with shaggy hair of a medium brown hung down his back. The eyes turned to Cean were blue though the brows above them were so dark as to appear black. A good-looking lad, and the stubborn chin marked personality though the face itself was sensitive in general. Cean bent again to look at the arm.

"What do you think of this, Lubran?"

"I think it does well as to the wound-sickness. How it will do for the arm's use I cannot say. The damage was great."

"Gentle exercise, building slowly perhaps. Very slowly and with care?"

"That is wisdom." He turned to Dauldi. "Hear our words, Dauldi, son of Venlo. The boy's arm was greatly hurt. He must take care not to strain it for if further damage is done it may be the arm will become useless to a warrior." Dauldi's look changed to one of anxiety.

"Nay," Lubran continued, "we do not say it will be so. Only if he rushes the use of it. Would you take a foal and have him bear heavy loads? He must build up the arm's strength again slowly and with care. Let him exercise it a little more each quarter moon. The muscles must be coaxed into work as a foal is coaxed into carrying. In time the arm may heal well, though a weakness may remain in it. Let him practice with the other when he becomes frustrated that the injuries heal slowly. It is good for a warrior to be able to fight with either arm."

Dauldi nodded. "That is true, Lubran. My father himself said so to me and I learned thus. I will see my son takes no foolish chances. He shall exercise both arms, and the one which was injured he shall train with care." He looked at Cean. "I thank you, healer. You are no kin to us yet kin could have done no more to aid us."

Cean smiled, the sudden open grin which had appealed to Boadicea. "I am joyful I was able to render help. Moreover have I not been paid? And royally? The foal skin the woman of your house gave me is the finest I have ever seen."

"Aye, she does well with such things." Dauldi's look was proud. "Yet a skin does not buy a life, and a life you have given us. We shall remember this."

He ushered them out with ceremony, making it clear to any who saw and would be inclined to spread word that Dauldi of the Iceni treated Cean as a well valued friend. Cean felt a small warm glow at the kindness. His journey here had started as an abstract obsession. In a way he had never seen the Iceni and their tragic Queen as more than the background to his desire to save them, perhaps saving the future in the process. Over the past two days he was coming to see these people as more.

Lubran, who had eagerly opened his home to a stranger. Lubran who listened and shared his own wisdom. Here was no ignorant hidebound old fool, set in his ways and reluctant to learn. His home was clean as might be in these times. Tidy, and solidly built. Lubran's person was clean too. Oh, there were fleas. Cean had expected them. Even body lice. But Lubran strewed a dried herb which kept them well away, something he named flea-bane. The old man had his clothing washed regularly, too, and washed himself each day.

Perhaps others in the tribe were not quite so careful, yet Cean had noted none who were as filthy as he'd expected. Their hair was a little less frequently washed, but otherwise they were a clean people. And hard working. Verli's arms were dense with sinewy muscle. Even so young, he probably practiced as a warrior already. Cean had seen children herding the cattle, and young girls spinning wool, all industriously working to provide for their lives.

The Iceni were prosperous in this time. They traded cattle and tin with Gaul, sometimes even the gold that traveled from Ireland. But prosperity came with diligence, and these people had earned their wealth. He smiled to himself as he followed Lubran back to their home. He liked these people. And there was Dauldi, who loved his son; Siharni, the woman of his house whose grateful gaze followed Cean. And Verli, a brave child who trusted the healers. Cean would not let him down. Or the rest of these people, if possible.

His mind turned back to the Queen. Boadicea, too, had not been what he'd believed her to be. There was a power there, but also a blazing intelligence. She had listened to him, agreed with what he'd said. If that continued, his dream could come true. Once he'd imagined a kingdom stretching from sea to sea within this country, ruled by women who were more sensible than Roman men or tribal kings, and less warlike without good cause. He could almost see them, red of hair and temper, but all with that power which drew others to them, and the intelligence to use their skills then for good.

There were ways to make a country theirs: Alliance, marriage, treaty, and conquest. But little of that last. The conquered had an understandable habit of rising against their conquerors. He'd make that point to her one day. She'd understand. Were not the Iceni planning exactly that?

"Cean, do you dream now while you walk?" He came back to himself with a start realizing they had arrived back at Lubran's hut.

"Aye, I do, Lubran. Good dreams." He looked at the old man. "It seems I will be staying here for some time."

"Do you mind?"

"Nay, I like you and your people well. I would see how Verli does, and if my dreaming was true. I am content to remain. Yet I would not be under your roof if you wish me elsewhere."

"And if I do not? Would you wish to lodge under another roof, one of your own perhaps? I think the Queen would send men to help you build should you wish it."

"Let me think on that." Cean laughed. "I may think so long I will never leave and you will have me here longer than you could wish."

Lubran shook his head. "I have watched you these past days. You are a true healer, concerned with those you aid. Also it is good for a people to have more than one healer. Your customs, I believe, are somewhat different and your beliefs also perhaps, but you respect ours. Before the people you asked me to bespeak our gods saying that surely they would answer one of their own. That was wisdom and kindness both. I say to you, Cean, I would like you to remain with us. I am not a young man. If we go to war I may not see the end of it. The people should have a healer."

His gaze lifted to meet Cean's. "Hear my words. Twenty years I learned, and seven more I trained. To me you have that first twenty, although you be too young for it in years. If the gods do not forbid me, I would train you for the other half of my work." He paused, looking deep into Cean's eyes. "I say no more now. Remember my words and if your heart does not bid you leave us, we shall talk more upon this."

They ate and went to their separate beds that night. Cean lay awake for some time after he had lain down. He couldn't be certain but he thought Lubran had offered him something rare. There'd not been much on healer training in the books of his time. Nor much that was known for truth about the druids of the Iceni period. Neither Iceni nor druids had kept written records.

Also, the Romans had hated and feared the druids, wiping them out where they could. And as the druids were the keepers of knowledge in their time, their learning had been virtually erased in Britain. The invaders had distorted much of the remaining information, filtering it through the cloth of their own fears as they recorded it.

Something in Lubran's talk had alerted Cean that not all druids were so obvious, too. If Lubran was not wholly druid, he was at least partially trained in that discipline. It was not surprising. In the generations before Cean's own, medical missionaries had been common. Lubran might not be a missionary, but Cean thought it likely he combined healer training with training as a druid. Learning from him would be useful and interesting.

If he was not mistaken the old man had been asking that Cean stay. And suggesting that if he did, he could in time take Lubran's place. Clearly, Cean could not go back to his own time. Nor did he really wish to. His friends were still there, but if Fort's promise held true, they would be leaving that world as well, and for some other time. Aside from that, his arrival in this time might already be changing this world, so that if he could return, it would not be to the world he'd left.

However, he ruefully allowed, his desire to stay might change if he was injured or the Iceni turned against him. He hoped they wouldn't. If they didn't, he thought he could find a place here, make friends and a home within the tribe. Or so he hoped. More importantly he must not forget why he'd made the journey. He could also change what was to come. No, not "could." Would!

He remembered Dauldi and Siharni's gratitude, Verli's trusting gaze, Lubran's eager face as they discussed healing. *Yes.* For their sake, and for Boadicea who drew all to her with her fire, they should live and not die. He swore it again in the silent darkness of the hut. He *would* change what was to come, or die trying.

* * * *

Three days later they visited Verli again. The boy was drinking broth obediently but he scowled up from his bed.

"What, you do not like your mother's cooking?" Lubran teased gently.

"The broth is well enough but no food for a warrior."

"Ah, but a warrior who is hurt must drink broth as he is told. That way he heals swiftly and may return to his spears."

"That may be so," the boy admitted grudgingly.

"I have said so. My brother Cean agrees. If you do not try to hurry your body, in time you may be as you once were. But hear me well, Verli. A warrior must be as patient as he is brave. Attack too soon and you frighten away your quarry. You must be just as patient with your body. Let it learn again but slowly. That takes time and haste may ruin all."

Verli looked across at Cean who nodded. "Your healer is wise. Heed his words." The boy's shoulder drooped a little but he nodded. "Good lad. A warrior obeys. If he cannot discipline himself, how shall he learn?"

Cean strolled away with Lubran who was amused. "No warrior is so disciplined."

Cean remembered all he knew of Rome. "Are they not? Yet what of the Romans, are they not disciplined? Do they not fight with many acting as one?"

"Would you have us be Romans then?"

"Nay. Not Romans. Iceni who have learned to discipline themselves in battle." He faced the old man. "Listen, Lubran. Rome holds many lands because they obey their leaders. They have both discipline within themselves and from those they follow. Thus those they face in war are slain as they do not fight together but attack one by one. Their strength is not combined against their enemies. If the Iceni are to survive, they may have to learn some new ways. Those who are not open to learning are closed to life's future," he added, a little sententiously. "Nor do they survive well, if at all."

"These words are hard."

"But true."

"I fear they may be so. Now, I go to gather plants for medicines. Would you come with me?"

"If you like the company."

"It is good to talk to you."

They foraged peacefully for the remainder of the morning but afterwards, Lubran again left Cean within his hut and sought out his kinswoman alone. Boadicea smiled up at him.

"Where is your guest?" she asked him.

"Learning the plants that heal. I set him to tying them for drying and then to tidy our house."

"What have you learned of him?" was her next question.

Lubran had sat then, taking the wine-cup offered by one of Boadicea's women. "His thoughts are strange. He speaks of battle discipline, saying that this is why the Romans win in their battles. I asked if he wished us to be like them, but he said not so. He wishes us to truly be the Iceni, but if we would live free of the Romans, our warriors must be open to some new ways." He paused to sip his wine. "He is an unusual man. He dreams as he walks and they are not ill dreams for I have seen him smile as a man smiles at the thought of a good future."

The Queen grinned. "Maybe he dreams of a woman."

"Mayhap, yet I do not believe so. He smiles at the girls of the tribe but his eyes do not follow any as a man normally would." Again he stopped before continuing. "But there is one thing he hides from me. He wears a cloth wrapped about his chest at night as well as the day."

Boadicea laughed. "That may be caution. He is a stranger."

"Nay, there is nothing in his eyes of desire when he looks at the girls. Only such a look as you might wear when you see a fine spear, a spirited horse." He had struggled to convey the impersonal appreciation Cean gave to the laughing girls of the Iceni and succeeded well enough to make the Queen thoughtful.

"He admires them without desire. Maybe he is one who desires men?"

"He gazes upon the young men in the same way."

"Then perhaps he is not a man, but a woman." The Queen continued. "This would be something to hide from us. Women who are healers are rare, and not often welcome among the tribes."

"I have seen him pass water, my Queen. He does not do so as a woman but as a man."

"An accident," Boadicea said delicately. "Such are not unknown. One who can no longer desire as normal men. I have seen it happen; a slip of the spear, or the hard shock of a stave between a man's legs."

"That may be true. I cannot say. He is careful that I do not see him without clothing. Even in bed he wears shirt and loincloth as well as the cloth about his chest. I asked of those and he said it is the custom of his people."

"Ah, the mystery. Did he say more?"

Lubran sighed quietly. "Little. He has friends in his homelands where ever they might be. He spoke of them once with sadness. As if he fears never to see them again. I asked of his land and he said it was very far across great seas. That there the Romans have not yet come, though of them his people know much. His tribe do not leave their lands, he says. Only he has ventured from their homes in many more years than he can count. As a people, they learn, growing great with wisdom, but he wished to learn of other lands though they did not. For that he wanders."

Boadicea thought on that. "He knows much which might be useful?"

"Very much," Lubran confirmed.

"Then continue to learn what he will share. We can only be the better for it." She smiled then, dangerously. "Meanwhile his suggestion is well. Word has gone out with gossip and rumor that Prasutagus lies sick. However, secretly I have also sent messengers to our friends in other tribes asking that we speak together. More people than the Iceni grow tired of Roman insolence and the way they enforce their laws, favoring their own over those with whom they trade." She stopped, thoughtful.

"I have begun the brew of a fine potion, old friend. If the gods favor us, it shall poison the Roman dogs in time."

"Just be sure they do not make us drink of it before we are ready."

Her serving woman, Maara, brought them cups of a tea steeped from the petals and roots of a chamomile. As she put it down, she murmured, "May the Great Mother be with you," before departing again. Lubran lifted his eyebrows in question.

"She still speaks of her people's beliefs?"

"Aye, she does," Boadicea responded, "and it matters not. She may not believe in the life, but she has a strong faith all the same. It harms no one, so I say nothing."

"As you say," Lubran agreed. "It harms none." He wondered if Boadicea listened to the stories Maara told. In her marriage the Queen had to have been lonely at times.

"And she has a strong good sense that comes from that belief. That also makes her a good servant to me, a helpful one."

The Queen drank from her cup, the brazier's light glinting in her hair. Prasutagus had not liked Maara, Lubran knew, because she amused the Queen with her stories. The king had been afraid they would interest the Queen enough to turn her away from the faith of their people. And further yet from him.

As Lubran reached for his cup, he looked into it before he drank, "I hope this isn't the brew you plan to give to the Romans?" Boadicea laughed, as he'd hoped.

"No, old friend. This is a more healthful brew. One that is safe to drink." Her mood lightened, and they talked of her plans. But when he left, she again commanded him to speak of her intentions to no one.

"I will not," Lubran replied. "It is good that you know the Romans for what they are. But be careful not to let that show too much."

"I am careful. Go and be the same. And if our young friend is not to be trusted, we will know in time. If he is false," she added, her voice grim, "his head shall join those of our enemies before our gods."

"In spite of his dreams, kinswoman?"

"In spite of them. Our people deserve it thus."

But as Lubran returned to his hut, his thoughts were of his Queen. He knew she'd not particularly wished to wed Prasutagus. The Romans had insisted, however, that he be their king once the old, failing king had died. The soldiers had implied that the Iceni people would share in the Roman wealth if they agreed. And they had consented. They hadn't felt there'd been much of a choice. At the time, there'd been too many Roman soldiers near them, and they were a people without a leader.

When it came time for their Queen to marry a king to rule the tribe, Prasutagus had been willing. She was of the royal blood, daughter to the ailing king. Though much older, he was of the royal line, and thus their children would be acceptable heirs to the people they were to rule. For the sake of her people, Boadicea had agreed. But there'd been little desire between them when they were wed, and it had guttered out in a short time.

Lubran would never have said so openly, but the man had been a fool. She could have given him wise council but he'd have none of it. He went his own way, paying lip service to her position in public, ignoring her in private. Worse still, after the birth of two daughters, he'd taken another woman secretly, although that dalliance had not succeeded, either. Mayhap he'd hoped for a son.

But the king's death had been abrupt and unexpected, and the old healer feared he was to blame. After the second daughter had been born, Lubran had made the Queen a potion which took away some of Prasutagus's desire. It might have done more than just that since she had fed it to him for so many years. Perhaps just as well. If the girl he'd bedded had quickened with a boy child, then it might have been Boadicea who had died, her husband wedding swiftly after her death that he might proclaim a son to rule after him. Deposing her daughters, royal women and the true royal line of the Iceni.

Then, too, perhaps Boadicea had taken revenge. Lubran did not know. If she had, she wouldn't be the first woman who'd resorted to it. Prasutagus had given her many reasons to wish him gone, that much Lubran did know, and a queen of their people had to have more than one good reason to set aside a husband. Divorce was possible but unlikely in a royal marriage.

Whatever she'd done, though, she'd done for more than herself. Prasutagus had liked the Romans all too well. Now came the Romans to make her less once again. They should not. She was queen here, the Iceni her people.

* * * *

Ten days later all the Queen's messengers had returned. The wait had been worth it. The Queen's smile turned savage as she and Lubran listened to the replies. All, *all* the tribes would speak with her. Their words were cautious, but plain. The tribes she bespoke would join the Iceni in rebellion if they believed the omens were good and the chance of winning fair.

Within the dun the hut built for Cean was completed in days. But not before the mystery of the cloth about his chest had been solved.

"Kinswoman," Lubran announced one morning as he rushed into the Queen's quarters. "Our friend has been certainly sent to us by the gods."

"How do you know this?"

With one raised hand, she stopped Maara from cleaning away some of the stale rushes. Lubran looked from the Queen to her maid, but it was clear that the Queen wished Maara to know what he was about to say.

"This morning early, Cean rose from his bed, not fully awake and thus careless. The cloth had slipped, its ends undone. My lady, he bears a woman's breasts. They are not of a large size, but they are truly those of a woman, and not those of a man such as some bear." He waited for the idea to register with his Queen. "He is both man and woman. Blessed by the gods as all such are."

Her eyes blazed. "He is man and woman? You are certain?"

Lubran nodded, his eyes equally on fire. "He dreams as only such can. It is the gods' mark: a shape that is not one, nor is it another. It is a rare gift. He brings us the gods' blessing."

Los Angeles, 2048 C.E.

"Hi, Fort?" The telephone screen was off, with no picture but Cean was sure he'd recognized the voice. "Fort? What's wrong?"

The picture abruptly returned. Fort looked awful, his face seemed to have become haggard overnight; his eyes shadowed by pain and a deep anger. Cean's stomach clenched tight.

"What is it? What's happened?"

"It's Mel. She was mugged. Badly. I've been at the hospital for hours, I just got back. They think she'll make it now, but for a while there they weren't sure."

"What happened, who was it?"

In the phone image, Fort's face twisted in bitterness. "Vigilantes of some kind. They told her she was an abomination, a thing to be eradicated for the good of humanity. They said they'd show her how to be a man. Then they beat her to the ground, kicked her damn near to death and left her lying in the gutter choking on her own blood. Someone saw the attack and called the police. Not an ambulance—the police!" He was outraged. "I don't know who. Just someone who didn't want to be involved." He sucked in air, unable to speak for a moment, as Cean spoke up.

"But, Fort, my god. Mel! She's never hurt anyone in her life."

"I know that," His voice was impatient. "That sort don't care for the real person. Mel was just a symbol. A message to all the Tensen's profiled to stay off the streets." His voice became harsher. "Mel wasn't the only one. There were several attacks spread city-wide. They killed a second victim and a third person probably has brain-damage from the beating they gave him. The bastards had quite a little rampage. An organized and vicious one. When are you free? I need you at the hospital."

"I'll catch a taxi at once. Tell Mel I love her. Get her flowers or something from me. I'll see her as soon as I can get there. God, Fort, this can't be happening."

Sick terror clutched at his throat. Like the AIDS killings. They were history, in the past, not something that happened to Tensen's victims. Time, he thought, it was time to do something, to save these people. Maybe if he could go back to Boadicea's time, he could change what was happening here and now. If time is like a fan of streams spreading out through the ages, then minor changes in the distant past would radiate out as they moved up along the timeline. The druids had been holistic, healers and masters of the age's knowledge. If he planted a seed in that past, it could grow in the future, which was this now. It would alter beliefs, perceptions down the timeline—and perhaps even prejudices.

Hopefully. With the right seed.

His hopes hardened into fast decision. He could save his friends: Mel, Fort, the others in the Coalition, everyone profiled with Tensen's. He would change that past and save every one of them. Cean was alone, but even he felt the growing obsession flush his face, the frantic shifting of near madness in his eyes. His lips twisted wryly at the image and put it from his mind. For them both, Boadicea and Mel, for all the victims who had been or would be. He must go back. He must succeed.

He ran to catch the next hover train to the hospital. At the hospital Fort was expecting him, Janet and Max from the Coalition at his side.

"Thank God you got here quickly." Fort was haggard, his face etched by deep, exhausted lines with bruised pouches of skin surrounding his eyes. He looked ten years older than the forty-two Cean knew him to be. Pain twisted in Cean's heart.

"Mel? Fort, she isn't …"

Surely if Mel had died Fort would have told him on the phone. It couldn't be that. In the back of his mind a voice was muttering that it mustn't be that. He liked Mel. She was a good friend, an ever ready support, and a decent, hard-working person. Someone like that shouldn't die. Not like this.

"No, not yet and," Fort added fiercely, "not ever, if medical knowledge and money can prevent it. But she's still critical." He sat down abruptly with the look of a man too tired to stand any longer.

Cean sat beside him. "Fort, how bad is it? Have they caught the ones who did this to her?"

Fort turned an exhausted face to him. "Sorry. I haven't slept. It's bad, but yes, they've caught some of them." Over his shoulder Cean noticed a hurrying figure approaching.

"This is Ambera, Dr. Romares. She's been looking after Mel."

Cean liked the look of the woman. Her skin was a warm brown and her eyes quietly calm. She looked the sort of doctor you could trust to speak the truth, even the whole truth, but never brutally, never without compassion at the grief it caused.

She nodded to them all. "Your friend will live." She waited out the exclamations, the sighs of relief, of joy. "But it isn't all good news, I'm afraid." There was a tense waiting silence into which her words dropped like a wrecker's stone.

"The list of injuries is rather long and most are severe. Your friend is a fighter, though. She never gave up, not for a moment. We've managed to save her right eye. We've started a clone of it already and with a transplant, the sight should be fully restored. Several of the tendons in her right hand were severed and many of the bones crushed. We've tidied that up but it will require a further operation, maybe two to replace the bones we can't save. We've reconnected the tendons and they'll eventually heal. We think that in time she should have full use of that hand back. But it takes more time for the nerve damage to regenerate."

Max was crying softly, Janet and Fort grim-faced with impotent anger. It was Janet who finally asked, "What's the bad news?" as they realized there was worse to come. The doctor was waiting for them to brace themselves.

"Her back wasn't just broken. A whole section of her lower spine was crushed. We may be able to repair it in time but at the very least she will be unable to walk for several years."

Max was stammering. "Aren't … aren't there other ways? Surely she can get walkers? Those outside braces?"

"Not with an injury this bad. Maybe if the damage had been nearer the top of the spine where it could be braced from any jarring. Using walkers would put more pressure on the weakened bones that need to re-grow. No, she'll have to be immobilized in traction while we continue therapy and operations. Later she'll be able to get around in a wheelchair but that'll be some time."

"Dr. Romares, what's the minimum?" Fort spoke, his rage under control, his eyes hollowed out and his cheeks skin pale and tight. Mel was more than just a friend. She'd been part of his life for far too long for him to be able to say that she was just a friend.

"The minimum is three years. The minimum. If all goes exactly right. If not, then perhaps twice that. The maximum …?" She spread her hands in frustration.

"If the operations aren't successful then there's no date I can give you. She may be looking at another five years of recovery. They smashed so many of the bones, they'll need to re-form entirely, and that takes time as well as patience. The damage they did to her skin is another matter. Some of the scars from the burning will never heal, not properly at any rate, and if stem cell research had been encouraged, we could do better for her. Grafts will repair some of it, and fortunately most of the burns are not on her face." She shrugged, hopeless.

Fort spoke up quickly. "Thanks, Dr. Romares. I'm sure you'll do what needs to be done. Mel does have very comprehensive health insurance if that's any help …."He spread his hands wide, mirroring the doctor's gesture, the movement not enough to stop their visible trembling.

"That may not mean a lot," she told him, her voice low. "Many of the HMOs are now claiming the profiled knew what they had and concealed it from the health care companies. So far the courts are supporting the HMOs and some coverage is being denied. I'll keep her profile out of the record if I can. She hadn't even begun the hormone treatments. But even here, word spreads. Most of the staff are careful, but there are always one or two who are not."

When she left them, her shoulders drooped slightly. She was one doctor fighting something she couldn't cure: human prejudice and its violence.

"Who did this?" Cean couldn't wait any longer. The glare of the overhead lights fractured in his sight, the glitter refracted by the tears he was holding back.

"A para-military group," Janet told him. "Mel wasn't their only victim. Five others were attacked, and two of them didn't survive. They were burned badly, doused first with gas and then set alight. Fortunately, neither of them were conscious when it happened. They'd been beaten so viciously they were out cold. Mel's attack was hurried. A police squad had almost reached her when the first match was lit. Two of them were able to smother the flames before they spread. The others went after the men and caught a couple of them. But Mel was still conscious and in terrible pain." Janet couldn't stop herself, she was sobbing hard.

"Why?" Max could barely get the word out.

"She's profiled. Somehow they knew. The police told me the group retrieved information from somewhere on who was listed. Maybe even from the HMOs or a hospital, using hackers to break into their files as far as the police can tell. Right now who knows? One of the men declared they did it to protect other people from Tensen's. That the world needed protecting and if the government wasn't going to do what had to be done, they would."

"Maniacs!"

"Maniacs with boots. And gasoline. Damn them! Fucking damn them all." Fort's face was wet with tears, his eyes stark with rage. Cean could think of worse, in a way.

"At least it wasn't guns. Guns wouldn't make the right statement, apparently." Fort rubbed his face hard. After a moment he added, "Cean, would you go in to sit with her for a while, talk quietly even if she seems oblivious? She may be unconscious but she might hear your voice. It'll let her know there is someone around who cares about her. We've been here a while and I need something to eat, if nobody else does." And calm Max, Cean thought. He needed a break.

"When we get back I'll look in. That's if you don't mind?"

"I want to."

And it was true. There was no place Cean would rather be than with Mel. Fort gathered up Max and Janet and they left, heading for the hospital cafeteria. Cean felt wired, tireless, the adrenaline flooding his veins. He walked quietly into Mel's room. She lay motionless, her small, normally so animated face in repose, the bandages sprayed on to cover much of it.

Cean felt sick. Mel was so alive usually, hands flashing in an attempt to keep up with her rapid-fire chatter. It was a joke amongst her friends that if you tied Mel's hands down, she wouldn't be able to talk.

She wanted to be a male, but had no real problem with wearing clothing that could have been worn by either sex. Nor did she compensate by acting overly masculine. She was simply Mel—kind-hearted, generous, and understanding. She'd listened to Cean's obsession with Boadicea and given him tips on the ins and outs of doing research on the Iceni, as well as spending a long afternoon guiding him around the university library. Mel was even the one who had found the language teacher for him.

He sat down slowly on the old hard-seated chair and took her limp hand in his. Her eyes were shut as if she wasn't there, as if this body held nothing that had been her. Perhaps Fort was right. Maybe somewhere inside, she could feel him there, know a friend was with her.

He began to talk. He spoke of the Iceni and his family legend about England. How his grandparents had said they came from that area of Norfolk. Of the tests. That his mitochondrial DNA showed he was provably Iceni by descent although not necessarily from the Queen, despite the legend, his family stories validated in blood. Mel was the first and only person that he told. He talked of his plans, rambling on about Fort's discoveries and how they could tie in with Cean's own intentions.

"If it works, Mel, if I can do it, then this will never happen to you. Not in other timelines. Not if I can change the past, it won't. I'm sure I can change things enough for that." He heard footsteps approaching the door and bent to touch the back of her hand with his lips.

"Hang in there, Mel. The doctor said you're a fighter. Keep fighting. Don't quit on us. Tomorrow will be better."

Fort entered in time to hear Cean's last comments. "It will, I'm sure of it. Janet took Max home; they're exhausted, and if you wouldn't mind, I think I'll do the same. Would that be okay?"

"Sure. Come back after you get some rest."

* * * *

But before Fort returned, Cean had to call him with troubling news. "She went into arrest an hour ago. They almost didn't bring her back. Now she's on life support." Cean's fingers rubbed at the lines etching themselves ever deeper into his forehead.

"She had head injuries," Fort protested, "but she was doing fine. Wasn't she?" Cean watched the vid screen as Fort sunk back into a chair.

"It was the shock," Cean went on. "Her body just couldn't take anymore." He glanced aside, towards Mel's door and two policemen standing there. Before Fort could ask, Cean told him, "They're hoping she can identify her attackers. That is if she pulls through."

"But I thought ... at least I've always read, that with that kind of trauma she wouldn't remember much."Behind Cean's head, Fort could see a nurse hurrying down the hall towards them, her stride intent and determined.

The look on Fort's face became both savage and triumphant. "That'd be true if there was a fractured skull. There wasn't. They were keener on causing her pain so one of them hit her across the eyes. She fell when one of them smashed some kind of pipe across her knee. Once she went down they stomped her, but she must have managed to cover her head. The doctor thinks that's why her hands were bashed so much. Her hands, her nose ..." Fort's voice drifted off.

Cean's voice shook with sudden rage. "So she might remember it all?"

"Uh huh, Dr. Romares thinks she could. You know Mel. She's a fighter, as the doctor said." He grinned briefly. "She doesn't lie down under intimidation. If she remembers, or can identify any of her assailants she'll testify no matter what the threats are. So it's in her attackers' interests to see Mel doesn't get well enough that she can testify. And there are still a few of them out there, the ones that got away." He looked at Cean closely. "We'll have to watch over her, even with security there. Do you mind?"

Cean quickly agreed. It wasn't as if he was currently employed, not like Fort. His friend thanked him, whole-heartedly, then added, "If there's any problem, stick your head out of her room and start yelling."

Cean returned to Mel's room, watching the blanket lift and fall as the machines pushed air in and out of Mel's lungs, helping her to breathe. Cean shook his head, furious and frightened. If only he could do something! Whatever he did in the past couldn't change this, but it would stop other Mels in other worlds from suffering this, or even worse.

He went over his plans in his head. He had the costumes and jewelry by now. In his closet, he'd folded the rough woolen cloth of the tunic and loose pants he'd take with him. He didn't want to look too rich, but he had tried his hand at a bit of embroidery on the tunic's front. Natural colors, natural threads where he could find them.

He had a clasp made from filigreed silver set with red garnets in the Celtic twisted knot popular, he knew, in that time. It would pin his cloak together at the neck, and for that he had two short-wool sheepskins he would stitch together by hand. Fortunately, the Iceni cloaks were simple: long and straight with the upper edge sewn together for a rough hood.

He'd even had some coins made, a few gold but mostly silver, imitating the ones that had been dug out of Iceni ruins near the eastern edge of what was now Thetford, Norfolk. Cean had carried the coins in his pants pocket since, hoping to wear the shine off of them a little, and secretly enjoying the clink of the metal. He'd had a small few bronze mirrors copied as well. These he'd tucked in with the tunic to be ready. He could use them for trade once he was among the Iceni.

He'd begun to bleach his hair to a lighter red as well. Most records indicated that the Iceni were mostly red-headed or blond, and while he had the blue eyes and pale skin that fit the type, his own hair was a very dark red, and he needed paler hair so he wouldn't stand out too much at first, he planned to take a small container of concentrated bleach as well so that he could maintain the look for a year or more. People related better to those that resembled them. At least he was of a height that matched theirs. In the time of the Iceni, few men were tall as his own age counted it, and Cean by his age's standard was a short man.

From online museum souvenir shops, he'd also ordered a few enamel pieces, brooches and rings, like some he'd seen in the books, and from jewelers he'd picked up a few rough gems, as well as some pieces of jet and amber. Those could easily be sold as well, and could be hidden in the hems of his tunic for safety. A few larger items could be sewn into a slit between the sheepskin layers.

He was almost ready. He'd kept Fort abreast of his plans, and now it would be soon. Eight weeks would be enough to finish his plans.

He had a book and decided to read that aloud to Mel. It was a Doreen Tovey book his mother had inherited from her parents and adored, and Cean carried it about with him to read on the train. He loved the stories about Siamese cats and pet squirrels. Now, in this quiet, strange-smelling room, he hoped Mel would, too. If she heard him. He opened *More Cats in the Belfry* and started to read aloud.

Almost three hours later his voice was hoarse, but he'd enjoyed the story so much he'd kept reading, wanting to know himself how it went. He laid the book down, marking the page. Only then did he realize Mel's one uncovered eye was open.

"Mel … Mel, it's Cean here." He took her hand, speaking gently.

There was a tiny croak in reply, not much more than a breath. She couldn't speak with the ventilator down her throat. Then a blink of her good eye. As if recognizing him pleased her.

"Yes, it's me," Cean told her. "You'll be all right. Fort, Max and Janet were all here earlier. We're taking it in turns to sit with you."

Her mouth tried to move, to whisper something.

"No, don't speak," he told her quickly. "You can't with this thing, anyway."

He touched the alarm and stood back as a nurse arrived. There was an interval in which he waited outside. Dr. Romares whisked past him to enter the room, stay briefly then pause beside him as she exited.

"Tell Fort it's good news. Your friend is conscious. Don't ask her questions just now but don't stop her if she wants to tell you about it. We've taken the ventilator out so she can speak if she wants to. She's getting enough hydration from the IV so don't give her any water. It could upset her stomach and she's in no shape for that as well." She studied him for a moment. "She has good friends," she added.

"Thank you. She deserves them," Cean told her fervently as she walked away. She had no sooner gone than Max and Janet arrived for their turn to watch.

Max smiled at him. "Good news. Five of the coalition will come in later to stand guard after they get off work. We're to call them as soon as we want a break."

"Great. Well, I'll see you tomorrow if you're on then."

He'd reached the hover rail stop before realizing he'd left the book behind in Mel's room. Cean swore as he headed back. He'd really been enjoying that, but it wouldn't take too long to return and get it. He headed back towards the hospital, clumping down the flight of stairs from the raised hover rail track. Once at the hospital he padded silently up the long angular corridor from the elevator. All was silent, empty.

Where the hell was the guard? Gone for coffee? Wasn't he supposed to be posted near Mel's door? Cean swung around as he walked, looking. There! He spun, running down a corridor he'd just passed, stooping over a slumped man in security uniform. A large purpling bruise had swollen up across the back of his neck.

Cean didn't even think. One moment he was looking down, the next he was tearing back along the side corridor then rushing down the main hall. His speed gathered with each stride.

From Mel's room there was a roar. Cean ripped the door open and stood in the doorway. One swift look was enough: Max lay sprawled to one side by the window, half dazed; Janet had fastened like a bulldog to the arm of a young white-coated man who was desperately trying to pry her off. In one raised hand he waved a med spray and under his white coat Cean could see the over-tight pants, and cod-piece of a paramilitary gang member.

As Cean leaped, the man struck Janet hard enough to loosen her grip. She sagged away. The intruder reached out, face intent, the med spray heading towards Mel's arm.

Cean had him before it touched skin. He'd never been violent, nor was he trained apart from his kendo and quarterstaff lessons. Very fortunately for Cean, neither were needed. His running shoes had brought him silently up behind the intruder. The man swung around, alarmed. Not knowing what else to do, Cean gripped his opponent by the arm. He simply heaved the man in a half-circle away from the bed and Mel. The young man tottered, colliding painfully with the door.

He yelped in stung fury and gathered himself to leap back. He still held the med spray in one hand. The fluorescent light glared on the tip as it came down like the point of a blade.

Cean seized the striking arm as the man staggered towards him, bent the arm savagely inward and heaved again with all his strength. Off balance, the intruder simply flailed about, his hand savagely smacking the door edge a second time. He recoiled, his right hand slapping back against his left arm.

The med hissed sharply. A fine, powerful, and directed spray penetrated the raised hand. The man screamed, shrieking incoherently. He wrenched himself free of Cean and fled.

Cean went after him but the chase was short. Halfway down the corridor the man faltered, staggered once, then slipped to the floor in a long, sliding, lax-bodied fall. Cean left him. He had a strong suspicion that whatever had been in the med-spray would keep his opponent down for some time. If not forever. Cean wanted to know how Mel was.

Back in Mel's room, Max was trying to get to his feet, a hand roughly rubbing one side of his head. Mel was twitching, frantic in her bed. Janet was bent over her making soothing noises and trying to hold her still. She calmed as soon as her eyes caught Cean returning.

"What happened to that man?"

"Dose of his own medicine," Cean told her briefly. "What about Mel?"

"She'll be fine. She didn't know what was happening until that man tossed Max across the end of the bed and onto the floor. But what the hell happened to our guard? He was there when we arrived."

"He's still around," Cean assured her. "Only flat on his face in a side corridor with a nasty-looking bruise across the back of his neck. There should have been two guards as well. There was before." He shook his head, appalled at this further turn of events. Where had the police gone?

"We should ring the police and notify the hospital desk immediately. Someone should look after that cop, and we will have to tell them about the man with the spray."

What a terrible night! He looked over to where Mel's one-eyed gaze frantically searched him to see if he had been hurt. He hadn't. But it had been close. Outside, light rain pattered against the window, barely streaking the layer of dust dimming the glass. In the distance, in spite of the rain, the glow of night fires reached out, spreading.

Iceni Homeland, 59 C.E.

Cean had dropped into the pool of the Iceni as if he were another trickle of the same water. He fitted in well since he was liked. He made no trouble, was quick to offer aid to any who might need it, and the rumor of his shape passed swiftly and secretly about the dun.

He and Lubran talked constantly. They learned of each other, Lubran saying privately to the Queen that he would be a better healer from Cean's time here even if the stranger did move on. He had much to teach the old healer. In fact the old man wanted to take time to travel to one of the druid strongholds to quickly pass on his new knowledge there. It would take him two moons of time, and the Queen gave him leave to do so. Cean could act as healer in the old man's place.

"You have my leave to depart, kinsman," she told him. "Have you spoken to Cean about this? If you are gone we can rely on him to be our healer."

"I have asked him, lady. He is willing to take my place for the time required. In some ways he knows less than I about our life, but he has walked different paths of learning. If he fails in some areas, still he is well-versed in others. In the time we have worked together he has learned well of my skills. He will do not so badly."

"Go then, but return as swiftly as you may." She stood and hugged his shoulders. "Be wary, Lubran. I have need of your wisdom, nor would I wish to loose you."

"Cean knows what to do if any come demanding to bespeak your husband." Lubran chuckled. "We have worked on poor Tilutegan until he knows by heart what he must say and do. Cean knows as well how to provide the outward signs of a man far gone in fever. So long as he has time to act."

As Lubran watched her, Boadicea smiled grimly. About the Iceni lands she had flung a net, as a fowler flings it about wildfowl. Even the children knew to watch that no one entered their wide lands without her knowledge. As soon as they passed the borders of the Iceni domain, she would soon know it.

"Tell me while we are alone, kinsman," she said, "which road you take. If there be great danger I shall send messengers after you."

He drew close to whisper steadily for several minutes. She nodded as he described the ways he would take.

"That road. I see. Yes, it is wise for none shall see as you pass nor will the Romans know where to look even if they stand watch upon our borders. I shall look for your return in two moons. Walk in the gods' power, Lubran, until I see you again. Send Cean to me once you have spoken to him."

Taking his leave, Lubran returned to his hut to pack and talk earnestly with Cean as he did so. "I may be gone a full two moons. Watch for the Queen while I am gone."

"Of course."

"Nay, not so casual, brother in healing. She is a good leader, but she can be impulsive, willful. It has been for me to temper that since she trusts me. Long has she known me and I am kin. You she does not know so well ..." He stopped, thinking. "But she might listen if you are polite." He smiled. Even in so short a time, he couldn't imagine Cean being anything else.

"Also I am not so trusted," Cean added dryly.

"Would you expect otherwise?" Lubran was surprised at the unexpected bitterness in Cean's words.

"No. However, I will watch. If I can give her council then I will. After that it is for her to listen or reject my words." He watched as Lubran took up a staff, heaved a sack to his shoulder. "Take care, the Iceni would miss you as would I."

"I walk as with my eyes like a dun's walls about me," Lubran told him gently. "Nor do I take the high way. Let those who want me seek, but I shall not be so easily found. I know this land better than the Romans and their spies. Guard my people, Cean. Where there is need, heal them." He swung his pack up onto his shoulder. It rustled with dried plants against the stiff wool of his spare tunic inside. "Before I forget, go to the Queen once you have seen me upon my road. She would speak to you."

"What does she want?"

"That is for her to say." He reached out to draw Cean's arms into a quick grasp. "Until my return."

Cean watched the old man slip away up the slope into the cover of the trees and scrub from which Cean had emerged less than two weeks earlier. His stomach dropped as Lubran entered the trees, even knowing there was no way the old man could learn how he'd arrived. That felt so very long ago. In time. He laughed wryly at the unintended pun. Longer in time it was, far longer than any here knew. But this was no time to stand about. He grinned again. Boadicea had asked for him and that, as it had since first he saw her, lifted his spirits. He found the Queen considering a legal question and glad to be interrupted.

"Healer. Lubran is gone then?" He nodded. "May the light of the gods shine on his path." Cean echoed that, then waited. "You may have seen Sharn building a new hut close by that of Lubran's?" He nodded. "Good. That is for you. It is not fit that a healer to the Iceni must guest with another when he works. He should have his own place and privacy. The hut is now ready for you. Go and take possession of what is yours."

Cean stared. "And if I do not stay? I promised Lubran I would be here until his return, but after that?"

"That is for the gods and you. While you are healer here you shall have your own place. Honor demands it." She dismissed him.

Cean almost forgot to thank the Queen for the gift of a new home before he went to look it over. It was as large as Lubran's home. Within the sheepskins were already laid in a bed-box along with his own foal skin. Clay platters and cups stood upon a shelf. A backless stool waited by an open hearth, a small hole above it in the thatch. On the hearth the wood was ready, waiting only for the touch of flame. Cean stood admiring his new domain for many minutes. His home! Here among the Iceni.

He scurried back out again. Best he move his backpack and other possessions in. After that he was busy. Half the tribe seemed to come with small ailments or minor injuries. He knew they were watching to see how he dealt with each but he was conscientious; a dab of ointment on an open sore, the hot water used to clean a fresh scrape on a child's leg, the drink, his "secret" potion many were coming to expect. Putting a few herbs in one drink, Cean thoughtfully kept from using his antibiotics unless he was sure they were needed. Best not to waste those until he found a reliable way to produce more. That information was on a disk in the casket beside his bed-box.

* * * *

Gradually the people began to approve of him, to trust his work, to believe that he could help them. It also amused them he was no spearman, nor archer. For that he had a ready answer.

"Tell me, man?" This to a spearman who came with a fox-bite. "How many years have you trained with a spear?"

The spearman counted on his fingers. "All my life, healer, and always there is something more to learn."

"That is wisdom. A prudent man understands he may live a lifetime and still not know everything," Cean praised Alieki. The spearman flushed proudly.

Cean nodded. "You have learned the spear only then? You are no expert with another skill?"

"I use a sword, a dagger. I have a little skill at drawing a bow."

"But nothing beyond weapons-skill?"

"No, healer. One has no time for other training."

"Exactly. I am a healer. Why thus would you expect me to know of weapons?"

The spearman's face lit with understanding. He repeated the conversation to others and the teasing stopped.

Time passed quickly. Barring any unforeseen delay, Lubran was due to return soon. Siharni brought word from the Queen as he was preparing his herb supplies for storage.

"She bids you come. Word is that the procurator asks after Prasutagus's health. The Roman hints that he may come to see his friend, since his friend has not traveled to see him in some time." She spat vigorously. "Friend! A king does not travel to visit an un-noble man. And the Queen's man sold him hunting ponies at low prices in return for the right to sell to the Roman army. A right that was promised yet never given. It is money he misses, not his friend."

"Go on, I'll follow once I've done this. I'll be there shortly."

He finished and stood stretching in his doorway, holding the door curtain in one hand. He noticed a movement as a girl crossed the path between the huts, a free-swinging stride to her walk. He'd seen her before. In the conversation with Lubran, she'd passed nearby. Tall, red-haired, yet young. She looked a bit like the Queen, but of slighter build. Lubran had told him who she was. Ancha, fifteen-year-old niece of Boadicea. He'd asked about her with careful casualness. She was the daughter of Prasutagus's sister, now dead. But the sister's mother and Boadicea's grandmother had been the same person, thus Ancha was blood kin to the Queen and loved. The girl was yet unwed, a member of Boadicea's serving women with property in her own right. She was also the only niece the Queen had.

If Cean had been truly descended as family legend had described, from the escaped niece who subsequently bore children of her own, then it could only be from Ancha. In some ways the girl had given another face to his purpose. The Queen would die fighting if he failed. Ancha, child of the Iceni, would be dragged off in chains. Abused, enslaved, impregnated by her owner, and eventually freed. But that was legend. There might have been some descendant putting a better face on events than what had actually occurred.

Cean knew he risked the future. If the family tale was true, she would bear a Roman's child, a child who was Cean's own ancestor. By changing the outcome of the rebellion, he risked his own eventual birth. She would not become the pregnant slave she had been in his history.

Would time tolerate that major change? Or would it not matter since, if Fort was right, this might not now be his own world? He didn't know.

But nevertheless, he had met her. She was a bright-faced laughing child. Beautiful in a slight way. He did not want to see her become the abused slave she would be if her people lost. If Cean could not prevent the destruction of all she knew. Even if he risked his own life. He went to the Queen in a somber mood.

4

"Time has this strange ability to adjust itself," Fortescue said in his first interview with me. "It's virtually elastic in the sense that it self corrects with minor events. If I were to send a pregnant rabbit back to a time where there were no rabbits, that rabbit and its offspring are likely to die off from disease or natural causes. Or they might find they are unable to reproduce given the change in their diet. A vital mineral might be missing in the new vegetation that they need for hormonal development. All kinds of limits are placed on the ecological evolution of history. The point is that time will take advantage of them."

When I asked him about major events altering the past, he mentioned the way history is controlled by the events of whole populations rather than individual actions. "Except in the case of technological change," he added. "There an individual can have a great causal influence on history's, hence time's substance."

—from *Conversations with the Time Master*,
compiled by Loreen McDawaldien

The Roman legions were defeated long before the battles with Britain's tribes ever took place. Rome's legions were beaten when they first refused to deal with Boadicea upon the death of her husband. By the time the actual armed conflicts took place, the error could not be corrected, and the Roman advantage of power and technology was lost.

This mistake was the first of many the Roman governor Paulinus Suetonius made in his attempt to administer the island's affairs. His procurator was willful and greedy (*Tacitus*, tr. by Alessandrea Bethenes, Vol. 33). Suetonius did nothing to govern the man as he extorted monies and goods from the tribes who were legally client kingdoms of Rome (*Tacitus*, tr. by Alessandrea Bethenes, Vol. 34) and therefore exempt. Instead, Suetonius tried to subdue the hostile tribes rather than govern his own men.

Elsewhere I have discussed Boadicea's intentions for her people. She further incited rebellion in the Trinovantes, and through them the Catuvellauni. Where no one else had before her, she made a common enemy of the Roman incursion, and as a justifiable consequence of the rather laisser-aller control of their own administrators, united the Britain tribes. Thus a new nation was begun, with Boadicea, the Iceni ruler at its head.

—from *The Warrior Queen's Rule*,
by Sylman Wershing

Iceni Homeland, 59 C.E.

Boadicea was with her women spinning, the drop spindles twirling gracefully as the creamy wool edged into thread. Nearby a hand-loom clacked as Myla, wife to Alieki, wove a length of cloth. Cean bowed.

"There is word, lady?"

"Aye, Decianus Catus, the Procurator, sends word to my husband that it is too long since he has seen him. He comes now," she scowled down at the thread, turning in her hands. "With his hand out as always and with fifty men whom we must guest and feast."

Cean stood in thought, the Queen allowing the time to pass in silence before she looked up. At last Cean raised his head. "How well does he know your husband? Is he likely to see the trick we play?"

It was the Queen's turn to think. "I think he knows him not so well, but Prasutagus spent time often enough at the Roman camp about which I have no knowledge. If that time was in the company of this Roman, then it could be he shall see the man he meets is not my husband. The procurator too is a man quick to fancy himself unwell. For that often a physician comes with him, a Greek slave who is like to know if a man be truly ill or not. What are your thoughts?"

Cean nodded. "That we make plans which are like the branches of a tree. If this happens then we reply thus; if another thing happens we reply another way."

"You have these plans in mind then, healer?"

Cean grinned at her, the grin bringing in turn one of Boadicea's rare smiles. It lit the strong angular face with beauty.

"I have them in mind. Would you speak in private or shall all hear?"

She stood. "Privately in my house, healer." She turned. "Myla, none are to disturb us or draw near." She waited for Myla to nod agreement before leading Cean inside the house. There she strode ahead, her steps strong, quickly taking her to the far side of the room where she drew back the hide door and stood to look out across the land. Her land. Her People's land. "I think now comes the time of danger. I smell it, even without the dreams. The gods warn me to be wary of the viper which lies in the grass. What say you, healer?"

Cean took in a slow unobtrusive breath. If he advised her well now, she would be more ready to listen the next time. Should he claim a dream, as he had before? No. He'd spoken of Roman attitudes to Lubran who'd probably passed the words on already. Cean would build on that. He talked as the Queen listened. Now and again she asked questions, always sensible, often cunning. He began to feel more confident.

"What of the other tribes?" he asked her.

"I have spoken to them. They stir under the heavy hand of Rome, many would rise if we showed the way." Her voice turned slow, thoughtful. "If they had a reason, if perhaps they were given one."

Cean spoke again, quietly, his voice dropping so she strained to listen.

Los Angeles, 2048 C.E.

The police questioned Cean, Max, and Janet for hours, unwilling to accept their first statements. Mel slept through most of it, but only after she was given more medication. Enough to make her sleep and, Cean hoped, to take away the fear. Forensic technicians quietly dusted and swept around the group, picking up the details with fingerprint brushes, swabs and tape. The two detectives seemed intent on going over events again and again.

"Tell us again, Mr. Rowan. You never actually struck the intruder at all?"

Cean looked at the speaker a little shamefacedly. "I never learned to fight. I don't think I've ever hit anyone in my life. Not with my bare hands anyway. But he was trying to hurt Mel. All I could think of…" He paused. "Well, no … I didn't think. I just grabbed and heaved him away from her. When he started back I did the same thing again, only harder."

The detective waited. "What then?"

"I guess I really swung him as hard as I could the second time. And in the same direction. The first time he hit the door …"

"How did he manage to do that?"

"I left it half open when I ran in."

"All right, so the first time you swung him away he hit the door. The edge of it?" Cean nodded. "After that?"

"Well, he headed back for Mel. That time when I swung him away again I sort of aimed him for the door. I thought maybe I could throw him through and shut him out until help arrived. I missed. He went flying back, the door edge caught him right across one shoulder. It must have really hurt because he yelled and I guess he clenched his hands in reflex."

Max struck in. "I was trying to get up to help and I had a better look at what was happening than Cean did. The man, whoever he was ..." he added before stopping while he thought it through. "Hitting the door the second time wasn't only very painful, it jarred him unexpectedly."

"Why do you think that would have been? He'd hit it once already according to Mr. Rowan." Cean couldn't help noticing a slight edge to the officer's voice.

"No idea. Anyhow he yelled, and threw one hand up. But when his hand hit the door, the med-spray discharged. It may be faulty," he added, running over the events again in his mind. "I think Cean's wrong and it wasn't the man closing his hand that discharged it. I think it was the impact when he hit the door so hard. Those things are designed not to be that sensitive usually. You should look at that."

The man was grim. "I think we can manage that." The dry edge was definitely there.

Cean spoke quietly. "Look, detective, I'm sorry someone died, but I would point out that he was trying to kill someone else at the time."

"You have no proof of that." There was a glint of some kind of satisfaction behind his words.

Max snorted. "I'd say the fact that he got the dose intended for Mel and died in less than a minute is pretty good proof. Mel's severely injured. If whatever was in the med spray was intended to help her, it's rather odd it killed a grown man who was anything but weak."

The detective looked disgusted, turning to his notes. What the pathologist would say on the subject of the hypo's contents would come later, when all was said and done here first. The questioning went on until the very early hours. When at last everyone was released it was with the suggestion none of them take any long trips.

"You understand?" the taller detective asked before leaving.

"Yes, we understand quite well," Max put in, angry with the way they had been treated. He snorted as soon as they were out of earshot. "Humph! *We're* the victims here, but that doesn't seem to matter to them."

Janet put her arm around him, but Cean couldn't help noticing the worry dark behind her eyes.

W hen Cean finished speaking to Boadicea, she sat down at last on a backless padded stool.

"These plans seem well to me. Go now, I shall bespeak my men. Prepare Tilutegan that he be ready when that strutting cock Roman appears. From the word he sent he shall be in the dun by this evening, a good time for our plans." She eyed him warningly. "But remember this, healer. I have no mind to make an enemy of Rome without cause. None are to move unless there is no choice."

Cean nodded and left hastily. He too had preparations to make. Time passed quickly, and the dun was in a ferment all that day as her people obeyed the Queen's orders. By nightfall Tilutegan lay in the king's bed, face gaunt with herbal diuretics and his skin asweat in the lamplight from a lightly applied oil. A basin stood beside him along with small stoppered jars containing other potions. As if ready to help an ailing man.

Cean, in one of Lubran's long hooded robes, stood nearby doing his best to look stern and impressive. He heard the commotion as the Romans arrived, waited until he heard the tramp of marching boots then gave Tilutegan a potion. The man swallowed it swiftly before lying back.

Procurator Decianus Catus tramped in already speaking. He was not tall but rotund, his shoulders wide and heavy. He was a strong man, used to people obeying him.

"What is this? I hear my friend is ill. How long has he been so? Why was word not sent to me?" Behind him his second-in-command stood at attention.

The potion worked quickly. Tilutegan heaved, retching violently. Cean leaped to hold the basin under the foul stream which splashed the Procurator's boots as he halted too closely. The Roman stepped back in hasty disgust.

"What is wrong with him?"

Boadicea entered behind the procurator in time to hear the question. "My Lord, he has the spring sickness. He has been so for some weeks. Our healer has done his best yet all his skills have not yet availed."

Decianus Catus snorted like a fly-plagued pony, speaking to his second in their own tongue. "Of course. What does this savage know of medicine? Call my doctor. He should have dismounted now. Let him tend the king."

From behind the procurator the Queen's gaze met Cean's. Cean spoke Latin fluently. Boadicea, though she did not speak it well, understood enough to know what had just been said. They'd planned for that possibility too. A genuine Roman-trained physician would not be fooled by outward show. It would have to be the second plan. A pity. They would lose time they might have gained but there was no choice.

The Queen slipped from the doorway speaking in a swift whisper to Ancha who stood waiting. Then the Queen allowed herself to be swept back into the hut by the arrival of the physician and the Roman second-in-command.

The healer bustled in, his grayed hair a ring around the top of a balding head, his uniform tight around his portly middle. He gasped as he walked into the room, the short distance from his horse to there winding him. He bent over Tilutegan, running his fingers across the man's face, smelling the sweat. Raising his eyebrows, he examined the false king carefully before opening his mouth.

To denounce them, Boadicea knew. As if in great distress, she brought one arm up, pointing towards him and pre-empted his words.

"*Aieee!*" she cried, a long shuddering wail of pain suddenly breaking free. "My man is dead! I have tried to deny the truth. I couldn't bear that it be so. Forgive a woman's heart, Roman. I loved my man and could not bear to know him gone." She covered her face with her hands, sobs shaking her chest. She was very convincing, even to Cean, who was expecting it.

"What? What is this? A trick! That man is not Prasutagus!"

She cast herself weeping to the hut floor and wailed, tossing dirt over her bright hair, tearing the breast of her robe with hooked fingers.

"*Aieee!* My man died of the spring sickness last week. I fell into such grief that my people feared to lose me also. They brought my husband's kinsman to lay here instead and told me my man was not yet dead. Yet I knew the truth. I wished only to pretend my man still lived, just for a little while, that I might cling to some happiness. This man is ill, and thus I could pretend to myself that he was truly my love."

She looked up, her face twisted in sorrow. "The sharp eyes of the Romans have discovered my secret, yet forgive a woman who is weak, who wished to remember the days of joy for a while longer."

Cean held his breath. She was magnificent. What man would not believe her? He eyed the procurator. A strutting bandy-legged man, his neck and arms heavily muscled. He had greedy eyes, sharp with intelligence.

Cean saw the brief flicker of contempt. Ah, good.

The man thought the Queen was a fool, or a trickster. Either way he despised her as a mere woman. Should Cean betray the Roman's plans? He must so the Queen would know Cean's knowledge of Roman beliefs and his advice on them was good. He moved slightly, catching the Roman's attention as he spoke in stumbling Latin.

"Lord, it is as the Queen says. Her grief over her man's passing was so great we feared for her reason. Besides, she is queen. She has a people to rule now the king is dead. Prasutagus's will ..."

"Ah, yes. His will. That left his fortune to the emperor."

"Half his fortune, Lord. What of the Queen's rights?"

He caught the greedy gleam and bit back triumph. *Yes!* The man was about to betray himself. Decianus stood straighter as the greed glowed in his eyes. Here was a chance to make himself rich, and as Cean knew, Paulinus Suetonius, Decianus, commander, had been clear about Prasutagus's will. This would enrich the Emperor Nero and hence Paulinus Suetonius and his soldiers at the same time. Bringing wealth to Rome would make his name, gain him a higher post.

And if Decianus sheared these sheep deeply enough, both of them might even aspire to a post in Rome itself. Paulinus Suetonius had hoped to make himself and his men rich just as Corbulo had done in Armenia. A brilliant campaign that had made the man wealthy beyond belief, and taken him to Rome in high favor.

Decianus looked down casually at the crouching woman. By Roman law, a woman could not rule anyway. If she was stupid enough to think so, he would teach her the dangers of thinking herself more than she was.

"There is no queen."

Cean gestured to Boadicea. "Yet there she is. And the king sired two daughters, the ones who are to inherit the other half of Prasutagus's wealth."

"Not in Roman eyes, healer, and make no mistake, this is a Roman kingdom now. Prasutagus is dead. No son comes after him. The royal line is ended. It was for him or his son that the Iceni were a free client kingdom. Now they are a province under Roman law. With a man appointed to rule over them by Rome's will. Rome takes no account of *queens.*"

The last word was vile in the man's mouth. "It is for a man to be king. Daughters we do not count. All the people own now belongs to the Emperor, since there is no one else who may own property here."

From where Cean stood he could see a portion of the Queen's face. For a moment it showed a fury which was almost inhuman, the eyes burning with rage, her mouth twisting to prevent a howl of outrage. Before the procurator noticed, though, it smoothed to blankness as she turned to look from under the edge of her arm at the Roman.

Cean asked his final question, already sure of the answer.

"The king's wealth then, you will take all?"

"Of course. His woman and her daughters will not starve. They have their own jewels, a few ponies. They will live well enough on the portion that Rome allows them. Until they find husbands, that is." He moved briskly towards the door. "In the morning the people are to gather the beasts, horses, cattle, along with a century of young men to join Paulinus Suetonius's legion."

Cean nodded. "And if they have no wish to be soldiers?"

The procurator frowned. "There is no greater calling than to serve Rome. Look at the soldiers who ride with me. In time they will retire with land of their own and the slaves to work it. How would any man of this lot do better?"

"Our young men do not wish to leave their land or their people, Lord."

Decianus smiled patronizingly. "They have no choice. It is for me to command, the Iceni to obey. With Prasutagus dead, I am in charge here. But I have ridden far and I thirst. I hope you have made my men welcome. It's been a poor guesting for me so far. Where is the renowned Iceni hospitality?" The man's callousness was overwhelming.

Boadicea raised herself from the floor, her hair in strings about her face. Just as he expected her to. No one disobeyed Roman law unless they were fools. She twisted dirt into her eyes, blackening them to bring forth tears.

"You do well to remind me. I am remiss towards our guest. Come let us offer the most noble procurator the welcome cup, healer. Tell my people to begin the feast that his men may eat. It is wrong they should stand hungry within the Iceni dun, regardless of the cause." She nodded at the couch where Tilutegan yet lay.

Cean obeyed, passing on her orders—all her orders—before slipping into the background to watch. His advice had done this so far. Instead of coming with two hundred trained soldiers and the knowledge of the king's death, the procurator had arrived with only fifty men; nor were all of them trained soldiers.

Although he'd suspected something minor amiss, Decianus had not known Prasutagus to be actually dead before his arrival, and now he did he had also betrayed his intentions towards the Queen and her people. His greed had made him unwise.

Rather than believe Cean entirely, the Queen had doubted any one in authority, even a Roman, could be so stupid. Cean knew this. But Decianus had revealed himself to her in all his greedy glory—and Boadicea knew Cean was right. The Romans would make slaves of her people. The Romans would take all they could, even the Iceni's freedom.

Too many young men leached from the tribe would weaken it for years to come. That is if there was any tribe left, after the soldiers had taken what they wanted.

Cean had plans for this, plans he would pass on to the Queen quickly. But now she was putting into practice what they had plotted together. History's change had begun.

Cean could barely contain the wild glee bouncing around inside him. His feet felt lighter and he was sure the procurator was eyeing him with avid distrust. But Decianus strode from the hut. Before any could move he gave a quick order. Boadicea and her daughters were seized.

"What? What is this, Roman?"

His face showed wounded pride. "Did you deem me so much a fool, lady? That man in the hut, the one you claimed to be your husband? It wasn't grief which made him play a sick king but greed. Your greed. You wished to rule. If your man was ill, then you could rule in his name. If he was known to be dead, however, you'd have to give up your kingdom, your wealth."

Her gaze flamed back. "I need no Roman to give me leave to rule my kingdom. I am the royal woman, life and heart of the people, their connection to the Gods. I rule in my own name."

"Not in Rome's name however. It seems, lady, you require a lesson I am willing to provide." He spoke quickly to his second-in-command. Orders in such swift Latin only Cean could understand them.

He took in a quiet deep breath. This would do it.

Two of the soldiers dragged Boadicea to a hut, holding her upright against the side as a third dragged her mantle back, slashing it from her with a belt-knife. Others had her daughters in a savage grasp in each hand. The girls writhed and fought, but their arms were as frail as grass in the soldiers' hands. Decianus walked over to smile into Boadicea's outraged face.

"You shall receive a lesson you will remember in future, woman. Rome is not so easily fooled. I will stripe your back well, just as Rome brands any disobedient slave." Behind them her daughters screamed as they were forced to the ground.

"My children, what do you to them?"

"Oh, a lesson there as well. A few of my men shall show them what women are made for."

She stared at him in an oddly concentrated way. Great eyes dark-ringed, holding his with the power of her own. "They are not yet full-grown women. Is this how Romans behave? Raping children?"

He chuckled easily. "Romans do as they will. A pity you didn't believe that before you tried your tricks. But the sting of your back and the squalls of your brats will forge it in your memory from now on." He turned. "Strip that pair and get on with it. Bring me a whip."

Cean shifted near to the children as soldiers held them. A long staff stood by his hand. Seemingly forgotten, it had been used to prop up a portion of house wall under repair.

He waited. Alieki would give the signal, but not yet. The Queen would not let her daughters be harmed. But she was less careful of her own skin. She wanted to be certain.

And she wanted her people to see clearly just how far the Romans would go.

From the corner of his eyes he saw the Iceni men had drifted away. He knew they were circling the huts to position themselves once they had been handed the waiting weapons.

The attention of the soldiers was all on the scenes before them. By the hut, Boadicea was held flat against the wall as Decianus took up the driving whip. Behind them the girls were spread-eagled on the ground, tunics ripped away. They writhed and snarled defiance. Daughters of the Queen. There was nothing passive about them.

The whip came down. It left a thin bright red line the length of Boadicea's back. She grunted through clenched teeth. The ten year-old Iessin shrieked as the first soldier fell on his knees over her growling at his friends to keep her still. From his position Alieki whistled, a long clear call like that of a bird suddenly wakened by the growing commotion. But it was not. The Romans ignored the sound until the Iceni dun exploded into chaos.

Decianus was the first to die. Alieki burst from the path between huts. His spearhead flashed then vanished beneath the spouting blood from a Roman's chest.

The Queen struggled, shouting. Her struggle concentrated the attention of the men who held her upon her alone.

Myla appeared, knives in hand. One she thrust into the back of one soldier. The other she tossed to the Queen as one of her hands tore it loose from the dying soldier's grasp The two women circled the other soldier. Playing him from one to the other until for a second, he was unfocused. Boadicea's strike was the flicker of a bird's wing. It seemed harmless, but when her hand drew back the knife was red to the hilt and the soldier was crumpling.

When Alieki's signal came Cean had seized the staff. The soldiers holding the girls hadn't yet realized what was happening. Cean leapt, driving through them before they understood. Iceni swords and spears struck them, but it was Cean's staff which took first toll. He crashed it against the temple of the man who was about to use Nessan. The soldier fell unconscious on top of the child.

His comrades acted quickly. One flung the child down again as she squirmed out from under the dead Roman, the other man drawing a knife.

Cean had feared just this. They would kill the children if they could do nothing else. His staff spun in his hand, lashing out in a ferocious blow. The knife fell away as the soldier collapsed. Cean whirled back to stand before Nessan.

For a brief moment he was busy, two other soldiers attacking the tribesman who dared to kill their own. Cean thrust, parried. Pieces of his staff flew up and then as he misplaced a stroke the flat of one of the swords took him along the side of his face, the force of the blow still there even if the edge was turned. He staggered but fought on. They *must not* reach the children.

He did not realize that it was Nessan, a long-knife now in her small hand, her lips peeled back in fear and fury, who guarded his back. Cean shifted to the French style of fighting. *Moulinet.* The staff spun like a whirlwind in the air. It held back the soldiers for the critical seconds while he recovered. Then there was no need.

Striking from a circle about the Roman soldiers, the warriors of the Iceni slew, and then slew again. Dead Romans fell around the healer and the two girls. Even as the last few tried to run when they realized they could not win, the tribesmen cut them down, thrusting with their spears, stabbing necks, chests or even legs, to finish off the fallen wounded quickly with knives.

The Iceni took some losses. But the soldiers had all been concentrating on other things: licking their lips with amusement at the sight of a naked queen being whipped, anticipating too their own turn at the two young girls. A few of the first to fall had not even noticed the rising of the Iceni warriors until it was much too late.

The Romans were no more than fifty against four times that many. They were scattered, without the time to organize a defense, in a block with overlapping shields, the kind of fighting that served them well on their campaigns they might have lived. But there was no time and their shields were still with their horses, lashed uselessly to their saddle harnesses.

One by one they were taken like deer by the Iceni wolves, their blood a dark wine seeping into the soil of the Iceni dun. When at last the final man fell the Queen moved to stand by Cean. Her stare was savage, her eyes showing white all about the rim.

"You spoke rightly, healer," her voice like thunder boiling in the air. "I heard him clearly. Rome counts no queens. I and my daughters are nothing, neither royal nor rulers. My people will not bow as slaves to Rome! We, who were born free, know no masters. As you said, even Prasutagus's will was denied. He would have taken all which was not his to take or have." She stirred Decianus's body lightly with one foot. One hand held her mantle about her throat. But rage drew her lips back in an unvoiced snarl.

"This was in his eyes. His greed was a fire which eats and eats and is never satisfied if there is fuel still about it. He would have had all from me. Then he would have cast his eyes on my people's beasts, their homes, until all they owned was stripped from them, even the food from their mouths. We would die under his heels, robbed of everything that would give us life." Her eyes met his. "You dreamed I'd be beaten, my daughters used before the people."

Cean spoke flatly. Fear shivered in his stomach. Did she blame him? "That did not happen."

"Nay, it did not. Yet only because you spoke beforehand so that I made plans. Even so, we were close enough to that end when Alieki gave the signal." Her shoulders shifted. There was a rumble of glee in her voice now. "Beyond close. I have one stripe to remind me of Rome's customs towards a queen, of how they see her. Decianus said he would teach me. That lesson I will remember. Indeed I shall." She turned to study Cean.

"This also I shall remember, healer. I saw how you fought for Nessan, how you stood between my daughter and the enemy, striking down the man who would have been first to fall upon her. Then the man who would used his knife on her. I saw well. I do not forget."

Cean was embarrassed. "I did no more than any other, Lady."

"Perhaps. No more than any warrior of the Iceni at least, yet you are not of our people. You are a healer as well, unused to the ways of killing. You could have stood aside, saying this was not your fight."

"I couldn't." His fear had subsided, but she could kill him with a word, suspecting him of complicity, of knowing what the Romans planned because he was their own.

"Because you protected what they would have taken, aye. But there is work to do now. We may talk further once that is done." She walked away in long strides.

"Best we be about our plan then," Cean said quietly to her, to himself, his stomach now full of relieved fluttering.

"Aye. Alieki, to me," the Queen called out. The spearman came at a brisk trot. "Bring their saddled horses to the edge of the dun. Halt them before the bare ground that they make no deep hoofprints in the mud. We shall bear these bodies far and far again."

Cean stood back. Let the Queen manage this portion of her plan. She was not in a mood to brook interference from him. Not yet.

The Romans were carried to the far side of the Iceni lands on their own mounts. On past the borders, and miles across country to a bend in the main highway that split the island. By the time they halted, it was almost dawn. There they were far from the Iceni territories, indeed from many of the tribal lands. Alieki was hunter as well as warrior. He studied the terrain, conferred with the Queen and with great care and the aid of many others of the tribe, curved back onto the road to leave tracks there.

"They will believe this?" Cean queried. He would, but then he was neither hunter nor warrior. Alieki nodded.

"Aye. See here where they rode." He pointed to a spot in the road where the horses had scraped the stone, leaving in the soil between it the right tracks. "The Procurator before them. Then, see, he spies something upon the hill to the left. He races his mount across the road to follow what he sees. His men ride after, far down the slope of the hills. There at the bottom where the ground is marshy they are taken in ambush. They dismount to fight on foot with the beasts held to one side."

The Iceni were trampling about in the muddy ground, denting it with marks that would tell this tale. "The soldiers fall, they bleed and die. Several escape, most of the loose mounts running with them. Their trail is lost in the stony patches between the heather which shows no footprints nor signs where men have trodden no matter how hard their feet fall upon the ground."

"They die?" Cean said looking at the sprawled bodies.

Alieki's face was grim. "Aye, healer. We are warriors and hunters also. We know how the bodies stiffen in death. Yet the stiffness passes. Two of us will remain waiting. Once this is so we shall lay them as if they had fallen after a hard fight. Those who find them shall believe this story because with their own eyes they will witness the signs left to tell them so."

He waved his companions on. One by one the bodies were brought as Cean left shivering. In the grass the bodies spread out like stiff dolls, unyielding to the rocks or mounds of soil. In a day, when the rigor mortis had left, they would be moved into their positions.

Four Roman corpses, supposedly those who had led an escape which never existed, would be found deep in the adjacent lands. Their bodies had been chosen for this site because they'd died from knife thrusts alone. Into the wounds the Iceni would thrust unmarked arrows, deep. There would be no tribal designs on the arrows to cast blame on the innocent. The Roman mounts would be driven farther into another tribe's territory.

"What if the Trinovantes find the horses?"

Boadicea smiled. "There is no blood on the saddles. They will take the beasts as a gift from the gods, and bury the Roman saddle fittings. If the Romans then come looking, they will see nothing. Likely the tribe will try to hide their booty anyhow. If the beasts are noticed, they will look like others the Trinovantes possess."

"What about those who have the horses?"

She looked at him blankly. "What of them? They are not Iceni. Nor are the Trinovantes our allies. They have been friends of the Romans too often for my liking. If the Romans discover them and slay some they believe are the thieves of horses, when the tribe knows their own innocence, will the tribe not turn to us? Let some die. The Romans will make them enemies if they act so, and allies for us at the same time."

Her smile was hungry. Frighteningly so. She was not a woman who would be kind to her enemies. Not after her own wound and their attempted rape of her daughters.

"The more the Romans oppress their Trinovantes slaves, the more shall their slaves rise up against them. We shall offer them the freedom to at least to die honorably in battle." She turned to look down at Cean where he stood. "I think many shall chose our way." She turned her horse's head. "It is well, Cean. It is well. Tonight we shall feast. The grain has been sown; the harvest will come."

He rode back beside her in silence, considering her words. The grain, the real seed had been sown so the Iceni need not starve. But another seed had been sown in the past twenty-four hours, and he knew it.

Historically, Decianus had lived. Boadicea and her daughters had been outraged, their tribe despoiled. Now none of this had happened here. The Romans could still punish the royal women, despoil the tribe. But they could not raise the procurator to live again. History was irreversibly altered. By how much and how far it remained to be seen. For now he could bend what would be.

Another problem. They would feast tonight, celebrate their victory, and then return to their everyday lives, content with what they'd done. But in Cean's history, that would destroy them. When all the tribes' warriors left with the major battle as yet unfought, and celebrated the smaller victories, satisfied with the looted goods, Boadicea had been left with fewer men, fewer people to fight when she needed them most. As a result, she'd lost that final, greater battle.

He must think of the right advice for Boadicea to prevent this. As yet, he didn't know how he could convince the other tribes. He had fallen back as he rode. Ahead of him he admired the lithe powerful figure which led the returning warriors. She *must* survive, she and Lubran his friend, Ancha who would become his ancestor, Dauldi, Verli whose life Cean had saved, and Siharni, the boy's mother who had given him his prized foal-skin. *All* of them must survive.

Somehow, in this time he felt at home. The people were decent, honest, hard-working, and free. Particularly free. No one should be a slave. He remembered the greed in the procurator's face as he turned Boadicea's wedding cup in his hands. Bandy-legged, muscle-bound *pig*. And that was the man who in another time and place had casually ordered two children raped before their mother and their people. To teach them their place in the Roman scheme of things.

He'd had Boadicea flogged because she dared protest his thefts from her tribe. The man hadn't deserved to live. Cean felt no qualms about his murder. The Romans had started this. Let the Iceni finish it with his help. Some things he didn't like doing, or even seeing, but hadn't it been Napoleon who'd said one couldn't make an omelet without breaking eggs? So long as most of the broken eggs were Romans, Cean could live with that.

He remembered Mel and Fort with a sudden pang of homesickness. He was saving them, after all, and Janet, Max, Marion, his other friends of the Coalition. What were they doing now? What would they think if they knew what he'd done? Would it matter? This wasn't exactly a question that would ever be answered. But somehow it still mattered for Cean.

They mattered. And in this world's timeline, maybe it would save Mel. Maybe save all of them. Maybe even stop Tensen's from happening. He rode on to join the feast and was merry all that night.

5

Separating the myth from the reality is very difficult when religious belief is under consideration. Many view it as faith, not subject to evidence, or rationale. But how does that reflect a whole people's conviction? Of how it is applied across a culture? Such a simple view can't, of course. What is absent from that equation—a cold word to be applied to a faith so warm and full of life—is the effect of worship upon the context of the world it permeates.

Druid beliefs animate the world: they give it cause and value; belief gives the world a spiritual life that is connected to the people who worship it, offering them a place within its fabric. How can that be rejected by anyone without the moral, transcendent perceptions necessary to judge a religion? Druidism is. Druids are. As the gods are.

—from *The Passionate Spirit*,
by His Reverend Holiness Colm Herraster

"Of what use is religion if it does not meet the needs of its people? And that this is true of government goes without saying. We are a people of the land, a people of our beliefs, a people who will go to war at need when Roman soldiers break down our walls! We will not willingly become their slaves!"
—Boadicea, from her first speech to the tribes of Britain,
collected in *Anla's Annals, Vol. 3*

Iceni Homeland, 59 C.E.

Alone the next morning, Cean worked on a timeline. Snugly shut in his hut, the hide door lashed tightly across the opening, the hearthfire glowing dully before him as he jotted down notes on the mini-computer from the casket, he recalled events as they had occurred in his own world and time. They'd taken almost two years, from Prasutagus's death to the destruction of the Druid's Isle of Mona, to the failure of Boadicea's rebellion and her subsequent suicide. *Supposed* suicide, Cean reminded himself. No history mentioned anyone finding her body.

A lot of the delay, he thought, had been caused by the long wait for news to travel in this world. The same incidents were happening again, but with his advice, the Queen was altering some of them. In this time Prasutagus had died as he had in Cean's. But Boadicea had successfully blocked word of that from leaving the Iceni duns. It had taken almost four months for Decianus Cattus to discover the ruse. Now he and his men lay in a far Trinovantes valley, food for the crows.

Once again none knew the Iceni king was dead and long since buried.

It was possible that could win them some months yet that could be worked to their advantage. Time for Boadicea to talk to the other tribes, and give her people a chance to bring in the harvest, and plan further through the long winter. The Romans would be reluctant to campaign during that season of food shortages.

For a start, all fodder for the horses would have to be carried with them. There was little or no decent grazing to be had as they traveled. Hunting would be difficult to impossible, and in consequence, the soldiers' rations, too, would have to be brought with them, including the increased winter portions of reserve grain. Cean's smile was harsh. He'd bought the tribes some time, and the Iceni gods willing, they'd have more now the Queen listened to him.

The next day, as the sun began its slow descent into night, Lubran returned from the Druid's Isle. He swept his door curtain aside and beamed at Cean as he stood hanging bunches of dried herbs from the roof supports of Lubran's hut.

"Ah, it is good to be home. The gods only know how I have missed the sight of my own hunting runs."

Cean found he was hugging the old man. "It is good to see you, brother. I have cared for your people as I promised, but I have been lonely while you were gone."

The old man's brows drew down. "None have kept you company?"

Cean laughed. "Indeed they have. But they are not healers. I have missed learning from you, talking over our knowledge. I gather herbs alone."

Lubran's eyes went to the hanging herbs. He crossed to finger them, pinching the leaves between hardened weather-beaten fingers. "You have done well. A tincture made from these leaves can be used to bathe sore eyes."

Cean looked at the goldenrod. He'd been fascinated to learn that many of the native herbal medicines were based on solid knowledge. In England, before he'd jumped back in time, he'd obtained two disks crammed with information on the plants of Britain, with particular reference to the Norfolk/Anglia area. His tiny solar-powered computer should work for many years to come, so he could access and cross-reference the entries on the disks with the things Lubran taught him about his plants.

Lubran began emptying his pack. "I brought knowledge from the Isle. The Romans press them hard. It is strange how they fear men of wisdom."

Cean didn't think it so strange. The druids had controlled much of the gold trade between Wales and Ireland, but that was perhaps something best not mentioned to Lubran. It was the kind of knowledge that sounded duplicitous, as if he knew *too* much.

"They fear their influence upon the people," Cean answered instead, sitting down near the hearth to light it. "They want our people to hear no one's voice but theirs."

"We are not Roman subjects."

"That is not what the procurator said."

"Aye. Of that tale I have heard. I went first to the Queen. You advised her well, Cean. The Roman deaths will not come back to shadow us, and now we know the truth of how they see us. Beneath their honey-eyed words lies the venom of their sting." His gaze was hard, unforgiving. These were his people. "I see a time when they shall learn how free men fight led by a queen their Rome does not count."

"Aye. Yet that time may be far off. I tell you, Lubran, once a man begins to break a pony it is not well to cease its training partway through. Nay, if we once rise up against the Romans we must defeat them, and not in a few battles. We must beat them so soundly they are swept from the lands of all the tribes, driven back over the seas whence they came. If they linger here, if we permit them to build their forts, and garrison their men here even in a small way, they will always be a threat to the tribes."

Lubran stood musing on that for some time as he stowed his pack's contents into their accustomed places: herbs into the chests where they would stay dry, spare clothes to the side to be washed later, his cup and bowl into another chest next to the first. The fire was lit and Cean had a meal warming there for the old man. The smell of venison and rabbit stew filled the small hut, making Cean's stomach rumble.

"You may be right. I have heard much from the isle. Other tribes may have defeated the Romans, but it has always been a temporary victory. Every time the Romans have returned in greater numbers until at last with too many warriors dead and the people weary of war, the tribe has yielded. Once they have done so, the Romans have driven the druids out so that the people go without their wisdom, and fear the wrath of the gods. In these kingdoms, the people's lives are changed, and not for the better. This is not a good thing for the future of any people."

"Because they fought only as one tribe. Or even one or two together." Cean blew on some broth to cool it before tasting it carefully. It was almost ready to eat. "Once a battle was done, they quit the field and returned to their homes thinking the war was won. I say to you, Lubran, the tribes win battles, but the Romans win wars. They fight well. Is it shameful to learn from a strong enemy?" He scooped out stew into Lubran's bowl, spooning a bit into a bowl for himself.

"Nay." Lubran accepted the wooden bowl and began to eat. "Do you think it shameful to learn from me?" The old man waited for the younger man's answer as he ate.

Cean grinned. "I am young. It is right I learn from you. Ask rather is it shameful if *you* listen to *me*?" There were many older men who would think so, but Cean was certain Lubran did not.

"Not so." The reply was very definite. "How shall I call myself wise if I do not take up knowledge where it is to be found?" He ate slowly, looking thoughtful. At last he laid down the empty bowl. "These things I shall say to the Queen. She is impetuous, yet she is no fool, and she loves her people well. Whatever advice may save them she will heed." He paused. "And she will be certain now that the Romans do not wish her well. Your advice thus far has been good. Between us we shall keep her from folly, and the Iceni shall be great."

"Greater than you know." Cean kept his voice low, as if he stared into the cup he now held in his hands.

Lubran's head jerked up. He had come to believe whatever the young man said. "You have dreamed?"

"Aye, a dream of two paths. In one the Iceni were ground as between millstones. Ground smaller and smaller by the Romans until our people were no more. In the other they grew great, like grain ripening in a field, until the rulers of all tribes of the land bowed before the Queen." He looked at the healer. "And in that dream, Lubran, the Romans wept along far shores, not daring to return."

"This dream, it came the night after the Roman pigs were slain?"

Cean was surprised. "Why do you ask?"

"The gods send dreams to men after a great event. They show whether the path the men took was right or wrong. They may even show new paths. It is as if the great event lifts aside a curtain for a wise man to see beyond to what lies behind it."

Cean hadn't read of that belief before, although as Lubran told it, there was sense in it; the future is determined by each event, particularly ones that alter people's actions. The young healer could agree safely and be believed.

"I cannot be sure. Aye, we worked all that night to take the Romans away from the walls of the dun. We slew them in the evening's dusk and carried them away to lie in their blood. I was weary beyond words when I returned." He spoke louder, feigning excitement. "I think you may be right, Lubran. I was too agitated to sleep that day. I gathered herbs to dry and made myself a fine stew as well. At dusk I ate and went to my bed. I was so weary it took time to fall asleep, but when I did, yes, it was then truly that I dreamed."

His companion sat back looking satisfied. "Aye. The night after the slaying of the Romans. That was a dream sent by the gods in truth, Cean. Now tell me all you can remember of it."

The old man was eager. The tales he had been told at the druid's isle indicated that something was brewing, a new force that was about to change their world.

Cean talked slowly, with careful words. They would undoubtedly be relayed back to Boadicea and could be an influence on her future actions. He spoke of a fire which had flamed up in his dream, a warrior flinging water upon it until it was no more than wet ash. Yet it was lit again and this time banked to stay alight, fuel added piece by piece. Again the warrior moved to put it out, but he failed as the fire blazed higher. He tried again and again until at last he walked away alone, cursing the blaze behind him, leaving it to burn.

Cean rambled, apparently, but each picture was designed to appeal to Lubran's belief in dream-seeing. A man already disposed to accept Cean's ability to dream, and who was well versed in the language of dream interpretation, would have little difficulty understanding what the images implied. Lubran listened intently, marking every word of it. When Cean was done, Lubran turned his eyes inward, thinking, and presently nodded.

"I think I understand this in the message of the gods. We must move with caution. There must be no foolish haste. We are to be as a man who builds his house. With strong foundations, it shall withstand even the hardest winter. If his friends aid in the building, then can the house be larger and stronger than if he built it alone. Aye, the gods send to a man. It is for a man who is wise to understand their speech."

"You are the wise man. I am only the poor messenger."

"Not so poor." Lubran's eyes glimmered with amusement. "I shall tell the Queen of this and I think she may not see a messenger go empty-handed."

"I don't think I am sent dreams so I may profit," Cean said slowly. "Tell her so if she should ask. I want nothing save to remain here and be counted as one of her own people. I am at home here as if this place is where I once lived and had forgot for a while."

Lubran spoke soberly, nodding like a man about to sleep. "A man lives, he dies, and if the gods will it, his spirit goes west of the sunset by the warriors' road. Yet one that does so, may return to live again in another body. This is the secret teaching of the druids. Yet you too, are wise though you have not learned at the Holy Isle. I say to you, brother in healing, what you feel may well be truth. If the Queen asks, I shall answer as you say."

Los Angeles, 2048 C.E.

Fort had called in the morning, waking Cean from a deep sleep. "Mel has been asked to leave the hospital."

Cean was sure he'd misheard. "What?"

"The bastards have asked her to leave. They said they don't have the facilities to handle the profiled." Fort was furious. "They said they can't risk any disruption with other patients. Their lawyers have informed the hospital board that her presence is a liability to their health." Fort was furious, his voice snapping with his anger. "None of the other hospitals will take her, either. I've called them already."

Cean was just as outraged. "She can't walk yet! What's she supposed to do?"

"I've managed to find a nursing home that will take her until she's able to get around on her own. But they're covering their backsides. They said they can't keep her permanently. I think they're saying that just in case any of their patients complain. Then they'll turn her out on a moment's notice, just like the hospital. The bastards! I should sue them. They're endangering her health."

It wouldn't help, though. No court at the moment would side with someone who was profiled. If what was happening these days, the watch they suspected had been put on many of the Coalition—the rumored secret list that was now being kept by the police—was true, Cean knew Fort wasn't overstating matters. He went on.

"Doctor Romares isn't available, apparently. Somehow I doubt she'd go along with this kind of behavior." He sighed. "An ambulance will take Mel over to the nursing home but I'll need your help settling her in."

Cean quickly agreed, then hurried to get dressed and out the door. When he arrived at the hover car station, he realized it was 7:00 a.m., barely rush hour. The hospital must have called Fort very early. Fog held in by the smog had yet to boil away with the sunlight, and mist clung wetly to the steel posts and rails, the metal drawing moisture out of the air. Cean shivered. Yesterday had seemed so hopeful.

At the hospital, Mel was lying on the bed, the attendants standing around waiting beside a gurney ready to take her. She lifted a hand, a simple wave, as Cean hurried up. He picked up her fingers to hold onto her, to reassure her. He looked around for Fort and saw him down the hall arguing with the duty nurse. He slapped his hand down on the counter as Cean listened.

"She can't use a wheelchair yet. She's braced while the nerve tissue in her back heals. She can't sit up at all!"

The nurse was adamant. "I'm sorry, sir. It's not my choice. The gurney will have to be broken down and sterilized if she uses it, some of it lost. Other patients will refuse to touch it even then. The hospital administrators have asked that you take her another way."

She frowned. This was not something she enjoyed doing, but she needed her job.

The ambulance attendant who'd followed Cean onto the floor spoke up. "Doesn't matter, sir. We have a stretcher we can carry her on. Not expensive and they can burn it if they have to to prevent further infections."

The nurse peered at him over her glasses. "It's on your head, not mine if you do that. You understand?"

"Yes, ma'am, I do." He lifted his eyes at her. "I *surely* do." She might have been willing to make recovery even more difficult for one of the profiled, but he wasn't. He nodded at Fort.

"Let's go, sir. We could get a call at any time, and an emergency would take priority over this."

They hurried back to Mel's room. The second ambulance attendant had spread a stretcher over the top of the waiting gurney. They'd shift Mel to that and carry her out from there. Both Cean and Fort readied themselves to help. Tears streamed from Mel's one good eye, and Cean scrubbed them away for her. None of it made sense. Cean wanted to scream: Tensen's couldn't be caught by touch!

But they were lucky. No emergencies occurred during the hour it took to transport Mel to the rehabilitation center. There, the ward supervisor led them to a room at the far end of one wing. It looked out on a small grassy slope, with pathways between dusty flower beds and birdbaths forlornly attempting to lure birds in among the bushes.

"It's rather nice." Mel managed to say, more for their sake than hers. The attack had occurred only two days before. Cean was amazed she could do that much. He leaned down to hear her. "Cleaner air, that's for sure, and no speakers shouting 'stat' at me in the middle of the night."

Indeed, it was much nicer, more quiet and restful than the hospital, but Cean had noticed the room was as far away from the other patients as it could be.

Fort patted her hand. "You'll get better much faster here. You'll have your own physiotherapist, there's even water massage, and you'll have your own private control for the monitor."

Mel tried to smile for them. She'd not have anything to do except watch television, even poor television, while she recovered.

"Patience," Cean murmured to her, trying to reassure her that all it would take was time.

They stayed with her for some time to be sure she was settled comfortably and there'd be no future problems, or at least none in the immediate future. But when they left, Fort was still furious.

"They didn't have the right!" he exclaimed as soon as they'd flagged an automated cab. Seat belts slid over them both as the car pulled out, and Fort punched the destination into the control board

A quiet, calm voice issued from the speakers: "Please sit back and relax, sirs. Your destination is forty point two minutes away. Your comfort is valued. If you have any suggestions, please refer to the destination board attached to the dash, and type your suggestion in. Then press the 'Enter' and your suggestion will be logged in." After a brief burst of static, it added, "Will that be credit or debit card, sir?"

Fort furiously stabbed the keys, entering a code before slipping his debit card into the appropriate slot, and turning to Cean once the card was accepted. "It could have done permanent damage to her spine to move her like that. Regenerating nerves are fragile, new bones are frail."

Before they left, they'd been assured by the nursing staff that exrays would immediately be taken to be sure no damage had been done in the move. The facility had an MRI and that would be used. Only then had Fort been willing to turn over Mel's medical file to them.

Neither Cean nor Fort said anything about what was foremost in their minds: the hospital had required Mel's move the day after a prostitute had been charged with murder. She was profiled and had deliberately used her Tensen's to kill a few clients. She claimed God had given her the divine right to punish sinners, she may even have believed it. Of those who heard her, very few agreed and many of those who did not were now more strongly motivated to act against the profiled.

Iceni Homeland, 59 C.E.

Now that Lubran was back, Cean's work was lighter. Summer was slipping away. There had been no word of anyone finding the bodies of the procurator and his escort. Harvest came and went, the Iceni celebrated and the year dropped quietly towards winter. If Lubran had spoken of Cean's desire to the Queen, she had given no word to him in return. Not yet.

On a clear chilly day in late autumn Cean and Lubran hunted herbs together. Cean wandered a little away from Lubran near some shrubs growing next to a copse of trees. Wild chives had rooted themselves in the soil there, and Cean fancied a taste of them in their nightly stew. As he was stooped over them, a bird's call sounded in one of the trees.

A chaffinch, its rusty color and gray cap reminding him of all that the 21st century cities had lost.

He looked up, searching for it. It hung in the branch of a tree, looking down at him, and Cean chirped back at it. It wasn't frightened, and in a moment spoke again. He repeated the phrase, and suddenly, with a single chirp the bird flew away. Cean watched the bird's swoop and glide away with pleasure, until a rustle in the bushes drew his eyes.

Two boys grinned up at him, and at his look, they chortled, happy, and ran away. Cean laughed and returned to his work, joining Lubran a short time later. Together they returned to the dun laden, to sort and string their gleanings before eating together companionably at Lubran's hearth.

"You have learned well, brother. The people trust you almost as they do me. You have a place here. Have you thought perhaps of taking a woman for your hearth?"

Cean shook his head, shyly. "Nay, I have no wish for another to share my roof. I have work I love, a companion who shares knowledge, and friends among the people. That is enough."

"Is there one left behind you?" Lubran queried delicately. "One for whom you could send?"

Mel. The thought of her brought a sudden pang of loneliness. But she'd been only a friend. There'd never been desire between them. More than friendship, but no desire. Nor could he send for her, not in this world or the other.

"I walk alone, Lubran. I think the gods would have it so."

Cean left for his own hut a short time later. For a long time after he had sought his bed he lay awake in the dark, with only the tiny glow of the banked coals for company. He thought about Fort and Mel, wondering how they'd managed, if Mel had recovered as she should.

Cean shivered, cuddling deeper into his bedding. A slow, powerful feeling took him in its grip as he remembered his own history. If he stopped his plans here, made no further changes, he would be like the Iceni. Winning the first battle, but losing the war. Perhaps the future had already been changed. He had altered the outcome here, so much so that he had to have established already a different history. Or not.

Fort had once talked about what he believed to be the resilience of time to any alteration, its elasticity. Cean wasn't sure he understood that entirely.

Fort had pointed out, too, another possible consequence to Cean's actions. "Which brings us to the question of what we really think is going to happen," he'd said. "You know, my friend, that if the time jump creates a parallel universe, what you're doing there won't affect this one?"

Cean hadn't wanted to think of that. He gulped a mouthful of tea before answering. "Yes. But perhaps I'll help the world where I do go. Or create a better history there, safer and cleaner for people who become profiled, perhaps even stop Tensen's before it develops. And if it is this world, maybe I can change it enough to do the same."

Fort looked at him appraisingly. "I hate to say this," he began, "but quantum theory lends more support to the parallel universe, or the splitting off of a new parallel world at specific points. What those are we don't know yet, nor why they happen." He smiled at Cean, fondly, his eyes grave.

"But if anyone could change an entire world, it would be you. I'm sure of it. I just wish I could be sure it would save this world. Because I don't know what's going to happen here. You are well out of it, I think."

Cean agreed. And if what he'd done so far hadn't changed this world's future, there were still other changes he could make. He had come very prepared.

He fell asleep finally, realizing he couldn't predict anything with certainty, save that he would have to stay always on the alert. He woke early next morning, rose to stir the fire, and fasten the door curtain tightly. He removed his computer from the bronze casket and recalled its origins. The Queen, too, had had a casket, or so legend had run. Was it like this one? He would like to discover that one day.

He sat, quietly adding to his tale of events on the tiny disk. Usefully the small piece of technology could be accessed by voice or keyboard. Once he was done, he saved the material before putting the palm top computer with its flat, fold away keyboard back in the casket. He checked the timeline from his own time again. Mona, the attack on the

Holy Isle, would come in a few more months. Perhaps he should dream again? Or perhaps he could "read" it in the motions of the stars?

He studied the disks. One day he might tell Lubran of this, the computer, the casket, the tale of Cean's journey. Not yet, though. Not until he was certain history was really changed.

He grinned suddenly. One day very far in the future his story and the casket might turn up as an archaeological treasure. Scientists would excavate it, find the code to open the casket and learn how their history had been altered by one person's compassion. They would see their escape from events which had devastated Cean's world. He smiled at the irony of the thought. No, it didn't matter if anyone knew why or how. He just wanted a better world. That would be enough. He'd never sought anything else.

"Cean, are you within?" The voice was Ancha's.

Cean closed the casket and tucked it beneath his bedding before opening the curtain. "I am here."

"The Queen summons you, healer."

"To speak or to heal?" It was a valid question. If he was required to aid Lubran, then he should bring his medicines.

"To aid Lubran in healing, wise one. A messenger has come who is injured. He has given his message. Now the Queen would see him healed."

Cean grabbed for his satchel and followed her through the dun.

At the Queen's hut he found Boadicea, Lubran, several of her women and a wounded man. Cean's gaze sharpened. Not a man of the Iceni. After six months here he had begun to learn the look of the nearest tribes. This man was Trinovantes. Well, well. Maybe Decianus's death had come to light.

In silence, apart from the necessary professional discussion, he aided Lubran in tending the man. The wound was unpleasant, a deep stab in the thigh. The type of wound taken when one was on horseback, though there had been no sign of a spare mount outside. With the injury clean and treated, the Queen waved her hand, directing the injured man.

"Go with my woman here." And to Siharni. "Take him to your hearth. Feed him well, let him sleep. In the morning, he returns to his tribe. Bid Dauldi find him a suitable mount since his own is dead." She remained silent until the man had gone limping after Siharni, a spearman supporting him on one side.

"I would be alone save for the healers. Go!" Her women chattered their way out, leaving the three of them in the hut. The Queen relaxed, taking up a cup from which she drank deeply. Her eyes were bright, alert.

"Your fire begins to burn, healer," she told Cean. "Aye," seeing his gaze fix on her face. "Lubran told me of your dream. Being wise he also told me of the meaning, the warning the gods sent to me. I have heard them. In the silences of the grove the gods have spoken to me that I should pay heed." She sat, her cheek propped upon one hand before she went on.

"And so the Trinovantes will join us if we rise against the Romans. A Roman patrol went astray on Trinovantes' lands two moons ago. While hunting their path, they came upon a valley." Cean looked at her. "Aye, that valley. The foxes and crows had done good work upon the bodies, but enough remained that the patrol might see some of what had happened. It seems the disappearance of the procurator had been much talked of in Camulodunum. Yet none liked him so well that there was any urgency in their search. But upon finding him and his men, the urgency became greater. None may slay men of Rome without reprisal. They had only to discover who had slain their brothers and meet them with swords."

"From the messenger I gather they leaped to conclusions rather than making any real discovery?" Cean queried dryly.

"Indeed. Since they found Roman-branded mounts within the Trinovantes' horse runs." Cean winced and the Queen smiled. "Even so. The Trinovantes are rich and powerful, with many warriors. Even the Romans did not wish to begin a war against them, yet they dare not let the assault go unpunished. They fined the tribe many beasts, and demanded also of them that they give a hundred of their young men for soldiers."

Cean was surprised. "They could pay so much, so many?"

Her smile became grim. Wind whispered under the door hide. "They could, and so they would have, but that was not the only demand. Paulinus Suetonius said that since the crime was so foul, his soldiers would take the king's son to learn Roman ways." Her fury transfixed Cean. "The boy was but six summers old. He refused to go, so soldiers seized him. The messenger was present. He cannot say the blow was death-meant. But the child fought, a soldier struck him, and he died."

Lubran's quick gasp was a hiss louder than the sift of a fire's embers.

"Thus the Romans deal with those they hold less than themselves. And would have done so with us," Cean pointed out.

The Queen lifted her chin, her eyes clear like bright glass, a fire lit deep within them, as she looked at him. "Thus indeed. The tribe rose then, but the soldiers were ready. Of the tribe, four hands lie dead, many are wounded. The king himself was slain and his brother, Cran, rules now in his place. A vengeful man, with his brother and brother's son dead, and too many of his warriors lost to the tribe, yet he is cunning and careful. The Roman soldiers slew also the druids who bided with the people, saying it was they who urged the people to rebellion.

"The soldiers have taken many of the horses and most of the cattle, enough to beggar the nobles of the tribe, claiming the fine should be still greater because of the deaths of more of their men. Moreover they have said that when spring comes, so shall they, to tear down the palisade about the dun. They claim there is no more need for it since Romans hold peace over the lands. Cran, I am told, did not believe this."

"What does he plan?"

"He holds his people back. Now is not the time for war. The harvest is gathered but winter presses. Last winter we lost people, a family caught without fire in their hearth. Two children died of the cold, and their mother lost several of her fingers. We must be ready for winter this year so this cannot happen again. In spring once the grain is sown, he will be more ready and when that time comes he has the blood of his kin to avenge." Cean waited. However, what she next said was something he hadn't expected at all.

"Healer, I never told you this. I wanted to watch and see what you did here before judging you. Months before, when spring was just upon us, the priests told me a stranger would enter my dun. And then you came. You have become a messenger of the gods to me. Think on this war you see coming, and tell me what the gods say to you of this now." She paused, adding a moment later as she rested her chin on her hand. "I hear, too, healer, that you speak with the birds. Listen to them well. Perhaps they will speak in your dreams."

Birds? Cean was dumbfounded, before he suddenly remembered a child's laughter. The chaffinch. Word of that had very quickly been passed on to the Queen. Boadicea had said all she wished as she nodded. The clearness of her eyes had hardened, darkened as she finished speaking.

Lubran took Cean's arm to lead him from the hut. Once they were outside, the younger man looked at him.

"What will they do?"

Lubran strolled towards the forest edge. "Let us gather supplies. After the messenger's tale, I fear they may be needed soon."

Cean hurried to catch up, trying to find the question which would unlock the whole story. Lubran must know Boadicea's thoughts. No one else was that close to her.

"What will the Trinovantes do once winter is gone?"

Lubran eyed him in dry amusement. "They will prepare for war, Cean. Thus the messenger. Cran seeks an alliance. He is young; he has no woman. The Queen has two daughters. In a year the elder will be thirteen and marriageable. Such a wedding would be in secret since the Romans think they have the right to say nay to a king. But Cran will wed Essault this coming spring. He will not take her to his bed until after the harvest, when she is of age, and that too gives her time to learn of his people. But the wedding itself will bind his people to ours."

Cean walked on, thinking. It would be a powerful alliance. It would link together two tribes which ruled the whole of this corner of England. If the Atrebates and Catuvelauni could also be brought into the alliance, the entire land would rise up in arms against the Romans. As might have happened in the past of his world. He must check his disks for the original history. That could suggest a way for him to offer aid in this. He was quieter than usual as they worked so that Lubran returned early, parting from Cean at his door.

"Think well on what has been said, my brother. Maybe the gods will send another dream for you."

"I shall hope for it."

But it was not a dream he sought when he opened the disk onto the screen. It was a way forward which would bear a more certain victory, and shed less of the Iceni blood. He considered the Trinovantes. If word went to the Romans this tribe was brewing rebellion, even that they and the Atrebates might become allies …

His eyes were caught by another possible date. He'd always known Boadicea was a priestess of her tribe. But the histories had not told much more. Conquerors wrote history, and the Iceni had certainly not been in a position to record their side of the story. The druids had told her a stranger would be coming, a prediction passed to them from their gods in smoke- and blood-influenced trance, and so she'd allowed him into her dun, listened to him even though she did not know him. But her beliefs took second place to her people. She was a realist. The Iceni mattered most to her. He believed he could work with that.

* * * *

Autumn slipped into winter, which moved along after the long chill months into spring. His timeline suggested he should dream shortly and it would be fulfilled. Cean rose early, rushing to Lubran's hut to cry at the door.

"Brother, I have dreamed so ill I fear. Share your wisdom with me, be the sun which melts the ice that claws away at my insides!"

Lubran flung aside the door hide, his face drawn. Cean realized his friend had been waiting for just this. "What dream, brother? Come sit … I'll heat wine to warm you. Say no more until you cease shivering."

It was still mid winter and Cean had lain near the hide door naked for some time, waiting until his shuddering was definite, his skin like ice. Lubran took that for the chill of the dreams. He heated the liquid swiftly, thrusting the cup into Cean's shaking hand.

"Drink!" he urged. Cean drank obediently, sipping the sour ale laced with herbs, enjoying its warmth in his stomach, and the outer warmth coming from the sheepskins Lubran had flung about his shoulders. When Cean's shivering abated he spoke.

"I dreamed again. She said I would. There were many, men like yourself in robes of white. The Romans came with swords, and when I looked next the men lay on the ground, their blood turning the dirt to mud around them. The soldiers became animals, tearing down their huts, cutting down the many trees of a grove. All they saw they burned. They destroyed everything, leaving desolation, all the time calling out that it was peace." Another quotation stolen, he thought, but Lubran wouldn't know that.

Lubran's gaze was horrified. He spoke very quietly. "The place where this occurred. What could you see of it?"

"Little but the few things I recall." He shared the minor items he knew of Mona from his reading.

Lubran's eyes widened, his face paled in shock."The Holy Isle? Oh, gods, it cannot be! My friends, my brothers, my teachers. None escaped? You saw none able to flee?"

"The druids? None." Cean's voice was solemn, heavy. "Yet my dream may not have shown me all. Nor may this yet have happened." Or so Cean hoped. "You could send a warning?" That would annoy the Romans, to arrive and find the druids alerted.

"I shall do whatever may be done." Lubran rose. "Wait here." Before Cean could ask any questions the old man was gone. He did not return for several hours. When he came back it was to say only, "Boadicea has sent a messenger to the Isle. We can do nothing but wait."

After that it was as if he put the matter from his mind. Boadicea, too, did not speak of it, at least not to Cean.

* * * *

Spring sowing that year had been heavy. The Iceni opened more land, and more grain than ever before was planted. A Roman patrol guested two nights with the people, hunting with Alieki spearman as their guide, and bartering for two hounds and a good hunting pony.

On a small piece of rabbit skin, Cean wrote a note in soldiers' Latin while they were there. He found an opportunity of slipping it into the officer's baggage where it would not be found until the man was back in camp.

That might bear fruit—or it might not. But if it did, it could bring two other tribes in as allies against the Romans. He regretted those who might die, but he did not know them. He knew the Iceni. And these people he badly wanted to save.

Boadicea's messenger had been gone several weeks, it was time he returned. He did so before the spring planting had finished. Cean was nearby when the man staggered, bleeding and exhausted, through the dun gates. He saw the fixed look of shock, the eyes of a man who has looked on horror, and screamed for Lubran as the messenger fell.

"What is ... oh, gods, *Brache*."

Lubran kneeled down to turn the man's face towards him. Behind him others of the tribe had crowded up, Boadicea in the forefront. She might have ordered Brache carried away into privacy, but before she could, he opened his eyes and spoke in a thin, eerie voice.

"Mona has fallen. The Holy Isle is no more. They defiled it. They burned us, all of the druids! Even within their own huts. They cut down the sacred groves, caved in the wells. They ringed the shore with steel that none could escape."

The Queen stood as if struck, her eyes staring, wide, ringed with white. Brache looked at her. "I was in a boat. I could do nothing but watch and bring word. How could the gods permit this?" His voice shook. "One of their patrols saw me as I fled. Their arrows wounded me but I escaped and they believed me dead. Lady, say I have not failed you?" His voice was imploring now.

To Cean, watching, listening, it was life flowing back into her, the need of one of her people. She stooped to touch Brache gently on the shoulder.

"You have not failed me. What use to die and have the knowledge die with you? We know, and that was your doing. We know, and through us other tribes will learn of it. You did what was best, Brache."

He sighed, relaxing. At first Cean did not understand the limpness of the body until he saw Lubran close the eyes and make a sacred sign.

He looked closer and gasped. Well might the Roman patrol believe they had slain Brache. That wound should have killed any man. It said an incredible thing for Brache's determination to return that he had fought his way across the water and then across the miles to his own dun, his body dying but unfailing until he succeeded in his mission.

Around him there was silence. He saw tears steaming down Lubran's face though he wept in silence. Boadicea stood above the old man. Her hands clenched so tightly they showed white. Her face was a mask of fury and desolation. She was a priestess, even though she put her people first.

About him the Iceni stood in the stillness of shock. For generations Mona, the Holy isle, had provided healers and druids for the tribes. To say the Romans had committed blasphemy was an understatement so vast it could not be measured. Along with the spiritual assault on the faith, they had destroyed with the druids the knowledge of all the tribes, the learning accumulated in memory over generations ranging back hundreds of years. In killing the druids, the Romans may have destroyed a way of life.

Could they have been saved? Cean realized he'd now never know. If he'd done something sooner, some might have survived, and for that he could only blame himself. What good was change at such a cost? The people had heard the words. The meaning was still to be completely understood.

Cean stood and went quietly to his hut. He did not wish to be present when the people felt fully in their hearts what had been done to them. To all the tribes. It was the beginning. Now the flames of rebellion would soar upwards. In that at least he could help.

The dream he had claimed would convince Boadicea Cean should be heard in any council. It had come true. They would remember that once the shock wore off. Now he must persuade the Queen to see the other tribes were made to hold back. They must not act prematurely. He should …

He felt tears sliding down his face and sorrow burned in him. So much knowledge and learning lost. He could have prevented it! He forgot his plans, lay upon his sheepskins and gave himself up to regret and shame, grieving as the Iceni did.

6

Although scholars have stated that the Iron Queen, Boadicea, is the only great queen of world history, I disagree with that assessment. Queen Juana of Spain was just as fierce, and just as innovative in coming to terms with church authorities in her time. Spain would be a very different country now if she hadn't. She molded an independent government that was a leader in implementing European trade treaties, as well as promoting exploration in areas where other countries were less willing to proceed, such as Arctic islands, and the northern lands of the Americas.

And in her turn I would also praise Elizabeth for her sense of the greater empire. It was her vision that has shaped the modern world into its present form of enhanced, responsible technology and civilized laws.

No, Boadicea was merely the first of the great queens, a significant honor in and of itself.

—from *The Queens' Legacy*,
by Dr. Antonia Luerting, Oxford

Our faith's priests and priestesses were a strange lot to the Romans wanting to conquer our land. Druidism is a religion of the spirit of nature, the cycles of life, a system of beliefs antithetical to the Roman and Greek gods. Their gods are arbitrary entities, distant beings who are remote and uncaring about us lesser mortals. I need hardly point out that they are also cursed with the emotional maturity of children. But when the Romans came to our lands, our panting, passionate cries to our greater gods dismayed the soldiers to the point that they were initially shocked still. Even with their superior tactics, that hesitation proved to be a fatal mistake.

—from *The Passionate Spirit*,
by His Reverend Holiness Colm Herraster

Iceni Homeland, 60 C.E.

All the rest of that day Cean moved through the Iceni like a ghost amongst them. They didn't ignore him so much as they didn't have the strength to look outward. Instead, they looked inward to the spiritual loss all had suffered with the razing of Mona. The Isle had held the most sacred of their people, the druids, masters of the knowledge passed down through time. It had all been savagely destroyed.

Always, as long as they could remember, the Holy Isle had existed, providing healers and druids for the tribes. On Mona those who would learn healing studied for as long as twenty years. On Mona those who would learn the secrets of the unseen studied, some their whole lives. There was not a tribe in the land which did not have its representative masters there. And without them, this was a desperate land to not have healers' knowledge among its people.

But Brache had said it was gone, everything. Those who dwelled there slaughtered, the sacred learning vanishing with their deaths, the buildings and consecrated groves all burned. Druid priests and priestesses dead and rotting, scattered about the island. The Iceni people drifted around the dun, shaken to their core. That which had been the solid center to their lives had been ravaged, destroyed.

No shock, no matter how great lasts forever, though Cean like the others about him felt as if it would. Three days later as the initial dismay faded somewhat, and life returned to the tribe, Boadicea called him. She sat in her favorite posture, chin on one fist as she mused. Her eyes were dark, the color of slate. She lifted her head as he entered her hut.

"This was what you dreamed." It was a statement and he merely nodded. "You come from afar, from lands over the seas. Therefore to you the end of Mona is an awful thing that touches you not." Her voice was husky, hoarse with anger

"Yet I grieve for my friends' sorrow, and the passing of a great treasure in this land," Cean said steadily.

"Aye, I know. But your spirit is unshaken. Not as ours is. Speak to me now, healer. What do you advise? Such an act must not go unnoticed. Yet I am uncertain. My desire is to rise up and slay every Roman I may find, to teach them with fire and sword that though they slay men, they cannot defeat our gods." Her voice rose, harsh. "Those gods remain and will have their revenge. Through *us*." She waited, her eyes intent on him, her face lined with deep fury.

"I think that is not wrong," Cean said carefully. Gods, let him pick the right words, show her the wisest path while she was willing to listen. "You have seen," he continued. "The Romans judge all people who are not Roman as less than themselves. Women they judge as lesser still, counting a woman of value only if she be wed or enslaved, since then she has value to her man or master." He saw her gaze harden.

"In other lands they have permitted the people the freedom to worship their own gods. Here they have made you slaves and your gods are overthrown. That riddle I cannot read save that I think they believe your gods dangerous, your druid priests a threat." Fire crackled in the open hearth.

She smiled bitterly. "That is true," she admitted before going on. "Listen, Cean, from far lands, the druids taught us well. Their knowledge made us one, revealed the secrets and mysteries contained by the trees, the fields, the very land we walk upon. In women there is another knowledge, a secret of their hearts. It is fever and fire, it is women's magic and it lives yet. But the druid beliefs are what make us 'man and woman!' The Iceni, the people of this land."

"This I know."

Her brows went up. "You know? Did your people believe in the old ways, the knowledge of the druids?"

"In my own lands, I, too, have heard the whispers of women's magic. In my own way, I have also bowed before the altar of the druids." True enough, he reflected, considering what he was. She might hear the sincerity in his voice.

She did and grimly smiled, her eyes calm again.

"The Isle is fallen, most druids are slain," Cean continued. "Those with the tribes remain and they, too, will burn for revenge, even as you do. Now may be the time to talk to the other tribes."

Boadicea eyed him with respect, and some lingering suspicion. "That is a ruler's thinking."

"You know the druids as I do not. Will they take allies where they can be found once word of what was done is known?"

"So I think." She turned. "Maara, bring warmed ale for us. The day is chill." The small dark woman who served her came shortly with steaming mugs. Boadicea smiled on her. "I think, healer, you do not know this woman of my house. This is Maara, she was my nurse as a child, a friend to my house now as well as servant. Her people had power of their own. They are few now and scattered, but the power remains.

"Maara," the Queen spoke. The woman looked up with old dark eyes as she sat down nearby. "Read me this man who is not of our people."

Maara's eyes met his. Cean felt as he had when he first stepped onto the Iceni lands in his own time. A bolt of power snapped through him, taking fire in every part of his body. He jerked with the force of it, the flare opening up something inside of him, something that this woman could then perceive. Panic surged in the wake of the zap of power. What if she could see his memories? About the 21st century, about Tensen's?

No, there was nothing to fear. If the old woman read anything at all, she would know how much he had risked for the Iceni. He had in fact given up his entire world for the Queen and her people. And if the understanding was only emotional and not in fact, she would understand his admiration of the Queen, his compassion for the tribe.

But the sparks sizzled throughout, hissing through him. Maara stepped towards him, reaching out slowly to take his hand. Her fingers were warm, rough and very small.

Cean felt the sparks flare between his fingers and hers. Her eyes rolled back in her head, showing only the whites as she tightened her grip. A good trick, he reflected, if it was fake. At the least it looked very impressive.

When she spoke the tone was a soft sound, a sigh shaped into words. "From afar ... so far. Time ... blackness ... afar. To us he comes ... he is sent. The Mother herself has brought him. A healer, a warrior who fought his way here, shedding blood to open the way ... spending life to buy passage."

Cean quivered in surprise. Jonathan Smith. How could she know that? But no, she couldn't. Maybe it was a good guess, or perhaps she had merely felt that somewhere he had killed.

Maara was still speaking. "He speaks the truth he knows ... his care for our tribe fills his heart."

Without intending to, Cean saw his twenty-first century print of the Queen again: The burning huts, the dead, and Boadicea, magnificent in her defiance.

"I see as he sees. He passes through time and blood to come here ... to warn the tribe. He is sent, truth in his mouth, wisdom on his lips ... hear him, little bird ... the goddess has sent him with her mark upon him ... I see it ... in a time to come you shall also see and know what must be."

Her voice faded into silence. Her hands lifted to rest on Cean's shoulders, dropping briefly to run lightly over his chest. She stood a while, her head hanging tiredly, before with a shake of her robe she straightened, her face grim but sure. She picked up the Queen's ale.

"This grows cold. I will reheat it for you, my lady."

"Do so, Maara." But the Queen's tone was blurred, her eyes staring after the old woman. She then turned to Cean. "As Maara speaks, so it is. I do not say I will obey your words, healer. Yet I will listen, for one sent to my door by the goddess will find it ever open. Come to me any time wisdom or warning is given you to bespeak me.

"Is there anything you wish to tell me now?" Her voice was cautious, restrained. "Have the crows spoken to you?" She was smiling as she said it, as if she joked, but her eyes were serious.

Ah, yes, Cean thought. She had heard about the chaffinch. He smiled before he spoke.

"No more than that wisdom lies in waiting. The Romans make no friends. That alone will encourage rebellion in the hearts of rulers. Let them hear of the Holy Isle, and have your messengers speak privately to the druids of the tribes." He measured his next words with care. "If there are ways to make the Roman yoke heavier upon those who waver, will they not then come willingly to you when you speak of alliance?"

"That is truth. The Trinovantes are ripe for rebellion, and they have come close before now. It will take little more to move them to take up their swords."

"How so?"

"They held lands before the Catuvelauni came, far more than the lands which are left to them now. Then came the Romans who allied themselves with the Trinovantes. In my mother's generation, Rome succeeded in their war to stay in this land, but left, thinking Gaul was about to rebel.

"When they were gone, the Catuvelauni again built their fences close to the Trinovantes' duns, pasturing their herds in Trinovantes' fields. The Romans returned, and they are now taking land from the Trinovantes as well, giving it to their own people near their towns, making the Trinovantes less than those who come anew."

She smacked one hand against the other. "Twice their lands have been taken. Now the Trinovantes have less than before, and yet before that which their fathers held." Her lips turned down. "Cean, the Trinovantes have not only been despoiled of what land was left to them. Now they must look up to their despoilers, a wound twice cut in the flesh of their tribe, a wound that is not near healing."

Cean understood. It was a story told by many North American natives as well. "Ah, my people would say it adds insult to injury."

"A good saying—and true. Yes, I think when they hear the fate of the Holy Isle, they will join with us eagerly. The Catuvelauni, too. They have ever bowed to the Romans, one ruler or another. Their queen made treaty with them to divorce their king. Yet after the fines and death of their ruler even they are not so fond of the Roman intruders."

Her head lowered in thought, voice trailing away into a deadly softness. "If they were given further reason you say. Yes, if ..."

Her head came up again. "Ah, well. That is for me. Yours the wisdom, mine to walk its path. Go now ... no, stay a moment. Lubran says to me you would wish to be truly one of the people. Is he right?"

He met her gaze, unable to hide the hunger in his own eyes. "That is truth."

"In times past we have taken one of strange blood into our hearts. Yet you wish to wed none of us. That way, I think, is barred?"

"I walk alone." He tried to keep the blush from rising in his cheeks, but wasn't certain he succeeded. And the Queen's eyes watched it flush his face.

"Even so." She paused before adding, "A man who has fought for us may be accepted as a warrior. Yet you are not a great warrior."

"Am I not? I have fought death beside Lubran for the life of Verli, Dauldi's son, and the victory was mine." He waited, breath tight in his chest.

The Queen grunted softly as if she accepted a shrewd blow. "Well said. I will think on this. Perhaps if you are proved over time to be sent to us by the gods, or goddess, as Maara says, then I shall have no choice. Who rejects one sent by them, whichever god it be? Go now, wise one. Remember, my door is never barred to you if you have dreams to tell or words to speak."

Cean bowed as he rose, straightened and bowed again. He walked out into the cold day, warmth glowing within his heart to fight back the chill. In time, yes. One day soon he would be Iceni, and once that was so, they would accept him fully. For the moment it was enough she would hear him whenever he saw a need for warning.

In his history she had been a wild-eyed savage, impetuous, and in the end defeated because she could not control those who followed her. But she was, of course, not quite what history had represented her to be, and now he had already changed some of what she had been. Her original actions had been in reaction to intolerable abuse. Cean had always believed that the beginnings of her revolt had been while she was still traumatized after what had been done to her and her daughters. If so, she'd barely known what she was doing.

But because of him that hadn't happened in this world. Instead, here Mona had been destroyed. That alone was ample provocation for rebellion, but not quite as it had happened in his world's past. There the rape of her daughters and her public flogging had incited Boadicea to rebel before Mona had been razed by the Romans. Revenge wasn't quite so personal here. Necessary, but not personal.

And Boadicea herself was unharmed. More, the destruction of the Holy Isle opened the way for her to lead a revolt. In this world, that gave her time to ensure the support and training of her warriors, while strengthening alliances with the other tribes, preparation she'd not had in Cean's history. After the attack, too, she had been quick enough to see what had been done would bring the druids into agreement as well. He strolled along the path towards his own hut.

Events were moving as he'd intended. He would shepherd them on into the best paths and in the end, at either end of time, all his goals would be achieved. He hoped. But he looked about him at their hard lives, the endless work just to survive, and what he'd done was not enough.

Although the Iceni prospered more in this age than at any other point in their history, it was still an existence Cean felt to be harsh almost all of the time. Children lost their lives to simple colds, women died in childbirth—frequently—and men labored with cracked hands and bent legs. Even the youngest worked. All of it necessary. Just to live. How good it would be if he could improve that for them.

Los Angeles, 2048 C.E.

Again Fort telephoned Cean in a frenzy. On the screen, his hair was clumped by sweat, his eyes frantic.

"I can't find Mel. I've been calling her all day, but the nursing home says she left. They won't say anything more. Not who she went with nor why." Fort gulped air as he spoke. "They just keep saying they cannot release that information, like something terrible has happened to her. I'm worried sick." So was Cean now.

After a number of unsuccessful calls to other Coalition members, eventually Fort and Cean went to Andy's office. His assistant ushered them in. Andy blinked, remembering.

"Sorry, Fort, we just didn't have time to try to contact you," he explained. "Mel's all right. She's in another home, a small one run by a nurse who isn't afraid of Tensen's and the profiled." Andy paused. "Uhm … You haven't been watching the news, have you?"

Cean shrugged his shoulders when Fort turned a questioning look his way. "No. Why?"

Andy turned to a monitor on the wall. He stated, "On CNN," and the television flicked on to the breaking news.

"Friends say Doug Chen was an athlete," the caster was claiming. Beside him another anchor was politely listening, and behind them both was a picture of a young Chinese man passing the ball on a basketball court. He was tall, well over six feet, with a large jaw. His face was blurred, his attention all on the ball as other players swarmed around him, a flurry of dizzying arms and legs.

"And he participated in any sports that were open to non-professionals. He played ice hockey in the winter, basketball in the summer, golfed when he could, and even organized the local little league. He was an all-around sportsman, and well loved by many."

"And his team mates just turned on him?" the other caster put in.

"Apparently. I spoke briefly with the team captain before he was advised not to comment any further."

The screen shifted to an image of a tall, blond young man standing on a podium, microphones clustered before his face. News bots hovered above his head, mobile cams slung below to twist in the air towards the boy's face and then to the crowd listening.

"We didn't know," he said, "not for all the years we've played together. Doug never came right out and said he was profiled, but lately he was acting kind of weird. Like feminine. And he didn't want to shower in the same room as the rest of us. He'd go home first and shower there. So some of us began to wonder." He had a rolled towel across his shoulders and tugged on its end, nervously.

"Not me, of course. But some of the others." He became a little belligerent at the reporters' questions. "Hey, we didn't all do this, you know. Just the ones who were bugged about him being profiled and all. He should have told us. He shouldn't have put us at risk like that. We were his friends."

Fort murmured, furious, "Friends who stood around and let him be beaten to death."

The image flickered to other streets, other crowds. "Since this cast aired two hours ago," the caster went on, "four more of the profiled have been killed, beaten to death by street gangs."

Andy murmured, "Off," and the monitor went black, reverting to the image of a painting. "We had to move Mel quickly for her own safety."

Fort sighed. "It's getting worse then." It wasn't really a question, but Andy treated it as if it was.

"Yes, much worse. Many of the Coalition are making arrangements to go into hiding, with friends or family members who are willing to take them in for a time." He took a deep breath before continuing. "I honestly don't know how long Mel is safe. But she's working hard on her physio, and the woman who runs this sort of medical half-way house says encouraging things about her being able to walk on her own eventually." He paused again.

"Sometime in the next year if there aren't any problems. She's improving faster than her original doctors thought she would. But don't worry. I'll keep a watch over her as long as I'm able. My staff don't know I'm profiled, just that I have represented some of them, so I'll be fine for some time yet. And, Fort?" he went on. "I don't think things are going to get any better. I'm saying this to warn you. You might need to make arrangements, too."

"Thanks, Andy. I appreciate it." Fort took down the phone number of the facility where Mel had been moved, along with the woman's home number.

* * * *

At home, Cean turned on the news again. Gangs were also attacking the homeless, fearing they too were profiled.

"Who knows how many have died so far? The victims of gang rage cannot be counted, and they are often the unprotected homeless," a female caster reported. "According to a recent study by the University of Washington State, their numbers can only be guessed at."

On the steps of Congress, reporters solicited views from any of the representatives they could pin down.

According to one, "We are considering a set of protective regulations for the profiled, beginning with curfews throughout the states, and if that doesn't work, perhaps camps where the profiled can be treated as necessary and at the same time protect other citizens from the risk. These steps had been tested in Cuba during the AIDS crisis, and we can learn from them.

"We are currently heading a commission on immigrants, even casual visitors, who cross our borders. Perhaps health inspections or certificates will be necessary for anyone entering our country in the future if Tensen's continues to spread. It is a disease that would be catastrophic if even 30% of the world's population developed it. However, the welfare of our great nation is our first concern and we are looking into all measures, emergency and otherwise, that might contain the disease."

Another man, a senator, a grim man attempting to hurry past the lingering cameras and newsbots, suggested that in the meantime, "the profiled would be required to report to a deputized official until such time as the camps were ready for occupation."

He looked around before adding that many of the states were considering new laws regarding "necessary force," stipulating that an officer had the authority to recognize when and if it was necessary.

Iceni Homeland, 60 C.E.

Only a day passed before messengers from another tribe came. It was high summer when they came bearing green branches for peace, fury burning on their faces. They bowed to the Queen, wasting no time before they spoke.

Cean listened avidly. One of his previous plans had finally borne fruit.

"They came, Lady. The Roman soldiers. Saying word had come to an officer that we plotted rebellion, each tribe with the other. They circled the dun, sweeping in to hold us at sword's point, then slaying our druids. All that they could reach. Men died trying to save the holy men until our king saw we could not win. He bid us hold our spears. Then the Roman dogs claimed a tithe for a rebellion we had never thought to begin. Nor would they listen to our rulers. Nay, rather it was the wealth of our rulers, the lives of our nobles which was stolen from us."

"So it was with our people, Lady," clamored the other. "Our king is wise. He came out to them bidding them search our hearths for signs of rebellion. The last of the wise ones he had smuggled away through a secret tunnel so they found him not. For that the Romans were the more angry and our tithe heavier upon us, for they said we had knowledge of where the druid masters hid. That they were now gone was proof we plotted." He went on. "We've sent word to all the tribes, that they must ward their holy men from the Romans."

Cean's gaze reached out to the Queen and he nodded as the messenger spoke. One of the messengers, taller than the other, noted Cean's nod.

Boadicea leaned forward."Where do the wise ones go now? Do they return to you, or seek out the Holy Isle?"

"They go to the Isle. There they will be safe. They will return when the Romans have forgotten us a little."

"Not so," Boadicea whispered in that intense rasp of a voice that always caught people's attention. "There *is* no Isle. Mona is fallen and crows count the bones. Foxes lair now in its ruined groves."Both men fell back a step their faces whitening. "I speak truth. In a dream our healer saw what would be. In fear I sent one to carry word to the Isle. But he arrived too late." She waited.

One man spoke, the words dragging from him. "He saw?" He looked again at Cean, knowing he was the healer who had dreamed this. "Is he druid that he dreamed this?" the man asked.

"He saw. The Isle was even as the dreamer had said. The Romans circled the shores with their swords. They slew until neither man nor beast lived. What they could they burned, along with the bodies of those who carried all our wisdom. The soldiers broke in the wells, despoiled all of value. They cut down the sacred groves. The druids' sanctuary is no more."

The faces of both men were aghast.

She looked at them significantly. "How will the gods see this, do you think? That we who worship them permit such a thing?"

Both messengers looked as if they were going into shock, Cean thought. They were a greenish tint under the white, shaking as they stood trying to absorb the news. The shorter one suddenly ran out of the Queen's hut, vomiting to one side of the open door. He wiped his lips with the back of his hand.

The Queen signaled to Maara who quickly brought cups filled with heather ale. The men drank deeply, the man who had sickened shivering in spite of the ale's warmth.

"Lady, our king must know of this. Have you words for them? Have you words for other kings? They all must know of the Roman treachery."

The Queen nodded, the red of her hair like the fire of her eyes. "I have. Say thus: 'One who would have a harvest must till the land in its due time. He who would have his house last must spend time and build it to stand strong. The hasty man reaps no seed nor does his house prevail against the great gales of winter. There is an enemy who has time. They work slow, with patience, and all they reap falls to them as they harvest. To take from them that harvest, we, too, must spend time like hoarded coin. If we are hasty or over-swift, we, too, shall be reaped like corn in the field. Let your kings talk with me. Let us plan our houses so they shall last against all a gale can bring.'"

Cean stopped himself from grinning openly. Talk about wisdom in riddles! But that'd be more palatable to the outraged tribes than straight advice of sitting about to out wait the Romans.

He looked up to find the first man's eyes on him. In spite of the Queen's assurances regarding Cean, there was distrust in that examination.

* * * *

But as he'd hoped, within days the Roman patrol returned. They feasted on Iceni hospitality, stayed overtly uninterested in any interference with their packs and departed—to search their gear hastily, Cean was sure, as soon as they were off the Iceni lands.

He'd written with a hot piece of pointed metal on the inner white leather of a rolled hare-skin. "The missing druids from the Trinovantes' dun have taken shelter among the Coritani."

Cean had also advised a Coritani trader quietly that the Roman soldiers had mentioned a suspicion of just that. The trader left, saying he'd inform them before trouble arrived on swift wings.

"This note too bore fruit in its time," Cean wrote one night in his hut, with only the glimmer of the computer screen to light his words. "The Coritani, protesting their innocence, paid high tithes to buy off the Roman soldiers."

Although Cean had believed he'd given enough warning to protect the druids, one priest had not fled. The Romans discovered one of the Trinovantes' druids within the Coritani dun. An old man, unable to leave quickly for a safer hiding place.

"He was murdered, and the tithe against the Coritani was heavy. Nor was that all. Their ruler was forcibly deposed, replaced by a kinsman who favored the Romans, or so they believe. Judging by the messengers he has since sent, the Roman soldiers are mistaken.

"Now the Romans, feeling that all about them the tribes seethe, have turned on the Brigantes as a result of a rumor suggesting they, too, sheltered some of the outlawed druids. Paulinus Suetonius has only made more enemies of those who might have been friends, and stirred strife in an area where there had been none before. By my advice it was easy for the Queen to stir up the hatred until the tribes at last sent almost continually to her for advice.

"The Holy Isle had priestesses as well as priests, the women sharing their own wisdom and sacred groves. They, too, died in the gutting of the island. Slowly, as the year moved towards another winter, thoughts of rebellion have settled more firmly among the tribes' leaders. The warriors themselves are all eager, but the kings and their queens are less certain. They've seen the wealth of Rome, its swift punishment and its well-trained legions. Nevertheless, they resent the violence already striking them, the deaths of the druids most of all. On the advice of the Queen, they are thinking of rebelling next spring after the first sowing."

He saved the journal entry to the disk, adding that to the stack beneath the small machine. What he'd intended was coming to pass. Gradually the Romans themselves had angered the tribes beyond the possibility of peace, inciting rebellion against the legions and their leaders. Most of the tribes agreed with the Iceni now.

Boadicea had been cunning in her use of the news of Mona's destruction. Men from many of the tribes had gone secretly to see for themselves. One of them had stopped by the Iceni dun to speak to the Queen.

"The grove is in ashes, the sacred trees no more," he told her, bitterly. He went to spit before suddenly realizing he'd been about to do so on the Queen's hearth. He stopped, sipping his her bed ale to hide his unthinking gesture. But his mouth twisted. He'd never forget what the Roman soldiers had done to Mona.

"The green life of the Isle is gone, burnt away. Perhaps forever. Who will restore our learning now? The wisest among us are gone, savaged by the Romans. They even pulled up the stones that led to the grove. Nothing is there anymore!" He slapped the cup down unsteadily. Dark ale swirled like mist, almost spilling over the side.

Cean stared into it, somehow caught in the shadow of the turning liquid. The memory of Mona was quickly becoming legend, another dream in the minds of the tribes. Meddle with a man's religion and you stir up fanaticism, Cean knew. And those who'd seen this happen knew who to blame. In fact, the Romans had not made any secret of it, thinking it was a good lesson for the tribes, and would in future frighten them into unquestioning obedience.

On their own, the Romans had themselves incited rage as well as fear, a combination that could be the death of them.

But in that moment, Cean realized exactly what he was doing. He would be causing the deaths of thousands in the rebellion. Saving the Iceni, if things went according to plan, but more Romans would die, as would many innocents caught between the forces in this very savage struggle. Their deaths were his responsibility. The thought turned his stomach.

And in the quiet dark of his hut that night, as he lay unable to sleep, he couldn't drive away the knowledge of this more brutal side to his plans. In the end, as he heard the birds first waken and begin their busy chatter, he reminded himself of the whip slashing Boadicea's back, the two daughters in the hands of the Roman soldiers, the druid priests and priestesses on Mona, and realized that there would be violence, no matter how he interfered with these lives. His choices were greater evil and a lesser evil, and he would chose the latter.

"Cean, come. It is time we gathered more herbs to dry for winter." Lubran's face was hollowed in sorrow. "On Mona, doing this was a time for great satisfaction. It was a celebration of well-spent seasons, a joy in the gifts of the land." He sighed, but continued, "Let us seek out our medicines and harvest all we can."

Cean trotted lightly to join the old man, both carrying wide baskets. "My people have a recipe for making a food which lasts for a time. One pounds a little salt and some berries into the meat, and then dries it well. Such a food will keep in winter's cold for many months without going bad if it's kept dry."

Pemmican was an American Indian food, but Lubran would never have heard of it. Cean talked of the different recipes and methods of preserving food longer as they worked. All autumn they labored harder than ever before. Food was gathered in and every scrap of horse fodder which could be harvested was hidden in double-walled sheds. Men disguised as ordinary traders with a string of ponies and Iceni hunting dogs culled out as less than their best, wended their slow way through Roman towns where they traded ponies and dogs for grain. The grain they purchased filled many bags. In turn all of it flowed quietly back to the Iceni stores.

Boadicea had it in mind to hoard what food they could before beginning the rebellion. That had been Cean's suggestion earlier in the summer. He had ripped open seams and hiding places in his clothing, gone to Boadicea bearing almost all his gems, along with the coins forged in his own time.

"Lady, we risk hunger if there is open war between us and the Romans."

Her reply was dry. "So it seems." But she smiled. She knew by now that Cean didn't bring up a subject without having some answer in mind. "Have you a solution, healer?"

"If men went out before the cold comes they could yet buy grain to store for the winter. The Romans sell bundles of dried fodder for horses. In the Roman towns there is always grain and such for sale. Surely they would sell it to men who came as traders of no particular tribe?" When she nodded, he held out his hand, the jewels and coins bright in the flickering firelight. "I bring to you what I carry of my own wealth. Trade it for grain that the children of the Iceni at least do not hunger as a result of our war."

She studied the gems and coins with interest. "From far lands?"

"As you say, Lady."

"Other tribes may know hunger when we go to war," she mused, eyeing the wealth in his open palms. "They would be grateful if even a little grain came to them. Perhaps *very* grateful."

"Aye, if lives are not ended because of what has been given, then those lives are owed to the giver."

She said no more, but Cean's wealth was used to buy grain and horse fodder, as was all else Boadicea could gather up to send with her traders. Despite having never fought a war before, the Queen learned quickly what might be critical to the survival of her people.

She truly was a queen, Cean thought, even more than he'd expected. The times may be barbaric, but she was not. She thought first of her people and their future. Always.

Throughout the fall, messengers came and went. Not openly but by secret paths and not to the dun, but to Lubran or Alieki spearman, who waited outside the walls, Lubran picking herbs and supposedly chatting to passersby. Alieki often hid within the copse of trees where Cean had covered himself his first night in this land.

* * * *

When the first frosts came, she sent for Cean. He found her sitting by the hearth in her hut, her mantle lightly covering her shoulders. An unseasonably warm wind dried the dead grasses outside, and Maara untangled the Queen's magnificent hair with a bone comb.

"The time draws near." Boadicea spoke calmly, resigned. Cean knew she had hoped for signs that the Romans would leave them alone after Mona's razing. But they hadn't. Any druids, priest or priestess, found among the tribes had been put to death, their heads mounted on Roman walls for all to see. And the tithes had continued, heavy on the shoulders of people about to endure a long winter.

"I have dreamed again."

Her eyes flashed up, meeting his. It was hard to meet that direct gaze and Cean wondered if she truly believed him, or just wished to.

Maara spoke quietly over the Queen's head. "So the Mother expected." She went back to her combing, humming lightly in the back of her throat. The odd sound, the strange firelight like a nimbus behind the two women, felt dream-like, as if this was the dream he was about to imagine.

"Speak your dream," Boadicea finally said.

"I dreamed the Iceni called a hosting of all the tribes in spring. Twice I watched cities burn in my dream, their walls crumble beneath the weight of warriors. *Our* warriors. Twice our people won great victories. Like death itself, the warriors of the tribes marched across barren fields, and none could stand before them. Romans fell before the spears of the Iceni, the Trinovantes, the Catuvellauni, the Coritani. And others I could not name. The fields drank blood and no grain grew there.

"But after the second battle, everything became darkness. The gods turned away from the Iceni and their allies."

"Why?" Her intense, marvelous eyes held him, waiting.

"The Iceni spearmen and charioteers lay in huts, feasting and drinking, wasting their strength on celebration. The foolish rulers of other tribes said they had won much, they would go to rejoice with their people, to take pleasure in the women they captured, and drink the Roman wine and ale. Yet they swallowed darkness in their ale, buried their eyes in the shadow of the shoulders of women laying with them, and so the gods brought darkness over the land.

"The warriors left the war-trail, and the enemy rose up, strong once more, attacking the duns of all the tribes. Here the Romans found you, your people their enemies, slaying you before the tribes of this land could rise again. Of all the warriors, the Iceni suffered the most. They died, their duns crushed and scattered. As I woke, only Roman soldiers lived on Iceni lands, the ground seeded with the last of Iceni blood. They were no more. Forgotten."

"An ill dream," Boadicea whispered, aghast. Maara had long since stopped her combing and stood still at the Queen's shoulder, struck dumb by the horror of Cean's words. "Yet it could be. The kings do not often look to the future. Even Prasutagus thought he could buy off the Romans each time they asked for more. It was thus the Romans beat us before. Only fortune took them from the shores of our land. We rested though they did not. When I send out the *crantara*, the sign for war, the tribes will rise to follow," she continued. "But we make war for as long as it takes, not just a season. Only then will we stop to take breath."

"Two sticks bound together are stronger than one," Cean told her. "Three far stronger together than three apart. Let the Romans and their armies be as unbound sticks. Nor shall you count the battle ever won until you count the dead after swords are sheathed. And ever leave a path behind you so that you can bend away from the Roman attack."

That was important! He had to get her to understand this. In his world, she hadn't, and her warriors had been pinned between the Roman swords, and the battle wagons she had brought. It had cost her dearly.

"Otherwise they will break your spears on their shields, your men on their swords."

Even though she looked down at the floor, he saw she was committing the words to memory. His advice was good, even if it hadn't been part of what had defeated her before, he knew. 'Divide and conquer,' had been a Roman system through all their history, and the organized tactics of the invading armies had won their battles over less trained tribes. Using the same methods against them would at least even the chances. If she listened, his second piece of advice also meant her forces could always retreat and re-gather to fight again later.

Boadicea spoke. "Healer? Are you still of a mind to be a true Iceni?"

He shivered. "I would give all I have."

"You have done so. I know this of you." She stood up. She was as tall as Cean, her eyes even with his. "Did you not say once that you had fought as a warrior against death to save Dauldi's son? Nor have you withheld your wealth, demanding it be spent on you alone—as is your right. You laid it in my hands for the good of all. You have labored with Lubran to gather stores, cared for my people as a healer.

"To us you were sent with your dreams. Shall we offend the gods and deny the gift? Nay, speak to the wise one. The ritual is very old and little used but he will know it. In seven days you shall be a man of the Iceni."

He knew she could read his face then. See and understand the joy that raced through him. She smiled and the smile was gentler than her usual look. "It is well. Go to Lubran and in seven days I shall see you again, healer. In seven days among the trees of the druids near here."

His heart rejoicing, he went. In a week he would be Iceni! The acceptance of his chosen people was so sweet he wanted to sing, to dance, to leap and caper in the air. Despite the coming war.

He settled for whistling so that Lubran, too, was smiling kindly when he pulled back his door-hide to Cean. The old man had thought this possibility might come to pass and he welcomed it.

7

"The way is not always easy," the Queen told me when I was young, "but it is often clear, whether it be found in the mists of prophecy or the paths of unclouded thought." And so she thought of the wars, and the future she set before her people.

—from *The Journal of Anla*, 2nd Edition,
translated by Ericia Thromheart

Where will the wind be
At our life's end?
Where will it stop;
What trees will it bend?

Will there be love;
Will there be us?
Will there be daughters,
To keep this our trust?

There will be flowers,
There will be sun,
There will be hours,
Of sweet love to run

Astride our great horses,
Upon this our land.
There will be stars.
There will be life,
That sings from afar.

Welcome the wind!
Welcome the sun!
Hello, my daughter!
Hello, my son!

Welcome my children,
To life and to love.

—Traditional Iceni birthing chant

Iceni Homeland, 60 C.E.

Lubran clasped Cean in his arms. "The Queen has told me. In seven days you are to be made one of us." His voice was elated. "I am very glad for you, I know it is your desire, to be truly Iceni."

There was a faint smugness in his tone, too, Cean realized. To the old man that anyone should wish to be one of the Iceni was only good thinking. Who else should they wish to be?

"Seven days, she said?" Cean was suddenly nervous. He hadn't asked exactly what the adoption rite involved.

"Aye. And I must prepare." Lubran was eager, his hands barely stopping as he spoke. "It is long and long since that rite was performed. I require time to prepare us both."

"Do we need anything special, herbs we may not have ready?"

"Nay, I have all that I need. Go to your hut now, my brother, and eat and drink well. For during the next seven days, you may eat and drink nothing save certain herbs and fresh water which purify your body and spirit in readiness for the change that is to come. Nor may you leave your hut in that time." He nodded towards Cean's home before walking briskly away himself.

Something else dawned on Cean with a sudden chill. In many of these native ceremonies, an essential part of the ritual was nakedness. Cean dared not reveal his body. He was halfway between male and female. His breasts, although confined in the fitted vest, were clearly the breasts of a woman once the flattening vest was removed. And his genitals were just as clearly male.

The tribe assumed he scraped his face in the style of the Romans. If anyone had thrust aside his door-hide early in the morning, Cean had feigned shaving in the Roman way, knife to chin and cheek. The truth was that with the initial course of hormones he'd taken, he now had no need to shave. He no longer grew facial hair. His chest, too, was naked and hairless as it had been for more than three years, since partway through the first hormone treatment. He'd had no more than that first one since he'd come here, but so far the effect had remained. He hoped that would continue.

His looks had always been slightly androgynous, even before he'd started the first round of shots and pills. After the hormone-initiated changes had begun, if he had stood unclothed, any would know his duality. But now—both male and female—how would the people of this time and place accept it?

In his hut he stripped naked after carefully lacing closed the door, lighting the lamps and placing a loose robe to hand. Then he studied his body using a bronze mirror. He placed the lamps to either side of him, looking himself over. Frantically searching for a way to disguise what he was. Even in the lamplight, he could see: naked he would clearly never pass as a normal man to the Iceni. Having breasts made him appear softer and more feminine. The lack of hair accented that softness. The hairless chest enhanced the look.

He stepped closer to the light to angle the mirror down. His penis fell flaccid before his testicles. But it was plain enough he still had everything a normal man possessed. Absently he began to caress the limp shaft. It stiffened quickly, the initial treatment had left him capable of that still, even if days had gone by since he'd pleased himself. His hand moved, slowly, then with swift urgency mounting into a sudden spasm. He groaned in the hard release, then swore quietly.

There wasn't any doubt. Anyone looking at him would know what he was: A person who was neither male nor female. Or perhaps they would say he was both.

He'd been an idiot. In all this time he'd never checked to see what the tribe would think. And if the ceremony required nakedness … in seven days he would find out. Without doubt.

On the other hand, they all accepted he took no woman to his house. Lubran understood Cean walked alone. The Queen, too, had said nothing against this abstinence. There'd been no insistence he should wed to join the tribe, or that he should wed after. And surely Lubran would have mentioned it if it was necessary.

Cean had studied Iceni customs and beliefs as far as they were known. But in his history they'd been a beaten, dispersed people, with no written history left behind. What had been known of them had either vanished under Roman swords, or been twisted in the words of their historians, until little remained that was the truth.

Their stories of the druids, for instance. Cean had lived with the Iceni for almost two years. In all that time there'd been no human sacrifices. When asked, Lubran had admitted that under dire need it was an option, but that he'd not seen it in his lifetime. But as Cean had explained it, the tale of a towering wicker man stuffed with men, women, and children, then put to the torch had caused Lubran to explode with laughter. Wicker wouldn't hold that many captives, and furthermore, why do it? Poles mounted with heads were much more effective.

Possibly there'd been human sacrifice on Mona. For particular and rare occasions. But not that Lubran knew. He admitted that something like that happened when a tribe was existing under extremely bad conditions, facing famine or slaughter. Then it was the king's entrails that were read, the king who gave his holy life—as he should—in the hope that his death would bring the knowledge his people needed to survive.

Cean dragged his wandering mind back to the matter in hand. Beliefs. Half male, half female.

Maybe he could edge up to the subject, or drop hints that it was a custom of his people that nakedness was only for lovers, or between husband and wife. That might work. Only if the ceremony's requirements weren't rigid, he realized. If they were, Lubran's next question would be, did Cean want to be Iceni, or didn't he?

* * * *

He began his campaign with Lubran's entrance at sunrise the next morning. His friend bore with him a beaker and cup which gave off a warm sweet scent.

"Drink this, brother. And listen to me."

Cean took the mug and drank. It was pleasant, some concoction of honey and herbs. It warmed him so that he felt relaxed and light. All would be well, he was sure of it. Lubran squatted before him to speak and Cean concentrated on the old man's words.

"The ceremony requires seven days because in that time you must change from the man you are into a man of the Iceni. It requires a full quarter of the moon's passage across the skies."

Lubran then became mystical and Cean lost track at this point. He'd been hungry, and the drink on an empty stomach was making his head swim slightly. However, he understood enough to learn that the seven days was tied to a belief in the phases of the moon ruling lives. His remaining in the hut was tied to a kind of passage from dark into light. Lubran paused for Cean's acknowledgement.

"I understand. It must be seven days, of course."

"Good, and on each of the seven days you mimic the growth of life. Thus, today you eat nothing. You drink only the sacred drink I bring. It is the sweet drink a baby receives from its mother while yet in the womb. This cleanses your body. Tomorrow you shall have milk only. The day after that, milk and barley-cake."

Cean felt he was beginning to grasp the progression. "As a baby would eat?"

Lubran nodded approvingly. Cean half laid in his bed and the old man was bent over him, a great smile on his face. "As you say. On the seventh day, then, you feast on meat as a warrior should after the ceremony is complete. Fear not, Cean. I shall stand with you at each step. There may be omens I must interpret but I believe they shall be favorable. The gods sent you to us. They would not permit anything be done wrongly in this."

Cean hoped fervently the old man was right. If he had to strip at some stage, he might be able to use their belief the gods had sent him to be both brother and sister to them to pass off his hermaphrodite state. They might listen to him. He'd prefer not to have to tell them such a fabrication, though. They might misunderstand. Cean could easily step awry if he tried to claim something which turned out to be completely against current beliefs.

At Lubran's urging he finished the drink. "Good. I will bring more at each change of the sun."

Oh great, Cean thought. That meant he got a beaker of this again at midday, a third at sunset, and that was it. No food, and one cup alone had made him as tight as an off-duty soldier. By tomorrow morning he was going to be starving and then getting only milk. His mouth was already watering at the thought of the following day's barley-cake.

"If I thirst, may I drink water?"

Lubran nodded. "That is permitted, but nothing else. Nor may any food pass your lips. Nothing!" He emphasized this with a raised finger.

Cean was feeling still more light-headed. He wondered just what was in the drink. "What if a fly flies into my mouth and I swallow it accidentally?" he asked the old man, half facetiously, half rambling.

Lubran shook his head. "Try not to. Such a thing would bode ill. I would then have to consider the omens again. If they were favorable, we could begin again from the beginning, but to be certain I would have to make the ceremony two weeks instead of one."

Cean gulped at the thought, then saw a small twinkle in his friend's eyes. "I think I'll be careful not to swallow flies."

"That would be best. Until high sun then, brother. I'll see water is brought for you. You have your chamber-pot?"

"Yes." Now he was reminded of that he needed to use it urgently. He hoped Lubran had arranged for someone to empty the pot for him. In the chill of early winter it wouldn't draw flies, but after a few hours in the warm hut it would begin to stink.

"That is well. Whenever you use it, cover it with a cloth and place it outside your door. It shall be emptied, cleansed and returned. But be careful to remain always within the door curtain when you do this. No more than your hand may leave the hut." Lubran straightened up, ready to leave.

"I understand." Cean's hand was limp as he lifted it to bid Lubran good-bye. Cean stared at it, surprised.

Lubran smiled down at him. "Then I leave you. Sleep, dream if you can. A dream at such a time would surely be true-dreaming."

Cean listened to the retreating footsteps before reaching for the chamber-pot. He used that hastily, covered it with a rag and thrust it carefully beyond the door curtain. He lay down on his bed. His head was going round and round. What in all the gods' names was in that drink? Nothing harmful, he was sure. He trusted Lubran. Besides, why would they agree to make him Iceni then poison him?

He drifted into a half-sleep, a doze in which he dreamed. He saw the battlefield, the Roman dead carpeting the ground. Beyond them, tribes-people hunted down the last Romans, slaying without mercy. From one side he heard a soft wailing and turned his head. It was hard to do that, as if he fought a reluctant body to make the movement.

There Boadicea stood beside a war-chariot. Tears fell slowly from her eyes as she gazed at a small body by her feet. Iessin, her younger daughter, torn and rent by swords, her teeth still bared in battle-frenzy, the war-spear she held bloodied past the collar of feathers at the hilt of the blade.

Slowly Boadicea's head came up, her eyes bleak. "She died as a warrior, with blood for her going. The Romans are beaten and our losses far less than theirs. Yet I grieve! Who now shall lead my people when I am gone? Iessin is dead, Essault is wife in another dun. Who cares for my people?"

The grief in her face was more than Cean could bear. Wordlessly, he took her in his arms, holding her gently, her head falling to his shoulder. He'd always known intellectually that people had been shorter the further back one went in history. Now it came home to him in his heart. The Queen, formidable in battle, scourge of armies, leader of the war-host, said by the Romans to be unwomanly tall. Boadicea was no taller than he was.

He held her. No word was spoken but when at last she stepped back, freeing herself quietly, her eyes were calmer. She looked up, a hand rising to touch his cheek.

"The gods give, and to them is given. I have seen the mark as Lubran said. I shall do what must be done, yet there must be something for my people." He hadn't the faintest idea of what she was talking about so he said nothing. She smiled up at him then. That rare whole-hearted grin which lit her face and eyes.

"Drink this." Under her urging, he drank the mug held to his lips. The honey drink swept him away again deeper into the dream and the darkness, taking with him only the insistent voice: "You dream, speak your dream, my friend."

"No."

The voice was commanding. "Speak what the gods give you to know."

He could not resist. He spoke as from the bottom of a deep well, the words rising like a tide to foretell, the images in his dreams describing the future, like the land claiming him when he first stood upon it. His words flowed up and out of him in a dark stream.

"That is well. Sleep again … drink when you wake. Forget you dreamed. All is well."

He obeyed, falling into a deeper refreshing sleep in which he forgot dream and voice.

Los Angeles, 2048 C.E.: six weeks earlier

Life had been different for Cean before he met the people of the Co-alition. He was lonely then, but comfortable with it, since his parents had passed away, he didn't have many friends, preferring to stay on his own most of the time. A little afraid of anyone learning just how different he really was. It was his secret, he believed. In a city of secrets.

Since he started taking the hover-rail to work, Cean had rarely looked out at the mounds of wind blown garbage clinging to the curbs in the streets. After passing the clean inner city enclaves the night before, however, he couldn't help but notice the decaying streets that morning.

The inner enclaves were like gods sitting in their towers above the dirty business at their feet. There, beneath the residue of oily smoke left over from the night fires, plastic bags slumped over debris, broken wedges of styrofoam were lit in places with their own blue flames, shredded streams of newsfilm had been dumped willy nilly to crowd the people-less streets.

A membrane of soot clung to most of the bits, leaving some as unrecognizable lumps that grew larger each day, almost as if they had a dreadful life of their own. There had been cases of the desperate homeless, sheltering beneath the miasmic layers for warmth, then dying of suffocation when the night fires really got blazing and oxygen was sucked out of the heaps of garbage. Suddenly, it all seemed strange and horrible to Cean.

What had happened to the California he'd known as a child? It was a different land now. Then, it had been clean, the country's golden hope for the future. Every day the sun shone on the prosperous streets where children inline-skated and played innocent games. The beaches gleamed with white and tan sand, cleansed by the continuous rolling surf. Families picnicked happily in the open, clear air.

Now even the waves sometimes glowed with oily fire. The slicks left by careless boats, big and small, clung to the shore to be lit by gangers as they spread with their unprosperous lives over the beach. They lived under their own tribal laws in what had now become their land. Cean turned away, taking out his book of Doreen Tovey stories to read instead.

At home, the yard was dark. He ignored the shadows around him, and the quiet. He'd come home late before, the walk up the sidewalk uneventful, the dark of the night hiding the neighborhood, the street lamps shattered at some point, bulbs and fixtures left like gaunt skeletons lining the suburb ways.

They were waiting for him. As he keyed in his personal code, they struck. Two dark figures fell on him before he could defend himself. The voice of one was hoarse, unrecognizable, full of hate to hide the deep, unreasoning fear.

"Fucking Tensen! Dirty shape-ape! Stay around and you're gonna get more'a this."

The first blow exploded in his face, dropping him. He was unable to fight back. He sprawled on the chill ground curling into a ball to protect himself, arms wrapped over his head. Feet thudded home viciously as he screamed at the pain. Their hard shoes like rocks smashing into his very bones, again and again, quickly bashing first his ribs, then his back. Cean dug his knees in tighter, but the blows came faster, harder. He soon lost count of them. Down the street a light came on, the whir of a neighborhood security watch-car speeding up. A last savage kick struck the side of his head, and a snarl descended out of the darkness at him.

"Fuck off outa this place or it'll be worse next time." He heard the thud of feet racing away down the street.

No more than half conscious, Cean lay there. His back was in agony where their kicks had landed. It felt like they'd used steel-toed work boots. His legs and head ached and the shock made it all so much worse.

When he was sure he wouldn't pass out, he staggered slowly to his feet, leaning on the lightless lamppost near the sidewalk. If only he could stand! But his legs shook, and he hugged the iron to keep himself up. He had to make it to the house. The watch-car had passed, seeing nothing, and they might come back. He didn't want to be here, out in the open, if they did.

The security car was passing again, slowly, its cameras twisting this way and that, signaling all was dark and undisturbed to the group in a distant building monitoring its images. As if the car were suspicious of him, as if they hadn't heard him scream. Cean let the darkness swallow him as he turned back to his yard, this time keying in his personal identity code to open the door quickly. It clicked shut behind him. Quietly.

That night he slept only after taking a hefty dose of painkillers. The next morning, though, the pain from the blow to his head thundered inside his skull. Should he complain to the police? Would it help? He decided not to. They'd been shadowy shapes, no more than bits of violence borne of the darkness, and Cean had heard no voice he could identify. A harsh whisper would sound the same from just about anyone.

* * * *

In the morning, though, he did stop at the hospital for x-rays and an examination. They were able to say there'd been no real damage, only heavy bruising. Not wanting it to show up on his company medical, he paid the bill himself and left. He wanted no surprises there. Not just now.

Later that afternoon at work, however, things became worse. He wasn't expecting the two police officers who asked for him. So far that day, work had been a nightmare of aching bruises, a headache, and more tasks than he could get through in one shift. He was tired and worn out when the two detectives approached his desk. Out of the corner of his eye, Cean saw his supervisor, get up and wander over, intent on listening.

"You Cean Rowan?" one asked.

"Yes." His supervisor drifted to a stop behind him.

"You were at the hospital this morning. They have to report anything which looks like a violent assault, so they called us. According to them, you got beat up pretty good. Want to tell us what that was about?"

Cean looked at them, standing slowly. Two nice clean-cut men, hormones in balance, securely masculine. They had to recognize him for what he was.

"I'm sure you can guess," he answered them. Politely. "I came home late last night from work." At least his supervisor would hear that much if she was so curious. "Two people jumped me just outside of my house. The security light was out so I couldn't see who they were. Especially not once I'd been beaten to the ground. I was too busy protecting my head from their boots. They threatened me but it was in such a low whisper, I didn't recognize the voice."

He paused as one of the officers flicked a lever on the micro-reporter. It taped everything he said as he said it. "I didn't think there was much point in reporting it," he continued when they didn't say anything, "because there was nothing I could tell you. I had a rock thrown at me a while back. And I have no idea who did that either." He waited, his head throbbing, his pulse heavy.

The taller man glanced at him kindly. Cean was sure he would have patted his shoulder if the supervisor wasn't so close. "Look, I know it isn't easy. But give us a shot at it for you." He looked hard at the woman. "Come and sit in the car and answer a few questions. Maybe we can come up with something. If we get an idea perhaps we can dig out a few local names. Is he free now?" he asked her. When she nodded reluctantly, he added, "Who knows? It's worth a shot. If we talk to them, they may back off—for a while anyway."

Cean nodded. "Okay, I'll do my best."

But in the end, the two officers told him it was unlikely they could pin down the perpetrators. Cean hadn't recalled anything else that could help them. But later that night there was a phone call.

"Cean Rowan?" The accent sounded eastern, the broad long vowels of the New England states.

He was cautious. "Who's calling?" He'd had his number unlisted for some time.

"I'm Leogold Fortescue. I represent the Coalition of Tensen's Profiled and their friends."

Cean hesitated. "Which means what?" He wasn't about to trust anyone who called him up out of the blue, not after last night.

There was a small sound which might have been a patient sigh. "We're a group of those whose profiles are such we may well eventually be affected by Tensen's Virus, through no fault of our own. As you may know …" the voice developed a tinge of irony, "many people are beginning to discriminate against those with such a profile. We have lawyers in our group who can give free advice if you experience this. As you may expect, we aren't advertising ourselves; the groups that have have only drawn fire from the prejudiced bastards who fear them."

But Cean wasn't about to divulge information over the phone to a stranger. "How did you get my number?" he asked before he'd admit to anything.

"I think a couple of policemen came to visit you today. Isn't that true?" Before Cean said anything, Fortescue continued. "We have contacts within the police department who will refer us to anyone who is a potential target for hate groups. Or the government."

When Cean didn't say anything, Fortescue calmly continued. "If you wish to come to one of our meetings, be at the hover-rail stop on the corner of Madison and Dehenly tomorrow night at seven. Someone will be there to pick you up. Look, it's not a formal thing—just casual and friendly. And all of us have had similar experiences to yours, so you won't be alone there. Some of us know what you can expect in the future, as well."

Cean hesitated. "How will they know me?"

"We were given a good description of you. You don't need to carry a red carnation or tuck a newspaper under your arm or anything."

Fortescue chuckled. Before Cean could say he would or would not go, Fortescue—if that was his real name—had hung up, leaving Cean to sit holding the humming phone. He pocketed it, thinking. He'd finally placed the accent. New England, an educated man, one whose status was secure: possibly either this Fortescue or his family had money. The real question was, was it a trap of some kind?

* * * *

He dithered all through work the next day, so divided between his job and his indecision over the meeting that he overlooked his co-workers' comments, even the remarks he was meant to hear, a slip that bothered some and satisfied others.

Her eyes like acid, his supervisor watched. She didn't fail to notice his inattention. His work-file was longer, his colleagues less inclined even to give him a "good morning,"and the talk about the lunch tables was a little louder, a little more invasive. They'd obviously heard about the police visit the day before.

"You just don't know. There could be other things."

"Like what?"

"Well … *you* know. Other diseases."

His workmate managed to invest the word with a shuddering distaste as her gaze flicked across to him and away again. She wasn't trying to hide that she was discussing him. None of them did any longer.

"Oh, you mean …?"

"There were before, weren't there? Who's to say …"

"It makes sense."

Cean wanted to scream at them that if he had the virus, he'd have to have sex with them in order to trigger the allergy-like response. But he wouldn't have sex with any one of them!

But the talk went on. Their eyes were avid. It didn't touch them, they were immune, with normal partners, ordinary children, and socially acceptable lives. It was Cean they watched, Cean who could strike them down. Or even make himself ill. In disgust, he walked back to his work station early again, no longer able to bear their vicious whispers.

Despite the abuse at work, Cean couldn't stop thinking about meeting others like himself. Should he go? Who at the police department had told them about him? He shook his head, trying to stop the worrying thoughts bouncing around in his head. If he was at the bus stop he'd find out. But what if this was more of what had happened the other night? The bruises still hurt. The man on the phone, though, hadn't sounded like a ganger, too educated for that, but Cean wasn't sure if that was an accent that could be faked.

He snorted silently to himself just before work ended. Why would anyone bother to trap him anyway? Everyone here knew what he was. The last implant had begun to work. His breasts were sore as they began to swell, and the last two mornings he'd noticed his beard was thinner. There was less to shave. He'd almost sang as he flicked his shaver over the softening skin.

To hell with it! He'd go and see what this coalition had to say. Boadicea wouldn't have hung back—he was certain of it.

He finished work exactly on time, closed down his computer and walked away from the office. The Madison-Dehenly hover-rail stop wasn't far. If there was danger, he could run away, and he was faster than most might suspect.

He reached the hover-rail queue, and stood back a little from the line of people, surreptitiously watching the road. Above him, a banner of newsfilm hung in the air, flickering in the acid light of dusk. Headlines flowed along the film, then images of hospitals and patients smiling and healthy. It was an info-film, a bit of advertising with the latest updates on the most recent cancer cures and vaccines now available at Mercy Western, "the hospital of people's choice." Tensen's, of course, was not mentioned.

When the three-car halted, it still took him by surprise. The driver leaned across to open the door. The small vehicle swayed on its trio of wheels with the shifting of weight. Three-cars were good only on city roads.

"Cean, what a surprise!" a delighted voice called out. "Look, I have to go right past your stop. Get in, I'll give you a lift. It's been months since I've seen you."

For a minute, Cean wondered what on earth the man was talking about. A tall, well-dressed man with light brown skin and slightly blunt features. Cean didn't recognize him at all. It wasn't until the man began to look impatient and nervous that Cean realized he was making them conspicuous.

"Oh, sorry. Of course! I was daydreaming. Yes, thanks. I'd be grateful for the ride."

He climbed into the front seat, waited as the safety straps—activated by his weight—wrapped around his chest and waist, and leaned back as the vehicle accelerated smoothly into the traffic flow. It dove into the outer fast lane as soon as there was an opening and headed west towards the inner apartment enclaves. The driver eyed him humorously.

"Good save. I thought for a moment you were going to bolt."

"I wasn't sure myself," Cean admitted. "Do I know you?"

The wheel shifted under the man's hands. "Actually," he told Cean, "I do work in the same building, but for another company on the fifteenth floor. We've probably seen each other on the elevator once or twice, but that's all. I thought I might have made an impression on you, but apparently not."

He leant over with one hand, and wryly said, "Jackson Fittafa, call me Jack. Pleased to meet you." He checked his speed, and then went on. "Silly, really. Of course, these days it's probably a good idea that no one notices me. Or you. For obvious reasons."

Cean didn't quite know how to ask, but wondered.

"Am I?" Jack guessed what he was thinking. "Can't you tell? Yes, as a matter of fact I am, but I haven't taken the hormone treatments. I really didn't want to change my life that much. Doesn't look like we're getting much choice about it though, does it? No one at work knows. And I'll thank you to keep your mouth shut about me there, too. Some of our staff eat lunch in the same cafeteria."

Cean quickly nodded. "Good."

The car hummed as it accelerated into a narrow lane designed just for the three-cars. Cean remembered something else then. He had seen Jack before, meeting a woman.

"You're married." His tone was more puzzled than accusing, but Jack took it as a question.

"My wife has a similar hobby." He noticed Cean's confusion. "For god's sake, man. She's transsexual, too. We married when the first hysteria really started up two years back. It's the perfect alibi. Both of us work where we'd be tossed out if the office had realized.

"We're each other's excuse, the perfect companions for office parties and conferences, so we're covered. We don't have kids, but plenty of couples don't these days. She tells her co-workers I'm sterile," he grinned. "I say the same about her."

Cean missed family ties. His parents had died soon after he'd reached his middle twenties. His father succumbing to a virulent strain of colon cancer, and his mother dying soon after, alone in her living room. A heart-attack, apparently. Cean had lived by himself ever since.

The car slowed as it turned into a maze of apartment complexes, all of them with walled security and gates. Jack pulled into one and began the complicated checks at the entrance. The guards there were alert, one watching the street, while the other two examined the narrow back seat and looked over Cean carefully.

"Where are we?" Cean asked. On his own, he'd never find his way through the forest of buildings about them.

"A Coalition member lives in this enclave." Jack turned aside to look at him. "But you'd never get in again without her okay."

The guards finally waved them through, their hands resting on the weapons that hung at their waists. Cean stifled an abrupt spasm of paranoia. But it would do no harm to find out what these people could offer him. At the very least there would be some companionship. If a day came when he needed them, having the help of friends could save his life. Like alliances, he thought. The enemy of my enemy is my friend.

Jack knocked at a door that looked like any of the others. A woman opened it and led them in. They walked down a hallway into a large lounge, furnished in minimal black furniture against a starkly white background. Burnt sticks against white snow, very modern. But it reminded Cean of cinders and ash tossed out the door of a farmhouse onto a snowy yard.

A number of people turned to study him as he walked in the door, making him self-conscious at the sudden, unexpected scrutiny. Jack nodded to several of them before making a general announcement.

"Everyone—this is Cean Rowan. He works in my building. He's been having some trouble lately so Fort and I decided to offer him the chance to meet us all. If we all like what we see, he may become a member."

After that, as he made the rounds, hearing names and discussions of jobs, the memory of their faces was a blur. The discussion which had been in progress continued with him sitting quietly, a cup of coffee in one hand as he listened to their mutual tales of discrimination, the barely disguised sarcasm and disgust of the normal people around them.

And these people made sense. More sense than he liked some of the time. One woman was talking of the witch persecutions of the Middle Ages, comparing them to their own plight.

"Many of these commoners are not so much different to us—they're that close to the same genetic problem." She held up two pale fingers, almost touching. "But they'll never admit it. It's not about sex, although they don't believe that. They treat us like witches, like we have some strange, sexual power over them, and if they're not careful, we'll force them into perverted acts."

Someone laughed. "Well, in a way we do. We can make them be allergic to sex." But no one else laughed with him. Another man mentioned lepers, Cean listened, making small grunts of agreement rather than venturing any of his own experiences.

"You feel that way, too?" the man asked him.

"It was something I thought a few weeks ago. As if I should be warning people away." He thought about what he'd said. "No, not that exactly. More as if they expected me to do it."

"Exactly."

The talk went on until very late before Cean followed Jack out the door. It was a long drive to Cean's enclave, but neither he nor Jack spoke much. When Jack dropped him off at the gate, he leaned over to speak quietly before driving away.

"If you like what you heard tonight, you should come to our meetings. Call this number any time you think you want to join us." He reeled it off as Cean keyed it into his cell phone before looking up.

"The guy who rang me first, Fortescue? He wasn't there tonight?"

"Other fish to fry. He does make most of the meetings but not tonight."

The car purred away, turned the corner, and was off, the taillights like glowing red eyes disappearing into the city's blackness. Cean shivered. The night fires hadn't started yet, but they would. Soon. He hurried through the unmanned gate.

* * * *

In spite of everything he'd heard from the others, he was still shocked the next morning at work when he was stopped at the door. His supervisor actually smiled when she handed him an old shoebox holding his personal belongings, his cup broken in two. They'd even included his computer mouse and keyboard—everything he'd touched, in fact.

"You *understand*, of course," she didn't trouble to hide her sarcasm, "why we cannot keep someone here who has trouble with the police. Our clients' files are confidential and we cannot risk you handling them any longer."

She tipped the box into his hands when he reached for it. She wasn't even going to hand him that. Then he noticed she was wearing surgical gloves so her fingers didn't touch anything that was his.

Don't you know, you ignorant insufferable bitch! he wanted to shout at her. *It's only sex that would be dangerous to you!"* He fumed at her ignorance, but there was nothing he could do as the two company guards escorted him from the building.

When he looked over his shoulder, they stood at the doors, barring them in case he returned to cause trouble. Their faces were bland, grim and hostile, their hands ready at the guns holstered upon their waists.

They were quite prepared to make sure he never came into this building again.

Cean walked away. He had no other choice. He returned home, imaginings of what Boadicea would have done playing through his mind.

Three days later at the next coalition meeting, he told everyone what had happened. They were shocked and sympathetic, but not surprised. The same had happened to many of them. For once, though, Cean knew he was among friends.

Iceni Homeland, 60 C.E.

When he woke in the hut, it was dark again and a beaker of the drink was beside him with the emptied and cleansed chamber-pot set at the foot of his bed. He drank thirstily with a vague memory of something having happened. Perhaps someone had been here at midday? It couldn't be important or he'd remember. He used the pot again, placed it outside the door, crawled back into his bed and slept through the darkness.

The conditioning of his body continued. Milk the next day, milk and barley-cake the day after. Dry and unsalted though it was, he was so hungry it still tasted like a feast. Then another change. He was permitted a bowl of cooked grain flavored with crushed dried berries.

Inexorably the days passed until the seventh morning. That day he fasted again, drinking only water as his stomach growled with emptiness.

Lubran came in briskly as soon as sunset colored the sky, the clouds orange and wine as they darkened.

"Now, my brother. There is very much to do before moonrise."

Cean stretched lazily. He could recommend this regime—if only he wasn't so hungry. His whole body felt light and clean. Like air cleansed by the rain. Purified.

He'd written it all down and added it to his tale in the bronze casket. If that was ever found in the future, he could see millions of trend seekers queuing up for the treatment in places set up especially for the purpose—and paying a fortune to do it, too. He grinned cheerfully at the idea. He had the better of them there. It'd been free for him. Or not free, he corrected himself. It had cost him his heart. And gladly.

"What do I do first?" He stood up, feeling a little light-headed.

"Drink this, quickly. You must not lower the cup until it is drained."

Cean accepted the mug and tipped it up, opening his throat so that the liquid flowed until the container was empty. The taste hit him and he choked.

"Gods, what was that?"

Lubran grinned at him, reaching for the empty cup. "Milk, blood, barley-ale, and water."

Cean had the feeling he wasn't being told all of it. And wasn't sure he wanted to know."Tell me of what kind is each ingredient? What is the significance?"

"The milk is from Myla, who nurses a child to her man, Alieki." Cean hid a sudden desire to be sick. "By drinking the milk of a woman of the Iceni, you take in a part of us. The blood comes from the king-stallion of the Iceni herds. Boadicea drew it from the great vein in its neck with her own hands. Our horses are a part of us. Thus they are a part of you now." He shrugged. "The barley-ale is the best made by Tilutegan's son. The water is from a sacred place in the fen. To drink it is to be blessed by the gods."

Cean reflected that the water was probably stagnant and germ-ridden but any infection in it would be countered by the fiery barley-ale. Ale was a mild word for its effect. He was sure that had been the largest portion of what the cup held.

"I thank my brother for his explanation. A healer should learn all he can. What must I do now?"

"You must wash."

Here it comes, Cean thought. He forced his tone to be casual, and resisted the desire to hold his tunic close about him.

"Must someone be here while I do so?"

His shyness was clear to Lubran who noticed the flush spread up Cean's face. The healer considered this for a moment. "I may stay if you wish, or if you do not, there is no need I be present." He smiled at Cean. "You are no small child who must be watched lest he not wash all of himself. If you would be alone while you bathe, then the rites do not require I remain."

"Then, if I do not offend you or the ceremony, I bathe alone as is the custom where I come from."

"So be it. Wait and the cauldron and water will be brought to you."

Cauldron? It sounded as if he was about to be stew.

When the cauldron was carried in Cean was pleasantly surprised. It was oval and large, almost large enough for someone to sit in. He eyed it with interest. Siharni, who staggered in with two leather buckets of heated water, confirmed his guess.

"Of course, the Queen uses it. Should she bathe in public?"

"No, I'm sorry, Siharni, I meant no disrespect. I had not thought. Tell her, should she ask, that I am most grateful she permits me to use it. I shall feel twice Iceni."

Siharni laughed. "She will like to hear that."

She took the empty buckets out while another woman entered. The bath filled slowly, each bucket adding just a bit more. Cean laid out a drying cloth and ash for soap while he waited.

Finally he was left alone. He fastened the door and stood waiting, listening. From outside there was no sound. No indication any were there. Slowly, hesitantly, he undressed.

He stood in the hot water, wishing the cauldron was just that much larger he could sink into it. Even this much caused him to groan softly in ecstasy. Hot water, and a real wash. Long ago he'd seen a water-heating system the Romans had used, a stone bath filled with water heated elsewhere by a hypocaust. The system was something which could be used by the Iceni one day, if they learned to work more in stone. Before leaving his own time, he had read up on the mortar Romans used in their bridges and aqueducts. Once dry, it was thereafter impervious to water. That information was stored on one of the casket's disks.

He let the water wash over his legs as he crouched. He'd no idea how much he'd missed something as simple as a warm wash. Once all this was over he would talk to the tribe's smith. He'd given Boadicea much of what he'd had towards more grain, but there was still a pouch of gold and silver bits left, as well as a few pieces of jewelry. Several bits of jet and some rough amber were left, as well. Enough surely to make a cauldron like this, or even better, to buy the stone quarried by the Romans to make a bathhouse for the Iceni.

He kneeled into the water's hot embrace, letting it lap up over his knees and about his middle. He'd spent a chilly winter since he'd had enough warm water to do more than wipe himself down. He had to teach them about baths and bathhouses. It would bring a touch of luxury to the tribe. Even if they didn't want to bathe, a stone foundation to make a hypocaust would heat a hut well in the winter, and keep it cool in the summer. That way, fewer people would die of colds and flu during the cold months.

And winters were hard on the Iceni. Cean was surprised that they were not more cold, and with snow, but they were dank and chill enough to drive people closer to the open hearths in winter, often coughing through the nights in the smoky huts. The cold mud of the paths around the huts, the misty rain that brought mold and prevented anything from drying for months at a time, nurtured disease. Iceni lives were often short as a result. Cean had seen that much already.

The system he envisioned could be used to heat water for washing clothes as well, in great stone tubs. It was the only thing Cean felt the Romans had really brought to this chilly land: heated floors and bath-houses. Just thinking about it relaxed him so much he was all but falling asleep.

At last he dragged himself from the now cool water, standing beside the cauldron as he dried his body with the cloth. He was clean, warm and comfortable, and as he dried his groin he felt a different heat. His penis hardened.

He looked down. He'd never become a woman now; the surgery of his time was lost to him forever and soon the hormone implant would lose its effectiveness. Yet becoming Iceni would make up for much, he thought. He'd have to make the best of what he was here and now. His fingers stroked lazily but with growing eagerness.

Behind him a small sound broke the silence. He twisted, the jutting hardness turned away. In the doorway, the curtain down behind her, stood the Queen. Quickly, he held his hands over himself, but they were a meager covering at best. They certainly didn't hide his breasts. Her eyes examined him slowly, thoroughly. She nodded once as if a question had been asked and answered. Then she held out a new woolen robe.

"My gift to one who will be a new man of the Iceni." Her voice was calm and clear. Cean suspected someone stood outside, listening to hear the ceremonial words.

He was frantic. "I thought no one was to enter."

Her gaze were amused. "I am Boadicea. None may say I cannot enter any place of my people."

There was no indication she condemned him. He dared to hope. But he wanted to be sure. There was a tinge of desperation in his question.

"You have seen me as I am. Am I less in your eyes?"

Her look was one of faint but genuine surprise. "How so, healer? I have long known the gods sent you to us. Now and again one like you is born among our people. Always it is a sign the gods bless their own. You stand between male and female, a bridge between the tribe and the gods. Many of your kind become druid priests or priestesses. Lubran's mother's brother was thus. His birth brought us fair harvests for a hand of years. You are our healer. You, too, will bring good fortune to us once you are reborn within the tribe."

Cean let out an explosive breath of relief. Unsure what to do or say, since he was still naked, he settled for looking down at the cauldron.

"I thank you for the loan of your bath. My people ... those who were my people," he corrected himself, "they had a way of heating water for washing clothing or themselves. Like the Romans. It is swift and easy if the structure is built well. If you are interested, my Queen, I would be pleased to show the smith how to cut the stones and the method of mixing a substance that will secure the stones together so that water will not seep through. The tools for this are simple to make. Thus he could build such a thing for the Queen's own. That is if you wished it."

"That I would like, healer. But there is no time to talk of baths now. Dress quickly and be ready for Lubran, who will come to bring you to the sanctuary."

The door curtain fell behind her as Cean rushed to don his new clothing. The new robe was smoothly woven, smelling faintly of sheep and sweet herbs. He was ready when Lubran called his name outside.

"Come forth, child of the gods, youngling who is to be re-born. Come forth into the day."

Shivering a little, Cean joined his friend. To his surprise, two saddled ponies waited. Now Cean was glad he'd spent time learning to handle such a beast. He tapped an inquiring nose away with one hand as he vaulted into the saddle. Lubran was already mounted and leading the way as Cean gathered the reins.

"Where do we go?"

"To the gods' sanctuary, the sacred place of our tribe." He lifted a hand. "Ask no more … you will see."

They wound down long narrow paths, descending into a marshy area. Cean had heard it spoken about but was startled to see the land looked to be peat bog. He'd always associated that with Ireland, but here the peat stretched away towards the ocean, the smell of salt and sea drifting over the rise between them and the distant open water.

Light was leaving the land as they neared their destination. They rode through a deep, wide bowl of land which stretched out to a grove of trees at one end. There the land rose a little above the marsh, water pooling in a small pond below the trees. Standing about it, Cean saw flaring torches and waiting figures. Waiting for him.

As they rode up, Alieki spearman came to take the ponies. Maara proffered Boadicea's chalice, bowing as she handed it to Lubran in greeting. The healer took it and drank before handing it to Cean.

His voice was a low insistent murmur reaching only Cean's ears. "Drain it!"

Wondering what he was drinking this time, Cean drank, gasping at the blazing bite of hard barley ale, apparently undiluted, and very unlike the ale he'd tasted in his own time. The cup must have held half a pint of it, but he drank it all before returning the chalice.

Boadicea spoke then, the timbre of power ringing in her voice. "Cean, healer, son of far lands. Would you be one with the Iceni?"

"I would." He noticed in this ceremony she was using the law of three. All invocations must name a thing with three different names.

She turned to Lubran then, the flicker of the torchlight flaming behind her hair. "Kinsman, wise one, healer of the Iceni. Is this man purified from his past?"

"It is so."

"Is he acceptable to the gods?"

"Kinswoman, warrior, queen of the people. He is thrice acceptable. By the gods he was sent. He has dreamed truly for us, and the gods' mark is upon him."

"By the law of three he must stand. All must be known of the people, true Iceni, witnesses with cause. Nor may they be all of one sex or the other. Are the three here?"

Lubran bowed agreement. "I stand first. Lubran, son of Rahuili, the daughter of Faida who was of the royal line. I, Lubran speak for this man."

He lifted his head in command and two other figures joined him, facing the Queen. Wind caught at the flickering torches, rushing through the leaves of the trees about them, sounding like the waves on a shingle beach. Or the wave of time, Cean thought.

"With me stands Alieki spearman," Lubran continued. "He suffered injury which was healed by this man. He speaks for Cean."

Alieki boomed agreement.

"Third is Siharni. Her son was nigh to death. This man healed him with my help when I failed on my own. The hand of the gods is upon Cean's head, their joined hands shield him from the fire. Three speak for him, he has dreamed true thrice, and been purified according to the ancient ways. He is acceptable."

"Let him die then from this world. Then let him live again, as Iceni, blood of our land."

Lubran led Cean down to the water's edge, his murmur reassuring. "Do not struggle. It would be an ill omen."

Lubran thrust him deep into the water, holding him under while Cean held his breath anxiously. His head pounded beneath the silence of the pool, alcohol urging panic as he struggled to stay pliant in Lubran's hands. Druids had been know to place sacrificial offerings in rivers or sacred pools. He thrust that thought aside. They wouldn't! But in moments the panic began to take over, despite his belief in Lubran's assurance. If he didn't breathe soon, he'd die for certain.

Then he felt strong hands raise him again. He came up with a gasping whoop of indrawn breath. He was guided to the bank as he pawed water from his eyes, the dark and torchlight running together in streaks of red and black. The barley-ale shuddered in his head like an incipient headache crashing into his pulse.

Above, the rising moon flooded the clearing with soft pearly light. Ah, the new moon. He'd forgotten.

Boadicea met them, a green knee-length cloak lined and hooded with rabbit fur in her hands. From the assembled tribe, there came three times a deep-toned shout.

"A man is born! A man of the Iceni!"

The Queen stepped forward.

"I welcome a new healer to the Iceni. Child of the gods, be welcome amongst us." She flung the cloak about his shoulders. "A gift. It is not right a healer should not be known to all. Wear this that others recognize a healer of our tribe."

Everyone shouted again, some clapping him on the back, and as everyone waited for him to say the required acceptance.

Cean bowed three times: once to the moon, once to the land, and once to the Queen, saying, "I am a man of the Iceni by the will of the gods, the will of the people, the acceptance of the blood. From now and henceforth let me be one with the people as they are one with me. So shall it be now and forever." Into the silence Cean's stomach growled so loudly everyone laughed in relief.

"Meat for a man of the tribe!" Alieki demanded. "Let us begin the feasting before our healer fades away before us."

Lubran chuckled. "Aye. Come Cean, food awaits."

On the upper ground, wicker trays had been set. These had been covered with platters of roast meat, dried peas and beans cooked into a grain gruel, and loaves of unleavened barley-bread. Even some of the hoarded winter nuts were there. Around the edges of the clearing moved many of the tribe, men, women, and children, Verli grinning at him from amongst the older boys.

Cean ate until he could manage no more. It was close to sunrise before the celebration ceased, and Cean, both over-full and more than half-drunk, was hoisted onto his pony's broad back by Alieki spearman. Cean's final feeling as he fell fully-clothed onto the bed in his hut and slept was a warm glow. He was one of them, Cean of the Iceni. It felt good. Like having a family again.

8

When the Romans destroyed the sacred groves on the Isle of Mona, they only destroyed the body, not the spirit of our faith. They gave the people reason to rise up against them, and the strength of purpose to shatter them.

Some say that was the beginning of true belief in our society, not its end. I say that is so. Though the lore of generations of druid masters was gone forever, out of that destruction, we found our true spirit.

—from *The Passionate Spirit*,
by His Reverend Holiness Colm Herraster

Many people claim Boadicea was a warrior first and a queen second, that her focus was war rather than the government of her people. However, the manner in which she established her alliances shows that she had the government of her people consistently in mind.

Her first act was to build a new royal dun, an *oppadi*, one that would accommodate the meetings she intended. It was larger, grander than the former one. It had the necessary capacity to house delegates from the other tribes, and meeting areas where all could be included. It even contained shrines to bless the house. This was not an act of war. It was an act of consolidation and government. It was also a statement of intent.

—from *The Warrior Queen*,
by Leceister Murrane

Iceni Homeland, 60 C.E.

A combination of the past week's excitement, last night's barley-ale, and exhaustion kept Cean asleep until well into the evening. He woke shortly before sunset, stumbled over to use the chamber-pot, and then crawled back into his sheepskins. When he woke again, he met the faintly growing dawn of another day. He stretched luxuriously. For a while he simply lay, enjoying the warmth of the bedding, the glow of feeling for once he was in the right place. And the right time. He smiled.

Sounds from outside stirred him to rise and dress. He set the new rabbit-skin cloak aside. Something like that was not to be used for ordinary wear lest it be spoiled. He'd save it for special occasions. Cean stirred the banked fire to hearty life, placed his porridge on it to cook, and lifted the chamber-pot. He poked his head from the doorway studying the sky. It looked as if it would be a fine, clear, but chilly day, a good day to bespeak the smith. With the pot emptied and cleansed, he returned to eat quickly, adding a spoonful of honey to make the porridge more palatable.

With that done he tidied his hut and wandered out. Dari, smith to the tribe, was always to be found in his ancient forge well to one side of the dun. There he and his apprentice worked tirelessly to provide spear and arrow heads, jewelry for the women and girls, and various items of horse-furniture. To the tribes of England, a smith's craft was magic. Dari was an important man in the dun, and Cean waited politely to one side until the smith paused in his work and turned.

"You would speak to me, healer?"

"I would. There is a thing which might be made for the Queen. It is no easy task, so who else should I ask but one who has the metal turn in his hands, sharing in its magical change?"

Dari nodded seriously. "That is so."

The tone was matter-of-fact. He was proud of his skills but not unfairly so. The new member of the tribe should acknowledge that. He poked at the coals, encouraging the fire.

"I would not take you long from your work while light is in the sky. But if when you rest you would come to my hut, I have food and drink. We could talk together? I'd like to speak to you about some stone skills, and metal."

"Aye. At sunset then."

Dari returned to hammering out the edging of a hoe-blade, and Cean left him to it. He went out again then into the trees to search out a sheet of bark. He needed the white inner side on which to draw. With that, he sat in his doorway where the light fell upon the thick uneven surface and thought, charcoal in one hand. Although he was no artist, he could draw moderately well.

He summoned up a memory of the old house he had visited as a child. The copper had been shaped this way, and thus. He sketched lightly, scratched charcoal from a rough line and sketched it again, closer to what he remembered. At last he felt he had the whole diagram right. He held the bark out and ran his gaze over the work. Yes.

There was no concrete here but baked clay should do. Or perhaps mortar. He could teach them how to burn the mixture of ground up limestone and clay that made up cement, and then show Dari and a few others how to combine the cement with sand and water for mortar to use between the stones. Copper could be turned to make the pipes they would need.

The Romans had used lead which had over generations poisoned their noble families. He knew enough not to make that mistake. He sat turning the bark sheet in his fingers.

This was another thing which would alter history. An important change. Fort had believed that time was elastic and self-repairing, that minor changes could smooth out in several generations as time gradually returned to the original path. But that had applied to minor alterations in history. Alterations to technology, however, were not so resilient since often they lost or saved thousands—even millions—of lives over the centuries.

Decianus Cattus was now dead. That was a fact. He'd played a role in one event in history: a greedy fool who'd despoiled the Iceni and driven the Queen to rebellion. But there was no shortage of greedy fools amongst Roman administrators. And incredibly, in this world word of Prasutagus's death had still not reached the Romans, at least none now alive. Cattus and his men were the only ones who'd known that. His replacement did not. Those who came as patrols and visitors now had known the king far less well by sight than the dead procurator. If necessary, Tilutegan appeared on those occasions and acted Prasutagus's part.

Messengers from the other tribes would continue to drift into the Iceni dun even over winter. That much he knew. The feeling of rebellion amongst the tribes was still growing. But not all agreed. The Silures, carefully approached, had rejected the idea. They did well enough under Roman rule. What more was needed to have them rebel? And what would make alterations in time sufficient so that it would not settle back into the same path it had followed before?

He turned the sketch around again. It would be amusing if this were what changed history entirely. If Dari could understand the ideas and make them work. Dari arrived that evening and was interested in the idea.

"You say your people from across the great waters use these copper tubes to carry water? They will work through fitted stone?"

Well, they had a few generations ago. Not in Cean's time. "Aye. But I am a fool. I knew only that they were there, I did not study them nor learn the exact making of them."

Dari grunted, peering in the dim light at the sketches. "I see how this works. A strange idea to me, but it can be done. But the stone will have to fit tightly together to hold these in place."

Cean explained the idea of mortar, and how Romans used it to cement stone together.

For a moment Dari said nothing, then he grunted again, thinking it over. "It will require time to discover the proper chants for the metal. Finding these other things will not be easy." Cean had explained lime mortar to him; the sandy volcanic ash Roman engineers had otherwise used would be hard to find in Britain. Dari continued. "And coin with which to buy them as well. I will take the time and make the chants." He looked at Cean. "Do you have the coin, healer, or is the Queen to pay?"

"Nay, I have the coin. But make the first for me. If we make mistakes, then it is I who will suffer them. Let the next, the better work, be for the Queen."

"That is well said. So it shall be. I will talk with Sharn who works with stones. He will work with me to make this mortar, and I will begin to get the copper we must use."

"How long …?"

Dari grinned. "Longer than you hope, healer, but less than you fear. This shaping will take longer than the beating of a sword. It is tricky, small work. Leave a man to the work that is his, though, and it will be done when it is done."

With that Cean had to be content.

Los Angeles, 2048 C.E.: six weeks later

Fort dropped by Cean's apartment after work. "Want to get a bite?" he suggested. "My treat. That is, of course, if you have time." Fort smiled grimly. He'd started teasing Cean about having too much time on his hands now that he wasn't working. When they sat down and finally made their order, Fort wasn't even trying to smile.

"Apparently, I'm looking for work, too." He picked up the salt, avoiding Cean's gaze. "Today the Trust gave two more of my assistants notice." Cean raised his eyebrows. Mel had already been terminated. "The two grad students who worked part time," Fort clarified. "They made it clear that I'd be next. They're going to shut my project down entirely."

A harried waitress plopped two bowls of clam chowder in front of them before dashing away. Cean didn't know what to say, except a tentative "I'm sorry," as he dipped his spoon in and poked at the bits of re-constituted clams clotting the thin soup. He tore his bread apart and buttered it, his eyes on Fort, thinking.

Fort was stirring his soup around in the bowl, but not eating. Finally, he spoke. "I was so close! Just another month or so and I'd have the kinks worked out. Just a month!" His spoon clattered against the dish as he pushed it away.

"But if you did it once you can do it again," Cean suggested. "Elsewhere. Even on your own."

"Legally, I can't. The research belongs to them. I can do applications of it, but not the original work I was doing there. Even the theoretical basis belongs to them."

Cean was still clinging to hope. "Surely you can convince them. Maybe if you go before the board, you can persuade them to keep the project going," he pleaded. All of his plans depended on this! "There are lots of reasons why they'd want to be the first to succeed with a working time machine."

Fort looked him in the eyes. "The thing is, I don't think it's the research they're objecting to. It's like they have another reason for not wanting me around there. For a time after Mel was attacked, I thought they were disgusted that she was profiled, and were eyeing me differently, but in the end they didn't say anything." He shrugged. He'd worried about Mel keeping the job then. "Everything returned to normal. For a while."

A suspicion drifted across Cean's mind. "Do they think *you're* profiled?" he asked.

"That's a thought, but it may be what's happening." Fort sighed. "I hate to say it, but Mel's beating and then your visit on top of it might have precipitated this." He held up a forestalling hand. "Not that it's your fault. That is entirely theirs. But they may have decided they didn't want anything to do with someone who could be associated with Tensen's. Bastards. They're ducking their heads and running for cover."

Cean knew exactly what he meant. Attacks on the profiled were happening every day. As if echoing people's anger, too, night blazes in what had been the suburbs had escalated. Sometimes the fires started up during the day as well as the night. Fire departments now often refused to go out to them any longer. And businesses were trying to keep from becoming involved. Hence the firings, the laying off of people remotely associated with the profiled. Like a country washing its hands of the tainted.

Cean realized there was nothing for it. He was going to have to tell Fort exactly what he'd planned. His eyes on the table, his words surging past Fort's few attempts to interrupt, Cean told him everything. He told him what he'd hoped to do by going back in time, how he wanted to change everything here, and even described the gathering of the items he needed to take back with him.

When he finally looked up, Fort was grinning. It was a hard grin, but a grin just the same. Fort approved. "Good. I'd hoped you'd tell me. Or did you think I wouldn't notice when you took the time-jumper?" Laughter and fondness for his friend showed in his eyes at Cean's shock.

"Mel confided in me. One day at work, when we talked about the possible uses of time travel. She started asking some rather pointed questions. It wasn't hard to guess something was going on. Then one day you asked exactly the same questions. I confronted her, and she admitted what you had up your sleeve. Or should I say tunic?"

Cean felt sick. If Fort knew, then he'd never be able to get the machine from him!

Fort's next words stopped him dead in his tracks. "So where do you think we should build it? Your apartment or mine?" Fort's grin spread. "I really do think under the circumstances that the sooner we begin, the better."

Iceni Homeland, 61 C.E.

Early winter became full winter. Branches cracked and broke off in the freezing nights. Wolves howled, and twice there were wolf-hunts organized by Alieki spearman, including shepherds as well as others fearing for their stock of sheep and goats. Along with Lubran, Cean was kept busy healing everything from a wolf-bite, to broken limbs caused by falls on ground slick with the treacherous winter ice. As with Dauldi's son, the compound fracture of an arm or leg could be fatal here.

He chose to join the second hunt and ended up with a fine tanned skin given in gratitude by the woman of Talcan's hearth when Cean's quick aid saved her man from bleeding to death from a mis-shot arrow. Still the cold increased.

Cean shivered in his hut though he kept the fire blazing. Snow blanketed the land, damp snow that melted about the walls of the hut, seeping inside in places to wet the floor and keep it chill. Then he swore at his faulty memory one cold night as he fed the open fire. The old house he'd visited hadn't only had heated water and a bath. It had had a stove. A great cast-iron stove which flung out waves of heat while its flat top could be used to heat water or cook. Why in heaven's name hadn't he thought of that first? Iron was easier to find and work than copper, particularly in this time.

Then he tapped his forehead. Even iron was expensive here. What about a fireplace? Stone was cheap and plentiful, and with the use of mortar, chimneys and flues were possible; even rudimentary bricks could be made.

The primary problem with the huts, though, was the thatch roofs. Cean thought the tin they traded to Europe's continent could be made into flat strips to cover the thatch near a chimney, inside as well as out. But then he remembered the weight of metal involved. It was probable Dari could not produce such an item.

Unless—he reached for a sheet of bark, turned it over to the white inner side, seized charcoal and began to sketch. They could use an inner firebox of metal, but make the casing of mortared stones. Dari might be able to make a cheaper version of a cast iron stove, one that was supported by stone. A small one would be all that was needed to warm an Iceni hut.

Dari was marvelously skilled. By the standards of Cean's time the man might have incredibly primitive tools, but what he could do with them was a miracle. The first copper tubing was completed and the foundations of a bathhouse built, the tubing installed for pipes leading from the foundations' hypocaust under the floor to heat the whole structure since heat rises.

Beside it a cast-iron fireplace was installed. The thatch of the roof was laid over the mortared-stone of the walls, then protected with tin sheeting about its chimney, as much of it as they could afford. Cean could think of no way to improve the Iceni's fire-fighting techniques, but dry thatch was wickedly flammable. Perhaps come spring he would talk to them about wood, and the ways to mill it flat.

"You expect us to wash our bodies in that?" Alieki spearman asked Cean. It went against many of the Iceni traditions, and to wet yourself in winter was risking severe illness in this country.

"Yes," and Cean described to them how they could keep warm even after they'd bathed.

Once Dari had seen how the fireplace worked, he made improvements. The next one, installed the day before mid-winter solstice, was placed within the Queen's house. Boadicea approved. A ruler should be able to endure any hardship, but there was no requirement they do so unnecessarily. The third, a smaller one, was installed in Cean's hut.

Dari would have begun a fourth fireplace but for Cean's producing his sketches of a stove. The stove would be more efficient, throwing off more heat over a longer period of time; it could heat water and conserve fuel as well. There was no point in the Iceni deforesting their land to heat their homes, although Cean swore to himself he would drum into them the need to replenish the woods they cut down.

"I see, aye, I see." Dari was running his forefinger over the lines, studying the results in his mind. "Clever indeed, your people, healer. Yes, such a thing could be made. The inner thing you call a firebox could be made as a man makes a war-shield. Aye."

He muttered his way out and off down the path towards his forge as Cean looked after him. This change in time would not so easily correct itself. And if he'd done nothing more for his adopted people, this winter at least he'd given them warm huts and hot water.

He chuckled softly. To be sure the new inventions survived amongst the tribes, he needed to have the ideas spread. He went inside to think about that, only to have Lubran call softly at the door.

"Cean, are you busy?"

"No, come in, Lubran. I was only thinking."

"Ah, a good idea, one more people should do." The old man's tone was gently amused. He entered and went at once to stand by the fireplace which gave off a pleasant heat. "These ideas of yours are good. The gods must favor us indeed."

Cean felt guilty. Lubran had no source of warmth in his own hut as yet, nothing but the inefficient open hearth. Dari was just beginning a cast-iron stove that could be used for Lubran. Several of the tribespeople had taken to sleeping in the new bathhouse for the warmth. Cean would see to it that Lubran received the first small stove quickly.

Those built at a time closer to his own had been intended to heat anything up to five rooms. One half their size would be more than sufficient for the average Iceni dwelling, and use far less of the expensive metal. After that there would have to be a halt for a time. There was not enough metal remaining and more must be bought. He felt that twinge in the mind which signaled an oncoming idea.

"Lubran, tell me, would it be wrong to show other tribes what we have done?"

"It is not well to share too many war secrets with those who may in another time be enemy to us." Lubran held out his hands again to the pleasant heat. "Yet this is no war secret. Warriors can live with winter. It is the old among us and small babes who die of it. This is a thing of peace. Nay, Cean. Let others learn of it. I think it would be well for all."

"Then when spring warms the land the Queen might invite other tribes to visit?"

"Aye, she'll do that. Messengers go forth even now. Do not forget, my brother, that we seek allies against the Roman thieves. Their raids are less when winter lies on the land, but with spring they will begin again."

"Tithes, not raids."

Lubran's face was grin. "What does a name matter? They say they levy a tithe for the roads they build, the commerce they bring us, but these are for their use more than ours. For their army to keep a peace which is not ours and bring us no justice. And for temples to worship gods which are not ours. For their people across the great sea to watch our men battle to the death for their ruler's pleasure, or see the helpless torn apart by wild beasts. They have told us these tales. What good do we get from their tithes, Cean?"

He had to admit it. "Very little. They make good roads."

"Aye, on which they may march the more swiftly to poke their long noses into our duns. Nay, brother. They bring nothing to us we wish or require. Let them go back from whence they came, and if they will not, the Queen plans to see they are shown the way with torch and our spears." Cean knew. "But let us not think of the Romans. It will be moons yet before spring is upon us. Let us consider instead the list of uses for the herb, fever-bane. Now, recite to me what may be done with it."

The conversation became entirely herbal after that. Lubran shared Cean's meal and left reluctantly for his colder hut. Cean noted the reluctance and understood it. He offered to share his hut with the old man, but Lubran refused.

"I am not so old, nor so soft that I cannot live as I always have." It was his pride speaking.

"But if I wish to have company, why not? We can talk some more about the plants that grow nearby."

Lubran was convinced, and gratefully brought skins over to bed down. But Cean worried. He was on Dari's doorstep the following day.

"How goes the small stove for Lubran?"

"I am almost done. The Queen's fireplace does very well, but she may wish for one of these when it is done. She rejoices that Maara is less pained by her joints on cold nights." He made a small amused sound. "Though in truth I think the Queen, too, takes joy in a warmer house."

He turned to glance into the smithy where his apprentice worked busily, hammer beating out a rhythm. "I shall bespeak Sharn into beginning the outer work on the morrow. By the time that is done, we shall have the fire-box ready. Host Lubran for a handful of days, healer. For speed we shall have to place this stove within the old hearth and until the work is finished, he will have no fire at all."

"Tell me when that shall be and I'll arrange all with him."

It was done a few days later. The winter was not an unusually bad one, but as always it was a time of staying more inside and spinning wool or repairing harvest tools. The rest was telling stories to the children.

With the new fireplace and stove, Lubran and Cean found their huts often overflowing with friends who enjoyed the heat as well as the company. By the time spring was near, many among them were planning to have these new inventions installed for themselves. But there would be little time for that, and less coin. Spring came early, and the Romans were soon out more among the duns. Tithe-gathering, fining, and—as Lubran had expressed it—sticking their noses into the tribes' duns.

Messengers from other tribes to the Iceni became more frequent. Then more frequent still. Now and again a Roman patrol stopped at the Iceni dun to guest a night or two. Sometimes a handful of officers stayed overnight hunting in the area. The foreign soldiers and their commanders clearly believed trouble was brewing. They were watching all the tribes very closely.

Los Angeles, 2048 C.E.

Vencanza: News-films across the country carried the story; a prostitute with the Tensen's virus had been killing her clients with it. The bodies had been turning up regularly in Las Vegas, abandoned beside garbage dumpsters in alleys, hidden from the neon glare of the strip by the buildings themselves. The police had long suspected one person was responsible, but had few clues to follow until an undercover cop saw her pick up the last victim. Her name was Vencanza. "Revenge" joked the others of her profession. Spanish for "revenge" is "venganza."

The screen changed on Cean's monitor. This time to a man reporting on Vencanza's trial. Behind him, angry protesters waved film placards at the cameras, the words a blur of rage just out of focus in the lenses swooping about them.

"I'm here on the courthouse steps. At the moment we're waiting for the judge to rule on a summary trial petition. The prosecution has claimed that Ms. Vencanza Moranna is a menace to any who come in contact with her and should therefore be prosecuted with all speed."

"What exactly does that mean, Robert?" asked the studio anchor. "Doesn't that change the basis of the prosecution's case?"

"Not actually, Don," the reporter glanced down to a PDA implant on his arm. "It just means that the court would have to focus all of its attention on this one trial. All others would be postponed until this one is concluded. Clearly the prosecution are hoping that a speedy trial will take advantage of the public opinion against the profiled, ensuring a jury that would convict rather than have sympathy for the woman."

"Does that mean she won't be allowed out on bail?" the anchor added. His voice betrayed just the right note of anxiety, the tinge of public fear that she could be released to kill again.

"That's right, Don." The reporter turned his full attention to the camera, away from the crowd behind him. "Even if she could raise the money, she wouldn't be released. We're talking about a very poor woman here." He appeared relieved.

Behind him the crowd were stomping their feet, banging metal tubes against the stone steps to pick up the volume, drowning out the deputy asking them to keep it down.

"And there's just been word that other prisoners are protesting her presence in the jail, citing the possibility of contamination. The guards have had to place her in isolation, away from everyone else. They're also burning her used dishes and clothes in the prison furnaces."

"Has she entered a plea, Peter?" The anchor carefully conveyed his concern.

"Interestingly enough, she has. But it's not what you would expect. She's claiming justifiable homicide. Ms. Moranna alleges self defense." Screams in the background of those shouting at the guards lining the front of the courthouse drowned out his voice.

Cean switched off the news before he drank his tea. This wasn't good news. Fort had predicted it, though. Or something like that.

"They'll find a focus," he'd said, "a reason that justifies their fear. Attacks against the profiled will escalate. What happened to Mel will happen to others. Then we'll have to go underground. Quickly."

Cean thought over all of his preparations for leaving this violent time. His clothes were ready to wear, the goods he was taking to trade were packed in the appropriate wool and rough leather packs, the gold coins and jewels sewn unobtrusively into his tunic. He knew the language as well as he ever would, he believed, and he was physically fit, enough to make do in the rough Iceni world. The only problem left was that he hadn't ridden a horse. If he had a couple of days, he could learn enough to get by.

The news on the profiled did not improve. Two more riots erupted the next day, in what was left of New York's Harlem, and downtown San Francisco. In Harlem, a man and a woman were beaten to death by the riot police.

"He spat at me," one of the officers screamed into the camerabot. "The ape-shape spat on me!"

Police chief Everard Burton promised the people of New York that there'd be a full investigation, but who was being investigated wasn't clear at the end of the interview. San Francisco's chief, Reg Rusmatsen, refused to comment on what had happened there, but tabloids cited rival gangs, one of which had members on the force.

Andy called everyone, urgently advising the Coalition members to stay indoors at night. He also set up a contact system with regular calls between each member to be sure nothing happened to any of them. Fort promised to cover Mel's safety at the nursing home.

"I can sleep on a cot in her room," he told Cean. "Wouldn't be the first time." Fort's mother had died of cancer five years before.

Construction on the camps to house the profiled were rushed ahead. Although the government stated they were for the protection of the pro-filed only, the fences around the newly built compounds were topped with razor wire, and the governors of each state were deputizing special forces of men and women to become guards. One news channel read out the oath for these guards:

"I do solemnly swear to protect and serve the people of this United States, and to obey all lawful orders given to me by my superior of-ficers."

Cean nodded to himself. His preparations were almost ready. The suggestion of a casket in re-translated editions of Tacitus had given him an idea. The extended version had included a description of the casket, along with the torque Boadicea always wore about her neck.

While Fort stayed with Mel, Cean hunted out a metal smith, a man in Oakland who made replicas of various historical items. Cean gave him the best description possible of the casket to make a replica in bronze. Well, bronze of a kind. The 21st century kind. It was fire-proof, annealed and tempered so the metal wouldn't corrode. It would last the two thousand years required—and many centuries beyond if needed—before it began to deteriorate. It would also have a coded lock.

As he'd explained to Fort, he was almost ready. He'd become mod-erately skilled with the quarterstaff. He spoke the requisite languages, probably with a thick and distinct accent, but hopefully intelligible. He'd had a friend of the metal smith make him distinctive jewelry while Cean stood over him, learning how to do the job. Not well, of course. That would take years of training, but enough to be able to explain it to a smith of Boadicea's time. Iceni smiths knew filigree work and enamel, but not the cutting of precious and semi-precious stones.

And there was, too, the lost-wax method of casting metal figures unknown to the Iceni. Valuable skills that might also change the tech-nology of the time. Since they used tallow candles and lamps, he'd have to teach them about wax, and also mortar. That knowledge was about to come north with the Romans, but it hadn't yet become part of the Iceni technology. The jewelry and bronze casket were concealed in his bedroom along with a rough wool pack containing his clothing and other items.

He'd also learned first-aid, and put together a pack of supplies including several medical disks hidden in the casket. Initially he could pretend to be an eye doctor. The period was rife with complaints such as cataracts and eye infections. And in that period to be blinded was to be helpless, and often useless. By 2037 medical science had developed drops which would dissolve the cataract tissue within hours. Antibiotic drops would cure local eye infections. The basic job could be done quickly, easily, and safely by anyone with an eye-dropper. For that he had a case containing some twenty small phials of almost unbreakable plastic with several spare droppers made from a plastic that looked like dried, tanned sheep's intestine.

And he'd included a large supply of Vitamin A, the miracle vitamin that prevented blindness from vitamin deficiency, a common problem in undeveloped countries of his own time. He added several thousand of the tiny broad spectrum antibiotic tablets to the medical kit as well. He also looked up methods of producing antibiotics. If he lost the tablets or they were destroyed somehow, perhaps he could make something similar.

Some seeds were included in his pack, some of them vegetable and tomato seeds, along with wild rice to grow in the marshes. If he was going to change history, he thought, why not change it all.

For himself he'd had vaccinations over the past year. He'd covered every disease he could think of and a few more suggested in medical articles. His teeth had been treated; two replaced by cloned tooth buds which had already grown into new full-sized teeth. He'd quietly added painkillers of real potency to his pack. He'd had a new hormone implant done two months earlier, but he knew, and was resigned that there would not be time for the final operations. Not in this world.

Iceni Homeland, 61 C.E.

In the dun, Cean kept the Roman discussions boiling like a pot, with notes accusing some tribes of harboring banned druids, or hatching secret plans for revolt. He knew the Silures would be hard to ignite into rebellion, but hoped they would yet be persuaded. Maara's cousin had lived as a servant in that tribe. He'd unobtrusively made opportunities over the winter to talk to her of them, learning the way the Silures thought, and what might antagonize them to violence. He didn't intend what came about.

Feeling beset and remembering what had happened to Decianus and his escort, Paullinus Suetonius became harsher and harsher in the penalties imposed as winter drifted into spring when his soldiers were able to get around more easily to the tribes.

It was well into spring where traders on the roads were becoming common, when a horseman came shouting for a clear path as he galloped up to the dun's gates. His mount stormed up to the Iceni palisade and the mud-plastered rider swung down calling for entrance.

Boadicea came, not running but quickly. "Let him in. Now, man," as he halted before her, "what is so urgent that you ride with the wind and wake the dun with your shouting?"

"Lady, word came last moon to Suetonius that the Silures planned a secret rebellion, urged on them by druids still in hiding on their lands. To foil it, he marched his men, beggaring the people with the tithes he demanded." The messenger paused for breath.

"Nay, more than that. He slew their king when the king protested, saying if the man could not keep peace in his lands, he was no true ruler. The governor raised another lord for the tribe. And thus he chose one the tribe themselves refused, being neither of the royal line nor one who understands the hearts of his tribe."

About him those who listened sucked in their breaths in disapproval. A ruler must be acceptable. A king could not be imposed on a people who knew him not to be one of the royal line.

Boadicea's face paled in rage. "What happened then?"

"The Roman said they would do as they were bid or they would regret any refusal of his authority. The tribe said they would have a ruler of the royal blood."

The messenger, too, paled in his grief, as he recalled the events. In the crowd Cean feared what was to come. No Roman officer took an open flouting of his authority well, and Suetonius was known for his stiff-necked attitude and pride as much as for his military prowess.

"Lady, it hurts me to say what was done then. The Roman governor took all of the royal line hostage before the people. The males he slew, down to the smallest babe. The women who were more than ten winters were used by his soldiers. Afterwards they were flung naked into the mud. Then he spoke thus: 'this is your royal line. It is no more. I make the lines I wish and it is for you to bow to them or perish. And lest you think to raise up a girl-child for queen, these others shall return with me as slaves.'"

Boadicea's face had smoothed into blankness but her eyes met Cean's. He knew she was remembering the scene in her own dun.

"What then?"

"The people were afraid. There were many soldiers, yet the tribe could not for their honor's sake bear what was done without repayment. In the night two men crept into the Roman's tent. He woke and fought them but was slain. The men with him also. He cried out and his soldiers came before the tribesmen could escape."

"They were recognized as Silures? They talked?"

"Nay, lady, they died fighting but who they were was already known to the soldiers. There has been traffic between the tribe and the Roman camp. Some of the soldiers recognized the tribesmen for Silures while they were within the camp. In revenge the soldiers ran mad. They killed all that moved, sparing not even the beasts." His smile was ghastly.

"The man the Romans chose as king went out to them saying he would not take his throne from such as they. But before he did so, he called me and others to him. He insisted I remain out of sight but watch what came, saying once I knew all, I should ride to the Iceni that you may know and tell of our fate to the tribes. The other warriors he bade escape the fight, taking all the weapons they could, and once the Romans had left, to save any warriors who were no more than wounded. He bade them to hide away those women and children who escaped, as well.

"Once the Romans had gone, these men should take those who yet lived into places where the soldiers could not follow. There they should train, preparing for war. He was a better man that we first thought. He went out then to the Romans, and was slain with many of the tribe." The man fell silent for a moment, grief taking what breath he had before he fought to speak again.

"I was to remain, Lady. I know our land and its hiding places. When the war-host rides, and it must, I will go ahead to call blood-debt to those of my tribe who yet live. They shall be scouts ahead of the host, fearing to ride nowhere for death is already at their shoulder."

He fell silent, waiting for her reply. Boadicea tossed back her hair in a violent shake, the wind whipping it across her face as she stared out across her land.

"To the pride and arrogance of these people nothing is sacred. They rape women. They slay children who are not even warrior-trained and unable to stand against them. The old are given to the sword, the young to chains. A wise man said to me thus: 'a house must be built with strong walls lest the gales of winter topple it to the ground again.' For seasons have I overseen that building. I say to you, man of the Silures, the day is coming. Bide with us until that day when blood calls for blood. For when it is here you shall go forth to call your people to the war-trail. Nor shall you be the last amongst us."

Cean saw that many about him had tears in their eyes. He was not ashamed to find his eyes stinging as well. That short speech had been as clear a call to arms as any trumpet. He returned to his hut to add another couple of paragraphs to his story before tucking the tiny disk with the computer back into the casket. He also felt this was a good time to add to the advice he had already given.

After the tribe had dispersed to their huts, grim-faced and anxious, Cean invited Lubran to his hut.

"I have thought, brother, perhaps even dreamed while awake of something which I pray will come true."

Lubran was eager. "What is it?"

"In the forest a battle." Cean became carefully mystical. "A battle between two hosts of great deer rising from the bushes under the trees, one side the red deer, the other the roe. Even deer have antlers with which to strike, yet some of these had none. When the two forces of deer raced towards each other and struck, those who had no antlers, died. And when the winning deer strutted from the forest, it was those with antlers who rubbed them, sharpening them even yet upon the trunks of the oak trees."

Lubran's gaze turned inward. He silently mouthed a single name before speaking. "So. Not yet shall I speak your words to the Queen, but a time is coming when they shall be spoken." He departed, leaving Cean content. Lubran would remember what he'd said when it was most needed.

After the massacre, the Roman soldiers pulled back to their own camps and stayed there for weeks. With both Decianus and Suetonius gone, the Commander of the Ninth Legion, Quintus Petillius Cerealis took over the campaign.

Cean raced to his hut the day the news arrived, looking back in the computer's notes on the Roman soldiers of the time. Gods, but that could be useful. In his history-line the man had been competent enough, but in a basic and mundane way. Cean had barely replaced the computer in the casket when there was a cry from outside his hut accompanying a scratch at the door hide.

"Healer, the Queen bids you attend her."

Cean shot outside hastily. "She is well?"

"Aye, but she would speak with you on a weighty subject."

Cean ran. If Boadicea wanted him, he'd be there. The suggestion, too, that the matter was important sped him on.

He arrived to find a spearman barring the door, but Cean was let in once the guard announced his name. Cean stepped cautiously inside. Facing him were Boadicea, Maara, Lubran, and another man Cean didn't know. A tall, powerfully-built man of middle-age. At his shoulder stood two spearmen.

Cean had been with the Iceni long enough to understand. Whoever the man was, he was of a royal line and an equal to the Queen. Trusted enough to have his spearmen with him in the Queen's hut, and in her presence. It was not a light matter that caused her to call Cean to stand before such a group. He bowed to the Queen, following that with respectful inclinations of his head to Lubran and the stranger. This was a time to honor the Queen before her visitor.

"Lady, you summoned me. I came in all haste to your bidding."

She nodded. "Cean, healer of the Iceni, dreamer, this is Sueno of the Trinovantes. Hear him, for Lubran has spoken of your waking dream. There is a decision to be made."

Cean shivered. It came now.

He listened as Sueno talked almost casually, quietly, as he told of his people's oppression. "Long ago we owned the lands. Our place was Dun Camulus where lived our druids, priestesses and those of the royal blood. Then came the Catuvelauni who crowded us more and more until most of the land was theirs. In a battle that was final, Dun Camulus was lost to us and we wept in our hearts. Yet at least it was held by those who understood it as sacred land, consecrated by our gods. But the Romans came then. From the Catuvelauni they took the dun, tearing down the hallowed places and building upon the ruins their own temples."

His eyes showed the grief of that memory. "Our holy places are no more. Upon them stand the Roman baths, their heathen circus, and temples. And we, who knew the peace of the holy groves of Dun Camulus, we are forced to serve the Romans in the temples of their gods. Our wealth is stripped away to pay for Roman games, Roman gods. Those of our people who are not noble are used like servants to bow their knees to the Roman settlers to whom our land is given. All things go ill for us. Our hearts are heavy. As a people, we are no more. Without our lands, we are homeless. Without our sovereignty, we are weaponless."

The tale died into a long silence before Boadicea spoke. "You dreamed again, healer, a waking dream, the kind that only comes to the greatest of our priests. Lubran has told me that dream. Sueno came to me and to him also I told this dream. He swears you dreamed of the city they raised upon Dun Camulus. The city the Romans name Camulodunum where his people are enslaved by common soldiers who are less than our beasts. Speak now, healer, if you would say you dreamed not of that place."

"I cannot." He waited holding his breath. His heart hammered below his throat, stopping his breath there. Camulodunum. Modern Colchester.

"Your dream foretold defeat."

"It did."

"And you believe it was a true-dreaming?" That was Sueno, leaning forward on one foot, his face angry. Cean shook his head. Sueno stared. "But you have said ..."

"I said I dreamed and you believe the place of my dream was Camulodunum. My dream showed a great defeat, but the defeat was among the forests, among beasts of the forest. How can I say thus the gods will give, or take away? They do not like to be taken for granted. I believe the dream was a warning, not a prediction. I say only that if we give battle as wise warriors, if we take no foolish chances, and have weapons ready, if we act as though the city could stand strong against us, I believe the gods will give us the victory and the city will fall to our swords."

Boadicea's gaze on him as he finished was fond. "Did I not say, Sueno, that our healer is a wise man?"

"Aye, in which you were right. What say you now, Lady?"

She straightened, seeming in that moment to grow. Her back was taller, her eyes deepened, and she was another: unearthly and great. Power shivered in her voice, striking them all.

"I say, Sueno of the Trinovantes. Long have I held back my spears and my men's swords. I knew in time the gods would show the path along which my chariots should ride to strike. That time is come. That place is made known now. Word shall go out to all who listen and have sworn alliance. In the space of one moon, the war-host gathers to ride ... against Camulodunum." Her voice rose in a sharp cry. "For the dream, for the people, for our freedom to be what we are, we ride!"

Beside her swords were tossed roofwards and caught again, spears raised to shake at the sky beyond the hut. Sueno's face was alight with hope.

Cean stood, almost unable to breathe for the feelings which swept over him. In a moon he would see the true beginning. The first battle.

Gods! Let it be the victory he had foretold. For their sake. For his people's sake.

9

Cassius Parellus once claimed that the tribes of Britain would be Rome's undoing on the island (*Tacitus's Annals*, tr. by Alessandrea Bethenes, Vol. XIV, 5th Ed.). He wasn't entirely right. In fact, what was Rome's undoing in Britain was their destruction of the druid stronghold, Mona. In Gaul the druids adapted, changing their ways to suit Roman rule (Herraster, *Land of the Faith*, 137): Romans followed the old gods, and the druids followed theirs, with little conflict between the two. On the continent the druid priests were never put to the sword. In Britain, however, they were (*Tacitus's Annals*, tr. by Alessandrea Bethenes, Vol. XV, Ch. 30).

The Romans were never forgiven. In consequence, the tribes united in rebellion against the foreign occupation of their land and drove Rome out of Britain. Why Rome changed its usual policy of tolerance towards local religions, we will never know. However, it was a lesson that still rings through time to all nations, all people: a religion is the heart of a people; attempting to separate the two will always incur war.

—from *Rome to Britain: the Failure of Vision*,
by Suedon Parsian

Iceni Homeland, 61 C.E.

For the next month, though little showed on the surface of tribal life, it was like a great flat stone. Above, nothing appeared visible; it was a featureless and level surface. Yet if the stone were lifted, a myriad of creatures scurry about. So it was with the tribes. To all appearances, there were few who traveled between the tribes. At least by day. But by night messengers rode from one dun to another, word came and quickly went between the compounds.

Twice nobles of the Brigantes came to speak of the tactics of war. Once a Catuvelauni leader arrived. To Cean's astonishment, this one was an elderly woman whom Boadicea received with obvious affection. The woman was royal and kin, Lubran whispered. Younger sister to the Queen's long dead mother. A woman who had wed into the Catuvelauni and whose daughter, Isla, now led the fighting strength of the women's side.

The Romans continued to seek out the druids where they might find them. Always the news of another death would trickle in to further inflame the tribes. Cean wondered if it was a desire for stability, or disgust at what the Romans saw as dangerous practises which motivated the hunt.

He began listening to find that in Cerealis's case it was political anger. He had noted at one time that the druid priests and priestesses had ties too strong with the tribes' rulers. If their beliefs were wiped out, then Cerealis hoped the Romans would stand a better chance of conquering many of the tribes of Britain.

Cean added to that with another well-worded warning note. He had not realized just how paranoid the man was, he reflected somewhat later. Quintus Petillius Cerealis had acted with a ferocity equaling that of any at war. Groups of soldiers had descended on a number of duns, slaughtering any druid found there.

Cerealis had flung two into a fire. They died agonizing deaths, being thrust back with Roman swords each time they sought to escape the flames.

Priestesses, however, fared better. They weren't recognized as such since to Roman officers, they were only women and therefore without power. In secret, the priestesses continued the druid practices, keeping alive the connection between the royalty of the tribes and their link to the land.

Cean talked to Maara. "I heard talk of sacrifices when I traveled amongst other tribes before I came here. The Romans believe the druids slaughter men by burning them alive in great wicker cages." Maara nodded, to his horror.

"It was true?"

She laughed softly. "Nay, Cean. Not as you say it. Now and again, in a time of great need, a king or queen would give their lives for their people, when one must go ahead to beg favor from the gods on behalf of the people, or give a life to bring renewal to the land. But they must be a willing sacrifice. And even that is rarely done. In my own lifetime I have heard of it only twice, and never by fire."

"But the cages?"

"Usually a he-goat, or a young ram is slain. And they suffer no more than any animal slaughtered for food. But a wicker man can be burned. That is a figure made out of straw, then set alight. It may be this the Romans have seen and thought it housed a man or two within it."

"Your own people worship the Mother?"

"Aye. It was from my tales that the Queen now considers what she is to believe. But it is hard. She is the connection in druid belief, her life a living link to the gods." She nodded, pursing her lips. "I nursed her from the beginning, I sang to her the songs of my people, taught her their ways, their beliefs. They were not so different, but the Mother's worship is strong in our tribe and has always been more to the Queen's liking."

She met Cean's gaze with her own. "Whatever else may be said, the Great Mother favors Boadicea. This I have seen. My nursling in turn shall raise the Goddess up so the tribe sees only the Mother." Her look was firm, and disconcerting for Cean.

"That is good." He saw her tension relax.

"That is so. When the war-host rides, we shall pray to the Mother as an aspect of the druid's Brighid for victory. For the people's hearts, we shall pray to Lugh and Samain as well as Belenos so they will feel their gods are with them. But it is Brighid the Queen will personally petition, the Goddess Brighid and Mother of us all," she intoned.

In his mind, Cean added two and two, and came up with a slight elevation in Maara's status. She was seeing her own form of worship become a religion of the people. With Boadicea a worshipper, Maara would be more important than an old woman who had once been a child's nurse, and was now her maid. Just so long as they didn't end up with a country split between those who worshipped one way, and those who insisted on another. He said something of that, carefully. Maara considered his words.

"I think not so, Cean. Mona is gone, that stronghold wrought with druid learning. They broke it open like a shellfish for its meat. Those who learned and taught lie dead there, and through the lands the Romans harry their remnants. But we of the Mother, we have no single place. And our training is of a different kind." She coughed quietly into her hand.

"The magic of women is not that of men, healer. But we have our own learning, our own magic and healing arts. Now the druids fall, the followers of the Goddess turn to take their place. We have no need to slay, to rival other beliefs. Time itself is the slayer. The tribes will listen to those of the Mother as she grants victories. Those the druids bowed to have granted their followers only death. But fear not, healer, we will not set ourselves against those who survive. Imbolc does not require it so."

A pragmatic view, Cean thought. A god's power was shown by his—or her—effectiveness. What Maara was saying was the druid system was a failure because the Romans had been able to take Mona, and since then, kill so many of the priests among the tribes. Because of Cerealis's persecution, the druids would foment an uprising. In the past two years most of the druids had died. Many of those who'd survived were the solitary healers, like Lubran.

The more intense worshippers of druidism, embodied by the mystics who were the teachers and the students alike, had gathered together, and been killed in one strike, wiping most of those inclined to fanaticism. The priestesses had managed to survive because the Romans did not recognize them, either for what they were, or the power they held. They would carry on a modified druid faith instead of the priests.

The sun was warm on his head and shoulders as he sat in silence beside the old woman. He stirred. He rose, content, and departed, leaving Maara to sit, enjoying the warming spring sunlight.

Los Angeles, 2048 C.E.

Cean stood before the apartment window, drinking a glass of chocolate milk. Outside, four separate night blazes exploded across the wide bowl of the city. Two were large, and their flames flared through what must be an entire city block. The others were single fires, isolated yet with jets of flame that spurted high like Biblical pillars of fire, subsiding only to well up in sudden explosions again and again. Gasoline, Cean realized. They're pouring jugs of gas onto the fires to make sure they burned. He hoped no one was there, that the gangs had caught no one with Tensen's this night.

Cean was in Fort's apartment when the police came by, and they were willing to take down his personal details without seeing where he lived. He wouldn't have wanted to explain the half a dozen machines spaced out so they could walk between them and taking up more than half of his living room floor. Not that they would have recognized the jumpers, but they would have wondered about bombs.

"Given recent events, we are listing the names of those who are profiled, and their supporters, sir, in case of accidents," the older of the two officers announced, his voice as gray as his hair. He didn't apologize.

Fort immediately asked, "How did you get our names?"

"The hospitals are required to give them to us, sir. They have to give us your names as the profiled have now been ruled a public health risk." This bit of information had not been on the news.

He asked them their names, the second officer checking them against the list he held in his PDA, a bigger version than the popular wrist model. "Just confirming you are who you say you are." Obviously he had pictures as well, and both officers had to identify them and add their thumbprints to verify it on the computer file.

"Thank you, gentlemen," the elder officer barely murmured as they left. The second didn't speak at all. Only his eyes moved as they glanced up at Fort and Cean carefully, glittering with fear and malice before he walked away.

After the door closed, Fort exclaimed, "You'd think we were criminals." Cean was just as unnerved. "I think I'd better look at what's come in and get on to the others." He was referring to the coalition members, and went into the second room to check his computer having heard the whistle that announced incoming mail.

There was plenty of mail, as he discovered. The police had already visited many of the coalition people. And many of them had lost their jobs as well.

That night at a meeting, it became apparent that the group was now being watched. Two dark, unmarked cars like shadows were parked near the entry, and beside the doors, a man and a woman stood, speaking quietly to the security guards. They were obviously officers, and made little effort to hide it. Nor did they try to seem friendly.

"I know," Janet said when she opened the apartment door. "They came earlier and said they knew about the meeting. They claimed they had no other purpose than to be here in case there was trouble about us gathering together."

"As *if*," Max seconded. "They just want to be sure they have all of our names." Cean was certain Max was right.

"Now I know what a rabbit feels like when he darts out to find himself faced with a fox," he told them. "Like I'm about to be pounced on!" He took the coffee Janet handed him and looked around for a seat.

It was a record turnout; almost everyone was there.

"It's like the Gestapo and the Jews," one of the members said, a short balding man who rarely came.

But Andy, a lawyer with thick eyebrows, added, "We haven't yet proved we are not a clear danger to the community. Until that is done, under the law we have no right to protest their actions. We do have a petition before the Supreme Court at the moment, but I expect they will delay a ruling on it until a judgement in the Vencanza trial comes through."

Cean gritted his teeth. She would be found guilty. Then what would happen? Fort agreed. As they left, he told Cean that government camps could be the upshot of the whole mess.

"We won't have a choice. They'll want to isolate us, for our own protection, or so they'll say. But their main reason will be to prevent the spread of the disease. And to protect their own hides. Voters won't be happy with a government that appears to do nothing. Approval ratings will go down, and politicians won't want that, no matter what's right about confining innocent people. It's history all over again. They rounded up all the Japanese-Americans in World War II and put them in camps, and they're about to do the same to us."

Although Cean hadn't been told he couldn't travel, that night he hid his passport, sticking it deep in one of the files among his other papers. It could be found, but not easily. Just keeping an honest man honest, he thought, or at least slowing him down.

Iceni Homeland, Spring 61 C.E.

With the spring, the tribes' messengers rode between the duns constantly. Coming and going, meeting the Queen and her advisers secretly, rarely appearing in the dun lest someone see them who should not. But the crantara was out. The branch burned at one end, blooded at the other, was carried throughout the area, and the Romans would have been unsettled had they seen who welcomed it to the duns.

With her own hands Boadicea had snapped rods from the felled hazel tree. She had slain the black goat beside Belenos's bonfire. Into the blood the Queen had dipped one end of the rod, charring the other carefully in the fire.

To all tribes who had shown a willingness for alliance, she sent the rods, the white of the peeled hazel rod showing between the rusty red and the charred black. Men now daily reported from the tribes who had received the summons and would ride with the war-host. The Queen's first question was always how many warriors would make up their numbers.

And ever Boadicea preached the tale of the house which must have strong walls to withstand the gales. Of the builder who must build slowly and carefully. Haste was ruin when the high winds came, she told them.

The going was hard. Cean saw her talk, smile, drink in friendship with tribes who had long been enemies to the Iceni, then smile and calmly speak again. She who never before had been a diplomat, was learning to persuade rather than command. A flame burned within her which tempered her words, her tongue. She had come so close to disaster already. Her people's lives were in her hands.

Cean saw in her eyes each day that she remembered standing gripped by callused hands, back naked for the whip. How her daughters had been held down, spread-eagled in the earth of the dun, waiting for the soldiers to fall upon them, they who'd stood laughing, arguing which would be first to outrage a child. Each time she remembered, her hatred burned stronger, hotter.

It was not enough to win a battle, or even three or four. The Romans must be driven out. Back to their kennels across the seas, to remain there. Or they would return. Next year or the year after that. They would land again on the island's shores, and enslave their people. Cean counseled the runners on this, recalling how Rome had fallen centuries later in his world.

"You do not love them, Lady," he said to her on one of the days.

She eyed him, the heat of her anger rising. "Love Romans?" Maara handed her a cup of watered ale.

"Even so. How do you think those other tribes around Roman lands love them? They who have been conquered and made slaves long ago, before the tribes of this land?" He saw her absorb that before leaning forward to speak a final proverb. "'The enemy of my enemy is my friend.'"

"That is truth. You do not know it yet, healer. You have missed the messengers in the night, the ones who come most secret of all. Rome's other enemies in this land." She smiled at his surprise. He thought he knew more than she did, coming from his time, but when it came to understanding people, she was startlingly perceptive, Cean thought.

"Another moon before we move. If messengers go forth they will know when we strike. They will approach Rome's enemies once we move, enemies already prepared."

Cean grinned, his breath shallow. "Aye. A hunt goes better when the prey is taken from both sides, better still if it be encircled. Is that not what you once told me when we hunted the fox?"

"You are a sensible man, healer. You listen."

"I listen to *you*."

Their eyes met and in hers he saw a sudden realization. What it was he did not know, but he knew she had abruptly come to know something which made her eyes widen in surprise.

She flung back her head, laughing, that marvelous hair a cloak of fire around her.

"Always listen, wise one. As I will listen to you. Now I must meet another legation. The Cornovii messengers come to list numbers."

"Many?" Now it was upon them, Cean was anxious.

"Enough, and all they can spare."

"Soon the Romans may notice there is much traffic between the tribes." He was certain she was being careful, but it didn't hurt to mention it.

"Soon they will notice nothing." Her voice was hard, flat.

He returned to his hut wondering what she had in mind.

* * * *

He found out three nights short of the full moon nearly four weeks later. Riders thundered into the dun. Twin fires blazed up by the gates, the dun's peace broken. Cean, wakened by the commotion came in his hastily donned clothing. A mud-spattered pony arrived wild-eyed, bearing a warrior who leaned over to speak to the Queen where she stood by the gates, the green mantle hastily thrown over her shoulders.

"Sempronius Astrican. All are dead." He swung the pony aside to make way for another.

"Igneus Octavius. All are dead."

Cean listened to the list of Roman names, recognizing some. They'd been the ones who'd taken a farm, built a villa, on a tribe's lands.

Gradually he understood. Boadicea had planned as she'd told him. Her warriors and those of some of the allies had gone out. If her plans had gone aright, every Roman in the Iceni lands, and in a great swathe between the Iceni and the city of Camulodunum, had died this night.

There would be none to see or give warning when the war-host marched. He turned away as another sweating pony arrived bearing a rider with names of the dead. Something told Cean he should stop standing about and make ready. A massacre like this couldn't be kept quiet. Not for more than a few days. After that someone would ride onto the farms and find the dead lying there.

Even with a ring of warriors around the area, standing between the villas and the roads, someone would notice. Even if it was only that none came from the Iceni direction, neither merchant, trader, nor courier. The forerunner of the first battle.

He packed, tucking the casket with the computer and the stack of tiny diskettes in it into a niche he'd carved in the hut floor. A flat stone placed over it and plastered with mud would hide it. The mud would dry in a day or two. He left his backpack, taking up instead the leather saddlebags he had purchased in the fall. Once he was done, he placed the bulging saddlebags by the door. Then he returned to his bed. He had a feeling sleep might be harder to come by in the coming nights. He was both wrong and right about that.

* * * *

The great killing remained unknown for three days while the war-host gathered. Already they had been on the way, travelling by night and stealth, answering the *crantara* sent out a moon earlier.

In another day the Iceni dun was the center of a camp. In two, the heart of a war-host. In three, the Queen addressed those who waited, silent in their war-gear.

"At moonrise we ride. A blooding of swords. A bath for our spears. Yet this is the god's warning. Even a wolf-cub has teeth. And a howl may alert the pack. Count no prey dead until you have its heart in your hand."

There was harsh laughter from several of the warriors who listened. Nervous laughter.

"Aye, laugh. Leave tears to the Romans. But be wary. This is the first battle only. The war is not done even when it is over. After this we must strike a second time, hard and fast, giving the Romans no time to gather against us. With the Iceni ride all the tribes of the host. The people of the Silures lead as outriders. They shall be first to slay in the name of their dead.

"But for the next battle," she continued, her voice a dark hum in the air, "I have chosen certain tribes alone to ride, and for the battle after that others again. Thus, all shall have their share of plunder and glory. All shall blood their weapons in turn. All shall have their revenge for the deaths of our people, for the slaves they have taken among us."

Cean bit back a whoop. By the gods, she understood her people!

In his history, one of the reasons for failure had been that after the third battle many of the warriors had left to celebrate their success and enjoy their loot. By rotating the tribes, she was not only ensuring they would have more warriors, she was also making certain each would be the more eager to take their turn in the fighting.

She would not have tribes leaving her, but clamoring to join and then rejoin in an orderly rotation that allowed some tribes to rest while others took their places. This gave them a chance to heal their wounded, and mourn their dead at the same time as they shared out their loot and bragged of its taking.

He was ready. The sturdy, sure-footed pony the Queen had given him was well fed and exercised. Saddlebags were tied across the riding pad. He'd done as the others and tethered his mount by the door of his hut. There would be no delay when the time came. He ate, then cleaned the pot, tidied his hut while he waited.

Outside the moon lifted above the trees. Within the dun a horn sounded. Clear and wild. Cean had expected more noise to sing of the coming battle. But in the moonlight there was little more than quiet curses here and there. The occasional whinny of a pony. The rustle of warriors' clothing and gear as they mounted. Followed by the soft plop of unshod hooves as the mounts vanished into the dark landscape.

He mounted, swinging his pony to ride beside Lubran. He'd been horrified his friend was going to war. Then amused to see the old man horrified in turn that Cean would think Lubran would not.

"Why should I not ride? I am not so old I cannot straddle a pony." He fussed with the bag he was tying to his saddle. "Maybe I am no warrior, yet shall they need healers when the battle is done. I am healer for the Iceni."

"I can heal," Cean mentioned diffidently.

"You have learned well, my brother. Yet better two healers then one. I think all healers who ride may be needed," Lubran added grimly.

"You do not think Camulodunum will fall so easily?"

Lubran sat astride his horse. "It will fall, aye, as a lamb to a wolf. But the Queen does not return. Without pausing, she rides on then to Londinium. With her ride the Iceni, the Silures, the Catuvelauni, the Brigantes, the Cornovii and the Coritani, and others.

"The Brigantes will turn aside with the Ordovices and other people from the north, leaving the Atrebates and Catuvellauni, Trinovantes and Cantii to carry on the battle. The northern host then rests, savoring their plunder, celebrating their victory before they return to the host again while the other tribes rest."

Lubran looked at the young man he and the Queen believed had been sent to them. "There will be a great need of healers before this thing is ended. Therefore I ride. Do you ride with me?"

"I ride." That was all Cean could say.

Ride he did through a long moonlit night until in the half-light of dawn they saw unguarded the buildings of Camulodunum rise out of the ground mist. Lubran reined his mount aside from the road, out of the way of the men who appeared silently behind them. A great host that followed the Queen of the Iceni.

"It is for us to wait a little now. Soon they will call for us."

The war-host streamed past. Then, harshly, desperately, a horn screamed warning from the city walls. The time for silence was gone, and the host cried out. A roaring confused shout like a blast of thunder bellowed into the sky. The patter of unshod hooves was a drum's roll across the ground as they attacked.

Camulodunum was all Cean had claimed. The Romans had been either arrogant or lazy. It was a city without effective walls, but its people would fight just the same. They had no other choice. They had neither chance nor hope, either. The war-host swarmed through the city gates, killing until the ground was sodden with blood. The hooves of their horses, their chariot wheels mixed it with the earth, churning it red and foul with the stink of spilt blood.

Boadicea's chariot preceded the crowd of fighting men, her spears striking as hard and biting as deeply as any of her warriors. She was the first, her voice as loud as her men's, her chariot ahead of them as she drove into the city. And she killed as they did, everyone they could reach. Then she took their heads, tying them to the sides of her chariot as she surged forward still, through the city, slaughtering everyone.

It was quickly over, the wounded crying out as they were silenced with the hosts' spears. Until none were left alive.

There was loot to be taken, amphorae of wine, fine fabrics, gold and silver ornaments and dishes, and victims' heads. Following the tail of the host into the city, Cean shuddered at some of the sights.

Yet had the Romans treated the tribes any less savagely? At least this land belonged to the people; they had a right to take it back. The Romans had come to kill, to enslave and steal all the lands of the tribes. Cean shut his eyes to the blood, and ignored the sound of the revenge of those who had been driven too far.

The air reeked with the copper-like stench of fresh blood. It was everywhere. Smoke choked the air, mixing with the odors of death. What could be burned had been put to the torch. He went from the wounded to the dying, helping where he could, again and again. His robe dripped with the blood of those he tended, his hands stained with it.

He kneeled to tend a man of the Iceni whose face was swollen and bruised. Dazed eyes stared vacantly up at him. Beside the man lay a dead Roman, a soldier from his gear, the shield still on his arm. Cean guessed it had been a blow from that which had caused the tribesman's injuries.

"Lie back. Let me do what I may for you."

"The battle …?"

"Is done. The tribes have conquered. Lie still."

"I promised the woman of my house gifts from the city. Let me rise that I may search for one."

Cean snorted. "Lie still! Drink." He held out his flask containing a mixture of water and the fierce barley-ale. "She will not have gifts if you do not live."

The man drank several mouthfuls before lying back as ordered.

"What sort of thing would your woman like?" Cean asked the man, relenting. The tribes had little enough wealth, and the woman had risked her husband, the livelihood of her family.

"Such jewels as the Roman women wear. Some cloth perhaps."

"If you swear to lie still and let the effects of the blow you received subside a while, I shall find these things for you."

He received a small smile. "I swear, healer."

He'd said he would. He must search through the nearest ruins to see what he could find to keep that oath. Not far away he could see Lubran caring for a woman of the Catuvelauni. Even the women's side had come to war in this battle. Two hundred of them under Isla, cousin to the Iceni Queen.

When he had done all he could for the wounded, he left to look at what was left of the city. He found a place as yet untouched, down one short alley between buildings next to the Roman market. The house had been a small villa, belonging perhaps to a merchant. Not a man of huge wealth but the home was well-furnished, comfortable. In the atrium stood several huge amphorae. Cean rocked one to find it was full, of what he did not know.

He walked deeper into the house to find it a place of the dead. Warriors of the tribes had struck down these people. All of them, in one room. The man and woman, an older couple, lay huddled beside their beds, their hands splayed out, their eyes lifeless. Their servants had fallen in the hall outside. An elderly man with his plump round-faced wife. Their veins had been split with swords, but they lay in each other's arms on the blood-soaked floor.

In another room two children lay, one's skull split and the other his head lolling over a broken neck. Grandchildren, from their age.

Cean wondered where their parents were. Fighting perhaps, or away from the city. With the children lay a middle-aged woman, a slave or servant from her dress. A knife had been used to stab her to the heart.

Cean felt the vomit rise in his throat. The stench of blood, the small forms, the woman's gaping chest. He had caused this. He … into his mind flashed the cherished portrait of the Queen.

No, this was not his doing. Who had asked these people to come as conquerors, invaders?

It had been a clear choice between the Romans and Boadicea. He had chosen long ago while still in his own world.

He fought back the sickness in his belly, forced himself to step to the bedside where the old couple lay. A small chest had tumbled to the ground near the bed, spilling its contents. He seized a handful of the jewelry, then searched a chest to find several lengths of fine woolen cloth, and one of a heavier weave. He bundled it all into a soft woolen stola, dropped the bundle into a magnificent iron cooking pot and bore it back in triumph to his patient.

"Take this to the woman of your house. I swear she shall not have less than many others." At least the old couple's things would go to a woman to warm her home, rather than as spoils to a merchant for sale.

"I thank you, healer."

"Good, then you are to lie still until your head ceases to spin. Once you feel a little better, seek out the battle wagons and rest there. I suggest you do not drink anything but water for the next pair of days." Cean forced a grin. "It is likely of little use to say that. I ask that you do not drink too deep though. Such a blow to the head mixes not well with ale."

He left the warrior investigating the bundle and moved on to another man he'd seen to before. This one was now dead. He signed the gods' blessing and looked about him. From the roar of sound in the distance, the battle still raged. Lubran appeared from behind a building. Sudden relief touched Cean.

"You are unharmed. How goes the fighting?"

"Some of those from the city have taken refuge in the temple." Lubran spat. "They did not guard the city but the temple walls are stout. It may take time to hunt out the rabbits from their burrow."

Of course. In his own history the temple had held out for two days.

Cerealis had marched to its relief and died. But the two days had been time wasted. It was the first of several delays which allowed the legions time to prepare against the rebellion. If the temple could be taken quickly that time would not be lost. As tired as he was, his memory stirred.

"Come with me." With Lubran following he returned to the small house, pointed to the amphorae. "Help me get the stoppers out." They forced the seals, Lubran dipping a cloth into the neck. Both of them sniffed at it.

"Oil," Lubran said with satisfaction. "I see your mind, brother."

He glanced about him. "Despoil this place while I go to seek warriors. Make certain nothing small of value remains. Others will come soon enough."

Cean wandered again about the rooms, avoiding where the bodies lay. Here and there he found items which were both portable and valuable, a small knife, a beaded bracelet of amber. He looked out of the doorway, seeing no sign of Lubran as yet. But beside this house was another.

He entered that, knife in hand. In the main hall, a warrior—Silures, by the look of him—lay dead. An arrow pierced his chest. The point had torn through his heart, killing him immediately.

When Cean turned him over to be sure he wasn't alive, he found a bronze casket underneath the man. In it there was jewelry, richer than that of the other home. He added it all to his sack. In the kitchen stood more amphorae of oil. Good, he'd have those. The warriors Lubran would bring back could take these next. Hoofbeats sounded near.

"Cean?"

"I'm here. So is more oil."

Lubran rushed in the door to help him. "Good. The Queen has said we are to bring all that can be found. We'll make a barricade about the temple, pour oil within, then fire it. Those who think to deprive us of a victory will be smoked out like rats from a grain field."

"I'll keep looking. If they brought a cart, we could take the oil more easily."

Lubran waved to where six men rode, one leading a solid horse who pulled a good four-wheeled cart. "We think alike. Go, as you say. Seek out more oil while we load the containers here."

Cean ran from house to merchant house after that. In most the warriors had seized what jewelry or coins to be had. But he still found a few items that the warriors had missed. And in most, too, there were the amphorae of oil. Some for lamps, others for cooking. All of it would burn.

Cartload after cartload went forth from the quarter where he hunted. The temple had a river of oil around it like a moat, and still the oil was poured in. They added wood until it was a ring of death waiting only for the fire's kiss. That came at last.

Boadicea took up the torch herself. "Stand back." They obeyed as her gaze swept over them. "For our dead, for our women outraged, our warriors slain. Our children beaten and used as slaves. Those within demanded we live under their laws. Let them now die under ours! Let justice claim them." She thrust the torch into the piled wood.

There was a roar of flame, a wall of it, towering up against the pale blue sky of dawn. Heat beat outwards, growing with each pulse.

There was no hope for those within. They could not fight through the great band of wicked flames. They could only give themselves a quicker easier death before the fire licked flesh from their bodies, breath from their lungs. Cean prayed the fumes suffocated them before the flames got that far.

It took hours for the wall of fire to die. It would take days before the ruins cooled. The city was theirs.

Boadicea sent for Cean that evening. "Sleep sound tonight. Dream for me if you can, and the gods send wisdom to you."

"If I can." She looked up at him, a smolder in her eyes that struck a chill in him. "I am no more than the mouth which speaks," he added, quickly. "But I will tell you all I see, Lady."

"Then sleep, mouth of the gods, and dream as they send you."

Cean already knew what he would tell her. The temple had fallen in this time as it had not done for days in his own. Decianus would already be marching towards them with the ninth legion. If he could be taken, totally destroyed, that would be one less enemy, and far fewer Romans.

When he slept, it wasn't peaceful. Cries from those he'd seen die, and those wishing they had, haunted him. But he rose with the dawn to tell his dream to Boadicea.

10

Tactics are a fact of culture. According to the words written by the ancient Roman soldiers (Bethenes, 318), and those described in the more modern journals of warfare (Semandes, 109), how people choose to distribute weaponry and forces is often a matter of what has worked in their culture down through the ages. When the Grecans broke down the walls of Newer Jersea during the civil rebellion there, the Grecans used bluff and deceit, just as they had in ancient times when they battled Troy. This strategy was part of their cultural tradition.

When Boadicea burned the temple at Camulodunum, she was only obeying the dictates of her culture: razing the enemies' duns had long been a standard battle tactic in the tribe's past. As was her approach to treaties with the Romans, or rather lack of. Her treatment of them was unforgiving and relentless: they were to leave the island entirely.

—from *The Treaties and the Wars*,
by Mierhan Perthwat

Iceni Homeland, 61 C.E.

Cean had slept the night away in the second merchant's small house. There'd been no bodies there and he felt more comfortable in such a place than outside among the soldiers mending their weapons. Lubran had stayed with him, and they had taken in a handful of the more severely injured as well so the two healers might watch over them. Many others were near death, and there was little Cean could do for them.

Others had deep wounds that would likely fester, even if they were well-cleaned. The water was unfiltered, and often dirty, as likely to corrupt the wound as not. Cean had one of the young boys boil water to use instead, and quietly given the Iceni wounded a potion containing, amongst other things, half a broad-spectrum antibiotic each as well. He couldn't afford to give it out to all of the wounded.

"They do well." Lubran said after inspecting the patients soon after dawn.

"Aye, I think between us the Iceni loses no more warriors from this battle."

"Battle!" Lubran snorted in amusement. "A shearing of sheep, it was, a hunting of rabbits. Such weak walls, with few guards. I say to you, brother, they must have been mad. Or confident beyond belief."

"Maybe, but they're warned now. They'll not be sheep to face the next time. It's Roman wolves who'll meet us then."

"True enough. Where do you go?"

Cean paused at the doorway. "To the house beyond this one. Romans often have medicines." He grinned, "And honey. I go to seek out what may be found."

He returned in triumph bearing a large pot of honey and a number of small pots of wound-salve. With these he had found several rolls of bandages and a small keen knife.

Lubran held his hands out to take them from the younger man. "You are summoned. Alieki has come and gone, saying the Queen bids you come to her."

"I'll go at once." He walked away looking about him as he hurried for the square where Boadicea held council.

It was mid-morning. Warriors of the Atribates, the Silures, and the Ordovices were combing what was left of the city. Already plunder stacked on ponies was leaving in a steady stream with laughing men and women. He noticed one thing as he walked slowly through the grim chaos. Unlike a Roman conquest, here there were no lines of slaves being led off in chains.

Twice he saw a woman of the war bands carrying a toddler or baby. He smiled. They might be Roman or Romanized, but he'd wager in a few years they were as the other children of the tribes. That was good. They would provide both replacements for any who died in this war, and the vigor of new blood for the tribes' future. He could comment on that as well, if the Queen permitted that is. He reached her camp and Alieki spied him as he walked up.

The big man beamed. "Cean. Lubran said you are well? No war wounds?"

Cean chuckled, even though he was tired. "He spoke truth. We have patients but we ourselves are unharmed." He grimaced wryly. "How could I be other since my careful teacher would not permit me to enter the city until the fighting was far past us."

"As well," Alieki said sternly, leaning on his war spear. "Warriors we have in plenty. Trained healers are harder to find. But come, the Queen asks for you."

Cean followed him through the press of people to where Boadicea sat, enthroned on a large carved wooden chair someone had found. They had found also a cloak, and he studied that with sudden interest. It must have belonged to someone very important, indeed. It was made of violet wool, knee length he would guess, with a band of gold embroidery running right around the hem and up both sides to where gold clasps set with pearls held the collar.

It was the color which caught Cean's attention. Close enough to purple, the same as worn by the emperors in Rome. Could it be the first subtle sign by the Queen that she planned this war to end with her as supreme ruler of the tribes? He nudged Alieki as they stood waiting to be noticed.

"From where came the cloak? It is the finest I have seen."

Alieki grinned, showing his missing tooth. "So it should be, Cean. Dauldi and I looted it from the governor's spare house, the one he used when he had business here. The house was empty and I thought the place would have the finest loot of all. I, Dauldi, and some of our warriors took what was there for our Queen. Being first into the city, none disputed our right to do so. She slept soft in her new cloak last night, and this morning we gave her the throne which is her due."

Cean grinned companionably back. "The plunder in such a place is of a sort to please your women as well."

"You are a shrewd man, Cean. Indeed, we shared what we found that any could carry away. We have made up packs and Verli returns home with them across his pony. He will give our shares to the women of our houses and rest a while."

"Verli? You didn't let that child fight, did you?"

Alieki peered at him in puzzlement. "Why not, Cean? The lad is now twelve summers old. His arm has been well enough for him to wield a spear for many moons thanks to your care."

"But ..."

Cean subsided, still shocked by the attitude that in this time a twelve-year old was as much of a man as a twenty-year old in his own time. Alieki would not see why a boy who was, in tribal terms, already half a man, should not fight. He was only glad that from Alieki's report Verli was unhurt.

In fact he had not seen many with serious wounds. The twenty or so men he and Lubran had cared for were the worst amongst the Iceni, and they, along with the Silures, had been first into the city and born the brunt of the strongest resistance. Five Iceni warriors had died. Twenty with deep wounds, the rest uninjured or with scratches, as they would count them. They had come off very lightly. He listened to the talk about him. Many praised the Queen for the victory.

"She is cunning," said one man, stooping over the open fire.

"A good fighter too. Did you see her strike down that soldier who would have stopped her when …"

"Lucky … I always say that to be led by a lucky ruler is as good …" Cean's attention was seized by her voice then.

"Alieki? Have you brought the healer?"

"He is here, Lady." He nudged Cean forward. Boadicea rose from her chair.

"Come with me, healer. I would speak without so many ears near us." She smiled as she said it and her warriors nodded happily, unoffended. She swept him with her into a guard's quarters, pausing to look about her. "Here, sit here." Cean sat on one of the mess benches and waited.

"The first battle is won, but I know, if those outside do not, that one battle does not make the war. If you have wisdom I would hear it. Also, if you dream, I bid you tell me of it. I will need your advice this day."

"Wisdom I have first …"

She caught at that last word. "Then the gods have spoken again to you?"

"They did. A strange dream, like waking to smoke. Yet I think it may be clear to you who knows the clash of spears." He paused. "But will you hear my advice first?"

She nodded, sitting back attentively on the plain bench of the room. She rested her cheek on one hand, but her eyes were alert, intent on Cean. No lamps lit the room, her mass of hair falling down her back, golden-red where the light from the doorway, and deep auburn where it faded into the shadows behind her. She seemed like a creature taking shape out of the darkness surrounding her.

"As I came to your call, I saw some of the tribes. They take their plunder and depart. They should not. They have more wealth than they've known in their entire lives because of this battle. With it to satisfy them, they might not return. In fact, they may feel that there's no need now. They've beaten the Romans, and taken what they would. Why should the Romans come again?"

"Indeed. I had not forgotten your words, healer, but knew no way to tell them differently. How can I stop them from taking what they think is their right?"

"By sending their plunder in carts or wagons to their duns, but keeping the warriors here."

"Aye, but it will not be easy. It goes against our ways." Boadicea looked at a window set high in the wall.

Cean continued. "Yet warriors now name you lucky and cunning. Men may come to ride with one they name thus. And the fame of the plunder they've taken waiting for them in their huts, will carry wide and far. Then, having ridden with you, they may remain out of loyalty to one who has led them well and cared for them as warriors." Cean waited, anxious. So much depended on this.

"I see your meaning, healer. If I bind them to me," her eyes found his although he felt he was as far from her as the sky through the window, "then shall they follow wherever I lead though it be further than they thought to go."

"Even so."

"Good advice, healer." She called in Alieki to pass on directions to stop the outflow of laden warriors before turning back to Cean. "Continue then."

"As I say, I saw a warrior leaving with laden beasts. I saw more, for some women of the war bands carried babies or very small children. I know they take them not as slaves, but because their hearts are kind. They could not leave them in the ruins of the city. That would be certain death for these children. Yet they have taken only those they found without searching, those who have caught their eyes. Likely there are others yet, unfound or unwanted."

Boadicea smiled. "Do we not take wolf-cubs in the spring? They run with the dogs and come to hand. They hunt with us and are a part of the pack. Thus it will be with such children. What has this to do with advice?"

"Two things, Lady. Do not let the Romans guess you do this. How would it be if they stole away children of the tribes? How then would you act against them?" He saw she understood. They would assume their children had been sacrificed in the druids' bloody rites. The Romans would then double their assault, swarm the island with more soldiers, and the tribes would not be able to stand against that fury.

"This, also. Once any battle is done, if there be such babies and small children, let any of the tribes who will, take them. Search them out." His look hardened. "Let Roman babies grow up to replace the warriors of the tribes Rome slew. It is just."

She was nodding slowly. "That is wisdom. That the Romans do not know what we do is also wise. I will give orders that the city be searched. Any babes found here shall be brought to Maara. I will give her the sharing of them. Amongst the host there will be enough who desire a child in their huts that none of the children must be left behind." She held up her hand. "A moment. I will give that order as well."

Maara hurried in at the Queen's call. They spoke quietly, briefly before Maara left, almost trotting away, and the Queen returned. Sunlight had dappled the wall behind Cean's head in the short space of time he'd been with her.

"What have the gods said to you? Was it a dream?" she said flatly. As if she braced herself for bad news. "Tell me."

Cean bowed his head. "I dreamed I lay in smoke, and out of it came a great hunt. Warriors encircled many deer without antlers and pulled them down. They died and not one escaped. But from the north came a wind which swept down upon the hunters, carrying the smoke or mist away. When it was gone, in a great meadow stags stood to battle.

"The hunters returned, and fought them. Once again they won, but in the fight some stags banded together. Being the swifter of the stags, they escaped. Later, when night settled down about the meadow, and stars marched like white flowers across the skies, they returned with others and again gave battle. This time they won and the hunters bled, dying. Others fled in their turn.

"My dream changed to daylight then, and I saw a hunter who picked up sticks for a fire. One he broke in half easily. Two together he still broke, but not as easily as one alone. Three he could not break, and laid them down to take each up to break one by one in his hands." He looked at her. "You are the Queen and the warrior. Priestess too, I am told. I am only the dreamer. Will you tell me now what my dream says?"

Boadicea looked at him thoughtfully for a moment before speaking. "As to the second dream, that is easy. It tells me I should always strike my enemies before they can join together in greater force against me. That you dream it now says there must be some chance of this happening soon and that I must watch for just such a tactic." She leaned her chin on her fist as she thought, turning her eyes darkly away from him. When she spoke, her hand dropped, her voice becoming hollow, as if she were a great distance away.

"In the first dream, Camulodunum was the deer without antlers. A city without defenses. We encircled it and slew all who fought us. A wind from the north says to me that danger may come upon us now from that direction. More Romans, I think. Soldiers from their forts and cities. I must give battle cunningly, letting none escape lest they return with others in such greater strength that we cannot win against them." She stood, clasping her hands together on her spear shaft which had been at her side since she'd left the dun two days before.

"Your dreams are fair and wise, man of the Iceni. The gods did well to send you to us. I trust you will see in the stars and your dreams what is best for *our* people." Her tongue softly emphasized "our" with pride before she went on. "Go, watch over Lubran who rests not as often as he should when there are patients to tend. He is an old man and he forgets he is not a boy any longer."

Cean smiled. "I know. I will see he rests if I must drug him to sleep. Fear not. He is your kinsman but my friend." Perhaps that had been bold but Boadicea was smiling.

"Go then to seek your friend. It is good to have friends."

He nodded, wondering if as Queen she ever had real friends. From what Lubran had said, her husband hadn't been one to her, not truly.

Cean slipped away as she went to talk with her tribal leaders again in details of what must be done next. He could relax, he hoped. His warning was given, Quintus Petillius Cerealis would be marching to relieve those besieged in Camulodunum's temple. He had no way of knowing that Boadicea was warned, nor that the temple had already fallen. Those within would not be there as reinforcements when Cerealis closed with the tribes.

Nor would his cavalry escape as they had in another time and place.

Boadicea would see to that. He wondered how far towards the city she would allow the Ninth to march against them? Almost to it? Or would she find a better killing ground? He would ask Lubran. He did as soon as he re-joined him, and the old man thought for some time before replying.

"Not too close to the city, I think, lest their hearts be strengthened by anger at the sight of it." His finger tapped thoughtfully on one hand. "Nay, if she would bring them to bay where none may flee, it must be in a place where a trap can be set. Some miles to the north of the city there is a wide shallow ravine. The road runs through it. They have cut the brush back from the sides, even to the top of the slope so none may lie in ambush there."

Cean was seeing the layout as Lubran described it. "But if the ravine is wide and shallow, then warriors could fling down spears, shoot arrows from the top down at those trapped within. Even if they sit atop the hills and hold the soldiers below without food or water for as long as they could hold out, that would also defeat them. That would be warrior cunning."

Cean paused and allowed his next words to sink in. "But not if the ravine were narrow, and the battle allowed a few at a time to come at their enemies. The Roman legion would just keep coming and coming, those at the rear rested and fresh for the fight. That would be folly and great danger for those who attacked."

"Aye," Lubran murmured.

Cean hoped his comment would be remembered. As a kinsman and friend Lubran was often enough with the Queen. If she considered giving battle as she had in his time—against a soldier who trapped her into fighting that way—if Cean was elsewhere, Lubran was warned. And this old man forgot very little. In turn he would warn Boadicea of the dangers.

Cean had not given up everything he had back in his time to see the Iceni slaughtered and enslaved yet again. One way or another, if he had his way, this time they should prevail. He dreamed that night, not of the Queen but of his portrait of her, and in that she smiled on him.

Los Angeles, 2048 C.E.

"We'll have to do it soon, you know." Cean looked over at Fort. He was packing up the machines after the last tests. "They'll be coming to force us into the camps soon. You have to be here to help Mel if you can. And the others. You're not profiled, nor do you have Tensen's, so the police gangs won't be watching you so closely. But the others—they will need help. I'm sure of it."

Fort nodded. He put his arm over his friend's shoulder for a moment. "I'll help them. You're not the only one who can go back in time, you know."

The thought took Cean's breath away. Of course not. The others would do what he was doing, in the parallel worlds where their presence altered that timeline.

Two days later, the first call came. From Janet. "They've advised Andy that he has to report to the first camp tomorrow morning." She was reading then from a piece of paper. "'Be warned that you may not bring all of your possessions, and thus must take appropriate measures to secure them in your absence.' Bastards. Even if he could, Andy couldn't do that in less than a day. And his children can't go with him. They have to be cared for by someone else if they are not profiled. The notice states that 'only the profiled, and not the children of the profiled if they do not carry the same genetic markers, will be permitted in the camp.' That means Andy has to find a home for them tonight as well."

This would devastate families, ripping them apart for who knew how long? The children, too, would be unlikely to accept their parents again if the separation was for long, particularly if they learned the prejudices of their peers.

Fort turned to Cean. "It has begun. Are you ready?"

He was. As ready as he would ever be.

Iceni Homeland, 61 C.E.

Boadicea had good advisers, and to them she listened as well as to Cean. Her scouts rode far on the roads across the island. Not only to the north, but in all the other directions as well. She wanted to be sure that all of the tribes knew what was about to happen. It was from the north they brought news. Cean came running with Lubran as word spread.

"Quintus Petillius Cerealis marches." The boy who spoke grinned hardly. "They are as old sleeping hounds before a fire. I crept up in the dark, scaled a tree and listened as they camped below. One escaped from the city to tell them that the governor and many of the soldiers planned to hold the temple against us as they could not hold a city without walls. They know not that the temple is fallen and their governor's bones lie in the ruins."

"That was brave. Heard you anything more of their plans?"

The lad blushed at her words. "Nay, my lady. Save that with dawn they send out scouts."

Cean turned to Lubran, speaking softly. "Aye, scouts to see if the temple yet holds against us. If it does they will march on. If they see many tribesmen still looting the city, will they not assume all are there? That none lie in ambush elsewhere, and that they may march on in safety because of our carelessness?"

The old man gave a muffled grunt of grim amusement. "Likely, lad. Very likely. The Queen will be discussing plans now with other rulers. If you will forgive me, I will see if I can be one whose voice is also heard in that."

Cean patted his shoulder. That was exactly what he'd hoped. "Of course. Who else should she hear but a kinsman who is wise with years." And who's just heard some of my thoughts on the subject, too, he added silently. But that was fine. Because of his age and standing, Lubran was more likely to be heard by the other rulers.

Cean went back to tend his patients. With no infections, all but two had recovered sufficiently to be cared for now by kin or comrades. In the healer cloak given by Boadicea at his adoption, he was able to pass anywhere he wished. No tribesman would assault a healer or bar his way. That would offend the gods and worse still, offend the healer. A man never knew when he might need the services of one who could cure his ills.

Cean prowled the city ruins. Some of the houses remained intact even after the looting. Those he searched, explaining to any who asked that he sought out medicines, salves and bandages to be salvaged for the wounded of this or coming battles. He had a better idea of where civilized people might hide valuables as well.

The Queen could use this wealth. Not just as rewards for her warriors, but for money after the war was finished. As often as he found salves, he found also caches of gold and silver coins. Sometimes brooches, rings, and other small items of value. Some he took, the smaller, more valuable pieces which he could easily carry. For the others. He would call whoever was closest.

Alieki marveled, taking up two handfuls of mingled coinage. "You are generous above nobles, Cean."

"I have no need of it," Cean shrugged. "I am a healer. I seek medicines I can use. I have my fill of plunder, and a man may carry only so much. Let others have their share." He laughed. "In my lands, we had a story of one who was so greedy he would never leave food on the table for others. One day he was bidden to a feast. He ate so much he burst and died. Thus it is told to our children one should be wary and not be too greedy."

Alieki bellowed mirth. "Ah, Cean. That is a good story. I will remember it and tell it to my children also." He stuffed the coins into his pouch and went away still chuckling.

That night Cean shut himself away in the room he'd been given in the fort, and laid out his own plunder. Gems weighed less than gold or silver, and were worth far more. Often he pried them from massive ornaments or heavy jewelry to leave himself with a growing heap of the sparkling stones. Over the past two days, he had found many. Plunder from cities is finite. One day when there was no more left but if he had the need, he would have the wealth still to do whatever he required.

To the tribes almost everything the Romans did was bad or wrong, but some Roman customs did have their advantages. They lived in greater comfort, built good roads, could read and write, and some of their writing was quite fine. The tribes could do worse than to learn some of these things.

He put away his pouch of gemstones and slept. The next morning, a subdued bustle woke him early. He dressed to emerge yawning from his room. Lubran was talking to Dauldi at the door.

"What is happening?" Cean asked.

"Nothing for us, Cean. The scouts have returned with word of Cerealis. The Queen gathers the host. They will give battle by high sun. We must only be ready once the fighting is done and the wounded must be cared for."

"I see. Well then, I shall seek more salves."

He moved away to the stable beside the house where his pony peacefully munched fodder. He brought water in a leather bucket for the placid beast, and laid out his riding pad and bridle. Once Lubran was busy elsewhere and the army had departed, he would ride after them. He'd be more useful caring for wounded on the spot. And anyhow, he admitted to himself, he wanted to see. He'd keep out of the way, he just wanted to know how the battle went. To be sure the Queen was unhurt when the fighting ended.

He waited several hours while the war-host passed. It went in groups, bunches of laughing, chattering warriors who flourished spears, waved swords, and boasted of the Romans who would die at their bite.

They were undisciplined, he thought. But if the Queen lived and continued to win, the battles themselves would teach a growing discipline. The poorer fighters, and the foolishly reckless would die. Those who remained would have experience and also have learned caution and battle-cunning. The more great battles they survived, the harder they would be to slay or beat later.

He shared a midday meal with Lubran then pleaded a desire to see the temple's ruins. If they were cool enough in which to dig by now, there might be useful items among the debris, he told the old man.

Cean bridled and saddled the pony, tossed across the riding pad saddlebags filled with medical supplies, and mounted the animal. Riding around the bulk of the house and stable to block himself from Lubran's view, he passed the temple ruins. They must have cooled; already a number of the wounded were digging inward from the edges.

Cean had no interest in what they might find. He pulled his cloak about him and sent the pony jogging steadily towards the north. Once out of the city, he pushed the small beast into a choppy canter and hung on. After an hour he could hear the battle ahead. It sounded like surf roaring in a gale's teeth against the rocks. A long moaning roar which rose and fell. Over and over. The clash of metal against stone and wood like a woodsman's axe chopping again and again.

He reached the ridge above, and looked down. Below was the ravine's rim. Along it stood the war-host. He moved to where he could see down into the area where Quintus Petillius Cerealis stood his ground.

The eagle standard flew bravely still, but in the two or three hours since battle had been joined the Romans had suffered. Their dead lay in heaps, their wounded still standing but staggering in the concentrated heat of the ravine. But where was the Queen?

Screams and shouts grew loud at one end of the ravine and he saw her. Here the ravine flowed out, flattening up and outward into open ground. Part of the host stood their ground there against a Roman escape. Here, too, were the war-chariots. He could see her in one, a warrior driving the running horses, her arm raised. Sunlight glittered in her hair, her mantle dark, highlighting her pale face, her anger and determination burning there like a fire.

She allowed the soldiers to reach the wide part of the ravine before halting them. With the wider ground about them, she could make sweep after sweep with the chariots. The horses sprang forward. Tilutegan was driving. Leaning over the pole, his mouth open as he encouraged the small fiery ponies in their hurtling gallop. Behind him, feet planted firmly apart on the plaited rawhide floor, body balanced to the bounding leaping motion, Boadicea waited.

There was a sheaf of throwing spears in a holster within the chariot. She would cast them as she came in range. The chariot bore down on the Roman line. Then in a smooth maneuver, it turned, almost canted up on one wheel, to run along the line. The spears flew. One, two, and a third. Two men struck, one dropping immediately, his blood covering his head and shoulders in a red cloak. The chariot wheeled again and came rushing back to rejoin the host.

But after it came others. A stream of them, bringing death to the Romans' frontline soldiers. But the tribes' warriors did not rest. At the ravine's open mouth, the Queen had gathered every war chariot of the tribes. They could run endlessly, each having time to rest before their turn came again.

She held Quintus Petillius Cerealis's attention fixed on the chariots. Focused on the danger his soldiers faced. He had moved up to lead the fight against her. Behind him his soldiers died from arrows, spears, and stones cast down from the ravine's rim. Cerealis didn't notice. All his attention was on the chariots and on the wild fire-haired woman who drove them on against him.

Behind him his ranks thinned. Thinned again. And fell. Until only a few remained. But his eyes still followed the Queen. It was not until his cavalry master came to drag forcibly at his shoulder that he understood how he had been tricked.

"We have to get out, sir." Cean imagined the shouted words between them.

"We can hold!" Cerealis was wild with fury.

Cean could see the white in his rolling eyes as he shouted back at his cavalry master. A few words trickled up to Cean over a lull in the battle cries, the screams and moans of the wounded.

"For what? We're no use here, we can't reach the temple and we're losing men all the time. The foot soldiers can't keep up with the cavalry. Leave them to hold. Ride with us, sir! If some of us escape, we're free to warn the other legions! We'll teach the barbarians a lesson another day."

Cerealis nodded, his face savage. "Sound the *bucina*. The foot soldiers are to hold as long as possible. The cavalry will break out of this hell-hole." He scowled. "I don't like fleeing from savages or leaving good soldiers to die for me, but this isn't the end of it! We'll chose another day on which to beat them."

The cavalry master nodded shortly. Cean heard no more, but saw the man turn to give Cerealis, orders to the soldiers as the Roman *bucina*, the war-horn, sounded. The foot soldiers were veterans. They would stand. Even as each one fell, the ones left stepped up to hold their positions. Cerealis mounted his horse and waited. The high piercing call of the *bucina* cut though the shouts of battle. The cavalry had drawn to one side. Now, in obedience to the cry, it charged. The warriors above were falling back, splitting away in terror to allow the Romans passage: They were out, away!

Cerealis galloped across the ravine rim. From the trees where they had been hidden, the mounted warriors of the tribes closed in. Thousands, blocking the way. Behind the cavalry those warriors on foot who had seemingly fled in terror now filled in the gap they'd left. The cavalry was surrounded. Isolated from help. The tribes remembered children starving after tithes had been forced from their parents.

They remembered women raped. Free women of the tribes! The images of men dragged off to slave in Roman mines for no greater cause than that some Roman had not liked their look.

They advanced. The cavalry fought back. Horses whirled, spun and reared. Swords struck, the clash like the fury of the gods, and spears glinted in the hard, unforgiving sunlight. Blood flowed to saturate the ground. Unable to do more than turn on the spot, the cavalry could not use their greatest weapons: speed and weight. They died. Not alone by any means. But they died as the circle about them tightened. In an hour there was no rider in Roman uniform to be seen.

The Celtic warriors then broke apart, flowing back to stand along the ravine rim, looking downward to where the last of the foot soldiers fought their hopeless battle. Behind the rim a few mounts stood bearing their Roman saddles. Their riders broken and stilled. In the ravine Boadicea rose in her chariot as a rider reached her. He spoke quickly, withdrawing at her signal. She turned to the war-chariots, their drivers and fighters.

"The Roman cavalry is broken! They are slain! Only these here remain. Now is the time." Her spear swung up. "People of the tribes, follow me to victory!" The spear swept down as her chariot shot forward.

On the ravine rim watching, Cean caught his breath. It was as he'd dreamed: the woman leaning forward over the chariot edge. Sunlight blazing from the spearhead, a light like a burning flame in her hair as it flew loose behind her in the storm of her attack. He could hear her scream, high and savage like a striking hawk. A shout. The chariots rolled. A tidal wave of spears like the edge of white danger on a wave. They struck the Roman line, crumpled it, and tore on. His breath caught in his throat.

The Roman foot soldiers fragmented, broken into tiny groups of men fighting desperately to live. Then, here and there one man who fought on, briefly, only to fall. The Queen's chariot swung around to return and there was no longer any Roman in her thundering path. Her spear shot high, out of her hand and into the air, to be caught and tossed again. The collar of feathers waved in the wind of her speed. And in answer came a deep-toned roar of acclamation. Victory she had promised. Victory they had. They screamed her name as on the hill above Cean stood weeping, overcome.

He might live to be an old, old man, he thought, as the tears ran down his face. But he would never forget that last charge. Nor her victory and the tribe's acclaim. If he had ever feared what he had wrought, he would fear no more. He only wished Fort and Mel could have been here to see this. He mounted his pony, plunged down the hill and joined the shouting throng.

One more battle to win, and he could be certain history as he'd known it was changed. His cloak caught her eye and she beckoned. He thrust through to join her. Eyes blazing, she smiled at him out of a dust-smudged and weary but triumphant face.

"You dreamed well for me, healer. I shall not forget it. When the time comes, you shall have all the honor I can bestow. You shall never be forgotten."

He shook his head. "It is honor enough to see your victory." And then, from some half-remembered tale and out of the fullness of his heart. "If you must give me something, let me lie at your feet when we are both returned to the gods. Then I may dream for you yet, west of the sunset beyond the Warrior's Road."

Her hand grasped his. "That shall be. I swear it."

She whirled away in the press of the exulting tribes. Cean sat his pony alone looking after her. Then, slowly, he set his pony in motion. There were wounded to care for. That was his job as much as any dreaming. He smiled, emotionally spent.

11

"War is the tool of the gods. It is what shapes humans to the gods' wishes, and not to our own. If we must, we are forced to take that tool into our own hands, and wield it with dreadful purpose. Only then can we take the gods' will and make it ours." And so the great Queen advised her handwoman, Maara, before the war began. Even then Queen Boadicea had a goal she shared with few.

—from *The Journal of Enla*, 2nd Edition,
translated by Ericia Thromheart

But then, when the centurions finally realized that our Queen was as much a Druid as any of the priests, they knew they had to do battle with her as well as us, or nothing would save them.

From that time till now, we have preferred the goddess Brighid. She is the goddess of the smith, the goddess of the hearth, and the goddess of our thoughts. Brighid blesses our homes and our hearts. She is, after all, the most savage, the most warm, the one that requires the best from Her worshippers.

—from *The Passionate Spirit*,
by His Reverend Holiness Colm Herraster

Iceni Homeland, 61 C.E.

They celebrated that night, but Boadicea made sure the ale was watered. She remembered what the scouts had heard in Cerealis's camp: At least one from the city had escaped to ride for aid to the legion there. If one, then perhaps others. Nor did it mean because one had sought that particular legion that any others fleeing the war host had gone the same way. By now word could have gone out to several Roman commanders and encampments.

Cean made sure she knew of the house in which he and Lubran had slept. "From what I could find, Lady, they were educated, and they left hastily but not in a panic. This makes it possible they will have friends in other cities and can find refuge with those who might listen. They rode—there are signs of horses in the stable. But no mounts were left there and their gear, too, was gone."

Alieki snorted good-naturedly. "How could they have known? We rode all night; we killed every Roman between our dun and the city. No, one of the other tribes took their mounts. As they should." He sounded sullen, jealous, obviously wishing he'd taken them.

"Am I the only one who dreams?" Cean asked quietly. All eyes focused abruptly upon him.

Lubran sucked in a harsh breath before speaking. "It is possible. From the dung in the stable I believe they departed a full day and night before we came." Alieki looked down, shrugging. "But Cean forgets something. Who shall believe them if they run to others with their dreams? The Romans follow different ways. Also, the news of our victories will take time to spread, and then again for the soldiers to march. Let us strike now, hard, before any know."

There were cries of agreement at that. Alieki's booming bass over the rest. "Aye, Londinium, I have heard the roads there were paved with Roman gold."

Boadicea smiled. "A children's tale. But it is true it is a city of merchants. Moreover, many spears, many arrows have been lost already. These merchants will have war-gear with which we can re-arm ourselves. Enough weapons' stores to see every one of our warriors has all they can carry. If we continue this fight—as would be wise—the time will come when we will need such supplies more than gold. We march then for the city. Celebrate tonight, my warriors. Sacrifice and give thanks to the gods. Before the sun is high, we ride for Londinium."

So the ale was watered, others talked of the incredible plunder which would come from the city, and Cean believed those tales, too, were Boadicea's doing. They encouraged the tribes to be ready by sun up to leave the ruins of Camulodunum. The army straggled out by midday, the Iceni and Silures at their head. At Boadicea's bidding, several of the tribes had chosen to send their plunder home on a few carts, returning to their people.

"You fought well," she told them. "You were ever in the heart of the battle as I would expect of warriors such as you. Send your plunder back to the dun on the wagons, share what has been taken as rightfully yours, and here dance and drink to our victory that we may be ready tomorrow for the next."

Her voice rang like a trumpet then, "And forget not who gave you that victory. There are yet more Roman cities, more plunder to be seized for your women, for your children. More glory to be won and Romans to slay. While you are with us, you will all share in this."

One of the men stepped forward and inclined his head. "Lady, how can we know that our families will get what we send? When the carts get there, it is all one." He had already packed to leave the host.

"Is there one among your wives who might read? Send a list with the driver and wounded. There will be plenty for your wives, your daughters, and your sons to come."

Cean was amazed. They listened, nodding. She had gained that much trust already.

"Lady, we will stay and fight at your bidding," the warrior had told her. "For our people as well as yours. For us all."

"Well said. Stay with us and enjoy some of the gains we have made from this victory. The sooner we continue on with our war, the quicker we drive the Romans from our land."

The few who were taking the wines and fabrics, the bronze pots and mirrors, back to the duns departed. Many had been wounded, with broken legs or arms in slings, and were unable to fight with the rest of the warriors. Taking the plundered goods back as guards saved their pride, and they were grateful for it. As they filed away, out of the ruined city, behind them trotted laden pack ponies and carts. But the rest of the host stayed.

Cean bit off a howl of triumph. Events took shape that were further and further from those in his own history. In that time, many of Boadicea's allies had returned to their homes, their plunder all they desired, they deserted the Queen when she needed them most. Surely with this change in events, in just a few more weeks those two histories would lie so far apart that this world would have altered for good, its future with it.

Los Angeles, 2048 C.E.

Cean ignored the notice to report to the camp long enough to update his will. If all things went well, if he caught the plane before he was tagged by the police, he wouldn't be coming back. This wasn't a journey that had a return trip, and he wanted to leave things tidy. A few weeks before, he'd quietly given Mel several favorite possessions, a couple more to Janet and Max, then helped them all to put their favorite things into storage. Four of the completed portable jumpers had gone to those that would use them.

The last five years of his paid-up lease had been left to Mel along with his furniture, just in case she and Fort were released before that time was up. Her rehabilitation had cost so much more than she could afford. Not in basic medical expenses, since her insurance was paying those. Her accommodation and physiotherapy, however, went above and beyond her immediate hospital charges. She had no money left over for storage or rent while she was huddled for an indefinite time in the camp.

He'd left the balance of his money to the Coalition, with Fort as administrator. They'd use it wisely—for the good of the whole group if they could. Surely the government would give them ways to manage their affairs while they were held in the compound. Surely? And if not, they had the jumpers.

He'd also purchased open plane tickets from New York to London and return with car and hotel vouchers for Mel. He smiled. These were an outright gift. He placed them in a large envelope with his will, sealing it. She'd get those from his lawyer if he didn't return within a year. Especially if she'd been released from the camps. He hoped she'd be able to use them then, to make it to England where the prejudice was less—thus far at least.

He talked to Mel on the phone that night.

"I'll see you in a couple of weeks. Have fun." She gulped air for a moment. "I do wish I could come with you but the physical therapists won't let me. It isn't fair. I've always wanted to see England. Something always seems to happen just when I think I may." She sighed. "Another time, I guess."

Yes, Cean thought, another time. He took in a deep breath. Neither he nor Fort had told the others about their immediate plans to escape this world. Fort, however, planned to take a suitcase with the sixth time jumper in it with him to the camp. His research, he'd tell them if they searched his bags. Harmless, and non-explosive, and that much he could prove without showing the real purpose of the machine.

"Another time, I swear. You'll see England and have a ball."

He rung off. Dear Mel. Maybe, if his plans worked out and he created a new world, she'd not have Tensen's in it, nor be in a wheelchair. She'd once confided that she'd always wanted to be an archaeologist when she was younger. She still read all the archaeology magazines she could, and in the past few years, organized her holidays with Fort so they could visit sites like Rome, trekking the ancient road system built around the original city capital and into Europe's southern countries.

The night before, Cean and Fort had decided it would be best if Cean went to the airport alone. "We can't risk it. They're sure to stop us if both of us take a taxi to the airport."

It was their final goodbye. Even if Fort succeeded in getting others out, even if everyone used the jumpers, they wouldn't be jumping to the same timeline.

"Don't worry," he told Cean. "If anyone can get them out, I will." They hugged. Long and hard. The tears trickling down Cean's face he made no effort to hide. Nor did Fort. They had become close in a very short time.

"Knock 'em dead, kid." Fort thumped Cean on the shoulder as they both broke into laughter. They'd always howled when they'd heard that line in old movies. Then they hugged again, unable to say another word.

The next day, when Cean walked away from the apartment complex, he was certain the plain car parked near the gate held two police. Watching, he was sure, for him.

Iceni Homeland, 61 C.E.

The remaining men injured in the Camulodunum assault were healing. Cean was amazed all over again at their vitality. If the wound-fever or wound-sickness did not kill them, they survived and recovered from injuries which would have killed most men from his time. The rewards of a hard life, he realized. Of them two had to ride in carts still, but the others had returned to their mounts and rode proudly if shakily.

Cean thought about the Roman situation he remembered from books of his own time. With Decianus murdered, and Cerealis assassinated, someone had to rise up now to take charge of the war.

Paullinus Suetonius had gathered together the Fourteenth Legion, veterans of the Twentieth, and scoured up many of the men from nearby Roman camps. He'd had almost ten thousand soldiers when he turned to give battle—at a time and place of his own careful choosing. But Suetonius had been an experienced fighter. He'd known exactly what he was doing. Thanks to Cean, that veteran now lay dead among his own cavalry. He was not around to give battle to anyone.

Someone would rise to take his place. That had to happen. The question was not so much who would, as would he be a capable veteran like Suetonius? That question would not be answered for some time, but Cean saw another problem resolved quickly enough. He had ridden up the line to check on one of his wounded. From ahead came shouts. He rode forward, listening, until he recognized cries of greeting.

"The Regni, they are come."

"Two hundred warriors with two hands of war-chariots!"

And from an older tribesman near Cean. "They too have deaths to avenge. Yet I would have thought them too much in the pay of the Romans."

Cean managed a look at the Regni and agreed. They had a more Romanized appearance. Their dun was far to the south, on the other side of Londinium near the shore of the English Channel. In the area that was modern Kent in his original time and place. They rode by the war-host, yet apart from them. He allowed his mount to drift back to walk again by Lubran's pony as he thought.

It could be. The Romans might not know a lot of what was happening, but between the tribes and the war-host there was always coming and going. They might even have traveled around the Roman strongholds of Londinium and Verulamium. The Regni could have heard all about the victories from the Queen's messengers if they'd gone secretly, quietly.

In fact, the Regni could have decided they had better be a part of this or they would become part of something else—a losing side closely identified with the Romans. There was no middle ground in this war, no proverbial fence to sit astride. But just how honest was their joining, and how big a part of their tribe had they sent? He turned to Lubran.

"The Regni, are they many?"

"Not one of the greatest of the tribes, but they have numbers enough. Why?"

"I heard shouting as I rode ahead to see Anra where they bear him and Cradoc in the cart. I heard shouting, men saying the Regni had come to join us."

"That is well, surely?"

"They have sent two hundred riders, ten chariots. Is that so well?"

Lubran drew down his brows in thought. "Nay, it is not. They could have sent thrice or five times that number."

"We have a saying: 'to run with the hare and hunt with the hounds,'" Cean commented softly.

Lubran drew their mounts to one side. "We say 'sending brothers to mother and father.' It is possible. Nay, it could be likely. I will bespeak Boadicea when we rest tonight. Those who join us will fight honestly I believe. But if others of their people come out of the dark to sit by a fire and talk, what will they learn and to whom shall they speak of what they hear? If those who have not joined us may be doing such a thing, I would wish to know it. We have men familiar with this territory. They should range ahead, in Catuvellauni lands as well as before our line of march."

"If we continue to win battles, more of other tribes will join us. If we begin to lose, we'll see no new faces. They can claim if they are questioned that they sent a few men for fear of what the Queen would do if they did not. But they sent as few as possible and they were not conspicuous in the forefront of battle," Cean said.

Lubran's smile was slow and dangerous. "Would they say thus? That can be altered before battle is given."

He called for Cean later that evening as camp fires blazed up in a thousand places and the scent of food drifted upon the cooling air.

"I go to the Queen. Walk with me. It may be she will wish to hear your own thoughts on the Regni."

Cean stood up and walked away with the old man, passing many of the thousand fires. Warriors murmured greetings to them as they walked by. By now they were known to all.

As it happened, Cean waited patiently beyond the circle of figures around the Queen as they talked quietly. He could see Lubran, dark against the fire as he spoke, his hands flickering in quick gestures. He could see the Queen as she listened. At length Lubran came back to him.

"She is not Queen without reason. She already thought as we did. Though she thanks us both for our care, she should listen to what we feared. Yet she makes her own plans in this."

The proof of that came as they approached the city. The leaders of the tribes and war-bands were called. Boadicea stood flanked by some of them while she faced the Regni king, Cogidubnus.

"You come late to battle." Her eyes were dark, the light of her hair like flames flickering in the firelight. A spirit out of the dark framed by the light.

"We are here." He was a man younger than her, and he frowned as he spoke.

"Of a certainty, and I am sure the fault was not yours that you join us only now." Her smile and voice grew stronger. "You have had less chance to gain glory, to blood your weapons, to take back to your people proof of your valor." She lifted one hand and paused, earnest. "Therefore in this battle you shall have the place of honor. As the Silures stood with us at Camulodunum, so shall you ride even with my own, men of the Regni. You strike as soon as we do. Your war-cry shall rise up that all know you are not least among the tribes."

From where he stood Cean could see the face of the King Cogidubnus. Cean stifled a quick grimace. The man looked as if he'd wet his pants. His eyes had that stricken look of knowing he'd made a terrible mistake and hoping like hell no one would notice. Boadicea was waiting.

Cogidubnus turned to the two nobles who stood beside him, one with his mouth wide. He drew himself up and looked patronizingly about.

"We are not the least of tribes indeed. It is fitting that we are among those who lead." He was hoping to antagonize one of the others into claiming that honor instead.

"You are not the least truly," the Queen replied. "Nor would we wish to deny you your turn for glory and the blooding of spears. All of us," her hand swept out indicating the other leaders, "have each led in our turn. Now the Regni shall draw us on to victory."

The Regni king could not stop himself from staring sourly back. A few of his men murmured behind him, and with a quick chop of his hand he silenced them. "As you say, Lady."

He tramped heavy-footed away leaving the Queen and other leaders to look after him. Several had thoughtful looks on their faces, men who'd been enlightened or confirmed in their original beliefs by the discussion. Cean reached Lubran's side.

"What if they vanish before we arrive?"

"I think they will not. They ride in the thick of the host from now on. They camp tonight by our people. How can they vanish so easily without others asking very loudly where it is they would ride?"

Cean grinned. "I see." He did. He'd bet that after the coming night, the Regni would see as well, if they didn't already. They'd joined up, they were going to be in front when the battle began, and that was that. If they tried to flee now, he thought, the other tribes wouldn't hesitate in killing them all, tying the bodies upright on their mounts, and still having them first in the fight.

The march continued, if not as swiftly as Cean thought it should, then still quickly enough. Communications weren't good. The roads had dried enough to take wagons, but few traders had yet appeared. Those who did, if they were vouched for, were simply added to the war-host. Others known to be Roman puppets were killed cleanly, and their goods taken for the use of all.

Boadicea was careful to be seen sharing everything. Any of the traders' gear and beasts were given in turn around the tribes. As the war-host passed, smaller places were taken by different tribes in turn, and what plunder there was that tribe kept. Sometimes a war-band would drop away from the march to take their wounded and plunder home, but not easily. After Boadicea spoke to each publicly, most stayed with the host, unwilling to look greedy or afraid in front of the others.

Gradually, the Queen established herself as the central authority. The other leaders deferred to her once they saw her plans worked well.

Arguments among them dwindled. And the few druids left who went with the host deferred to her, listening to her counsel. She was priestess as well as Queen.

Cean talked often to Lubran, knowing that his warnings and suggestions were being passed on to Boadicea. She listened to every one, or so Lubran told him. In turn, he talked and listened amongst those who traveled as well. With his strange accent, his aura as a far-traveled man who could talk entertainingly of his travels, cloaked in his healer's mantle, Cean was a welcome visitor to many camp fires. And there he heard useful talk he shared with Lubran, who took it in turn to the Queen.

Some began to share their ideas or complaints deliberately with him, having noticed what was said to him went where it would do most good. Boadicea recognized the system and used it. There had been war-hosts in the past. Never before, though, had one been so free of strife or remained together on a march as long as this one. Even so it ended quickly enough. In another day, word came back from ahead that Londinium was in sight.

With it came word of another Roman who would lead. Decianus Cattus had died in the Iceni dun. Quintus Petillius Cerealis had been assassinated. Paulinus Suetonius had died amidst the slaughter of the Ninth's cavalry.

A new leader had arisen in the Roman legions. A man named Lientus Quintorus Falcus, not Roman by birth, but a seasoned soldier. Cean sought out one of Boadicea's lead warriors to speak with him; the man had earlier mentioned knowing the city and had relatives there.

"This Falcus, what do you know about him? What plans is he making? How is it he leads his men?"

The warrior grinned. "I had a cousin within the city who sneaked out of the gates with the darkness alongside a passing wagon. This Falcus was promoted after he'd raided some wine-merchant said to be a spy, and gave out all his stock to the soldiers. Then, when Suetonius marched with the Ninth, Falcus stayed behind. Suetonius was that glad to be rid of him as a drunk and troublemaker, that the governor left the city in Falcus's hands."

"But from whence came this Falcus?" Cean was surprised. Suetonius must have been very sure he'd defeat the Queen's warriors and then return safely to his city.

"He was with the Fourteenth they say, but he retired early. He still had friends with the Fourteenth, and it was they who raided the wine-merchant at his suggestion. My cousin thinks the man no great warrior. He's the sort who sees what is there, and thinks that must be all."

"Is he so?" Cean said slowly, assimilating that. "You mean if he sees no warriors he assumes there are none, not that they might be in hiding?"

"He's not quite so foolish as that, but aye. If there were little cover and he saw no one then, aye, he would think none were there."

Cean worked out the possibilities. "And if his enemies broke and fled because their leader was slain, he would assume they had indeed panicked. He and those under his command would chase the enemy ..." He broke off as he followed that thought where it led.

"Into places they would not otherwise run so hastily, aye," the man continued for him, but diffidently. "A good thought. Do you mind if I take the idea to the Queen, along with the report of my men and my cousin's words about Falcus?"

"How should I mind?" Cean told him blandly. "Did you not think of this yourself?"

The man grinned widely, leaving to share his information—and the idea. Cean went to check his wounded to find Lubran about the same task.

"Is there word on when we attack as yet?"

Lubran turned. "Tonight." Cean stared. "Nay, I mean the Queen will give word after darkness falls tonight. She waits to hear from all the outriders. Have you seen Alieki and Dauldi? They wish you to go hunting with them, and have sought for you, that is if you have nothing else to do."

"I must have missed them. My thanks, Lubran. If I find something tasty. I'll bring it back to our fire to share." Lubran waved him away and returned to the man he was re-bandaging.

Some time after sunset, Cean was eating well-roasted pig. Very well-roasted, despite Lubran's protests at the time it took. Cean didn't know how he'd explain trichinosis to the old man. A Roman villa had been in the war-host's way. Now it was not, nor were the inhabitants, and the stock had become roasting meat on a number of campfires.

Cean had averted his eyes from the dead. No one had asked them to come to this country, and they'd died quickly, the women as well. He forced himself to remember Roman ways with their victories. They'd been given quicker deaths with less torture than they would have given out. Boadicea had given strict orders against the rape of women. Her warriors would not do what they so despised in the Romans. And a clean death was more than many the Romans had meted out to the tribespeople they seized as slaves.

Maara appeared silently out of the darkness. "The Queen bids you come, both of you. She would share a thought with you."

Cean was on his feet, the pork forgotten. Lubran took up both shares, handing Cean's back to him. "Eat while we walk, brother. Talk fairs better when stomachs are full." He patted his own contentedly.

They had time enough to finish the meal as they negotiated their way through the sprawl of camped tribes. Twice as they approached the Queen they were challenged by Iceni. Each time they were passed as soon as they were examined. More suggestions bearing results, Cean thought. Each new idea should be making it harder for time to return to its original path.

The Queen met them on her feet, smiling. With her was the warrior Cean had spoken with earlier. Boadicea looked from one to the other. "This is Daldren, leader of the outriders. Son to Bralch of the Trinovantes and kin to me in a small degree. Daldren, this one is Cean, healer to my people and adopted son of the Iceni. A wise man and a dreamer."

Cean hid any surprise. He'd had no idea the man was that high among his tribe. With a warrior aristocracy prevailing among all the Celts, many he rode with were noble.

Daldren nodded. "A wise man indeed. A generous one also for when we thought together of an idea, he gave it to me that I might appear well in your eyes."

"He has good ideas," was all Boadicea said.

"Aye, and this one seemed good to me also. Listen, Lady." Daldren detailed what his cousin had said of Lientus Quintorus Falcus. Boadicea listened intently. "Now my men have found this man's soldiers, not far from the city's walls. There they have taken their stand and there they will remain. I think we should seek them out now and leave the city until the soldiers are beaten. The city will fight, make no mistake and we will lose men. Also war-bands will glut themselves on plunder and fall away.

"Falcus's soldiers have taken up their place in a river ravine. Nor is it like to the one in which we slew the Ninth. This one is steep-sided, narrow at the entrance and encircled by thick woods in all directions save the ravine's mouth. We cannot wait in ambush, and to attack head-on is unwise. We need to lure them forth, for before them is the wider land, and once they leave shelter we have them, more so if we have warriors waiting at either side of the ravine's mouth. Once they are out, have our men run behind the soldiers when they leave the ravine so they may not return to its shelter."

The Queen nodded. "You believe that if this Falcus thinks I am slain and my people fleeing in panic, he will attack?"

"So I think, Lady. But we must be very sure the war-host does not truly think so, else they may panic in truth."

Maara spoke. "That we can do by claiming a warning from the gods. A dead crow, say, found by the Queen's guard. Let us say that the Queen should not ride in the forefront of battle this day. That another should take her place, one who looks very much like her. Who amongst the Roman dogs knows her now? Nay, all those who might have done so are dead. They know only that her hair is red and she is tall for a woman." The woman's hands were quick as she gestured.

"Let another ride her war-chariot with Tilutegan. Let that one pretend to fall so the war-host knows it for a game to lure the Romans to their death. Then even if my lady seems to fall, they will not fear knowing it was never she who led."

"Have you some idea who could act my part? I would not have anyone take great danger in my place." The Queen stood tall and looked down at the smaller woman.

Maara nodded. "Verli." She raised her voice to call his name. When the boy stood before her she took him by the shoulders moving him so he stood next to the Queen. "See you. He is of a size and height." She was right. The boy was tall for his age, thin enough to pass for a woman.

"He has no beard as yet, and I can dye his hair so it is of similar appearance. I can add dyed fleece to make it longer as well. He is a fair enough spearman, too, and he has ridden in a war-chariot more than once. He has only to make a pass or two against them before falling to the chariot floor while Tilutegan bears him from the battle."

Verli smiled. He'd come with his father to help, but now he could be the warrior he wanted to be. At the center of it all, and in the Queen's place. He was thrilled.

Cean feared the boy would take too many risks as he played the Queen's part. He opened his mouth to ask what if the boy was killed. Then shut it again. The boy saw himself as a man and a warrior. To say any such thing would shame him immeasurably before his Queen and other warriors. But something turned cold within him. He'd saved Verli's life once. He didn't want to see that life thrown away.

As soon as the Queen gave him leave, he slipped away from the discussion and returned to his fire to sit and think. Verli would die happily if it was for his people and Queen. Even Dauldi, his father, would not deny the boy warrior right. Cean sat still, finding the fire's warmth did something to counteract the cold within him.

His mind cast back to accounts of the original rebellion. He'd saved Verli once, but in Cean's own history, the boy could or would have died more than once already. There was his wound received in the fall from his pony. If Cean hadn't changed history, the boy would have died from that. Or he might have been killed or enslaved in Decianus's assault on the Queen and her daughters. Or killed when the war-host struck at Camulodunum, or later at the ninth.

Then there was Londinium. London as it would be in another time. They could all have died there, every one of the Iceni. His friends, Lubran, Alieki. The Romans had slaughtered more than half of the Iceni adults, enslaved many and dispossessed those remaining. Here Verli was doing what any Iceni warrior would do, and Cean couldn't deny the boy that.

Cean was coming to know himself as well over the time that had passed. He'd been bitterly sick when he'd killed Jonathan Smith. Not so sick, although he'd felt ill, when he'd fought for the Queen's daughters against Decianus's soldier, and killed that man, too. Later he'd had to prove he could fight in sparring matches within the tribe. They would not have deliberately harmed a healer but Cean still had to show his courage and skill or they'd not have brought him along.

He had done well enough that they accepted him, and admired his skill with a staff. One day he would have to kill again for his life. He couldn't stand aside in every battle. Not here in this time. Sitting by the fire, he realized he could kill again if he had to. He only hoped Verli would survive the coming battle. But he could accept the boy had a part to play that was his own.

He slept uneasily, half-waking often, wrapped tight in his sheepskins. In the morning, word was sent to all the tribes. The Queen's woman had found a dead crow near where the Queen slept. A bad omen. One would take her place in the chariot. An offering to the gods, the druids murmured. It might be taken or not, but the making of it was the sacrifice. And to deceive the Romans, the Queen announced, so they might not think she feared to face them, the one who took her place should look like her. Let the willing sacrifice live or die, it was a good omen for the war-host, one that countered the dead crow.

Only the Regni king, Cogidubnus, objected. "Does the Queen stand back now and let others go ahead of her?" His words were bitter with the remembered shame he'd faced in front of his own warriors.

"I do not hold myself back," the Queen replied, equally as angry. "I will lead two tribes behind the Romans if my war-chariot bearing my double is pursued. My warriors will hunt with me then, they and the Brigantes who have come to dip their spears again in Roman blood." Her look was direct, not haughty as she continued. "I, too, will share the dangers my warriors face." The tribes about her muttered agreement so that the king was silenced.

Cean moved off with the rear-guard. He was delighted when an order came down the line. Another crow glided above the warriors, a bird that could have been a raven. Perhaps a better omen, and all looked to Cean as it passed, as if he'd bade the bird to come. He kept his eyes down.

"Hold far back. The Queen's order. Very far back and do not form a solid line."

So she'd recalled his dream. He spoke quietly here and there to acquaintances among the warriors, reinforcing the order. Daldren appeared to check, making certain there were large gaps between the islands of wagons, carts, supply-wains and battle-wagons. They'd taken a number of the huge grain wagons in the sack of Camulodunum and these had been driven away by women from the different war-bands, those suffering some injury. They were to haul London's stores of grain back to their people. The tribes would not be the ones to starve in the coming winter.

If there was any connection to his own history, Cean believed those were the wagons that had endangered the war-host then. They'd blocked Boadicea in, preventing her host from giving way before the Roman onslaught. The Romans had smashed the host back, trapping them against that solid wall of wagons, defeating her. Here they could give way at need and then return in a pincer movement to trap Roman soldiers instead. That danger was gone.

The sun reached its zenith. From ahead Cean heard the battle begin. Gods, let no one have taken word of the ruse to the enemy, he prayed under his breath. Let the tribes recall all was as planned, and not panic except in pretence. The cries grew louder. The shouts and screams as spears bit flesh. The clashing of swords and spears against armor, against shields. It seemed to last hours. All of the time he waited for the signal. It came. He heard the cry go up.

"*Aiee!* The Queen, the Queen is slain! The Queen has fallen!"

The cries broke across the sky, above the screams of the dying, louder than the shouts of pain, the clang of iron against iron and thud of wood.

Now, he thought. Now came the time of greatest danger. The world hushed, waiting. The battling warriors must not only pretend to break and run, they must also turn to fight again once the Romans were lured from their shelter. From the cries he could tell nothing. Then gradually the whole mass of warriors in the distance began to fall back in his direction.

He sat his pony, watching. This was a new trick, one never attempted before by undisciplined tribes. If it worked, it could go a long way towards convincing them that there was such a thing as "tactics." And discipline. The warriors were falling back faster. But from either side galloped war-leaders. Men they trusted. Cean heard the shouts, the yells of command. The mass of the war-host wavered, slowed and halted. He held his breath.

From far away where the mouth of the river ravine stood guard, he heard a high, piercing scream. It went up, reinforced by war-horns blowing the attack. The war-host was turning, reversing. Now they were retreating from Cean, running back into battle. Seated astride his sweating, shaggy pony he closed his eyes.

"Guard her, gods."

She could die in any battle. If she fell, all of his plans fell with her. Yet it was not for that he prayed. It was for her.

12

"The best tactic of all is that which will win." In the journals of all the great generals, from Alexander to Titus to the greatest of the Iceni queens, this saying returns over and over again throughout history. No one knows where it first began, but the sentiment cannot be faulted.

There is no rule in warfare. That is the other ultimate statement that can be made. Winning is all, and if it must be by cheating, by skullduggery, by illusion, by cruel savagery, or even by the intervention of the gods, that is the wisdom of all battles. What comes after is the realm of government, not military expertise.

—taken from the Introduction, Decius Ovantes,
Rules of Military Engagement, 12th Edition

Finding wormhole signatures is an art, as well as a science. It certainly requires an understanding of the physics. However, there must be an instinctual feeling that goes along with the necessarily logical one.

When I pinpointed the first wormhole, it was literally a stab in the dark. I targeted a spot with the locator, and tested it. There was a feeling, a timbre to the exercise as there is with great music, that immediately told me whether the point was "right" or not. While there are many wormholes that appear to lead nowhere, there are others that have a definite direction into the past or the future. It is their echo, their resonance in space that like music I sense most strongly.

—by Leogold Fortescue in his Nobel Speech address,
as quoted in *The Time Doctor: How I Undid the Universe*

Iceni Homeland, 61 C.E.

Dust billowed up from the fighting below. Here on the open ground the cover was thinner, the land had dried out faster, and the trampling feet, the chariot wheels had pounded it to dust. The battle blurred in Cean's eyes. It was an endless time of shouts, the clash of weapons, the pounding thud of horses' hooves, the shrieks of pain, of rage or loss as warriors knew they died, the swift whir of swords, like a crowd of wings, the hum of spears. Flying above everything, the dust rose in a churning fog to obscure details. Of that Cean was glad.

From out of the cloud a man staggered, his right arm hanging limp, blood trickling from a wound along his left shoulder. In his left hand he clutched a broken spear, the feather collar about the spearhead dripping red with fresh blood. Cean knew him. Cruach of the Trinovantes, a spearman and hunter. He and Alieki had become friends on the march having much in common. Cruach reeled as Cean ran to provide a supporting arm, asking as he did so. "How goes the battle?"

"Water?" Cean hastily provided a waterskin, watching as the man drank eagerly. At last he handed it back. "My thanks, healer."

"Come and sit here then, where the grass is clean. I will tend your wounds while you tell me of the battle." Cean was determined to know what was going on.

Cruach smiled wearily. "Aye, a bargain, healer." He sat painfully, laying the broken spear beside him on the grass.

"First, how you got your injuries. Who gave them?"

The spearman smiled wryly. "They were no gifts, healer. I had to fight with all I had to gain them." He moved so Cean could better reach his shoulder. "Nay, I will tell you," as Cean glared down impatiently. "For the first I think my shoulder is broken. A Roman lost grip on his sword. He snatched up a length of wood and struck me with all his strength on my shoulder, here." He touched the point where the massive muscle bulged out just below the shoulder point.

Cean was already touching it, feeling the arm carefully. The area had blackened, swelling up. Cruach winced. It had to hurt terribly, and he doubted any 21st century adult would be as glib about it as Cruach.

"I do not think it broken," Cean assured him. "The blow has bruised the muscle deeply, and so heavy was the blow that for a while the muscles are paralyzed. I shall bind it for support, but I think in a hand of days when the bruising begins to fade you will find the arm undamaged. Let me now look at the other shoulder. How did you get this cut?"

"Ah, well." Cruach started as Cean probed the wound with a wet cloth. "Since my spear-arm could no longer raise a weapon, I took up my spear in the other hand. A soldier caught me with a sword." He looked apologetic. "I am not so good with a spear in the other hand. The spear shaft broke so that I must return to the supply wagons for another one. I thought I would have the injuries bound before I returned."

Cean studied the second wound. This one was more serious. The sword had sliced deep into the upper arm. Cruach was losing blood, and the gash urgently needed cleansing and stitching. Cean began his work.

The sounds of the battle drifted past on the stray dust billowing towards them. A chariot had crashed nearby, spilling the warriors in it, one wheel catching the dirt to fling it up into the air.

"While I am at this tell me now of the battle. Was the ruse successful?" Talking would distract the man from the bite of the needle as Cean stitched. He was using a sponge found in one of the Roman houses, and fresh water from a waiting leather bucket, covered by a cloth.

Cruach began hastily. "Aye, it was, so far as it goes."

"As it goes?" Cean's query was sharp.

"Well, man, the battle is not yet done. How can I say what happens? But we were cunning, aye. Our cleverness was that of a hunted fox which flees the hound pack laying false trails as he runs." He grunted sharply, in amusement or pain. "The Queen had some lad in her place. An omen, they said. He fell, or pretended to fall, I know not which. But when he did certain men cried out the Queen had fallen, she was slain. We broke off the battle and turned as if we ran.

"At first I did not think they would believe it was so, but it was well done. Once we began to fall back, that leader of theirs was out in front, shouting at his soldiers to hunt us down. To kill us all."

Cruach groaned, followed swiftly with a wry chuckle.

"I can hear him now. 'Kill them all,' he shouted. 'Hunt them down like rats. Teach them to attack Imperial Rome.'" He rocked in Cean's grip, a bellow of laughter cut short in a quick gasp of pain. "With him out in front, the rest came streaming after him. The Queen planned well. She had half our own leaders out behind to halt us once we had retreated far enough. That they did, so we stood. Then they turned us and we came back." He grunted as the needle plunged in for another stitch.

"Would that I could have been close enough to see their Roman faces when they found we were not fleeing them after all. And that the river ravine was barred to them. Aye," as Cean's head came up from his stitches. "The Queen and her warriors came racing in behind. They had to kill a few of the rearward Romans, but they took the ravine mouth. Then we closed with the Roman leaders who chased us, and there I took my wounds. What came after I do not know."

"Could you guess?" Cean invited.

"They were surrounded. The ravine no more protecting them. The Queen ordered before the battle that any who took wounds should leave for the healers to tend. Thus they would not hamper the uninjured and the fight—the unwounded yet outnumber them by very many."

"Then you think …"

"I think the victory may be ours, healer." The man made a sign to avert ill-luck. "Let it be so, and the gods not be angry that I have spoken thus before I know it for truth."

Glancing around as he knotted the last stitch, Cean was conscious that wounded warriors, so many he couldn't take them all in, were drifting back from where the battle still thundered, masked by the boiling dust. Strange cries still hurtled through the air, the shouts and thud of iron striking wood loud and reaching even to where he sat.

"I thank you for your words, Cruach. Find another spear, then return to rest here a while. I think you shall not be needed but best to be ready. When you wish, you may drink but you shall come to me before you sleep. I have a potion I shall give to ward off wound-sickness that might come with the night chill." Cean helped the man stand.

"Be sure I shall seek you out then, healer. I have no wish to be Cruach the one-armed. Roman or not, that soldier fought well. His sword bit deep."

Cean was sure Cruach would find him. A quarter tablet should ensure any infection did not gain hold. Hopefully he wouldn't use all his stores. Treating the Iceni through the winter, and the wounded of the first battle at Camulodunum had used up many. He moved on to seek out the next injured man. Then the next.

Los Angeles, 2048 C.E.

Cean turned around in the taxi, as if glancing at a woman walking her dog on the sidewalk. The plain car quickly pulled into traffic behind them as the cab drew away from the curb. His suitcases were in the trunk, Fort's machine in the first and heaviest of them. He knew he couldn't carry the time jumper on the plane. The security machines would bleat in alarm the second they detected the workings. These days, anything remotely mechanical was examined thoroughly.

While he waited to check in, he considered what he could do. The two men were standing near the main doorway, watching. Both of them were tall men, one heavy-set with cropped blond hair, the other dark and thin. Something as simple as a change of clothes would not work, Cean knew. Their eyes followed him everywhere. And they were definitely waiting. For what? If they were going to pick him up, why didn't they just do so?

Cean decided to try the change of clothes just before he went through the Customs and Immigration. A baseball cap, a different jacket of muted blue that he had in his carry-on bag. And it worked as he scuttled past them. But only for a few moments. Without a word, they dropped into line behind him as he waited to enter Customs. But they were stopped. Cean turned to look back. The security guard was holding back the two men, preventing them from entering the area. They were arguing, the two plainclothesmen holding up badges, pushing them close to the guard's face

"We have the authority," one was thundering. "Let us through!"

The security official's voice rose above them, drifting over to where Cean stood, listening.

"That may be, gentlemen," he was telling them. "But you need specific authorization to enter this area carrying weapons. Official authorization and in writing. You'll have to go over to the main office, just down there about half way along the building, and wait for someone to write it out. Then I'll be happy to let you through."

His two colleagues, both large enough to menace the policemen, stood firmly on either side of him. Cean glanced at his watch. Twelve-ten. He almost whooped out loud. The Customs office was bound to be closed for lunch. The flight left at 1:10 so the two cops were unlikely to get to him in time. Saved by a knot of red tape! He grinned.

He caught the security guard eyeing him. Cean's jaw dropped. The man had returned his grin! He looked a little familiar, but Cean didn't know him. He was sure he didn't. But the face haunted him as he made for his flight.

At the gate, Cean abruptly realized who he was. The man—his gray hair, the way he stood with his back almost military straight—was the spitting image of Wyatt, a Coalition member. Maybe his brother, even a cousin. But certainly someone who sympathized with the profiled. One little piece of luck to send him on his way.

And on the plane, comfortably seated in first class, Cean accessed his e-mail. A short message from Fort explained the reason the officers had not had the authority to pick him up or even follow him into Customs.

"Hope you're well on your way, my friend," he began. Cean could almost hear his friend's voice. He gritted his teeth, blinking. Hard. "Things are not going well here. But the camps are on hold for a few days. Andy and a group of other lawyers contested the order in a class-action appeal. The government can't incarcerate us—and no matter how much they claim it's for our 'protection,' that's what it really is—until the courts make a ruling. Unfortunately, they have said that will come in a matter of days.

"I took Mel out of the nursing home last night. She's here with me, her physiotherapist coming once a day, the nurse at night. She's improving by leaps and bounds, and thoroughly approves of our plan. I had to tell her my plans to leave via jumper and she's with me. She's looking forward to our own little adventure, as soon as she's able. The other three machines will go to Andy then, and he'll smuggle them into the camps, if necessary, to start getting people out. It's a great idea, and all yours, my friend! Have a good trip—in both senses of the word—and give my regards to the first century!"

Cean shut down his computer. He would.

Iceni Homeland, 61 C.E.

It was dark, and still Cean worked on the wounded, a haze of weariness descending on him. There were yet some with slashed arms or shoulders, others with the stabbing cut of spear wounds. If they were deep in the torso, there was little he could do for them beyond cleansing the shallower portion of the injury and giving them herbs to strengthen their immune system. If the wounds were severe in the wrong places, many could lose an arm or a leg before the coming night was over.

And for most, Cean could not do very much to ease their pain. Some he could not give aid to at all except to make them comfortable in their passing from this world. But he could not halt until all were helped. He wasn't a warrior. This was what he knew and after all, in a way, this was his doing. He'd brought this war to its present state. Lubran found him hours later.

"Cean, brother. It is time to rest."

"There are still wounded."

"Nay, most are aided and the other tribes brought healers as well."

Helped by a strong hand under his arm, Cean stood staring about him. It was full dark. Everywhere he looked campfires blazed across the rolling land. A host of twinkling flames which ran one into another as he stared. He staggered, his knees buckling so that he sat hastily.

"You're sure, Lubran? The wounded are tended?"

"I swear. Now, come to my fire and eat. When did you last eat or drink, brother?"

"Why? With you at sun-high." Cean realized his tongue was like sand, his skin dried like brittle paper. He realized, too, that some time ago, the sounds of battle had died away, leaving only the moans of those too close to death to care who heard them.

"It is now near moon-high. Come!" He led Cean to a fire around which lounged several of the Iceni. "Food for the healer. He has worked too long and is weary."

Alieki handed over meat and bread. So he, too, had survived the battle, Cean thought absently as he ate. He was ravenous. He accepted an ale-skin and drank cautiously. Good, it was watered. He sank further down onto a sheepskin laid upon the ground and relaxed. Then he bolted upright as memory reminded him why he was here. The battle! He'd almost forgotten it in caring for the injured.

"Who won?" He cast the question anxiously at those by the fire. There was a flickering of laughter around the circle. It grew into a gale which was taken up as other warriors from adjacent fires asked what was the joke, and passed it on in turn.

Alieki wiped tears of mirth from his eyes. "Aye, you are a healer indeed, Cean. Who else would remember to ask that of us so long after the fighting is done? Would we sit here around a fire eating and drinking at our ease if we were the losers? Nay, the victory was ours. More, too, not a soldier of the Romans lived. We slew until our weapons were weary and our fingers couldn't keep their grip for the blood running over them. But tonight the field is ours and death is the Roman portion. The women glean the field for weapons. In a day we strike for Londinium."

He saw other questions in Cean's face and sobered. "The Queen lives and is unhurt. Verli was injured a little but Lubran tended him and says it is not serious."

"It is not." Lubran struck in. "A scratch and bruises. Dauldi is unhurt as well. Indeed we were fortunate. Though our people chose the place of honor, to stand in the ravine's mouth so the soldiers could not break back and away, yet our warriors took few wounds they will not survive."

"How many died, Lubran?"

The old man sighed. "War brings deaths, Cean. Eighteen Iceni died this day. Two who should not have been with the war-host."

"Who?" He heard the answer incredulously. "Iessan and Ancha?" The Queen's daughter and cousin, he thought. How had that happened? "What were they doing there? They were children!"

"Aye, children of the Iceni." Lubran's eyes found the fire, stinging with either smoke or tears. "They were with the Queen last night, as you know. It seems they stole weapons, found themselves helmets for disguise and went with the Trinovantes to hold the ravine once the Romans were drawn out. None amongst the Trivovantes knew who they were, save that they were Iceni." He lowered his head to glare out under his brows. He'd known them both all their lives.

"They had danced the weapons'-dances with the women's side. I suppose they believed that since they were fine dancers, they could fight in a true battle. But war is not a dance. I am told they fought well, very valiantly. Both slew their man before they died in turn."

"The Queen knows?" Cean wanted to go, to speak with her although it wasn't his place.

"She knows. She is alone save for Maara and her grief. Cean, no one is to blame. In battle any who come to the field may die. They knew this as well as any, yet they would have a part in it. Ancha was angered that the Queen forbade her. She was fifteen. Other women of the tribes have fought at need by then. Iessan was too young under the laws to fight, yet she remembered Decianus and what he would have done. I think she wished to make a strike once for herself." He threw a twig into the fire and watched dying sparks dance upon the air.

"Did she?" Cean's tone was bitter enough to curl his mouth.

"I have said it. The Trinovantes had with them a war-band from their women's side. The girls stood with these. The women have sworn to the Queen both had blood for their going. Nor did the men who slew them live past another heart-beat. The girls died well, Cean, and swiftly."

"Can I see them?" Lubran looked up at him, considering for a moment.

"Nay, their bodies lie with the Queen in her wagon. Speak not to her of this, brother. She grieves and I fear her temper is short. Wait, and it may be she will send for you before too long has passed."

He turned back to the fire, and sorrow. Cean, too, grieved as he lay in his sheepskins that night. For the bright happy face of the girl who in another time and place had been one of his ancestors. In this world, centuries away from now, he would not be born, or if so he would not be quite the same, perhaps. He grieved for Iessan who'd been quiet, thoughtful, who might have made a good queen to the people in time had she come to rule after her mother.

His sorrow, too, was for Boadicea. Two of her blood were dead. Essault's marriage had been put off with the war but after London they might take time to celebrate it. Either way, she, too, was lost to the tribe and the throne. He had come to know Boadicea over the near two years of his time with the Iceni. She would grieve for the kin she had loved. She would grieve twice as hard moreover for the loss of the royal line. He slept, still wondering what she would do now. He discovered that in a day.

Rumor ran about the war-host as they ate by their fires. The nearby city was half deserted. Falcus had stripped it of soldiers with which to make his futile stand outside the crumbling city defenses. Since then many of the population had fled—empty-handed. How had that happened?

Well, said those who knew, the Queen had taken guards from some of the tribes. They had been set about the city upon the roads. When people began to flee, the guards let them pass, but without taking anything with them that each could not carry in their two hands. They may have been able to carry jewels and coins away with them, but no weapons and little food. The coins and jewels would quickly make their way back into the hands of those who had food to spare, such as the Iceni.

The war-host laughed in admiration. The Queen was cunning as a fox, and wise. Who wished to slaughter old women and babies? They'd gone, but their goods and war gear remained.

"What of those who remain in the city?" Cean queried. "They stay. They will fight, I think."

"Let them," Alieki answered him. "We ride tomorrow once it is light. In an hour we shall be at the gates."

* * * *

It was so. Cean straddling his pony was in the rear, the Iceni out front, but where he could still see them. His gaze swept the city walls. Considering their history and the number who had dared attack in the past, the poor earthworks about this town were barely a defense system at all. In places, even the wooden barriers set up as temporary walls had never been replaced when they'd fallen into disrepair.

Had the Romans believed they were so mighty they'd never face war here? Were they that arrogant? Yes, Cean thought, they were. But here they were far from Rome, far from the lands that had relied on them, and less aware of their weaknesses.

Boadicea rode out to the forefront of the host. Her arm swept down, the spear in her fingers pointed at the city. In the sudden silence she shouted a word, taken up by the war-host. Then they flung themselves forward. In a surging wave they rolled over the city, poured in their thousands through the streets, flung like wave spume through doorways, and courtyards. And as they ran they shouted the word she had used, over and over so loudly the sense of it was drowned by the thunder of their cries.

Those they met were cut down. In no more than hours, Londinium fell and the Iceni, the Brigantes of the north, the Silures of the west, the Catuvellauni and the Coritani from the midlands, the Atrebates and even Regni of the south, walked beside the Trinovantes and the Iceni through Londinium's streets. And they weren't taking prisoners of any who were left. Adults, men and women, were put to the sword as Roman allies. Babies and small children were taken away, many to be adopted out to the tribes. Most of the buildings around the marketplace were burning, and what was left of the Roman fortifications were being torn down. Londinium was taken.

Cean cantered his pony down a wide street. He was looking for a specific type of building, a merchant's shop which should hold medicines for sale. He dismounted, broke in the door latch, discovered he was right, and began to load the cart Lubran drove up to the doorway.

"That was well done, to find this place. We'll have need of these."

"So I thought. Let others find what they will. These will buy lives which is more than their coins will buy them."

Lubran smiled. "You have little regard for wealth, brother."

"So long as I have a roof which holds out the rain and the cold, food and drink to fill my belly, a fire to warm me and a bed to sleep in, what do I need with more? Though I am not so careless as you think, I have some small wealth I may use if the harvests are bad, or buy me medicines at need." He finished loading and grinned up at his friend. "Let us seek out another of these places. We can hunt medicines in the rich areas just as well as the poor."

He led the way. Archaeological sources said they were common: herbalists and apothecaries followed armies since there their services would eventually be needed.

"Be wary, all may not have fled," Lubran called from behind.

"Rich men? They'd have been first to run."

"Maybe, but their servants or guards may have remained."

It was unlikely. Rich people would have taken their servants to carry their gear, and keep their guards about them as protection. Yet it never harmed one to be cautious. Cean entered the next house with sword in hand, eyes darting about him. It was a luxurious villa, hastily abandoned with much remaining. He hunted through it, locating salves and herbs to add to the cart's load.

There, too, by a doorway, he found a small basket in the shape of a box lying upside-down on the floor. He scooped it up investigating the tangle of contents. From that he drew out a band made to fit over a woman's hair, and stared at it. The work was pearls on gold wire, with rubies set in the second, lower band. His gaze caught a glint of color by the bed. The warriors taking the city had passed this house, or run through it quickly. Cean stooped and found he had a second of the small crowns, this one of amethysts on gold wire, inset with jet ovals along the lower band. He thrust both into a cloth tossed flat on the bedding, adding to that the rest of the box's scattered contents, two armbands, earrings, and a ring.

From another room Lubran came smiling. "Look, this goes well." He held out a pot of honey. "Nor is it the only one. I think whoever owned this place liked the sweet."

"Why? How many are there?"

"Come and see." Lubran turned and walked back through the doorway.

Cean followed him to an open kitchen and gasped at the loaded shelves. He counted quickly. Gods, the owner must have been half bear. There were more than a dozen of the big pots, each sealed with wax for long keeping. A treasure in these sugar-hungry times. He would save the honey for their friends amongst the Iceni. He helped Lubran carry it all to the cart, added his cloth full of jewels, and then several of the fine blankets, and a huge beautifully sewn, fur-lined bed cover.

As they emerged carrying the final load, a war-band streamed by. They stopped, several of them waving spears at Cean and Lubran before one of them recognized the two healers. They ran on then, yelling the word Boadicea had shouted to begin the attack. Cean listened. It sounded like "boot-latch." He grinned to himself. He really couldn't see everyone roaring about the city yelling warnings at everyone else to make sure their boots were done up. It had to be a word he hadn't learned from his teachers. Some sort of slang perhaps. Lubran was tucking the blankets around the pots of honey.

"Lubran, what is that they're yelling? 'Boot-latch?'"

Startled, the old man looked up and smiled. "Nay, it is not what you said, Cean. They cry *buidealaich*."

That made things no clearer. "What does it mean? Why did the Queen shout it, and why do they keep yelling it?"

Lubran pondered, understanding Cean was asking more than the literal meaning. "It means a curse, Cean. A curse upon those we fight, but it can mean more. We learned it from the far north and here the meaning has changed somewhat." He paused finding the right words.

"Here it means that now Iessan and Ancha are dead, we accept no one's surrender. There shall be no mercy."

Nor was there. That day and the next until the city was reduced to blackened rubble, Cean stayed away with Lubran. They took their cart and medicines, set up a camp well out of the city and treated the injured from the battle. Lubran took the lesser wounded, and returned to the city hunting for further salves several times. But Cean refused to go back. He could guess what he might see there now and had no wish to look upon such things.

On the second morning after the battle they gave Iessan's and Ancha's bodies to the gods. Cean attended briefly beforehand. He found a red-eyed Maara dressing the bodies. Mutely, he held out the jewelry he had found, then the magnificent fur bed-cover. Maara accepted them.

"They shall be beautiful for the Mother. They shall sleep soft upon this also." He nodded, tears stinging his eyes. "They died well, Cean.

Do not grieve. They go as warriors. Nor do they go alone. They have an honor-guard to lie at their feet." Maara offered.

"Doesn't bring them back," he mumbled.

"Nothing can do that. Yet we must die, all of us. Better to go clean and die well so that you are remembered. Will you forget them?"

"Not because of their deaths. I will remember them for their lives."

"Even so." He felt her eyes on him as he departed.

But the funeral for the two girls was held that night, attended by all the warriors able to stand, and not on guard. The two young women were laid out on a single bier with oil-soaked wood piled around them. In solemn grandeur the Queen spoke briefly of these the tribe's loved ones, before touching the flame of a torch to start a fire.

"It isn't just for these two that we mourn. We grieve also for all of those who've fallen. Our daughters are our spirit, the wealth of our tribe. With their passing, I grieve for the losses, the lives they would have brought into our dun."

Cean watched her, the smoke of the fires still smoldering in the city, a darkness rising behind her, the sky's dusk rapidly turning into a dark cowl falling to meet the smoke.

"For my people," she began again, "for the lives of all those who've gone today. Let all believe they died with meaning, for the life that is in us all, and the life many will find in the sunset lands where we sit and speak with the goddess of Imbolc, Brighid, who brings us life, and meet Lugh where he will bring us purity, bring us renewal. For the life!" And saying that, she brought the torch down to light the fire under the bier.

As the smoke rose above the flames of the two girls, their skin blackened before the flames mercifully overwhelmed them, hiding them from Cean's eyes. But the warriors stood silent, watching, their eyes grim, their grief turning to rage. None left the pyre until there were just ashes upon the stones.

* * * *

In the days that followed, though, any prisoner caught within what was left of the city met no mercy from any of the tribes. Some women were found and executed before the warrior host, their breasts slashed off first before they were given the merciful strike that beheaded them. A few men were sliced apart, their bowels dangling out of their distended stomachs before they, too, were beheaded. Boadicea, grief-dazed and angry, at first did not care. But when she saw a group of warriors about to do so again, she stopped them.

"We are *not* Romans. We will not do as they have done."

She ordered that any who did so would be treated as a Roman. After the first tribesman was executed, none dared the viciousness of what had gone before. And many became proud of that, proud of the Queen's wisdom and justice.

Cean busied himself with his wounded, falling into his sheepskins each night so exhausted he slept without waking no matter what the sounds. Soon he saw messengers beginning to come and go once again. The war-host moved, gathering itself to march on the return north. They moved slowly; there was no haste. Not now. There was talk around his fire each night of other battles. Of Roman camps overrun. Some tribes had held back, because of the great distance, or because they had not heard what was occurring; if they had, they had been unable to reach the war-host in time.

Now, though, they burned to share in the glory. Some made certain of doing so, attacking isolated Roman camps and outposts. Sometimes they won, other times the fight was more even and the victory cost more than it gained. Tribe by tribe, the whole of the land was rising.

On the way to Verulamium, the Queen remained in her wagon. She saw messengers, spoke to rulers of the tribes, but not since the battle half a moon gone had she called for Cean to attend her. Lubran went sometimes but not her adopted tribesman. It was not surprising. She had no need of his dreams now, and he had no dreams to give her. Not any more. The Romans had virtually been driven out of the land.

The dreams had been lies he thought, lying in his sheepskins one night three quarters of the way back on the road to Iceni territory. All lies. He'd told her what would happen, been able to warn her only because of what he knew. But his history was failing him. Too much had changed from the original events. From now on he was guessing. She'd believed him because the dreams he'd told her had happened. If he guessed now and was wrong, how long would it be before he was ignored?

He was valuable as a healer, as an apprentice of sorts to Lubran. The tribe liked him well enough. The druids maybe not so much. But he had friends, a roof over his head, a trade and no one would thrust him out. But he'd been right in something he'd hoped far back, more than two years ago. The victors had matured. The warriors had learned that to fight Romans effectively, they must use the invaders' own tactics, combine and fight together. They'd done so. Boadicea, too, hot-tempered, hot-headed and impulsive, had learned patience and a growing statesmanship. And the brutality of her war, the savage vengeance she'd wrought in his world, had been tempered by his aid.

He was almost asleep when shouting roused him. He groaned. It was always something in the war-host. Anything from a quarrel to news.

Alieki had gone to listen. He came racing back, eyes wide in the firelight.

"The Romans. They're attacking!"

"What?" The question was sounded in many voices.

"Messengers have come from the Dobuni. They've sighted Roman ships approaching the coast. Listen!" They held silence. In the distance they could hear the war-horns beginning to call. "We march for Glevum instead."

The ancient Gloucester, Cean thought, and why were the Romans coming there? He was to find out.

13

Britain was never likely to welcome the Roman invaders. Even if they'd come well-armed and well-equipped, they would still have been defeated: First by the weather, and then by the strength of anger in Britain's peoples.

The first of these was of course Queen Boadicea herself (*Tacitus*, tr. by Alessandrea Bethenes, Vol. 34). Paullinus Suetonius saw a madwoman, a savage, a religious zealot possessed with a cruel faith. He was the first to make that mistake. But not the last. Each Roman who tried to conquer the island's wild people found that there was a strength in them that could not be subdued. The Romans found, too, an unexpected strategy in her decisions, as well as a land united by her fierce determination. She spoke for their outrage, their passion for self-determination.

—from *Upon the Shores of the Past*,
by Tringanta Delliant

Iceni Homeland, 61 C.E.

The war-host was energized by the news. Though the tribes' warriors were still undisciplined, they were learning. Nor did any lack the desire to fight. With a net of outriders flung out before them, the host rolled up the roads towards Glevum. The Catuvelauni granted passage eagerly, acting as forerunners who knew every inch of the land. The Silures, too, wanted to give as much aid to the war-host as they could. Glevum was between the Dobuni and the Silures' lands. Thus more news of the Roman approach came in as they marched. Lubran had been with the Queen and could tell Cean more.

"The messengers say there are many ships."

"How many? Could they say?"

"Six at least, they believe. It could be there are others which have sailed more slowly, so the fisherman tell. It is late summer. There may have been storms further out on the waters. Six arrived three days gone and have anchored well off the beach."

Cean considered that and shook his head slowly. "Nay, I think what you see is what is there, Lubran. If you wished to take back a territory you have lost, would you attack with half your force when you could wait a little and have the rest of it? If no ships have come in the last three days and they move now to the shore, then I think it likely that is their true number." Cean tied up his sheepskins to carry in the cart with his other gear.

"They are crazed!" Lubran said angrily. "Do they think they will take back all our lands with such small numbers?"

"I doubt it. Remember, brother, news travels slowly sometimes. Do you think they know yet that so many of their soldiers are food for the crows?" Lubran was shaking his head. "I think they know little and of a surety they have not heard of our battle before we sacked Londinium. They come as reinforcements, having heard only of the Queen's first uprising. They think to land in a place where they are not expected. Then to march cross-country taking our war-host unawares."

After a moment's thought, Lubran agreed. "A hope which shall prove vain. Cean, you think clearly as always. I go to bespeak Boadicea." He was shaking his head as he spoke and turned.

"Go. But ask her also this," Cean continued. "Where would you rather come in to land if you were an invader? On a beach where there seem to be only fisherfolk who stand amazed, or on a beach filled with angry tribesmen well-armed and ready to resist that landing?" Lubran nodded and left. He understood *that* very well.

The pace of the war-host steadied and slowed the next day. Boadicea had listened to the advice, improving upon it with ideas of her own. Cean heard nothing of her plans but did not notice, having his own thoughts.

His advice had been to send envoys to the tribes outside of Britain, like Gaul. Some had waited generations to strike back at the southerners who'd conquered their people. Now would be an excellent time for them to do so. The Romans had entered a war which could bring the uprising to their very own gates. Not all had prospered under Rome's rule, and many suffered with the injustice of their laws.

Six ships. From the description, they were the big-bellied transport type. All packed, he was sure, with soldiers. A thousand men, half as many again if they had brought few mounts and packed the men in very tightly. That might be a sufficient number to encourage Rome's enemies into attacking if they knew. Somehow, he thought they'd know.

The big question was when would the other news get to Rome. They'd made the rolling land before the ravine a killing-ground. Few soldiers had escaped. But amongst those who'd fled Londinium, there'd been clerks, minor nobles, and undoubtedly a few who'd make it their business to get word to Rome.

The cavalry of the Ninth was gone. Wiped out along with Paullinus Suetonius. The Fourteenth Legion, too, was no more. The veterans of the Twentieth had died, along with the auxiliaries from a number of other legions and stations. They'd never found the body of Lientus Quintorus Falcus. Rumor in the host was that he'd torn off his badges of rank, dropped his insignia, and fled the city as a common soldier.

A few of these had escaped the carnage, slipping past the tribes' warriors in the confusion. Not that anyone cared. Falcus hadn't been the sort of opponent his enemies minded surviving. His ways had been easily understood, and quite easily tricked. The war-host hoped he would resurface and lead another army. He would add to the odds against a Roman victory.

Cean's mind returned to this new invasion. If the war-host surrounded the invaders and wiped them out before they'd encroached further into the land, there would be few troops left alive in the whole country now to oppose Boadicea. If the Romans were foolish enough to want to take back the land, they would have to send a great—and very noticeable—army.

His smile showed teeth. The moment they did that, their enemies would attack them eagerly. The Queen had sent envoys to some of the tribes north of Rome's forts in Europe. Her message would certainly give them pause. Just so long as there were no traitors within the tribal ranks, Rome had no idea of how serious the uprising had become. But the tribes knew. They would know as well when a good time was to strike.

He hoped with all his heart they succeeded here. If they did, Britain was safe for the winter. And perhaps for the future. Once the Roman leaders learned of their losses, it would be too late in the year to send another fleet of ships. The autumn storms would be well begun.

The war-host was halted for camp an hour's swift pace before the beach near Glevum. They would wait here until the ships came in to land and troops began to disembark. There the Romans would be vulnerable: too late to return entirely to their ships, and not yet prepared to fight on land. Once that landing began, Boadicea's war host would run to be ready. A smaller group would move up, archers in place to fire the ships, outriders and healers following on their heels, including Lubran and Cean. No fires were lit while they waited. In the cold and the quiet, Cean fell asleep, waiting.

England, 2048 C.E.

Cean waited anxiously in his seat until the plane taxied to a standstill. He fidgeted with his carry-on bag, twisting it this way and that in his hands. What was in it, and in the suitcase in the cargo hold, was his future. He'd prepared everything he could think of to take with him, the small things that would keep him alive and valued. If Fort's time jumper was damaged, all would be lost.

"It'll be fine," he tried to tell himself. "It's well-packed and I can test it before I actually use it." Cean couldn't help himself. Everything he'd worked for depended on this.

At Customs, Cean knew he'd be unable to appear casual, that the guards were certain to inspect his baggage. The items there, though, would pass muster. Cean checked through on the automated system without a hitch, but they stopped him to look at his pack.

"Some sort of metal you've got in there, sir," one said. He smiled. But Cean was unable to do so in return. Frowning, the man dug down into the pack, taking out a small heavy bag. The man held out the coins in his palm, the light glinting off the burnished surface.

"Odd," he pointed out. "Not exactly what I could buy a cuppa with, is it?" He turned it over in his hand, examining the engraved head there.

Cean had an explanation ready. "It's a copy of an old coin. Like Roman, only a bit older."

The official passed it over to his partner with a snort. "We've got plenty of those here, mate. You didn't have to bring anymore." He was joking, of course. Most of those were in museums.

Cean went on. "I'm joining a dig down in the south. I wanted to do some research on the coins before I got there."

Many coins had been dug out of the ruined Roman forts and cities, along with coins cast by the ancient Celtic tribes. The movement of coins was the most reliable way to record the transactions of the times. Not many of their other belongings had survived the long centuries since.

The guards wished him luck as he tucked the coin back in with the others and Cean hurried off. At the hotel, Cean took out Boadicea's picture. He slid the print from an envelope and stared down at the furiously proud face. It was an artist's rendition of the great Iceni Queen, based in part on the Roman description, and although he knew it probably wasn't true to life, it had come to represent everything Cean believed her to be: the stubborn determined chin; the blazing red hair an aureole about the head and shoulders. He looked and something within him turned over.

Could he convince her? Would she listen and believe?

He'd change Boadicea's defeat and death, the Romans' public rape of her daughters. The nearly complete genocide of the Iceni tribe, the slavery of most of its surviving men, and the forced resettlement of what was left of her people. This time—*his time!*—the Iceni would win, sweep triumphant over their enemies, and grind the ranks of Rome into the dust.

Iceni Homeland, 61 C.E.

Cruach and Alieki woke him. "Cean?" Alieki said quietly, "Are you ready?"

He groaned, looking up blearily. "What time is it?"

"First light. The best. Be ready. The outriders believe the Romans will beach their ships tomorrow morning. The Queen has been searching for those who speak the Roman tongue to be near the shore among the fishers that remain."

Cean jerked upright. "What is planned?"

"Ask Lubran, he was with the Queen last night. For us," Cruach said quietly, "we go to join the host. Tonight is our turn to lead. This battle is likely to be long and hard. Here we win or die. Be safe, Cean." He smiled cheerfully. "If we see you not again in this life, be sure we shall see you west of the sunset on the Warrior's Road." They trotted off together, barely a whisper sounding in the brush as they sped off, spears at the ready.

Lubran was stirring a pot over the fire. It smelled of wound-salve, a clean astringent scent which cleared Cean's head. He moved to give some aid.

"Have you pots ready for that?"

"Over there. Hold them in a cloth. They will heat once the salve fills them." Cean knew. He'd been doing this for some days now, but Lubran needed to say something. The old man was worried.

For some time they worked in silence. Cean gathered himself to ask. "The battle? How is it planned?"

"There is no great secret, Cean. The Queen held back the host an hour away from the beach. The Romans sent soldiers into Glevum to search for signs of uprising, but they saw nothing. The fishermen plagued the ships, offering fish and begging for small items. They pretend to know nothing of the uprising, little of our Queen and her war-host. They act as friends, saying the Queen is a madwoman and no ally of the Silures." Lubran looked over at Cean, quietly.

"All has appeared so normal that the Roman commander has decided to risk a landing. He was overheard bespeaking his officers with commands to be ready."

"And when he lands?"

"There are archers with fire arrows. Once the Romans are at battle, the archers shall set fire to the ships." His gaze met Cean's, unrelenting. "The Queen has spoken. They have come to take our land. Land they shall have—but only enough for their graves. None shall escape. Not one Roman shall return to tell the news. We will have the winter months to rest and grow strong again. To talk in council. The Romans will come again in spring perhaps, but by then we shall be ready once more."

"To hold the beaches?"

"Even so. Thus she has said. That once they are driven forth, never shall they take our lands again. This she has sworn to the other tribes."

"What did they say to that?" Cean shivered with the cold. He was very tired.

"They have struck hands."

Cean allowed a long sigh to escape his lips. She had carried the day with the tribes. They finally understood the war was not one battle only, with its victory feast to follow. It was a true war and must be continued until the enemy ceased to fight. Roman excesses had taught them a savage lesson. If nothing further went wrong, next year Britain would be free forever.

A young man came trotting up, emerging out of the half-light like a sudden ghost. Cean caught him by the shoulder. "Verli, I am happy to see you. You are well?"

"Very well, healer. I am here with the Queen's orders. She says the time is now. You and Lubran must set your camp where I shall lead you. Other healers shall join you there once the war-host moves."

"What about Roman outriders?"

"They've drawn back to the ships. Besides, where I take you they are unlikely to come."

Cean was packed and the cart was ready. Lubran had said they would move earlier than the host. "Lead on then, warrior. We follow." The boy led them proudly along thin tracks.

"A Silures spearman showed me the way." Cean studied the landscape as they passed, and thought only someone who knew the land could have done that.

They wound through scrub and uplands. Then down towards the shore. Cean smelled the salt water on the air, heard the splash of cold waves. The ponies cantered where they could, and where they couldn't, they walked briskly for long periods of time. They emerged at the lower slope of a cliff that leaped upwards behind and above their heads. There they made a cold camp, caring for the ponies and giving them fodder from a stack of hay they'd brought along. The small beasts would eat contentedly there, then drowse. It was late afternoon.

Cean smiled at Lubran. "Rest, brother. I will stand guard a while. An old man needs more time to rest, and I have sat at ease enough on this hard wagon."

Lubran lay down on a sheepskin, nodding his thanks.

Later, Cean looked up at a sky that was growing light. He'd drowsed a little himself, even though he should have kept watch. Full dawn. Now was the time.

"There's water heated. Would you drink?" asked Lubran softly.

Cean glanced at his friend, then stooped to the fire that shouldn't have been lit. Fortunately, Lubran had made it of very dry wood. No smoke rose to the sky. Lubran smiled as Cean pretended not to have checked on what he'd done. He was an old man, but he knew what he was doing.

"I'll put it out shortly. But we will need hot water soon."

Cean didn't answer. He didn't like to think of the reason for that need.

"Both of us have rested," Lubran added firmly. "I can serve myself well enough. Why do you not go up upon the sea cliff? It is first light, and the attack may already have begun. From there you can watch the battle. Do not show on the skyline unless battle is fairly under way, but after that it will not matter. Lead the pony. You can then reach me swiftly when the wounded need us. I'll join you shortly."

"I will." He should be able to see much of what would happen below very clearly. Unlike the plains battle, there'd be no dust. He was leading the pony up the bluff in minutes. Just below the brow of the sea-cliff he halted the small beast, tethered it and crawled on his belly to look over the edge.

Dawn gleamed on a quiet, peaceful scene. Over the water he could hear barked orders, see the dark silhouettes of the ships. They were about to beach the flat-bottomed boats. The sea was calm with barely a ripple beyond the gentle wash of the waves on the beach.

"How many soldiers do you think, healer?" His whole body leaped in one convulsive shudder as his head jolted around. He could see who it was in the dawn light even if he had not known the voice.

"Boadicea! Lady? What do you here without escort?"

"The same as you, I think." Her tone was dry as it often was. "I wait to count the enemy and see what they do. Here … I brought barley-spirit against the chill."

He accepted the leather flask and drank, gasping at the harsh bite and the fumes surging up into his sinuses.

She reached over to take the flask from his fingers. "Tell me, Cean." As she spoke she was listening to the activity below. "If we beat back the Romans and they leave us be, should we fear your people? I have seen evidence of your learning. Lubran tells me your knowledge is very great. You have told me you come from a far land." She paused, looking down at the water before turning that direct gaze upon him. "When you return, could your people see us in turn as those who might serve them?"

Her eyes stabbed into his. "Are your people like the Romans, healer?"

Cean was so startled, he floundered a moment, unable to find words. Then, "No! I tell you, Lady. My people have no interest in the lands of others. The journey between our duns is very far. Farther than I could explain." His face and voice, both were desperately earnest with the determination to make her believe.

"We worship freedom. Our rulers say each person has their own voice, their own rights. We make no one a slave. Moreover they are happy in their own lands. To them no other place would be as fair. I swear to you, Lady, they would never come to take from you what is yours. What you take here, you hold. You and yours after you."

She waited, still looking closely into his eyes. He was aware again of the depth in her, the unfathomable thinking of a ruler about to take back by force what is her people's. Dawn flickered in her hair. He drank again from the offered flask. A long pull as the spirit burned downwards, warming him.

"Mine and those of my line to come." She finally said and turned from him. Her voice was soft, half musing. "Yet who shall come after me? Essault weds once this battle today is done. So long as we be the victors," she added. "Iessan and Ancha are gone west of the sunset. I have none to follow and I'm old enough that I'm unlikely to breed more."

Conscious only of the need to comfort, Cean spoke and continued to speak without thinking, the barley-spirit loosening his tongue and emotions. Perhaps that was what she'd intended. Dimly, he could hear drifting up from the sea, commands to close with the beach and prepare. Adrenaline surged with the battle nearing.

"You are yet young enough, and no man could be unmoved by your beauty," he told her.

"I have no great looks, healer. I am too tall and ..."

He broke in angrily. "You are *beautiful*, I tell you. Like a sword's blade. Clean and shining. A sword all men long to possess, to hold, to know the balance in their hands." The barley-spirit was working in him. He felt light, lifted into involuntary prophesy. What spoke—his knowledge of the future? Or the gods he was coming to believe in? He didn't even pause to wonder.

"You gather the tribes into your hands as a driver gathers the reins of chariot ponies. You shall harness them and the land shall prosper. In the name of the gods you shall rule the tribes. Nor shall any woman again be counted less because she is woman." He drank again. Above him the sky was paling with daylight. With whatever was reaching him. "You shall rule, and men shall remember you for a hundred generations."

Her voice was very quiet, so as not to break the spell. "What shall they say?"

His mind was flying, his words winged messengers to bear his hopes and dreams, the obsessions of so many years in them.

"That you were beautiful, that you ruled for many years. That you lived to be very old and were beloved of all who knew you …"

"And you, Cean. Do you love me?" She didn't turn to him. Her eyes rested again on the water below. In the brightening gleam of daylight, his gaze met hers.

"I have loved you all of my days," he said simply, honestly. This was not something he could hide, even if he'd wished to.

"Then love me now!"

At another time and place he would have hesitated, unsure of the moment. But here in the half dawn, she was the only woman he had truly loved, and he had loved her for too long. He moved to touch her, and her own arms went out fiercely about him. This was the gods' messenger. Voice of her goddess. If there could be a child to follow her, to become a new royal daughter of the Iceni, then surely it could be his. And Cean, as he reached for her remembered that the hormone treatment had been only preliminary and it left him able yet, he could pleasure himself, now he pleased her, his heart, his obsession.

Cean had seldom lain with lovers over the years. He had never felt himself sexually attractive. And recently his changing body left him more self-conscious than ever. But now on this cliff top, immediately before a battle, lying beside the woman he had dreamed of for so long, all his fears and doubts were gone. Perhaps blurred by barley-spirit, by his long fascination with this woman, and the adrenaline generated by the coming battle, his self-consciousness vanished.

He loved this woman in his arms as he had never loved before.

He came of an age where making love was a skill, even an art. A way to share all that people were. In turn, she brought a fierce, more savage vitality to the act. An involvement so total that when Boadicea climaxed, her soft shout was one of victory and fulfillment, his own groan of release blending into her last joyful shuddering.

She lay back in his arms. There was little time left. The battle was about to start. But a second love-making would ensure her desire. And there must be a child. They held each other silently, Cean reveling in the closeness.

This could only happen once. She could not openly take as lover someone adopted into the tribe, someone not even of the royal lines of another tribe. Yet he would never forget the hours of this day, the sky slowly paling above them as daylight grew. The warmth of her against his body, and after an hour or two of lying quietly, his growing urgency again as her hands strayed.

This time the act was slower, more paced. They had little time to linger, to touch and caress, but they did so anyway. Her hands sought his breasts.

"I have never loved one of your kind before, yet it is good. Like making love to one who is sister as well as lover."

He hugged her to him, hands stroking down her flanks, savoring the lean muscles, enjoying the feeling of equality. This was no soft woman but a warrior.

"The goddess be thanked I can be both for you." Well, the gods and modern medicine, his mind added.

"Do not fear, I shall thank her in due time, as shall you." Cean watched as her own thoughts drifted into places where he could never follow.

The last vestige of night's darkness was gone. The sky had paled to blue entirely, like the watered blue of winter morning. It would be a bright clear day of sunshine.

Cean heard a graunching sound from the beach. The ships' keels biting into the shore. The two rolled over to watch. The soldiers were disembarking in an orderly fashion, officers running about shouting faintly heard orders. A thousand men, he would estimate, and horses. Good ponies of fine breeding. A cavalry wing at least, all blindfolded as they were led down the gangways.

The Queen hissed in admiration. "Fine beasts. They will improve our stock."

"Very well," Cean returned absently as he looked out, shading his eyes with one hand.

Boadicea slid backwards from the cliff-top, reaching up to touch his hand. "I go. If I survive this day, maybe we shall lie together again." She saw the blaze of joy in his eyes, the worship. "Nay, do not look at me so. It is not a likely thing, just a possibility. Remember I am Queen. The things I must do as queen, I would not wish to do as a woman. And some of the things I would do as a woman, I cannot do as queen."

"I know." He tried to keep the regret out of his voice.

She was gone down the hill as he looked after her. He understood her warning. If she held to her word, they could never be more than the most occasional of secret lovers.

Yet that did not matter. He would never forget, and if this morning was all, it would be sufficient. He lay on his back recalling the sweetness of what they had done. As he remembered, the sounds from below on the beach increased. They became the shouts of attack and warning, then the clash of arms. The bucina screamed orders.

Below in the sand, the soldiers maneuvered clumsily. Well instructed beforehand, the tribes charged, only to halt at the line where soft dry sand gave way to harder land. Fire arrows arced to fall behind the Romans. Ships caught fire, dry wood in a brisk breeze.

Again the *bucina* commanded as officers called orders to their men.

One in every five of the soldiers holding against that line of warriors raced seawards to put out the fires.

The tribes pressed harder. The Romans could not advance. The fire arrows flew like flocks of fire-winged gulls. The Romans could not retreat. Caught between sea and land, between fire and sword, they fought as they'd been trained to do. Unprepared, under their sandals the soft sand shifted, throwing a man here and there from his balance, and always a warrior was ready. Several fell.

The tribesmen pushed ahead. The soldiers were ankle deep in the water, their Roman footwear slipping on the shingle beneath the bloody waves. More fell, and the horses were released to run as they would. The day wore on as the larger battle dwindled into many smaller fights.

Cean had gone to the back of the lines with Lubran where they set up their salves, their needles, and bandages to staunch the life-giving blood, prevent it from streaming forth. He healed where he could, bracing the broken bones and sewing shut the wounds that gouged between ribs, striking at the men's lives. He gave out the potion men had begun to swear was from the gods, the medicine that stopped the wound-sickness from setting into the flesh.

Boadicea's orders had been the same as those for the fight on the open land at Londinium: any with wounds which slowed them must retire to the healers. The able-bodied were to fight on to earn glory. A good decision, and one Cean was sure gave her warriors hope.

Increasingly, the battle-weary Romans faced fresh unwounded fighters. They could take a toll, killing as many as they could, but the Romans could not win. Behind them their transports had burned to the waterline. They were trapped, at bay with no escape unless they swam away in the cold water.

Desperate, they fought on still. They were the elite of two legions, veterans who'd held against too many enemies to count. They would not break and run. Over them the eagle lifted. Their officers still shouted orders, the *bucinas* reinforcing the commands. But against overwhelming odds even the best fighters cannot stand forever. One by one they died. The gaps in the line filled with those behind until at last there were no more to step forward.

Cean had returned to his cliff-top. Lubran had bid him rest a while and the young healer was anxious to see how the battle went. His eyes flickered over the ranks below. The entire Roman contingent all fought, even the sailors from the ships, the legion cooks, the grooms from the horse-lines. They had no choice, not facing the enormous force of Britain's combined tribes, not when confronted with the fury that drove the war-host at them regardless of casualties. The Roman line held yet, one man deep, fifty or so long, as it followed the curve of beach. Every one of them bled, and as Cean knew, they'd taken a fair toll for their wounds.

The tribe shouted, the deep savage cry of her name catching his attention as Boadicea's war-chariot rolled to the beach edge. She turned on the chariot floor, looking out across the open stretch of beach to face the enemy.

"Would I could give you mercy, for you are good warriors. But I am sworn. You come as invaders. You sought to seize our land, and so on this land you must die. I say to you your burial will be honorable. What do you say, officers of Rome? How shall we send your spirit? To your gods or ours?"

She gave him a choice, to be buried as the Roman gods required, or even though dead, sacrificed to hers. The man she was facing was short and thickset, with black hair, dark eyes, and strong bandy legs. He was middle-aged with a face weathered by years of soldiering under hot suns. There was no fear in his eyes, only bitter determination.

"How shall we send your soul to Hades, woman? Have you no man to speak for you?"

"Nay, and that is the difference between us. I am queen. I need no man to give me voice. Yet should the goddess and gods give you victory, you shall send my soul west with sword in hand." Their gazes held and clashed like spears. "What gives wings to your spirit, soldier of Rome?"

"Fire. If you win, burn us all and may the gods rain that fire on you in turn."

She inclined her head. "According to your word." She stepped from the chariot. Faced her people. "In my own name I rule, in my own name I slay. Let none say I had no true part in this."

Her sword spun loose from the sheath which she tossed away as the Iceni screamed her name. Cean cried out, helplessly, on the cliff. He knew the meaning of her gesture. She would take the field now against the Roman, not retreating until the battle was won or she was dead. It was foolish policy, but even in death she would win. None who saw would ever forget she'd risked all she had. But, oh gods, what if she died?

He crouched in the short salt-grass, shivering, unable to take his eyes from her advance.

The Iceni gave a war-cry, their warriors leaping to stand beside her. The Romans moved up, the scene dissolving into whirling battling figures. His gaze stayed on her. Twice a blow staggered her. Each time she gathered herself and returned to fight. He could see her hair, bound into a club at the base of her neck. Still glinting like fire in shafts of sunlight.

She surged forward against the man who had denied her. Her sword struck his shield while his sliced air. Again she raised her weapon. A strong woman with work-hardened arms. She swung it again. The Roman dodged the downward gleam of her blade. Again she wielded her sword, and again the Roman eluded her. Battle spun in clumps around her then, her warriors hitting out at the Romans still alive on the shore. In the dance of shifting figures, Cean could not see how it happened. But the Roman fell.

All down the Roman line they were falling. Then there were only tribespeople standing, the Queen in their center. He heard the shouts for her, over and over as they pressed in to touch her hair, her rent and bloody clothing, the unsheathed sword-blade stained red. She lifted it and her voice rang like a war-horn.

"Rome is gone from our lands. The gods give victory!"

Cean raced down to join them, shouting with joy, slapping the backs of all he met in his triumph. And when he found Lubran, he hugged the old man, lifting him off of his feet to swing him about in the crowd.

They'd done it! *He'd* done it! History here would never go back to what it once was!

When the cheering subsided, the Queen's voice rang out: "A promise I made to the last leader of these men. It shall be kept."

Still flushed with victory, they raced to obey, stacking wood dragged from the camp, from the land beyond the beach. They raised there a great long pyre, laying the soldiers upon it in rows, stacking more wood about them. Some of the oil they'd seized from the Londinium houses was poured out over the wood and bodies. The horses were led carefully away before the torches came near. They were too fine to suffer the injury that might occur if they panicked when the fire blazed up.

Atop the pyre, in the center, they placed the man who'd defied the Queen. Tears welled in Cean's eyes. The Queen honored a valiant enemy. As the healer honored her for that gesture. The flanking Romans lay limp in death. None of them had lived.

Boadicea brought the first torch, laying it against the wood. The fire caught, racing down the line, consuming the wood and then those who lay there. The wind lifted the oily smoke, the charnel-house smell, taking them away as if it swirled seawards with their departing souls.

Before the wild flames Boadicea raised her arms, chanting. A prayer of thanks to the gods who gave victory, a prayer and a promise she would keep—but not quite yet. She must be sure before she kept her oath.

14

Boadicea was surprised when the druids objected to some of her choices. This may be what first turned her against them. But there was also a darker reason for the hatred she developed of the druid priests and their ways, something that struck much closer to her heart.

—from *The Journal of Carigwen*, 2nd Edition,
translated by Ericia Thromheart

Iceni Homeland, 61 C.E.

The majority of Rome's military forces in Britain were killed with Cerealis in the great battle before the sacking of Londinium, and in the subsequent entrapment of the reinforcements from Rome. The whole country had taken up arms against the legions. Fire and sword protected the land from the southern invaders. Warriors streamed in to join the war-host, to lay sword and spear at the victorious Queen's feet. Boadicea had united them all. And her will drove them on.

The people regarded the deaths of Iessan and Ancha as sacrifice, their names whispered from dun to dun. The war-host marched on and where they trod, the last of the Roman settlements burned, their villas razed until there were none left to stand against the tribes.

Of all the tribes, the Catuvelauni had suffered the most. Their king was determined to be at the forefront of any battle, regardless of the danger. He'd demanded this honor, and the Queen had bowed to his wishes.

It had been statesmanship, nothing more. Of the tribes, the Catuvelauni were one of the largest, most belligerent towards others, and the most disliked by the others. She let him take the position he demanded for his people. Yet she made certain the other tribes saw that she bowed to his request. Then she made sure the Catuvelauni king and his warriors were ever in the front line, in the most dangerous positions.

When they were slain in battle, or were wounded without hope of recovering, she grieved for them. But the Catuvelauni who, wounded, returned to their dun were far fewer than those who had ridden to join the war-host. Most stayed with the host to die in battle. Ever anxious for glory and power, their king had stripped his lands of its warriors.

The Trinovantes flowed back to regain a fair portion of their own lands again. Now stronger in numbers than their old enemies, and with one of their princes wed to the Queen's daughter, a balance was struck, each as no greater than the other. The agreement would hold both in check.

In Britain, so far as Romans and their works were concerned, the cities and fields were a wasteland. A few Romans remained. Those re- tired soldiers who'd been given land, and consequently wed into tribes, and who had cared honorably for those who worked for them, were untouched. Here and there a farm survived where some darker Roman faces could still be seen. It had paid to be a decent man in the days of fire and the iron sword-hand of the Queen.

Apart from these, only a few Romanized merchants remained. They'd been honest, given fair trade and not cheated the tribes. And for that they had found friends to speak for them. The rebellion had stripped Rome from the island. Temples to the foreign gods had been pulled down, the stones used for buildings, for roads, the last of the druids virtually dancing upon their ruin.

Of the Romanized Britains, many had been killed, some had cast off their togas and returned to the tribes. Those who could afford to had found a ship to take them, their families, what portable wealth they could carry, and fled to Rome. Not that this was necessarily a safer place, as Cean knew from his previous reading, but all this he faithfully chronicled on discs that were tucked away with the computer.

On the edge of winter, some moons after the fall of Londinium and the massacre of Rome's reinforcements, Cean stood at the royal dun. The Iceni had circled about the land, and then returned to their own ter- ritory.

"What do you think, Cean? Will Rome send more soldiers?"

Cean sat with Lubran in his hut stoking Lubran's new small stove. The old man adored the innovation, his joints becoming less painful than they had been for many a cold season. Cean remembered that soon he should tell the old healer of willow bark for pain, and for its use against the inflammation of joints and tendons, although he wouldn't use those exact words.

"We'll know for sure when spring comes, but Rome has its own troubles."

Lubran chuckled. "Oh, indeed. The peoples held under the Roman thumbs have not been so happy as slaves, not as the Romans wished to believe. With the loss of so many soldiers here, they see a chance coming when they may throw off the yoke of Rome."

"Aye. If Rome sends more soldiers in spring, her enemies will know of it. I think the mighty cannot afford to spread themselves thin again so soon. Not now, not yet." His tone on the last four words was meaningful, sobering the older man.

Lubran nodded. "So says the Queen as well. She reminds the tribes that we hold our land only as long as we can fight. We have weakened Rome even as they weakened the Silures by their slaughter. But the Silures yet hold their own lands. In another generation, Rome may grow strong once again."

"Even so, and in another two generations, once they have taken more soldiers from other people for Rome's use, they may think it time to land here once more, and think to re-take the land as their own."

"Aye. For that the Queen warns that if we are not the guards of all our lands, who shall guard them for us? The tribes listen to her."

They did that, Cean mused. He'd feared the alliance would fall apart once Rome was driven from the lands. Boadicea had already seen how that could happen, and was working hard to prevent it.

Surprisingly, she was succeeding. In a loose, unofficial way, she was queen of them all. The other tribes' rulers had acquired the habit of consulting her throughout the rebellion, and continued doing so. Some of the tribes even had representatives lodged near the gates of her dun now, and she spoke of building a larger dun that would house all of the tribes' delegates. She spoke good sense always, and had become an efficient mediator between squabbling peoples.

The fear of Rome's return helped as well. That thought had been driven deep into the tribes' collective minds these days. Every tribe had their tales of atrocities, their memories of loved ones dead at Rome's hands. To prevent more abuses, the tribes would co-operate with each other as they'd not done when Rome first came. They'd learned that indifference to each other's plight was what had defeated them before. They would not see it occur again. Not when the price paid was so small a thing as an acknowledged queen.

Perhaps Queen of all the tribes, Cean mused, hoping.

Lubran broke into his thoughts. "We celebrate winter's end in two nights."

"It will be a time to celebrate. At least we'll have a season or two free of the Romans and their tithes."

"Free of the Romans. The tithes remain."

Cean straightened. "What?"

"Did you not hear? A council of rulers decided the roads the Romans left behind were not so bad. The rulers agreed to keep the roads in each tribe's land, repairing them as need arises. The Queen said it would be foolish to throw away good ideas. More cunning to throw out those who gave them and keep the idea in their stead. So the tithes remain, but smaller ones."

Cean started chuckling. It grew into great whooping gales of laughter until he was half bent over, holding his stomach with tears trickling down his face. Lubran was caught up in it, laughing himself until both were exhausted by the merriment.

"Boadicea!" Cean said between gasps for breath. "By the gods, that woman learns fast."

Lubran frowned a little in puzzlement, tugging at his beard. "She is no fool, Cean. She would not rule us elsewise."

Cean agreed. That hadn't been precisely what he was thinking, but he could not explain that to the old man. Not here. Not now. He thought back to the history of his time. There the Queen had been portrayed as both a deeply wronged woman, but also as hot-headed, savage, impulsive, and ignorant of statesmanship. How very wrong history could be.

The Boadicea he'd come to know was hot-headed and impulsive, yes, but willing to be advised. She might have been initially ignorant in the ways of uniting a country, which had always been many small tribes, but she'd swiftly learned effective ways of persuading the diverse peoples to do so. The advantages had been obvious to her. Immediately obvious.

As for his history's claims of her savagery, he felt perhaps there he could accept some of the credit for the change. The woman of his history had been flogged, her young daughters raped before her. In that history the girls had vanished after that. Cean had always wondered if what had been done to them had killed both because they were too young physically to survive violent sexual intercourse, or if they'd chosen suicide, unable to live after the degradation of the public assault.

Then Boadicea might well have become a madwoman in her grief.

To the tribes, under certain circumstances vengeance was almost a holy rite. Well might she have been a savage after what she'd seen and what had been done to her and her people. Since Cean had come back, what had happened in truth had here only been a threat. He'd saved Essault. Iessan and Ancha had died, but in a manner the Queen could accept. Her grief had been honest and deep. But in the months since she'd lost them, she'd made peace with that loss. Essault had wed and was gone. That, too, was acceptable. She lived, and her life went on.

Two years had passed since he'd come here. In that time he'd found his heart. He was Iceni. He spoke as they did now, he'd begun to understand their belief in the gods, and sometimes he wondered if the gods had even first put the idea to come here into his head. Who was he to say for sure? Perhaps the gods did exist, and it was he and his like, back in his original time, who were the fools not to believe.

"Will you ride with us, Cean?" Lubran asked him.

"Of course. Whenever I can."

It would be pleasant to ride out in the crisp air and see the horse herds. Watch the half-grown foals playing, woolly with the start of their winter coats, and—he bit back a smile—to watch the Queen as she rode ahead, lithe on her playful mount, sitting as if molded into the warm back while her beast cantered on ahead.

Actually, he had watched her often, whenever she was about the dun, saying nothing but remembering that short time of passion on the sea-cliff. He made no spectacle of himself and would have been astonished to learn two were aware of it besides himself and the Queen: Lubran, and Maara. They, too, said nothing. As Lubran knew, each had his—or her—own thoughts and talk was not required. The time for action would come when the wheel of seasons turned.

"You need a clean robe, Cean."

"What?" Cean was startled out of his reverie.

"For the celebration." Lubran eyed him. "It is time for Imbolc, the time to honor Brighid above the other gods."

Back in his own hut, Cean found a clean robe waiting upon his bed for him. It was dark green, with a paler green embroidery about the sleeves. The weaving was fine and the cloth soft. He donned it with appreciation. It could only have come from Boadicea. Dare he hope it meant something? He had not forgotten her words before the battle, and hope lingered. He was to be included in the druid celebration; that was something at least.

Not many of the druid priests remained alive. That morning two had ridden into the dun to meet with the Queen. One of them Cean remembered. He was the messenger who'd first come to tell them officially of Mona's fall to the Romans. Odessan was his name. He and his companion were to be at the sanctuary when Imbolc was officially celebrated. Each Iceni family, however, would celebrate the goddess in their own huts beside the hearth fire.

Brighid was the goddess of renewal, of purity, and her symbol was the swan. The wheel of seasons was turning upon the land. Winter was ending. The fall harvest gatherings had been good, and now the tribe looked to the coming year. In the sacred grove Boadicea and the priests would celebrate the changing of the year, the lengthening of days, the continuance of life.

They did so with the Queen first amongst them to make the offering to the fire, Lubran after her, chanting the ancient songs softly, yet with a passion ringing in his voice as he asked that the people be safe in the blessings of the gods. In their hands, the priests held small amphora of lamp oil to be blessed by Brighid. These would be taken back to the dun, and returned to the families who'd asked for the goddess's blessing. They'd celebrate Imbolc the next night with the blessed oil burning in the lamps.

But the afternoon beforehand there had been a meeting with Odessan. The Queen asked Cean to join them. Odessan's dark hair was long, and hung about his face in loose tangles; he had a thin mouth and it looked as if he scowled more often than he smiled. Cean discovered that the priest planned to restore Mona to what it had once been. The people were hopeful he would succeed. It would mean the beginning of a new peaceful time, a fruitful time for the tribes to recover what had been lost.

"This is the dreamer?" Odessan asked as he'd once asked before.

Boadicea nodded. "At Lubran's side, Cean is healer to the Iceni as I have already said. Sometimes also he dreams as the gods wish him to. Those dreams he has shared with us and they have indeed been the wisdom of those who dwell in other realms."

Odessan eyed him carefully, looking from him to the Queen. "Have you dreamed further?"

"No," Cean said quietly, "the dreams come when the gods wish to tell us what needs to be known. Not else."

When Cean left later, Odessan glared after him, a jealous stare that did not bode well. Cean was teaching Ancha's younger half-sister, Anla, to read and write, and the druid objected every time he saw them bent over a lesson. Committing knowledge to writing was against the druid way. It was sacrilege, and memory instead was the way of the gods. But the girl learned well and swiftly. Cean thought no more of Odessan's squawks.

England, 2048 C.E.

Cean wondered what to have for his last night in the 21st century. Chocolate milk? He wouldn't have chocolate in the 1st century. That much was certain. England just didn't have the right soil or temperatures to grow it. He hadn't been fussy about coffee, so that wasn't a problem, but he would miss a good cup of tea.

At the hotel, he stopped into the pub to have a small glass of Champagne to celebrate his leaving. The inn's small bar was smoky from the low fire in the hearth. There were few lights, and the other guests were hunched shadows grouped around the bar. A couple sat at a table, un-iced gin and tonics before them. The barmaid's laugh rang out as a customer flirted with her. Cean liked it. There was no loud music, no sports blaring on a TV, just quiet conversation among people who obviously knew each other well.

He walked up to the bar. The barman leaned toward him, asking, "What'll you have, sir?"

"Grimmer's Ale."

Brewed locally, it was as good as the Guiness he'd once had in L.A. The Iceni drank ale, and some wine the merchants brought in from Europe, but they'd not have ale as good as this. He eyed the thin layer of foam with delight. It wasn't the alcohol content he liked. It was the rare taste of the brew itself. He took one shallow sip, getting as much on his tongue as he could without filling his mouth. He let it sit there for a moment, savoring it, before he swallowed. He almost said, "Ah!" out loud, but noticed the barman watching, amused.

Cean grinned. "Nothing like it!" He ducked his head as they both chuckled. When he had been deeply into his research on how things were made, he had looked up brewing, but he doubted he'd find a way in 59 A.D. to make an ale quite as good as this. This would be worth the effort. He'd be the best eye doctor the Iceni had ever encountered, and make the best damn ale to boot. They'd love him.

He looked around the bar. No one he recognized. Although the man at the end of the bar didn't look local. He was glowering over a glass of something that looked like whiskey, and he wasn't wearing rough farm clothes. He had on a clean, sharply ironed shirt, and a sports jacket laid over the bar in front of him. All expensive clothing, more expensive than the average tourist's.

"Looks like a professor, doesn't he?" Cean pointed him out to the barman who was lingering nearby.

"That he does. And American, too."

But Cean didn't walk over. Somehow he thought, he'd rather not get into a discussion with someone he wouldn't see again. But the stranger had seen his look. He picked up his jacket, his drink, and walked his way.

"You don't look much like a farmer," he told Cean as he drew closer. "Tourist? I'll warn you: there's not much to see around here." He sipped at his drink, then held it up. "Not much in the way of a good drink, either. Just the usual, I'm sorry to say."

"Oh?" Cean was surprised. "I've found the food and drink here quite decent."

"I'm used to something a little more 'up market,' as they say here. Where are you from, by the way? You sound as American as I do."

Cean didn't like the smile that spread across his face. There was something calculated about it, a twist of the lips over abnormally white teeth. Very predatory. Cean introduced himself and told the man they were both from Los Angeles. Cean's stomach knotted up, a bad feeling sinking into his middle as he waited for the stranger to say his name.

"Jonathan Smith. I'm here to do a little research on the Iceni duns. That's if, of course, I find any. Haven't had any luck so far, at least not any substantial luck, if you know what I mean."

He glanced down into his drink before taking another sip, calculating even that. Cean believed the man measured everything, including those he met.

Cean didn't turn a hair. "No, I've heard that there's not much to be found. I'm interested in all the Iceni stories. I hoped to pick up an artifact or two, just as a souvenir, but no luck there." Cean dreaded the turn of the conversation. He didn't want anyone else hanging about when he was trying to make the jump.

"Well, I might have had a spare old coin to sell you, if I'd been more successful. And I might have been at that. But the people here aren't helpful." He chose to ignore the level glance the barkeep threw up at him. "They seemed to send me to all the wrong places, and any information was misleading as well. As if no one knows where the old duns are buried!"

Cean could barely hide his grin and quickly sucked on his ale. His grandmother has been a countrywoman before she and her husband moved to Los Angeles, and he'd heard of country ways from her. But Smith's eyes were closely watching him, along with everything else.

"Think it's funny , do you?"

"It's … ah … part of country technique," Cean stammered quickly. "If they know what you're about and don't like it, they turn a blind eye. Then nothing comes easy if they don't want it to." He was failing to deter Smith and he knew it.

"What makes you think they don't like what I'm doing?" Smith said, his voice raised belligerently.

Cean lowered his glass, his humor entirely gone. "Only because they're not fully co-operating with you. That's all. In farm country, if they like you, you'll find ten cooperative hands, all getting into your business. Which doesn't seem to be the problem in your case. My advice is to just let it alone."

"Well, I don't need your advice."

Smith abruptly swallowed the last of his drink and turned, walking away. He did glance back once, taking a careful look at the younger man before he strode through the door. It slammed hard behind him. Cean couldn't help noticing the barkeep watching from under his brows.

"A problem?" he asked.

The barman finished rinsing the glass he had in his hand. "If that one treated us less like what he finds under his boot heels, he might get some help. If he needs it, that is. That kind usually doesn't, no matter what they say. He's just looking for what he can get which is little or nowt here." He shook his head and walked away to see to another customer.

But that night Cean saw Smith again before he left his time.

Iceni Homeland, 62 C.E.

Casting off any ill feeling the druid priest directed his way, Cean looked forward to the coming celebration. He wore his new robe proudly to the ceremony, watching Boadicea make the offering at the fire's side, admiring Lubran's voice as the old man sang. Once the official offerings were made, the people scattered from the sacred place, leaving to make their own offerings in pairs. Nor were those gifts to the gods to be despised for the goddess loved the coming together of male and female.

Then Cean, returning to a hut warmed with the fireplace's heat, heard a scratching at the door-hide. The sound one outside makes when they wish no other to hear it. He pulled aside the hide. She slipped past him smelling of the wind and the bracken, her hair a tumble of russet fire, brushing his arms as she passed. He had no words as he turned, nor were any needed. Later they lay in the box-bed, warm enough with the heat they had shared to allow the covers to slide back. Cean leaned back against one elbow, looking down, filling his eyes with the sight of her.

"Is it right for you to be here?"

She laughed up at him. "On this night I am priestess to the goddess. Whatever I do is right, and this most of all." But Cean wasn't sure she meant it. Her voice spoke as if she thought of something else.

"You said on the cliff before the battle, perhaps you would come to me again. Can you say so a second time?"

"Ask that of me next mid-winter."

His hands stroked down her flanks. "Nay, am I stud to the mare only four times each year?" He said it jokingly, but he could not hide the seriousness behind the words.

She gazed up, her eyes firmly holding his. "I may not wed again. If I take a man of another tribe, then I fail in my authority over those tribes where I have not wed. If I take a lover from amongst my own tribe, the same will be true among my nobles. Here in my own place I could take a man openly to my hearth, but still my people would fear his influence if he were not of the royal blood."

What she said was true. That he had to admit. There was no way she could take husband or lover from another tribe and keep her authority among the tribes. She would automatically be allied with whichever tribe her husband came from. And he would have a say over her people that now she couldn't allow. If she took a man from amongst the Iceni, they, too, would fear she would listen to him, forsaking the advice of her councilors.

A queen who was above other rulers must not appear to be other than neutral. The other tribes accepted she was Iceni. The allegiance of other tribes, though, might falter if she emphasized it with an open alliance—however irregular—from even among her people.

He sighed. "We have tonight. Maybe mid-summer or next mid-winter. I can live on that, though it be little food for my heart."

Her arms went up lazily to pull him down. "Then I shall see to it that for tonight at least you do not starve."

He did not. She was gone before first light but he lay far into the morning. Body sated, mind relaxed, reluctant to leave the sheepskins still smelling faintly of her scent.

He was startled by a scraping at his door lacings. The hide lifted, and half asleep he was sure he saw Odessan look briefly in. But if he did, it was only a flickering glance that was quickly gone. No more than the quick guttering of a candle's flame.

After that winter crept still across the land. It snowed, the horses came in from the far horse-runs and a messenger appeared bringing news that Essault would bear a child to her Trinovantes husband in the summer. Cean was near when the news was given.

"That is well, very well." The Queen was gracious, sending gifts and loving words. Cean caught her eye and she smiled at him. Something strange showing in her expression like the sudden glance of a bird's wing. "Say to my daughter with spring I shall choose from amongst the best of the new foals for a mount for the child. It shall be broken and trained by the time the child is old enough to ride."

Cean grinned quietly to himself. Only an Iceni would consider a baby of two old enough to ride, let alone on a still youthfully crazy two-year-old mount.

"Take to her now these small gifts with my love. Say to her she is ever in my heart and with summer's ending it may be I shall ride to the lands of her man to see for myself the child she has borne."

Why late summer? Cean wondered. Perhaps she was anticipating possible Roman invasion or some tribal problems. She wouldn't want to say she'd be there and be late. Better to name the latest possible time and arrive early.

* * * *

Winter wore on. But the chill was easier this year. Outside it was as cold as ever but many of the houses and huts were warmer. After the battles, the Iceni smith had all the iron he required—and a new apprentice. The small stoves were beginning to appear not only in Iceni homes, but also amongst the Trinovantes. Other tribes, feeling the warmth and seeing the stoves when they visited, were clamoring to learn the making of them and the fireplaces that warmed the larger huts and provided hot water.

Cean lay in his bed a last few minutes on the morning before Beltain. Boadicea had come silently through the dark the night before to tell him this year the celebration would be special. He should dress in his finest, come to her hut at dusk to eat and drink with her. He hoped that meant they would share more than a meal, but he would not assume too much in case he was wrong. Still his heart raced.

He rose at last to bathe, using water heated on the stove's top. He stretched as he ladled warm water over himself and into the large basin about his feet. At length he dried himself, tossed the used water outside, and put away the basin. He dressed slowly. His good robe, and his best cloak. He would take the foal-skin given him by Siharni. He could sit on that and enjoy the soft suppleness and the feel of the sleek hide beneath him.

The day slipped by as he worked a little but more often sat, remembering. He'd come as a stranger, obsessed by hopes that he could change history. And he had, leaving behind everything familiar, and welcoming all that was unusual in this land and its people. And Enla had taken to reading and writing as a duck to water, moreover the knowledge was spreading. He had watched the child bent over her work earlier that day and wondered, could it be that in this world, *she* was his ancestor?

He had made a difference to their lives. And altered the shape of their history. There was no doubt of that. Thinking of them, he was certain no amount of elasticity in time's passing could over-ride them or snap this world back to its original path.

It had to be a different world now, a world where Tensen's might not develop. And if it did—if Boadicea had prevailed and druidism spread down through history—perhaps it would not seem so dreadful to the people of future centuries. He'd succeeded. He would pray to the gods of this world tonight, especially the goddess Brighid, that wherever his friends were now—Mel and Fort, and the other friends of that time— that they had made new worlds of their own and had no more to fear.

He wrapped his cloak about him before stepping outside. The cloak, too, had been Boadicea's gift. He loved the soft rabbit fur lining. Pulling the hood over his head, the foal-skin over one arm, he trotted lightly down the path towards her hut. Within, Maara met him.

"She keeps the spring feast tonight, but you and Lubran are not her only guests."

His face lit with happiness in spite of the disappointment they would not be alone, and he nodded. She smiled at Cean, ushering him towards the feast and those who waited within.

Odessan and another druid had joined them. Cean hadn't seen them arrive at the dun, and certainly hadn't expected them. But it was Beltain, the most important of the druid celebrations, in which all the gods were honored. It stood at the beginning of the onset of summer, the most unpredictable season of the year. In the summer months, crops could fail due to weather, and stock could be lost to sickness brought on the summer air. Next to Samain, it was the most important festival day of the year.

Odessan's welcoming smile was more like a sneer, and Cean suddenly felt as he had so long ago at the company cafeteria when others talked spitefully about him. He resented feeling that way—he'd come so far since then—and here, on such a night. He looked to the Queen and Lubran for a better welcome.

Boadicea's smile, though, was enough. Even if he felt her eyes were guarded, perhaps with a ruler's business, he still knew himself to be truly welcomed. She was beautiful in the fire and lamplight, her hair a torrent of flames, her eyes now bright as the light caught them, now dark with mystery as shadows fell. She wore a long white robe, embroidered with green and gold thread. He'd never seen it before but guessed it symbolized the coming summer, which the celebrations were designed to welcome.

The bonfire had been set ready in the dun's center, and people gathered around as the Queen and her guests emerged from her hut. The torches were ready, and everyone stood shivering in the cold. Boadicea stepped forward.

"Tonight is the night of the gods. The end to a cold moon and the start of a bright sun, which brings us the warm rains and sweet fields of summer."

Odessan was suddenly standing beside her, a torch in his hand as well.

"May all the gods bless us and bring our lives to fruitful bounty," he added, touching his torch to the Beltain fire as hers did.

Flames blossomed, running up the oiled logs in a furious race. The gathered people cheered as the bonfire ignited and drove back the night. Maara brought Cean a drinking cup of silver, filling it from a skin which gave forth a sweetly honey and herbal scent.

Odessan watched.

"Not the metheglyn?" Cean protested quietly. That stuff usually left him with a mighty hangover. He'd only had it a few times and didn't really want it now. He peered dubiously into the cup.

"Not quite, brother," Lubran assured him, his face kind. "We know you do not like that. This is a drink from the Brigantes. Prasutagus brought it to our tribe. Drink well of it as it is rare and expensive, difficult to make. You will like this, and it is spring. You are amongst those who love you."

"Spring is ending. Drink to summer," Boadicea said softly.

Cean drank. It was weaker than the metheglyn, he thought. Though honey must still be the base, he could taste it. But it was less sweet and had a lighter taste, with a faint flavor of mint and something else he could not identify. He did like it, though. They'd been right about that. He drained the cup which Maara silently refilled as the two priests looked on.

There was roast meat to eat, bread, small cakes made of honey and oats, even a nut dish, griddle cakes made of ground nuts and dried berries from last fall. He felt he had better eat something as well as drink, for even though the drink might be weak as they claimed, he could still have a heavy head in the morning.

"Think you the Romans will come again with spring, Cean?" Odessan asked him.

"They may, but if so then they may also leave again swiftly."

"Ah." The priest smiled. "Yes, those they have conquered and who lie about their gates, they will have their say as long as Rome empties herself of soldiers for wars far away."

"They may be weak now," Cean cautioned the man. "Yet strength returns with time."

"Aye, and for that I am warned, as I have warned those of other tribes," the Queen responded, giving Odessan a heavy look. "Do not fear. We shall be ready. I and those who come after me."

Maara was filling his cup again. Lubran nodded at that. "You find this drink more to your taste, brother?"

The lamplight must have been making Cean dizzy. "It is pleasant. Lighter than the other, less strong." He was sure it was, so it must be the lamplight, or the flames on the hearth as they leaped, their light dancing in ripples around him.

"Then drink up. Let summer come early and the Romans come not at all." The Queen was raising her own jeweled cup. It was the same one Decianus had eyed with greed, and the firelight again winked in the stones set in its sides. Cean lifted his cup and drank.

More meat, and the nut cakes. Both foods Maara brought him seemed to start a thirst in him. He drank deeply again, enjoying the taste of the liquid, watching the two priests crouched as they were near the fire. Like crows, he thought, a giggle almost erupting from his throat before he contained it. Black and with long beaks for noses, hunched down into themselves. He forced himself to put the cup down. He felt warm, a little too warm. He thrust back his sleeves.

The talk continued: the Romans, the tribes, training young warriors, and celebrations to honor the gods as summer came. He felt supremely happy. Here with his friends, good talk, good food, good drink. Cean found he was half-asleep, relaxing on the long bench, the soft foalskin under him.

Boadicea was speaking again. Her words slightly muffled, or was it his mind, swathed in something which made him strain to hear? He put up fumbling hands to move the cloth which must be about his head. He could feel nothing. He concentrated and her words became more clear. Was she speaking to him?

"The gods sent you to bring the tribes victory, to tell us what we needed to do to drive the Romans away."

Oh, yes. That is what they had done, with his dreams and his advice. For her. All for her.

He couldn't say anything. His tongue was swollen and filled his mouth. And dry. Bring me a drink, he thought, wanting to laugh again.

A whisper seemed to come from Odessan. "When the Queen is gone there will be none to follow her. Essault is gone to be queen in her time. Queen of another tribe. Iessan has gone on the Warriors' Road. After the Queen's great victory, she walks alone and none tread in her footsteps as she leads her people."

It was a sad thought, and Cean felt a tear creep down his face.

"Nay." He heard Boadicea speak loudly, over the priest's malignant whisper. "It is not so. I am with child. With the blessing of the goddess and the fires of Imbolc." She cast off the outer robe, her hands pressing over her belly, her smile a glory even to Cean's drunken eyes.

He could have sworn Odessan hissed at her words. His words, though, were unmistakable:

"And the father? Your husband, the king, is dead."

Boadicea replied strongly in the way she did when she was making a decision as queen. "The child is a gift, from a man of the Iceni. That is all that matters. And my people will welcome it. A new Royal Woman for the tribe."

Cean allowed the knowledge to trickle through him in small explosions of pleasure. There would be a child of his amongst the Iceni. He would watch a child of his own learn to ride under the sun, a child who would grow, and Cean would know he'd changed his own future as well as the tribe's.

"In late summer, I will bear a daughter. Your daughter, Cean," she turned to him openly. "Nor will anyone naysay this, for your blood is from the gods, a blessing to us from them and you shall be Iceni forever."

"A blessing to be sent back," Odessan put in swiftly. "A sacrifice that the gods require of you to ensure summer is as it should be."

It was an argument already held, Cean saw, words that had been previously exchanged and decisions made, for good or ill. That much he could still understand.

"For the good of the tribe," the priest continued, "as rulers have done for many years, given of their life that the tribe survives well."

"Only in time of great need!" Boadicea returned, her eyes like the fire.

"And need we still have," the second priest countered. "There is no guarantee that the Romans will not come again, that the harvest we so badly need will be good, that which all the tribes need. If you are queen of them all, you must sacrifice this to the gods that your child be safe and well when its time comes."

Cean tried to stand, but could not.

What were they talking about? Cean wondered dizzily. Were they speaking of the Queen? They couldn't be! Her own people would rise up even against druids did they plan to sacrifice her.

Lubran watched in concern. "There must be consent for it to be so," he quickly added. He'd agreed to what they planned because he didn't believe Cean would agree, no matter how much he'd drunk of the holy drink.

Boadicea bent over the man who'd come to her from the gods, her hands catching his. "Cean, do you consent?" She shook him a little. "Do you consent?" She, too, hoped that he had enough will left within him to resist what the priests demanded.

What had she asked? Oh, yes, that he be Iceni forever. He smiled. How could he refuse?

"I consent," he said clearly, grinning.

"And so it is done." Odessan was satisfied.

"No!" exclaimed the Queen. But it was too late. They'd heard him.

Odessan went on. "He shall return to the gods and bespeak them of your daughter, of our fields and the ripeness of the season, that the year will be good for us. For all of us."

Lubran was holding the cup to his lips, the old man's eyes sad and wistful. Almost tearful. Tilting it. He must want him to drink again. He obeyed, closing his eyes, swallowing the last of the sweet liquid until the cup was empty.

He could feel Boadicea's strong hands clasping his. He opened his eyes to stare into those wonderful eyes.

"All you came to do is done, son of Brighid. Sleep now. At moon-high when the seasons change, you shall go. Nor shall we forget you. The child shall bear your name, your blood as well as mine. Forever you will live on amongst us, in her and her line to come."

Why were her eyes filled with tears? What was she so sad when he was going to stay here with her?

Then she whispered to him in a voice that reached him even as he began to fall, "And I will not forgive what has been done by these priests, they who wish to rule as this hand of mine rules. Take to Brighid my message in return. That all the days of my life shall I honor her, as will our daughter and her daughters after her."

Then, slowly, like a sigh on the wind, a moment held long in time, he fell into the night.

15

Government is about the application of power. Good government administers itself wisely, promoting a good economy and bolstering the welfare of its people. Bad government is dominated by maintaining its ascendancy, and bolstering nothing more than its own well-being.

Take, for instance, the Roman occupation of Gaul. Until they permitted local officials to administer the tax system, and encouraged local religious practices to flourish as they had done for centuries, the Roman governors were fighting a constant battle for power.

Similarly, when northern Vikings first defeated the Jutes, although they set up political chiefs to rule the tribes, it was the religious beliefs that separated Jute from Viking. The British tribes under Boadicea were not the first or last to face this type of problem. However, they were the first to reach a suitable administrative solution.

—from *Public Administration: Course Text 1*, 6th Edition
(Hibernia Collective Publishing House),
by Lindaslass Bedwarn, et al.

Iceni Homeland, 62 C.E.

Lubran touched Cean's shoulder. The young healer did not stir. But the pulse in his wrist still throbbed, very slowly. The sacred drink laced with mistletoe was killing him, but it would take hours. Mistletoe, the miraculous plant without roots, a gift of the gods to those of the earth.

They had that time to prepare. The willing sacrifice, one who goes of his free will to Belenos to ensure good crops and a good life for the people. He took in a slow deep breath of relief. Cean hadn't fully understood, Lubran knew, but he'd consented. Lubran quelled his anger. Some things must be.

The druid priests had discussed this at length with both of them the night before. The Romans could return. The Iceni *must* have a good, nay, a bountiful harvest this coming year. In the midst of the battles, the Queen had insisted the tribe couldn't plant as they normally would. Without a rich harvest this year, the tribe would starve. And too many of their warriors were injured badly. The tribe needed someone to plead with the gods on their behalf. Odessan had insisted on this. Boadicea and Lubran had protested desperately. This young man was their friend, someone they'd come to love.

The Queen had paced around the burning hearth. "I would have him here," she'd said. "He is a gift—the brightest gift our gods have sent in many years." She'd gazed down at the burning flames, her arms crossing her middle, seeking reason to counter the druid's demands.

"Ay," Lubran added. "A fine healer with many ideas that bring us all comfort. There are many here who live because of him." He was not willing to even consider Odessan's proposal.

"It is for the people," the druid began.

"It is for the people that he stays!" the Queen shouted at him. "He is our healer, our wise one. It does not matter that he is not a priest of your kind. That he is a traveler from another far people. He is one of us now, and someone I would not do without."

Odessan's lips had twitched at that. "He is not druid. And he will never bring the tribe what one of the faith can."

His companion nodded, glaring at the other two. How dared they argue with the priest! "If he isn't asked for the sacrifice, we cannot bespeak the blessing of the gods."

"You *can't*," Boadicea sneered. "It isn't the gods who say this."

"Who else speaks for the gods but me?" Odessan went on. "We cannot give our prayers to a venture such as you propose for the tribes if you are not willing to make this sacrifice."

Boadicea stood still, her eyes ablaze at this open threat. "This is nothing to do with the holy way. It is to aid all of the tribes that we unite as one. Acting together, we help each other. Alone we are weak. It is Cean who has taught us this."

Even as she spoke she knew she wasn't persuading him. Cean was a threat to his power, a danger to the druid hold upon the tribes' beliefs. She looked at Lubran, desperately. He shook his head, his face pale as if ill. He could think of no other argument.

Odessan sensed their hesitation and knew he had them. "He will be willing—you will see. He thinks of the people and their well-being. You are about to build the new dun, the one where you will take counsel with all the tribes. This would bring you the gods' blessing to help you keep the tribes together." He paused before adding. "And our blessing, too."

The druid repeated his demand then. The man was senior in druid rank, and yet … How could she go on with what she had begun without the druids' support?

After that conversation, sleep had come reluctantly. Now Lubran reached out to pick up some of Cean's things, his face twisted with remorse at what he must do, and the stirrings of a sullen, deep anger against Odessan. He couldn't show that feeling, but it would never go away. He took up Cean's cloak and robe, Boadicea's gifts. The young healer had valued these. Though he must go on the final journey shrouded only in skins, he should have the gifts he had treasured, to take with him on the road.

Ever practical, Maara had already brought heated water. "Help me get his clothes off. The body must be washed and blessed before it is dressed again."

Cean was limp, heavy. They handled him with loving care; his spirit was still within him. Odessan watched them, his eyes spiteful, his mouth a tight smile. Stripped, Cean was the center of their stare.

Maara gasped. She reached out a hand, then drew it back.

"It is true. A shape-changer. A creature of the gods. Half human and half of them. *Their* mark, and none can deny it for I have seen with my own eyes."

"A child of the gods, a bridge between woman and man, a connection between this world and the gods. I'd never have agreed else. And he consented," Lubran admonished her, reminding himself as well. Tears streamed down the old man's face for what they were about to do.

Odessan called attention to why they had asked this of Cean. "If we make no mistakes, if all is honorable on the path he walks back to the gods, then they shall rain good fortune upon us."

"To Brighid," Lubran murmured. "*She* would not ask so great a sacrifice of us." He caught Boadicea's eyes and found agreement in them, albeit a grim one.

"To the gods, to Taranis, the God of Thunder, to Esus, Lord and Master, and to Teutates, the god of us all," Odessan intoned. "*All* of them," he insisted heavily. "They would ask nothing less of us."

His shadow nodded quickly, supporting him, always agreeing with him. Did Odessan believe he would lead the new community on Mona? Lubran wondered. The one he was trying to re-build?

On Cean's chest there was no more than a flutter of skin where his heart still beat. "He was given the burnt bannock?" Odessan asked quickly.

"Yes," Boadicea replied. "I gave it to him, as was needed." Her voice was cool. "And I shall be the one to cleanse his body before he is given to the gods. As is my right." She glared across Cean at the druid priest, Lubran at her shoulder. She could not fight the druids, not openly as she had the Romans. "You and Maara bring what else is needful," she said to him. "Maara, is the tribe ready?"

"I spoke to Alieki once Cean was here. They are ready when we call."

She and Lubran were briefly gone to return with a flask. In that time Cean had been washed and dried, Odessan and the other druid watching carefully. The flask was opened and the soft scent of wild roses filled the room. Brighid loved flowers; their scent was a blessing.

Boadicea touched her finger to the scent, and upon the points of life anointed Cean's skin, murmuring as she did so.

"With your eyes watch over us, who are your people. With your ears listen for us, speed our prayers to the gods where they live, waiting. With your lips speak of us, remind the gods that we honor them, always, and bring our names to their lips that they do not forget us who belong to them."

She looked up once at Odessan, then Lubran before continuing. "With your heart speak well of us to Brighid as you do to all the gods."

Odessan hissed behind her, but she continued. "We who love you, as you love us." She touched perfume to each nipple. "The goddess sent you with her mark. Let this part of you remember the women of the Iceni as sisters."

Her hands dropped lower to stroke perfume over his genitals. "Let this part of you know the Iceni were also brothers. Sisters and brothers are we ever to you. Remember this, Cean," she added, whispering close to his ear, "remember it well. Your daughter in time shall be royal woman of our people. Watch over her also." Lastly she bent to anoint his feet. "Be swift on the Warrior's Road, Cean. Run with joy to meet those of your kind."

Straightening up, she said briefly to Lubran, "He said his people were from a land so far away we could never meet them. He spoke truly."

Lubran handed her a shallow bowl. With the tips of her fingers she sprinkled mistletoe pollen down the silent figure before her. Between the eyes on the forehead. The sense of ritual dropped from her as she straightened.

"Shroud him now," Odessan put in before anyone could speak. He spoke impatiently. "We have little time left. The bonfire must be lit soon."

Lubran was ready, Maara holding the clothing. They dressed Cean with slow care as the priest tried to hurry them without avail. Once again

Cean wore the garb of an Iceni. His own jewelry had been brought, all of it: the Roman rings, and brooch, the heavy silver and garnet bracelets, and a silver circlet to bind back his hair.

Odessan objected once to so much going with Cean, but Boadicea hissed back at him before he'd finished speaking. "They are his! They go with him."

Lubran laid anxious fingers against Cean's wrist.

"Well?" Odessan spoke.

"He yet lives." The old man's eyes were clouded. "We must bear him to the sacred waters."

"Maara, call the people." Boadicea spoke from the shadows where she waited.

They came, crowding quietly about the door in the flaring torch-light, many with tears on their cheeks. Alieki carried a bier, a platform of four poles with hides laced between.

Boadicea came forth to look down at it. "After the battle in which Iessan and Ancha died, Cean came to me with a great fur bed-cover for them. That they might lie soft, he said. Jewels he brought to adorn them, but it is not that which I remember. It is the fur. Let him lie as softly."

Maara ran away to return quickly, holding the foalskin. Behind her, Alieki came holding the other Lubran had offered. The spearman lifted Cean, cradling the healer to his chest as he carried his friend from the Queen's hut to lay him down gently on the bier. He stepped back, looking down.

"He healed me when I was injured. He was a good man." If it was protest, he said no more. But he and the Queen looked long at each other.

Dauldi brought up four ponies wearing harnesses. The corners of the bier were attached to the rings at each girth. Then, in slow procession, they started out. Boadicea led, Lubran at her side, the two druids trying to be as close to the front as they could. A hide bag balanced on a pony's back, and Maara held onto it with one hand. After them came the bier, Alieki and Dauldi each controlling a lead pony. The Iceni people followed, somberly. Among them a slender child, her eyes burning as she watched the druids. One day ... one day she would avenge her friend. And before that day she would write of this and remember.

"He loved the skin I gave him in thanks for Verli's life." Siharni wept softly as she caught up with Lubran. "More than once he told me how much he enjoyed having it, how he admired my work." Lubran's hand patted at her shoulder, shortly, in kindness.

"He was kind to me when I was sick," Verli remembered out loud, daring the priests' anger. "He made me laugh."

Cean would have been surprised, Lubran thought, had he known just how many small kindness were recalled as the people followed their queen. Their voices were a reproachful murmur in the darkening air that shadowed the priests. And Lubran remembered something else as well. To Cean it had been natural to speak gently, to aid where he could. To them it had been a sign of his sacred origin, summed up in the end by Tilutegan.

"The gods sent him to us. Never did I know him to be other than polite and kind. It was well we took him as Iceni. Surely he will never forget us, even on the Warrior's Road, and in the House of the Gods. Did you ever know him to offend, to fail in his word?"

Siharni shook her head vigorously. "Nay. You speak rightly. He is one who is loved. He goes with his own consent." She didn't sound certain. "He will speak with the gods so that we be blessed." Her voice strengthened with that.

Lubran nodded. If anyone would forgive them this night, it would be Cean. After that they walked in silence until they reached the sacred grove.

Night had settled about them, a group of people trailing through the dark, following the two torches that led them on. In the grove's center, the small pool fringed with rushes lay at the bottom of a shallow dip. The grove straddled a small island in the heart of the fen, no more than a quick step up out of the marshy water. The ponies' hooves splashed out of the water, the Iceni on foot close behind them to stand cold on the soft grass. Like dark mist, they drifted into position about the upper slopes above the water.

Below them their Queen waited. The priests watched, their eyes eager and evil. Lubran stood at her side. He spoke. Not to her. To the priests.

"Let us begin this, if we must."

"The gods sent a messenger to us," Odessan began. "Your Queen dreamed of him before he came. That we might know him for the gods' own, a mark was set upon him."

"That this was so," Lubran continued, "I swear as does the Queen, and Odessan and Poletin, priests and masters of our faith. Cean is of the gods, sent for a time to advise us, to dream for us and to share their learning among our people."

Above on the hill, the smith spat. But he did so quietly, and not so as to distract the priests.

"His time here is done, and now we send him to his place with the gods." Lubran faltered. Could he do this? This was his friend, his honored colleague. Unbidden, the memory of them selecting and drying herbs together came to mind. He coughed, his throat swelling with the tears. He continued. "Cean goes freely, consenting. Already his spirit slowly leaves us. Yet he must be set upon the path according to ceremony. Our ceremony, people of the Iceni."

Poletin quickly knelt beside Cean, placing the thrice-knotted cord about his throat. Under its bite, the pulse of his vein fluttered, fading. Poletin tightened the cord, holding it.

Odessan took up the axe, taking it from the druid hiding place. Ancient above anything the Iceni owned: polished flint bound with horsehide to a haft of carved oak wood.

"Only the willing sacrifice is good enough to be touched by the axe, and only one who was trained over the many years of learning may lay hands upon it," Odessan announced, striking a quick blow to the back of Cean's head.

Poletin stabbed the jugular vein in the healer's neck at the same moment. Blood cascaded suddenly from Cean's vein.

Someone, Lubran didn't know who, cried out, once.

The old man watched. Even in the darkness he could see the Queen pale. Maara rolled Cean over, binding his hands behind him. She then held him so that he curled, making him appear to kneel before the priests. His head bowed to the axe.

The axe struck again.

Then a third time.

Each blow precisely placed. According to the rite.

The druids' rite. Hateful to Boadicea's eyes.

Odessan laid down the axe. Lubran aided Maara in placing Cean back on the bier, his hands folded upon his chest.

No one spoke, though all turned to listen as Lubran stepped to the bier. While Cean had lain on the horse-drawn bier they had stripped his hut of those things that had been his. They'd found the bag of gemstones and presented it to the Queen before Odessan could stop them.

"Do we send this with him, Lady?" they'd asked her. The druid priest had watched greedily over her shoulder.

She had poured them out into her palm, but it had been the druid priest who'd answered. "Nay, they are from the Romans. See how this one is cut, and this? He did not bring them with him. They will stay here with us to help rebuild Mona."

The Queen had broken in then. "What he brought, what is truly his, those things he takes—and the gems also. If they are anyone's they belong to the tribe since he was Iceni."

She'd stared down at the priest, deep anger boiling in her look. And as much as he resented it, he gave way to her will. He had, after all, won his much greater demand of her.

Beside the bier Maara was opening the hide bag she had borne here. Cean's backpack, his best knife, the bronze casket. They had filled the metal canteen with barley spirit, wrapped honey-cakes in green leaves tied with grass string. The gods would welcome those. Then, carefully they undressed him, placing the folded items under his head, binding the foalskins about him.

One by one Lubran held up the other items before placing the great knife in Cean's hands. "He fought for Iessan. Let him bear arms to that other place as a warrior should," Lubran added before the priest could speak. It was the finest knife he and Boadicea had ever seen.

All wondered at the bronze casket. It was heavy and when shaken, some contents within rattled. They could not open it, no matter how they tried. The Queen handed it to Lubran, who laid it beside Cean even as Odessan reached for it.

"Something of his people. Not for us." Lubran, too, glared at the priest, daring him to snatch it. Cean was gone; the casket didn't really matter, but it was something that had been his. It belonged with him. Yet both the Queen and Lubran noted Odessan's hungry stare following the casket.

At Cean's head they placed the backpack as all watched silently, still as the sacred trees. The only sound was Poletin's soft chanting, Odessan adding an odd discordant counterpoint. At Cean's feet the casket bulked, a darker shadow against his bare skin, like blood at the foot of darkness. All that which was Cean's would travel the path with him, nothing had been withheld. His friends had seen to that much.

Alieki and Dauldi came to join them, striding down the short hill, as they'd been told to do. Four from the people, two male, two female, were to aid the healer in the last step of his last journey. They lifted the bier, two hands clasping each corner. The Queen, Maara, Alieki spearman, and Dauldi who owed blood-debt, would not have had it any other way.

They carried the laden bier to the shallow pool and slowly lowered it into the water. The priests would pronounce, knowing by the way it was received, if all had been done rightly. For a moment it seemed as if the body would float, rejected by the depths below it. Then, as water seeped in, the bier and Cean sank from sight.

On the hill, watching the flicker of torchlight on the water's ripples, the gathered Iceni wept. The two priests chanted, waving the torches in the air. They sung of death, of its place in their lives. All lives. They beseeched the gods, calling to Taranis to stay his thunder, to Esus for life, and above all to Teutates to watch over them, to bless their servant's return, the Iceni's gift: Cean. They told the gods their healer would look after them as he had their people.

Boadicea spoke for the first time. "Brighid, our goddess of home and hearth, take him into your house. For along the road of death, all must journey."

Lubran watched her raise her eyes to the two priests. It was not her death, he was sure, of which she was thinking. He felt the same. All his years of training, his discipline and honoring of the way, were suddenly like ashes, something that had burned away in a deep fire of anger and was now gone. The gods would approve this night's work, Cean would understand, but Lubran himself would never forget what had been done here.

The bier sank beneath the dark water. Lubran had quietly placed a few stones within the foalskins. They'd not put any clothing on Cean other than the foalskins wrapped about him as shroud. His cloak and robe were beneath his head. He must go to the gods as he'd been born, but they had tied one strip of fox skin to his arm. Shape-changer.

The fen stretched out into marsh. Although the bier had sunk into the shallow water, it would, over time, work its way out and away into the marsh itself. In the past other, less meaningful sacrifices had been laid there to vanish into the fen. It would not do to have a priest celebrating sacred rites tangle his feet among old bones.

But for the true rite, the sacrifice must be laid in water. Thrice consecrated: by the cord, the axe, and the water. Thrice sacred to the gods. Only once before in his long life had Lubran seen this rite, and that had been the first time he himself had carried it out. Lubran had done as well as he could for Cean, the man he'd come to call brother and to love almost as a son in the two years since Cean had come to them.

They led the Iceni back to the dun, many weeping while others hid their feelings. The two priests strode as close to the head of the shadowy group of people, as near to the Queen as they could. As if their place was there, with her. At the dun, they all silently disappeared into their huts, clutching their angry sorrow like old mantles as they went alone to their homes. They would miss the healer. Very much, and the child slipping away into the shadows would miss still more the man who had been her teacher, mentor, half father, half elder brother.

Boadicea signaled to Maara to find beds for the priests in a room of her hut, but Lubran watched as she went to her own bed without speaking to anyone. He understood. She'd chosen for her people at Odessan's insistence. But it was a choice she regretted personally, nor would she forget who had convinced her to do this despicable act. A queen has to make choices, but they were based on her people's needs, not her own.

* * * *

A day later Lubran returned with only Maara and the Queen. Wordlessly they stood and looked down into the shallow pool. Above them, the sacred flame still burned within the grove, the ritual axe and ropes hidden where they'd always been. Nothing remained to show what had happened, or who lay deep within the fen's waters. The man they'd known was gone, out of their lives as quickly as he'd become a part of them. They felt empty as they looked down. Boadicea laid her hand on her stomach above the slight roundness there.

Lubran thought he knew what she felt. Here. Here Cean would always be with them. Truly part of their blood.

They returned to the dun as silently as they'd come. It was barely dawn, barely light, and the pale sky shot the water with a flicker of its life. Once there, Boadicea spoke quietly to Lubran before she turned away at the door to her hut.

"Look you through Cean's hut. I suspect our priests would wish to have more of the messenger's things if they could."

"I looked for all that was his," Maara pointed out.

"There might be something else, something our good healer had hidden. Be sure there is *nothing*. No drawings, not even clothes. His medicines he would have given willingly, but other things were his own. I will not aid these priests through the death of one of our own."

Lubran quickly agreed and walked on to Cean's hut. There was a flicker at the doorway, as if a breeze tugged at the door-hide covering it. But when he looked inside, there was no one. To the old man's quick look, the bed had been rifled, and some of the coals from the hearth had been poked about.

He looked outside. For a brief moment he saw someone standing at the edge of one of the other huts, a man in black, possibly one of the priests. But he was quickly gone, like the flicker of a moth's wing, as he dodged around the back of the hut. Lubran had disturbed him before he'd entirely searched Cean's hut. Just as well. There were still the medicines, and those the young healer would have wished go to his people.

Later in the day, Lubran went to speak to the Queen. She was somber, her eyes clouded. "Odessan may have been there in the hut," he told her quickly once he was sure she was alone.

"Did he take anything?"

"Nothing that I saw. I believe I arrived before he had the chance."

Boadicea nodded. "A good thing." She turned to look at him. "I hate to ask this, kinsman, but I fear for Cean's grave."

Lubran was quick to take her meaning.

"They wouldn't," he murmured, but even as he said it, he knew she was probably right.

"They have an island to rebuild, and this Odessan would build it to his own glory. I would save what was Cean's for our tribe's future instead."

Lubran's look was steady. "I will go. I will bring to you what was Cean's."

Before he left, she spoke again. "Not the gems. Those I would use only in dire need, and that is not yet upon us. Bring only the casket. Bury the jewels under the bier where they may safely rest beneath him." She had another use for those, something she would build and dedicate to Cean along with the goddess.

Lubran walked away silently to do her bidding. On the next dark morning, he sunk beneath the cold water to seek out Cean's body, and the bag of possessions at the messenger's feet. From it, Lubran took the bronze casket. It had not dimmed for its time there below the surface.

The small bag of gems he tucked below the bier, pushing them into the peaty soil beneath. The knife he took from the bag as well, thrusting it, too, beneath the bier. He'd seen the covetous gleam in Odessan's eyes when he'd looked on the weapon.

He returned, the casket beneath his cloak. Boadicea received it, sadness in her eyes.

"What have you in mind to do with this, kinswoman?"

"I have in mind a new dun, one that will house the messengers sent to me by other tribes. Within it I wish to build a hall for the council of our allies, a place to discuss and come together as one in times of need. This I will build in Cean's honor."

She held the casket before her, and turning, placed it next to the one that was her own very similar box, given by a Hibernian trader wishing to court Iceni favor.

With the next dawn the druid priests departed, and by the frustrated hate in Odessan's eyes as he bid them goodbye, Lubran was sure he'd been to the grave site and looked for Cean's treasures to take for his own. The rage showed he'd failed, and Lubran hid a faint smile of triumph. The Queen had been right.

Later, in his own hut, Lubran looked over the things he'd found amongst Cean's other belongings. He'd taken the tablets Cean had used to prevent wound-sickness, along with all the other medicines for which his brother had no further use. Cean had taught the old man once how he could make something similar with the mold upon bread. The old healer could use the tablets and he could make the medicines. And more.

He'd learned something of why and how they worked. It was all knowledge that he could pass on in his turn to the next healer he apprenticed. He wouldn't send anyone to the druids for teaching in the future.

It had been two years since the young stranger had arrived in their dun, to learn and to teach. Lubran had taught, Cean had admitted to Lubran's knowledge. But, in turn, Lubran had learned. He wondered now if Cean had ever realized how much he'd taught a man who had long been druid-trained.

Now Lubran must seek about him for an apprentice. He could not take the chance this new knowledge would be lost. The druid masters had not known it. And Mona was destroyed. Who knew how long it would be before it was restored? If it ever was, Lubran thought, as he hung Cean's pack next to his own. Patting it softly, as if it waited for its owner's return. The druids' obsession with secrecy would be their undoing, for once their knowledge, their rites, were gone, who would bring it back? Lubran no longer had the taste for it.

England, 2048 C.E.

Anxious to make the jump in time, Cean paused to look down at Smith's body. The absence of life turning muscles limp and rubbery, the arms and legs splayed out, appearing vulnerable. As they were without the life in them. This he regretted. It was an unnecessary death that would stay in his dreams, haunting them. He regretted, too, the first. That had been an accident, to protect Mel, this a blow in self-defense. Both robbing life of its habitation, a shroud of flesh that would now decay, eroded by time into the dirt.

He sent Smith's corpse through to another time. Then Cean stood, looking around for a moment. It was his last sight of the 21st century, and actually there was nothing to see. Just darkness, the pale starlight struggling to reach through a permanent haze blanketing the land.

If there's anything I'll remember about this moment, he thought, it would be the silence. A distant dog's yelp splitting the air made him grin. Almost silence, he amended. He took a deep breath, stepping onto the time jumper's pad.

This is it, he told himself. With that, he left the life he'd known.

Iceni Homeland, 62 E.E.

Spring was almost done. The Queen grew greater in size. She would bear the child towards high summer, but spring came first. Spring and perhaps other new beginnings. One day long after the fires of Beltain had died she sent out riders out to all the tribes who'd risen with her against the Romans.

She called together a council from among them, and called it the Tribal Cyngor, an assembly of advisors. She strode in front of them, her hair a flame, her mantle the strong green that blazed with the life that radiated about her. And the life she carried. Her stomach was small and round, noticeable to all.

"We have begun," she told them. "But it is not the least of what we must do. These thoughts the messenger of the gods spoke to me: that we make an alliance amongst us. A permanent alliance for protection and support. Instead of single tribes, open to the attack of Roman war eagles, we remain as one, ready to fight together against any invaders. And when there is want among us, when the wolves of hunger and need crouch at the gates of our duns, we can aid each other, and grow stronger together. For what weakens one of us will weaken us all."

The Cyngor listened, many unwillingly. They were required to return to their kings and discuss her message with them, to return by late spring with their final answers. But the Romans landed first.

On a wild windy day in late spring with returning geese crying overhead, a messenger thundered through the gates to leap from his winded pony in front of a startled Queen and Lubran.

"Lady, ships have been seen on the father of rivers." He panted so hard the words could barely be understood.

Boadicea wasted no time. "When? How many did you see? What do they do?"

"Lady, those who crept back to live in the Londinium ruins have said there are eight ships upon the river. They came up towards the town two days past, acting as if they went unnoticed. I have slain one beast and maybe ruined this one to bring word." He looked ruefully at the staggering, sweat-lathered animal. "As for what the Romans do, they do nothing. They anchor just within the river mouth and wait. For what we do not know."

"None have landed?" Lubran stood at the Queen's side. She had already sent word to Alieki spearman.

"None, Lady. Perhaps they wait for some to go out to them." He handed his pony's reins to a boy who slowly walked it back and forth.

Lubran snorted. "They may wait for that until they die of old age." There were snickers of amusement from the people who had gathered.

Boadicea thought a moment, smiling also.

"Nay, I think they have cause to wait. But you have ridden far. Alieki, let your boy and another care for the beast. Dauldi, take this man to your house and feed him well."

She motioned Maara and Lubran to follow as she entered her hut. Lubran spoke first, as soon as they were beyond listening ears. "I know what may be in your mind, kinswoman. Cean told us this, that if the Romans took from their city too great a force, weakening it from within, then the enemies who lie about their walls would likely choose that time to strike."

"Even so." The Queen faced him darkly. "I think they slay two hares with the same arrow. They sail hither, slowly perhaps. Should enemies attack them upon the beaches, they can recall their ships quickly enough to take their foes from behind as well as before. Therefore they wait. This is no true attempt to retake our lands. It is a dangling of bait to draw us out to them. If we strike, they could perhaps unman us from behind."

Maara nodded as she walked in. "Yet what if it is not?"

"Then we call in the tribes now," Lubran told her. "Not the war-host but as many of the tribes as can take to the roads at once. And as we march, we place relays where messengers wait ready. If the Romans land, we attack, holding them between wave and sand as we did before, burning their ships. The relays then ride with all speed to their people for aid if our war gathering is not enough. Messengers go to every tribe saying those who would make slaves of us are come again. The tribes then send their warriors that the lands be free."

"Good advice. Go, see to it the crantara is set again and the riders do not linger."

He obeyed.

The advice had not been his, in truth, but part of a long evening's discussion with Cean earlier this past winter. They'd talked of the possible future, how the Romans might act, what they might do. Cean had talked, Lubran had listened and stored it all in his druid-trained memory. Cean was gone, Lubran must live and the Queen leaned on his wisdom.

His eyes lifted briefly to the sky and none heard his whisper.

"You would have given me those words if I'd asked. Forgive me that I took them."

They rode, the Iceni about their Queen as her chariot drove slowly behind a smooth-paced horse. She was close to six moons with the child. Keeping the pace of her outriders would not be good for her. As she passed, the torque glinting about her neck with the bright red of her hair, warriors came from side roads and tracks to join her. Trinovantes, Brigantes, Catuvelauni, and Atrebates. Silures would again come before long, and even the Regni.

There were many, all grim men ready to fight again. She did not notice how they looked at her, but Lubran did. At nights about the fire he listened. He talked, joked and encouraged men to speak their minds. As a healer, they trusted him.

"Messenger from the gods, they said? Even from Teutates?"

"Aye."

"Consenting to the blood sacrifice? He knew?"

"Aye. A good man and perhaps something more than a man," Lubran often said to them, his eyes on the fire before them. Perhaps.

Who would know now? This question haunted Lubran. Should they have done what the priests demanded? He didn't know. But he would ever speak of Cean to others, and say that the young healer had been a gift who was more than just any other. Cean's name would live as it should, even as legend, if Lubran had any say in it.

A warrior Cean had saved after the slaughter of the Ninth Legion spoke up. "I had the wound-sickness. See, here, where a sword took me." He exhibited a jagged scar down one thigh. "Cean came. He spoke to me kindly, saying by the gods' will I should neither die nor be a burden to my tribe. He gave me a potion to drink and the next day the wound-ill was gone."

Lubran noted the awed looks. The breaths sucked in as they remembered with wonder. The strike of a sword or spear was not the worst blow a man could take in battle. What happened to the wound afterwards was. Cean had healed that where none before could.

"It is true. I have seen him do such things. And there is another wonder." He waited while they leaned close. "The Queen, she bears his daughter. Yet she is no young woman. He lay with her on the holy nights and the gods told her in a dream that her child was to be a royal woman to come after her."

He talked a little more before retiring to his sheepskins to sleep, well satisfied with the planted seeds of Cean's greatness. This was the least he could do for his friend. And for the Queen, as well as the daughter about to be born.

The other tribes in the end had come to accept Boadicea as queen to lead them to their battles before the winter had begun. But the isolated months of ice and snow would have loosened that tie somewhat. A belief that Brighid or another god had sent someone to sire a royal daughter upon the Iceni Queen would bring back much of that awe that had united the tribes in the first place.

They reached Londinium in two days, Lubran having an outrider bring at once one of the men who watched the lurking ships.

"Do they move?" the Queen asked.

"They have not landed," the man told her. "Yet they have shifted ground. They moved yesterday at dawn further up towards the city. We sent out boats in the night with oars wrapped in fleece for quiet. In them men who know the Roman tongue sat close and listened. They say the invaders prepare to land."

"Have them keep a good watch and let no word escape of what we know," the Queen told him, dismissing him with a small gift.

Lubran saw the man away and then reported back. "I think if no ship comes against them by tomorrow morning they may land." He lowered his voice speaking softly. "I have riders watching at the mouth of the father of rivers. If a ship comes swiftly, we may believe it to be their recall. I shall get word to you what seems most wise."

With morning the Roman ships had moved to the beach. The warriors lay within the city's ruins and waited. Hard-learned discipline fought with a lust to fight. Discipline won. They had been enslaved once, and would not be so again, as Boadicea had told them. The first ship was near the sand, just beginning to heel over on the outgoing tide.

From behind came the beat of racing hooves. Verli swung from his pony to hiss in Lubran's ear. The old man moved casually towards Boadicea where she waited, the reins of her chariot restless between her fingers.

"One of the Roman courier ships has been sighted off the point. It runs for the river mouth. I think word comes to the Romans."

She raised herself, concealed from the sea by buildings but visible to the warriors who waited. "The gods send warning. Today the Romans flee the battle. Tomorrow they will not come. But one day they will. Let us ever be ready, for when time passes, people forget. If we are not ready, the Romans will be, and they shall come when that time of forgetting is upon us. Let our memory be as a hedge of spears against them."

After a few minutes, as silence returned while they waited, a warrior grumbled, just loudly enough for his companions to hear. "I see no sign of flight. The woman is mad."

A cry came on the heels of his words. "A ship. They turn to it."

The army waited, spear and swordsmen restless. Watching as the later ships drew off from the beach. A boat rowed to and fro. Then, the half-beached ship was unloaded to aid its refloating, a kedge anchoring it from the shore, before it was reloaded.

In brisk convoy, the courier ship leading the way, they sailed off. Down the father of rivers and out to sea, setting course for Rome. They were called home to protect their own land, as Cean had warned, and nothing in this chill land would keep them.

Behind the ruined walls, Boadicea raised her spear high and shouted. The men cheered.

In the midst of the shouts came a wailing cry as those about the doubter stabbed him. He'd questioned the Queen who'd brought them victory. She who was priestess as well. Her warning had been true, as if she saw with an unnatural sight. They could all see proof in the retreating ships.

They turned to look at Boadicea, their eyes glazed in awe. She knew. The gods spoke to her, even in the midst of a camp.

Boadicea rode home in triumph. Messengers rode ahead spreading the tale, which like all tales grew in the telling. High priestess of the gods. Speaker for the goddess Brighid. Royal woman of the Iceni.

And when she asked them to build her a dun to suit this new Cyngor of the tribes, they listened, and hurried to do as she bid. This was their council, their rule, with counselors from all the tribes to listen to her, for her to listen to them. The Cyngor was for all, like a warm hearth to draw them to it and nourish their duns at need.

Thus the goddess Brighid, goddess of the hearth, held her own place in the hall built for the Cyngor, a special shrine dedicated to her to bless this union of representatives. She presided over them with Boadicea as her voice.

The Queen had built a second shrine within the great hall, a shrine to Brighid's messenger. Something of Cean's had to be placed within the shrine's base. Here she publicly set the bronze casket, the people claiming it was a wise choice. When many people saw the casket's unmarred surface, they said Lubran had been wise to take it up, and that indeed, Cean was from the gods. At Boadicea's command, Lubran tucked it within the second shrine of the Cyngor, the one that from the hall's other end faced Brighid's.

* * * *

On a warm night in late summer, the Queen returned to her hut near the new dun. She strained in labor. Yet despite her age the birth was quick. Another blessing of the goddess. The child rushed to be born. Maara aided but Lubran took the child to anoint it with Brighid's sign.

"She will never be for the other gods, not the ones who took her father from us," Boadicea whispered from her bed.

"A girl, as you dreamed," Lubran said.

"As was promised me," the Queen answered.

Lamplight glowed. He turned the babe so the light fell across the small head. His smile came then. "Look, she is her mother's daughter." The light glinted on a short, fine growth of copper hair.

Boadicea raised herself to see. "Aye. But see the shade." Both looked more closely. The hair was not the fire-gold of the Queen's, but the dark copper of Cean's hair as it had grown out over later months.

"It is well. In three days I show her to the people. The new Iceni royal woman." She brushed one hand across the babe's head, smoothing the fine hair down. The child did not cry, just squirmed to find a softer place, fist near her chin.

In three days Boadicea kept her word. Stepping from her house to hold the babe aloft, naked to the warm air so all could see the child was whole and unblemished.

Her voice rang out. "People of the Iceni. Behold the new royal daughter. Child of your Queen and of the gods' messenger." People cheered, and Boadicea smiled broadly. "Her name shall be Ceana, spoken as *Cee arna*, and in time she shall rule. Will you have her for royal daughter, to be your queen in my place? Say you now."

A great wave of sound rose to the sky. It rose like the din of a great flock of birds in spring, bursting with the sheer joy of life. The sound rolled about the dun, coming back to her in a great roar. There was no doubt. Ceana, daughter to Boadicea and Cean, child of the Iceni, priestess-to-be to Brighid, Goddess of women. She was acceptable in the eyes of all the tribe.

And if with that acceptance and her name, time twisted; what would never be, what had once been, what was now and for all time to come—all would be right. Again. A name come full circle, a bloodline shaped by something which could never have been, without one person's obsession, now and in another time.

In the sunlight, Ceana stirred at the noise which woke her and complained, loudly. She might rule in years to come, but just now she was a babe and hungry. The cheers broke into laughter as Boadicea put her to the breast. So the babe fed.

It was well for the Iceni. Very well. Like love's passion in the night, sunlight quickened in Boadicea's hair, spreading from that flame to flare in Ceana's. Behind them, the rising dun and the broad hall of the Cyngor framed them with solid permanence.

Brighid's living hearth in its home.

And on a night when the full moon rose the sky beyond the hall a woman came down the edge of ancient waters and whispered softly. "I swore you should lie at my feet when I died, that vow I dared not keep, but from your hair I cut three locks, for me Maara braided them into a cord, and that cord shall be about my waist when I am laid to rest. Thus shall your spirit ever abide with mine, that we meet again West of the Sunset. Sleep well, we prosper and your enemies are dead."

16

In the end, the Isle of the Iceni with its many tribes was not worth the effort. Their Queen was brave, but a savage. Conquest would have taken too many legions, too many trained men lost, and for what? A cold island of damp air and rotting thatch, peopled with barbarians who would make worthless, unskilled slaves at best.

There was little gold there, and that reputedly came from elsewhere, an island further to the west. As for settlement, the land was made more for horses and forest beasts than farms. There were more productive lands on the mainland, closer to Rome and with more amenable people suited to becoming citizens of the Empire.

And so the wise choice was made to forego Britain, a decision Agricola made himself. No one has regretted it, however. Even the great Emperor Nero counted it wisdom to have his legions return to the soil where they were needed instead of wasting their blood on foreign lands that were unlikely to contribute to the ultimate glory of this, our Empire.

—from Tacitus, *The Annals*

No one yet understands the nature of the universe. Even Einstein couldn't have predicted the complications, or simplicity, since he was always sought that elegance of a unified field theory of quantum physics. Much of that revolves around the essential nature of time. The concept of parallel universes doesn't explain precisely how they function: does one run into another, or is there a distinct separation from a single point in time? Can one universe influence one nearby if it is close enough to almost touch? We may never know. But it is delightful to think about it, isn't it?

—from *Conversations with Leogold Fortescue*,
by Ellina Martingale

Dear Janet,
    I've been planning on sending you computer mail for months, indeed, almost a year now, but things have been happening so fast I'm afraid you'll be getting a narrative of these events as a copy of my journal instead. Personally, all is well. Fort found himself a partner (as he often does!) soon after we settled into the Thetford site excavations. She is one of the assistant Anglish archaeologists and it is beginning to look as if this relationship might be serious.

Angland's history of died-in-the-wool matriarchy makes women even more assertive here. The women often see themselves superior to men. That attitude is not quite so strong at home in the United Americas, but Fort has always preferred strong women, perhaps the stronger the better. He has his hands full with his new "friend," but judging by the almost permanent smile he wears, he has no complaints.

Since the Thetford site, and the others, are showing so much of importance, it could be that we'll be occupied with them for the remainder of our working lives, so for him, this relationship could make him happy for a long time to come. And no, dear Janet, that doesn't mean we'll never come home. Only that we will do so in the off-season, during their winter in December and January when we can tour and lecture, put our notes in order, and give seminars at various schools around the country.

But I promise from now on I'll send you at least my journal entries by electronic mail every couple of days. I am sorry for the delay up to now, but things really have been a madhouse here since we arrived. You'll see what I mean once you start reading.

Mel

May 19th, 2048:
    Because of the heavy rain, it will be a couple of days before we can go out to the site Fort and I will be excavating. To overcome the frustration caused by this delay, I plan to spend some of my time writing this journal, in particular a brief commentary on how we came to Angland and why. Of course, this may become the foundation for a book, perhaps several books, so I would like to describe some of what preceded our arrival.

In years to come, I want to have the experience all written down to keep it clear in my own mind before later times obscure or blur my recollections. I'll try to avoid technical jargon. That may make the record easier for my family if anything should happen to me, and certainly easier for my publisher who is already making noises about a "popular book" based on the Thetford excavations.

We arrived in the midst of a downpour but I didn't care. This is Angland! Clean, glorious Angland! With ancient buildings at every corner, well-preserved, and covered with ivy. Just as I'd dreamed they would be. I am here at last, and the first thing I did was walk around Londin. The streets are wide, and there's a central park surrounding a bronze statue of the Iron Queen herself, Boadicea. She's standing with a young man kneeling at her feet, and an old man standing at her side. They even put a dove on her shoulder; her spear is held high. I was so excited, I walked for hours before I was exhausted enough to be able to sleep.

Finally, the place I've studied for years. And we have all the necessary permits, introductions, agreements from the Anglish archaeological societies, and all the appropriate signatures from government departments. I suppose they couldn't say no without looking as if they feared our theories were right. And for that reason, it's been difficult.

Because of the massive traditions and beliefs encrusted around the Boadicea legends, having two American males come in and say some of them were wrong isn't something which is ever going to be well received, no matter how true our theories may eventually prove to be.

But I've always wondered why, if tradition was so certain, they'd never been able to find Boadicea's Cyngor, or council assembly. The original dun was found long ago, but Anla's record also says she built a larger, grander dun for the gathering of all the tribes, and in it built the first Cyngor hall, complete with the shrines she was supposed to have placed in it. And that dun has never been discovered.

The original Iceni dun was found almost fifteen years ago now. It has been completely excavated and several small shrines discovered, along with a large number of artifacts. It is near Thetford, where archaeologists have long suspected it would be found, but despite all further exploration in the area no trace of the Cyngor was ever found.

I must have been twelve when I started to think about this. The story always sparked my imagination, and later drew Fort and me together as students. The tale of a warrior queen who swept her country free of the invaders, the oppressors of her people. The woman who went on to build a stable matriarchal government that ruled by Consensus—the first true democracy! One that not only lasted her lifetime, but for two thousand years to follow. Here in Angland that system still endures, as it does in our own United Americas, in a different way.

Legend says the idea came through a messenger from the gods, a creature neither woman nor man, giving rise to the belief in the holiness of the hermaphrodite (in later years, a child born as hermaphrodite was usually cherished by the community, almost given a Saint's rights).

When the messenger returned to the gods, that wo/man was said to have gone back to Brighid as Her spirit, kind of an angel-like assistant (which has always led me to wonder whether this being was real or no more than a dream the Queen would have had. Nevertheless, as legend also has it that the daughter of Boadicea, who eventually rose to follow the great Queen's rule, was sired by this same messenger; the story also goes that s/he knew the language of birds, and understood the motions of the stars and the moon—the messenger is credited as well with the invention of the first iron stove, but if all that is said of this wo/man is true, s/he worked miracles, and all in a very short time, which is very hard to believe!).

Another part of the tale states that in the Cyngor Boadicea built shrines, one for the messenger, and one for Brighid. Although these have never been found, judging from the description in one of Queen Arta's chronicles some six hundred years later, it must have been both large and fine.

All of this of course comes from Anla, and what survived of her writing. She wrote that she was taught to read and write by this same messenger, precluding the twenty-year druid apprenticeship of memorization. Her writing is the little original resource that we have from that time. There has been considerable scholarly dispute as to the truth of what she wrote, including her claim that this messenger brought strange seeds which she tended at his bidding. From her description two of them were identified as tomato and potatoes, and that lent some credence to her writing since neither are native here.

The dun containing the Cyngor and its shrines was burned to the ground during a major invasion partway through Arta's reign around 653 E.E., and they were rebuilt in a different place, one further still from the coast and thus easier to protect. That site is well known. But the interesting thing there was that those who rebuilt the Cyngor never recorded finding or moving anything from the old site.

All of this is very strange since Anla also mentioned that the shrine contained "sacred items brought by Cean to the tribe." That always made me wonder (and of course made me think of treasure, and there isn't an archaeologist in the world who doesn't think of these things, no matter how small, as treasure!).

Later, Arta's priestess wrote a document which describes both the Cyngor and the shrines. Unfortunately, assuming her readers would know exactly where both lay, she never gave any clear description of the area around the site or how to approach it. However, legend had already accumulated over time, and distinguishing how much of her description was embellishment, we can never know.

All of it could have been designed to make her own queen sound more important by asserting a stronger connection to the past (Arta's right to the throne was not as secure as she pretended, after all), and the origins of the site more supra-natural (a common problem with very old writings—exaggeration, particularly in the case of numbers, was normal to make things sound grander, more exceptional; their lives were so harsh that people loved to write and think about heroic acts or beauty that's so out of the ordinary nothing can be compared to it).

But there were things about the descriptions which made me think. Portions of the priestess's writing were assumed to mean certain things. In later years I came to wonder if the official belief was correct. But while I was a child I dreamed about the Queen, standing in her chariot, tears streaming down her face yet too proud to take comfort, the collar-feathers on her spear flying bravely as she led the charge against the Romans.

At university, Fort lived next door to me. He's half a year younger, and I talked often of my hope, one day, to go to Angland and find the resting place of Boadicea. I don't think my enthusiasm wholly influenced Fort, although I may have fired his own interest to begin with. But in later years he, too, saw that period as interesting in its own right, for his own reasons.

We went through university taking the same courses, working side by side. Our third year vacation dig in 2037 of a small site near Regina in the Upper United Americas, was a model of care and attention. It was a minor site, looking for the recorded "pile of bones" from over-hunting that started the settlement. But we took enormous pains to see all was done with perfection. In the end, because of our hard work, some new information was gathered on the trade matriarchies of early Indian tribes.

But that attention to detail brought our work to the attention of Tressider Carawaan, the leading prehistoric U.A. historian and archaeologist, and we were invited to join her the next season, after we completed our degrees.

Five years excavating first century Indian sites under her leadership was inspiring, but with her growing ill-health and age, Fort and I chose to seek other areas to pursue; she'd fairly made a name for herself by excavating all of the major sites, which left little room for recently graduated archaeologists like ourselves to make our names (note to self: Dig out the list of sites after that, cut and paste it here. If we are to publish our record of this dig, they would give a good background to our later ones).

By this time we were thirty, (I transitioned to male between digs when I was twenty,) and my own theory on the possible site of Boadicea's Cyngor and its shrines had hardened into a feeling that, at the very least, I must see if I could obtain permission to dig where I believed it might lie. The Anglish government rejected my request. I suspect at that time it was because relations between our countries were slightly strained. They may have resented the fact that a foreigner might find something they hadn't.

Instead, Fort and I excavated the summer palace of Queen Juana of Ispana that season. By a generous portion of both good luck and very hard work, we managed to shed a whole new light on the relationship between Queen Juana, Mary of Ferance, and Elizabeth of Angland.

With the discovery of her personal library bricked in behind a false wall, an attempt perhaps to hide her personal possessions from the dissidents rampaging through her city, we found her letters preserved inside the pages of her books. The chamber was so air tight, it had preserved the books and the letters almost as if they were months old, rather than centuries.

Fort actually stumbled on that—literally. His toe caught in a crack in the stone flooring, and when he reached out with one arm, he leant against the wall to the secret chamber. One of the stones came loose as he put his weight against it, and he picked away at it while a doctor looked at his ankle. That was a very fortunate sprain indeed! It kept him off his feet for a few days, but made our names in archaeology.

My championing of Angland's right to have Elizabeth's letters returned to her country after the special five-country exhibition seemed to alter their Ministry of Cultural Assets' attitude towards my theories. A woman from the department approached me and, after negotiating many imposed conditions, I was offered a permit. My only condition was that I need not specify the exact site, only the very approximate area, so no one else could claim my location before my arrival.

That was agreed to, but very sourly. I think she must have had her orders because she gave way once she saw I was adamant on this one point. What she did not know, what no one but Fort and I knew, was that he had quietly entered Angland the previous winter and toured the area ahead of time. He reported back that it was still farmland, though urban development was close by. We didn't see that as a problem. Purchasing supplies would be that much easier, and the excavations less of a problem.

However, if the site has been built over, that would be a nuisance. It would stop us entirely if the local people didn't wish to be inconvenienced by us digging in their cellars. I have, in fact, done such excavations before, but they take far more time and huge amounts of money as the buildings above the site must be shored up to keep them from collapsing.

That is, as I said, if one can obtain a permit and the occupants' permission in the first place. These are often not forthcoming. People do get annoyed when they can't easily step out of their front doors, and there are those, too, who want to be paid for the disruption in their lives. If only they could see how important this knowledge is!

But I am here now. In rainy England, permit in hand, Fort ready to move our supplies and gear on my word. I spent two days prowling the back streets of Londin, remembering how this city, too, had been burned. It is a constant surprise to me that in such a climate the inhabitants have still managed to burn so many important archaeological sites to the ground and then lose the knowledge of where they once stood. But I'm not complaining; that just makes more work for people like Fort and me.

May 25th, 2028:

Well, we're here, on site, lines laid out, strings and pegs all firmly in place, and the first trench started. I saw amusement on the faces of those local officials who arrived to watch (the urban build-up may be just a little too close for comfort!). They're convinced I'm a fool from another country with grandiose ideas and no conception of what I'm doing. But since they know they owe me for my support over Elizabeth's letters, they'll graciously allow me my dig, and equally graciously bid me farewell when it fails. I'm determined that won't happen.

May 31st:

That determination is unfulfilled as yet. The onlookers' smiles are growing broader, the sarcastic comments a little louder. But they'll fade. Archaeology is a slow process and they'll grow bored quickly.

I've moved the excavation lines out to the west. If the Cyngor the Queen built lay in another direction, it is most likely to be that way.

June 9th:

I can hardly say these words for tripping over my tongue in excitement. My poor computer misheard me at first so I had to calm myself, wipe what it had written, and speak more clearly.

We struck the edge of something under the site at 2 p.m. today. Burned timbers, charcoal, mostly, with only scraps of wood remaining. The officials watching were stunned. Now they are saying that it is most probably a much later site, one like Juana's summer palace in Ispana, burned during the war against the Dutch-Portuguese coalition in the 1500s. One of them added that it would still be important to their history. She was apparently attempting to placate me, but in a very condescending way, as if I didn't know this bit of historical record.

June 10th:

I have an urge to find that official and stick my tongue out at her. Fort started early on one trench while I worked parallel on another. Our graduate students did most of the digging, but we mapped out locations for them before beginning ourselves. We don't like to leave the digging only to our assistants. Neither Fort nor I mind getting our hands dirty (his mother says that's why he became an archaeologist in the first place, a chance to dig in all that dirt!).

We scraped down to the bottom, past the level of burnt bits, and into what should be the foundations of the original buildings. We've cut deeply into the soil already, as there has been little to find so far. However, we have turned up fragments of pottery typical of Boadicea's period. Fort found Roman-glass beads. And we have found traces of a dun, a large one. They used unmortared stone and wood to build the duns, but the one that housed the Cyngor would have definitely had more stone than wood. (The legend goes that the "messenger" taught them this, along with some iron work.) We've found the outlines of what look to be that shape. And it is large, so large it might be something built later than the great Queen's time. But I still have hope.

The small items we've found are beginning to accumulate in neatly labeled rows in the storage room (with any luck we'll have to rent a larger house, one just for the artifacts! I'm pathetic, I know, but I do have great hopes for this project).

Fort and I have made no claims yet about their origin as I believe that if we brandished our finds, the officials would say the site is significant to their cultural heritage, and take it away from us because we're foreigners (technically, we're from a renegade colony if you look at the history, but I'm not splitting hairs). We want incontrovertible proof that this is the Cyngor, and that we have credit for our work before we face them again.

June 27th:

We have it! I'm sure of it. Both the proof and a mystery to go along with it.

We have been excavating carefully, tending always towards the west. The tribes in the Queen's day believed that if a warrior had a worthy soul, it survived into the next life and traveled west of the sunset. So, perhaps a little superstitiously, I have pushed the excavations west. After I finished my work today, I had gone back to our building to catalogue some of the small finds when Fort came quietly in.

"Mel, are you busy?" He had an air of excitement, perhaps unnoticeable by others, but I have known him too long to miss it.

"You've found something? What?" I carefully put down the shards I'd been entering in the daily log.

He shook his head. "I'm not sure. Come and take a look, but don't be obvious. We don't want anyone to notice."

I trailed out after him, my hands in my pockets, appearing to consider only where we should place the next line of excavation. I must have looked a bit of a clown to anyone who knew me well! I never do anything casually, and it's impossible for me to keep my hands still. He took me to where the trench had deepened as we cut down, the ground rising above it.

Something stuck out of the leading edge of the trench. I glanced about before dropping silently into the trench with Fort, crouching so we were both hidden. The bell had rung for lunch and the area was empty of our helpers.

I brushed at it with the softest brush I carry, even though it appeared to be metal. Bronze? But from that depth it had to have been there since Boadicea's time, and unless the soil conditions were exactly right, it would be pitted and crumble at an uncareful touch.

Fort nudged my arm, knowing what I would be thinking.

"We could have been salted," he said quietly. "I thought we should keep this to ourselves, get it out and take a good look at it before we start yelling."

He was both right and wrong. I wouldn't have put it past a few of the Ministry's officials to put something that would later make us look like fools. We would have to be careful of just that. And if the artifact had been planted, no matter what it was, it had to have been done by an archaeologist far superior to us both. The surrounding soil looked old, with that weighty sense of time pushing down on the differing layers. And considering the debris present around it, this would be exactly the place where we'd expect to find something substantial.

But bronze? I dug into my memory. The Iceni had many bronze ornaments, like jewelry and brooches, as well as bowls and plates. But Enla had described a bronze casket belonging to Boadicea, supposedly left her by the messenger and later placed in the shrine to him after his death. It was one of the tribe's greatest treasures.

As I dragged these bits of information from my memory, I was still brushing at the metal bit. It came out of the dirt in my hand, leaving a jagged hole behind it. A metal clasp. It looked like the soil had etched time into its surface as I brushed away what would lift off. It was elaborate, the setting including a large bead of amber in a wolf's head.

I looked back at the spot where it had come out. There was more metal behind it, like corroded coins crusted together.

I started to pluck at the dirt, digging into it with my fingers, not caring whether I broke nails or not. It wouldn't be the first time. Fort scrambled to help me. In minutes we'd exposed in the trench wall a pile of coins that lay at our feet. And there was still more. Below them I could see what looked to be a piece of metal about ten inches long, and as I dug away at it cautiously, I found the top of it and the bottom. A square of bronze imbedded in the ancient earth.

This could be the casket. The shape was right for the corner of one. I dug into the surrounding earth, prying back from the past a little more of the artifact. It seemed to be plain metal, but ordinary bronze should not have lasted unmarred by time. The coins and the clasp were pitted as they should be. No, there was something odd here. I would not be taken for a fool.

"Fort, think of something to keep them away from the site tonight. One of us will get this out, but not until all can see. We can't make a mistake here!"

"What about documentation?"

He helped me recover the coins and pin. I looked around to be sure no one had noticed us. It was dusk, and the staff and graduate student volunteers had either packed up for dinner or had already left their sections for the night.

"That's why I want the site clear. I don't want anyone stumbling over this without keeping records. If this turns out to be some fake or trick, we can denounce it. If it's genuine, then we have everything we need to substantiate the find." He agreed.

But in the early morning, before I had time to go and dig out the coins and bronze, something else was uncovered. What we found excited even the officials.

The student, one of Fort's best, was calling everyone to come and look. The small statue was almost undamaged. A foot was missing, and one arm was cracked, but otherwise it was a fine piece of work: Brighid carved out of bone.

I leaned over to brush away as much of the caked soil that I could. The item was beautifully carved and detailed. The statue had to be from Boadicea's time or near to it. It alone was enough to prove our theory could be true. Fort completed the excavation while I did the photography then I took it to our records room to be photographed once more and measured once it had been cleaned.

Everybody returned to their digging with enthusiasm, eager again. This was obviously a site of significance, how much only their efforts would show. I had to smile. Archaeology is like a drug—you're either addicted to it or bored! There is no in between.

I returned to the trench where we'd found the bronze pin.

I had a tiny pick—like a dentist's—to use with great care, and an ordinary gardener's trowel. My camera hung about my neck (and believe me there are times when I'm very thankful for technology—digital cameras are so lightweight compared to what they used to be). I quietly photographed the coins once I had partially excavated them, and gestured for the official nearby to join me.

With his eyes watchful, I picked out the bronze corner below the other artifacts, brushing away at its surface. By touch I continued to work the artifact free as gently as I could, digging out the soil around it before attempting to touch it. (He isn't an archaeologist and did not recognize the small signs that showed it had earlier been removed, then replaced.) The casket was quite large as such things go, about ten inches long, and seven to eight inches both wide and high.

Digging it out took hours as I made the most of my day in the limelight, and Fort must have used an endless supply of film, but finally I had it again out of the grave where it had rested for two thousand years. With a start I realized that many more had come to watch. I laid aside trowel and brush, easing the casket from the earth and putting it where all could see.

"How quickly you're finding things." The voice was sour, and had to be another one of the Ministry officials.

I ignored him—there'd be more for them to be angry about if our theories proved correct. And would ensure there could be no accusation that Fort or I had salted the site since we'd been sure to take core samples, and the official too could testify the earth—around most of the casket at least—had been undisturbed.

July 30th:

There is now no doubt: this was the site of Boadicea's Cyngor, her ancient council hall, as well as the shrines for Brighid and her messenger. Since our finds last month we have trenched into the main square of the original dun itself, and discovered enough artifacts to fill a museum on their own (I hope someday that is exactly what is done with them). At some time it had been burned and then turfed over.

Since Arta describes it in detail in her own time, it must have been maintained for many years before it burned. Fort thinks it was buried purposely, but I have my doubts.

If so, that may have been done to prevent looters. But we'll never know for sure. It may have been some feeling of "out of sight, the less grief," since the new capital would be built elsewhere. But because of Arta's actions—if she was the one, and if that is in fact what was done (note to self: there could be a good article on just that, co-authored with Fort; run it by him)—the site has held its secrets untouched for almost fifteen hundred years. And "untouched" is exactly the word. Several hundred years of continuous occupation by the thinkers and decision makers of ancient England, uncontaminated by modern interference. The site is a treasure trove of information.

The bronze box we found has its own secrets. That was clear as soon as we cleaned it. And this is the strangest story of all, if anyone will believe it: this casket is not an artifact of Boadicea's time. It took hours of examination and discussions with Fort before I was willing to admit this. And then when we were finally able to open it, I had no doubts any longer.

The bronze is not Iron Age bronze. It has been tempered in a modern way. The clasp is a combination lock which took us more than a week to undo without damaging it. Inside is a computer. Yes, a computer, similar to our own in some ways but sufficiently different to make both Fort and me wonder about aliens and flying saucers (all of this sounds so absurd, but I will delete it, Janet, before I let anyone else but you read what I'm saying—really, this is all so strange, those are the kinds of explanations we've had to consider).

Who *was* Boadicea's messenger and from where had s/he and her/his strange computer traveled to the Iceni of the first century? Could s/he have been alien? Does that explain what s/he was able to do?

August 12*th*:

Fort flew back to New York, quietly carrying in his pocket what we believed to be the chronological first of the odd, small disks from the casket. We're hoping that it is a storage device like our computer cubes.

If so, it could be a record of who—and what!—the strange messenger was. A respected computer expert we both know (that's you, Jan, and a bow to your expertise) is taking on the task of finding a way to read the contents of this item.

August 30th:

The results have stunned all three of us. Our expert was able to read and decode the disk in two weeks. Fort called me and explained exactly what had been found. I shipped the other disks to him. With the key in her hands, Janet was able to give us a readout of them all within two days.

The problem now is to decide what to do about it. I am uncertain whether or not such information should be generally released. The messenger's name was Cean, and he was from the future. Not our future. A different future.

Sept. 10th:

I have been able to delay any action by convincing myself and the others that it is important we use this Cean's records to find and excavate the ceremonial pool of the Iceni druids. He describes it very clearly when he outlines his acceptance into the tribe. From his records, I believe that this was also a pool of sacrifice. It is clear his ceremonial entry into the tribe, and in particular the culmination of the rite, was a kind of ritual death and rebirth.

Enla records that "the messenger was returned to the goddess Brighid with all honor at the insistence of the druids." When read by an archaeologist, that sort of comment indicates sacrifice. Where better to complete it than at the pool where the man had first been accepted into the people?

His description of the area is meticulous. Each hill of the land is described. We already know where the dun had been. From that I traced the way to where the pool should be. Between two hills, a shallow dell looked like it might have once held water, but not as a pool. Near its center was what looked like an artificial hill or mound.

Sept. 14th:

I waited until Fort returned so we could both study this mound. He is better at watercourses than I am. He pointed out to me that the area to the east of Thetford must have been flooded by a stream from a low gully through the hills.

"There?" I asked him. "But there's no sign of a stream."

"Not now, but see there, Mel. Where the hills come together. Look how the land dips. Walk over there with me and I think you'll see something."

I obediently walked after him, striding along in his wake to where the land rose again. We climbed the small hilly area there and looked down on the other side. Below us was a lake. Not a large one, barely more than a pond, but fed by a thin stream on its northern edge.

Fort grinned. "See. That's artificial. I'd say it was made around the late 1700s, just when everyone was enthusiastically altering the landscape to make it look like a park. 'To see beauty ringed 'bout all,' if I'm correctly quoting the poet. The low-lying area farther on is bigger."

He pointed at it. "There. Can you see it? It would have made a larger, deeper lake. But when they made their artificial lake, they diverted the stream and cut it off from that one back there. I think they dredged the bottom before they diverted the stream."

I caught my breath in understanding. "And they dumped the excess soil into the depression which once was our pool."

"Which is why the area looks more like a barrow than a marsh or pond."

"How high do you think they would have piled the earth?" I needed to calculate how many extra hours we could ask our students to put in. I also wanted to know exactly how long it would take before we knew if our theory was correct.

Fort studied the lake. "Maybe twenty feet. At least fifteen. We could get in one of the small earth-movers to shift the top layer. The officials may take some convincing, but right now your name is high with them. Just say you believe something may be here. You'll be paying for the earth-mover yourself, and not touching anything that could be a cultural site." He laughed. "They'll jump at that. It's a free ride. If there's nothing there, we'll only look the more foolish for wasting our time and valuable money. It certainly won't cost them."

Sept. 15th:

I did a lot of groveling about "collateral sites" and "investment for the future," but the Ministry officials finally agreed to let us look at the mound. As Fort said, they saw the advantages themselves. It's poor, rough land, part of a Government reserve. They bear none of the costs, and if we make any real finds, this group of men and women would look as if they were very far sighted.

Nor have any of us been disappointed. There is something below the mound. Clearly this area must have once been the sacrificial pool, and not a grave mound (I actually dreamed that we carelessly dug out an army of prancing skeletons! I'll be so exhausted by the end of this, Jan, that I'm going to need a month of vacation. Know any good southern cruises?).

There are no accounts of ancient druid rituals, at least not in Angland (Caesar said a few things, but he was very biased by their failures here, and there is no corroboration for the "wicker sacrifices" where the victims were all pushed into giant wicker images, which were then set alight, burning all alive; although to my mind, he had no room to talk, given what occurred regularly in his coliseum).

But it is likely from what we know of Eirin's druids and some of those of Gaul, that those about to die were brought here first, killed ritually, and then their bodies were either tossed into the water or left to sink into the bog, eventually becoming buried under the peat. Angland's druids did not believe in the soul's continuance after death unless the person was exceptional.

If Cean met the same fate as others—and I believe this to be the case—we still haven't yet found what remains of his body. We may find nothing at all—it depends on the chemicals concentrated here in the peaty soil. Sometimes it preserves bodies, but not always. But if he is here, why was his casket not buried with him? It could be that the Queen wished to have it for the shrine, or she may have wanted something of her lover's always at hand.

The thing which has aroused our great interest has been the discovery of other bodies. On top were three males, druids from their tattoos. Nothing is left of their clothing, of course, or the flesh of their bodies. But their skin has been mostly preserved. Sometimes the peat's chemicals will do that, acting on skin like the chemicals a tanner uses on hides.

Sept. 18th:

We have had a chance to examine the bodies further. Each of these men died from a single killing stroke to the heart from behind (there is a tear in the skin in their back, and the ribs covering where the heart lie are broken; I think the evidence suggests one strong spear thrust, but that's a tentative opinion. I don't have enough laboratory equipment with me to do a further analysis; I can't make any further conclusions until a forensic pathologist has had a chance to view the remains).

None has any possessions with him, and they were killed over several years, not all at once, as may be seen from the burials. Still more interesting was the fact that they were laid to face north, south, and east. Beneath them was a single body, wrapped in what look to have been foal skins. It had been placed facing towards the west, the direction an extraordinary soul would take. West of the sun, indeed.

The articles found with this fourth male were minimal, but sufficient to suggest he was important, and therefore an important sacrifice. The skins, of course: they could be foal skins. Even now stained as they are, or I should say leeched of color (peat tends to remove colors, leaving behind the red), they look as if they once were beautiful and soft.

There is a leather thong wound around his arm, tightly enough to have dug into the skin. Carved beads are strung on its end, jet as well as other stones (amber would have perished in the peat over the centuries). He has a gold torc about his throat, covering what must have been the deathblow, a slit in the jugular (usually sacrifices were struck a blow to the head, then their throats slit at the same time as they were garroted—swift but not merciful). Unlike the others, this was a sacrifice of note.

But this must be Cean. His teeth show evidence of modern dental work.

Sept. 23rd:

As soon as we could move the remains, I called in Angland's top forensic pathologist and demanded the body be completely examined using all the most exact techniques. I want nothing to call this find into question.

The results are astounding. Few will believe what the pathologist has found. But no one can claim that we committed any forgeries or salting at the site. We have had continuous visual records of every move made by even the most junior of the students.

There is no question but that this man was killed around 62 E.E. Nor that he was killed before the three others. He was well below where they lay. They'd died perhaps five to ten years later, definitely within the time of Boadicea's rule. But his body is that of a modern man's, not one with the poor diet and hard life of an Iron Age man. I swear this is so.

I will allow the scholarly furore to rise to the heights I expect it to go before quietly producing the casket. A complete transcription of the records it contained will be presented at the same time, but only to a small circle of those who should be told. That record contains the explanation for all the anomalies of that fourth man, as perceived by the experts including Cean's own words that Enla was his student.

Not that they will be happy to hear that explanation. On the contrary, I'm sure I'll be showered with complaints about what I expect them to do now, along with demands to know why I said nothing before.

Fort plans to ask them what they'd have done if I had gone public from the start.

There will be ramifications which will create even more problems, if the public is told everything from the beginning. He notes, in that rather terse way he has, that there had already been enough suspicion about us, and our reputations were at stake, as they always will be.

(This is not really a find I want associated with my name—those who are suspicious of it will be just as suspicious of anything else I do in the future; however, on the other hand, I'm thrilled that our ideas have been borne out so dramatically.) Once we knew what the records within the casket said, as the authorities will eventually realize, we were right to first obtain further corroboration, and then to tell only those who should know. In the end they will agree.

I keep looking at the face of this man. It is a gentle face, somehow a person I know I would have wanted to count friend. That's not scientific—just my feeling.

Nov. 30th:

The amount of discussion has been horrendous. After enough meetings to bore us and all our ancestors to death, the Ministry has decided to release the information over the next ten years. They will do so in small news bites, which will allow the public to assimilate the facts slowly, and hopefully without any sort of panic. (Can you imagine how the Men's Rights' activists are going to react? Can you call Cean a man or a woman? I wouldn't like to answer that. It is hard to tell if the legend is true, since the muscles of course have rotted away, leaving the skin loose over what is left of the bones but there is evidence both of genitals and of possible breasts.)

The Ministry almost decided to withhold all the contents of the casket from the public. Most of them still believe that Fort and I are responsible for it. The fact that Cean claims to have known people with our names in the city he called Los Angeles was too much for them—or us—to believe. Of what he claimed, I cannot say. I can only say that it must be coincidence. Although one physicist who has worked in time theory, Dr. Estephana from Parisi University in Ferance, said that knowing our parallel selves in Cean's world was a real possibility.

She said that with each branching of time, if such exists, the parallel worlds would be distinctly similar to the first. The closer they are to the first, in fact, the more similarities there would be between them. And the further apart the branchings, the more dissimilarities there would be. I could tell many of the Ministry officials listened to her politely, but not with any great show of being persuaded.

However, in the end there wasn't any other resolution to be made. The casket's discovery, the site of the Cyngor, these are discoveries too great and now too easily stumbled across to be hidden for long.

And for the sake of science, I have to say that I agree with the final decision. To tell ordinary people that their entire civilization and much of their history was begun by the meddling of one person, then also tell them that it is possible to change the past and thus change the future (and I think that information should *never* be revealed), that we are only one of a number of branching worlds—all of that is likely to cause a great many problems, not the least of which would be a sudden enthusiastic pursuit in time research. (As I say, that information should not be released to the public. There are too many who would like to alter history, and not for the better.)

But the problems could be less, perhaps, than in Cean's world. The civilizations and populations there appear to have been far less stable. They were a hysterical people, prone to panic, apt to war, and they thrust their way into a headlong technological progress without first considering and solving the harms it could cause. He talks about nuclear bombs and a dependency on fossil fuels that also pollute the air. We didn't permit fossil fuels' use without examining the problems it could cause first, and then allowed it only with appropriate modifications to prevent just what he describes.

When comparing our world to theirs, we have progressed more slowly in some directions, but our civilizations have bred people more emotionally stable, slower to anger and less likely to fight. We have had fewer wars, we learned earlier to control our population's behavior as well as number, and our medical knowledge may be considerably greater. (In his day there still was no cure for cancer, if you can believe what he says; we'd discovered the different vaccines and treatments almost a hundred years before the time he left his world.)

With what he says of time travel in mind, several governments have combined to work on a possible way of shifting between these alternate worlds. Not that they really have any wish to do so, as it may cause more problems than we can imagine. But Cean may not be the only one who discovers this way of leaping from one branch of time to another. Should anyone from one of these other branchings find a way to reach us, it is well that we know how to return them, or how to prevent them from interfering in our affairs.

We have benefited from one such interference. We might not be so lucky if there is a second.

April 3rd, 2050:
The museum at Thetford is finished. Cean's remains, preserved in a form of stasis, will be held there. A replica of the body has been placed on display, rather than the actual remains—light alone would cause fur-

ther deterioration. The museum was opened by Queen Kaaren herself. A fitting tribute, as her DNA proves her to be closest to the pure old line of the original Iceni.

(You probably know that, Janet, but just in case you didn't, when DNA was first discovered, someone here suggested we really have no other way of showing that the Queen is truly descended from Boadicea; consequently, for the past two hundred years the Anglish have used mitochondrial DNA to determine who will be their queen.)

The public has learned some of what Cean brought to this world. But far faster than their enlightenment has been the knowledge gained by our scientists. By the time the world knows everything Cean did (and I do mean everything), we will also be in a position to bar the gates against any who would attempt to alter our history or our future. The scientists believe they can send back a sort of wave in time which will prevent any further incursions, while preserving our own history forever.

Someone has proposed, too, that a statue be raised in a park in the heart of Londin in five years' time. By that time the public will know almost all of Cean's story. The monument will depict Cean with Boadicea, and there will be panels around the base showing an artist's representation of scenes from the records. I wonder if he would be pleased at such a tribute? Perhaps where his soul now lives, West of the Sunset, as an Iceni matriarch would say, he *does* know. And maybe there he and his Queen are reunited to watch over the world they created together.

May it forever be so!

Yours,
Mel

www.ingramcontent.com/pod-product-compliance
Lightning Source LLC
Chambersburg PA
CBHW050355260626
47156CB00003B/745